HOMER'S PLACE

HOMER'S PLACE

A NOVEL BY

HARLAN G. KOCH

JOHN M. HARDY PUBLISHING

ALPINE & HOUSTON

2 0 0 4

First Printing: March 2004

1 3 5 7 9 10 8 6 4 2

ISBN 0-9717667-3-8

Printed and Bound in the United States of America

Cover Design - Leisha Israel, Blue Sky Media
Austin, Texas

John M. Hardy Publishing Company
Houston, Texas

www.johnmhardypublishing.com

DEDICATION

I dedicate *Homer's Place* to my unusual hometown and to two of its related business couples who played tremendous roles in preparing me for life as it really is: Louise, Esther, Virgil, and Aaron. They invested an inordinate amount of their busy lives to show me the right way, the fair way. They lent a hand before I was even aware I needed it.

The town was special because it seemed that its adults, in general, made a collective effort to mold every young person's character and to give each of them every opportunity for eventual success. Winelda's people epitomized Brokaw's *The Greatest Generation*. During the Depression, when the going became very tough, these people did not pull up stakes and head for greener pastures. Despite great adversity, they stayed, worked, and together they prevailed. What a superlative American town! A collection of these is what has made America great!

ACKNOWLEDGMENTS

Mrs. Georgia Parks of Muskogee, Oklahoma, was among the first who tirelessly guided me towards *Homer's Place*'s completion. At its inception, she made it abundantly clear that becoming a published author would be a trying task. Mrs. Sandie Olson, president of the Waynoka Historical Society provided invaluable historical and editorial assistance, and of course, I thank my ever-supportive wife, Judy, who probably re-read *Homer's Place* a zillion times, and put up with my long absences at my Micron word processor. My thanks to Evelyn Schlatter, editor at the University of New Mexico, who spiked my resolve just as I was ready to throw *Homer's Place* in the wastebasket, and to Professor of Creative Writing, Johnny Quarles—himself the published author of eleven novels. All of these people in turn gave me resilience when I began to discover the maze of literary agents and other time wasters who became determined obstacles along the way.

When it came to actually setting this story to galley proofs, and then moving ahead to promote and produce it, I'm deeply indebted to Mike Hardy of Houston. Of greatest importance to me, I found Mike's word and his uncommon Texas resolve to be as genuine as his sterling friendship. He honored me by taking *Homer's Place* from its loose manuscript pages to this printed book. Had it not been for him, there would be no completed *Homer's Place*.

My objective was to write an acceptable story. I hadn't thought much about the cover but Leisha Israel of Blue Sky Media in Austin suddenly brought that aspect of a published book into sharp focus. Her thoughtfulness and her artistry in cover design overwhelms me.

Also, I wish to thank some classmates who inspired me to succeed; each of them made the story better through their constructive advice. They catalyzed me at those times when I was ready to abandon writing novels so that I would have time to read them instead: Mayor Bill Overstreet (Juneau, AK), Gen. Frank Blazey and his wife, Joy (NC), Gen. "Black" Jack McWhorter (TX), Col. Dick Gruenther (FL—We rode Harleys across the nation) and Silver Star winner Col. Sewall Johnson (FL—We served together in Korea). Very important to the finalization of *Homer's Place* was the unstinting advice and effort of Col. Jay Olejniczak of West Point, New York, (Editor-in-Chief of Assembly Magazine). He unflaggingly contributed many hours toward professionally editing *Homer's Place*.

Many of the above also recognized even greater promise in my second Tom Cable novel: *Deception*. It will become a sequel to *Homer's Place*—a thriller of Southeast Asian diplomatic intrigue. It will soon complete its own grueling obstacle course toward publication.

Harlan G. Koch, San Francisco, 20 February 2004

Authors Note

The novel *Homer's Place* is by definition a work of fiction including its wild and wooly incidents, titles, ranks, and military decorations. Some place-names, characters, and geographic designations give rise to infectious speculation. The reader's first objective should be to relax and not to become concerned with reality or location. *Homer's Place* is a story based superficially on a purely fictitious town, Winelda, that appears on no map of the fifty states. This is a story of Winelda's people, its geography, and one family in particular. May all of them entertain you.

Harlan G. Koch, San Francisco, 20 February 2004

PROLOGUE

DRIPPING BLACK UMBRELLAS

Because Winelda had no church to accommodate the numbers expected for Homer's funeral, the American Legion held it in the auditorium of the Winelda High School. It overflowed with people and "Concho" Concepción Rodríguez headed the Mexican contingent.

This was all taking place where in two months I would graduate from high school, the great event that Homer would not attend. They placed Homer's casket in front of the stage on the very spot where last spring I'd worn the white suit and had turned with my companion to face the seniors in their processional. One of my classmates, Bessie Marie, sang two of Homer's favorite songs. I suppose it was just about as emotional a funeral as Winelda had had in recent memory. Primarily this was because Homer was so young and so constantly before the public, and everyone for many miles around felt as if they had known him. They also knew me, and people were genuinely sorry I had lost my dad.

After the singing came ritualistic words from my Methodist reverend. I wished they could've come from Aaron. The reverend had not once stepped inside the Majestic and had no personal knowledge of Homer, and Homer had never gone to church.

They wheeled Homer's casket up the aisle to the main doorway of the high school so that all the people could file by to view him. He still had that hint of a smile Mr. Floyd was so pleased with, but now he was dressed with a white handkerchief in his suit pocket, and his hands rested on his chest. I had retied Homer's tie the way he had tied it. Once again, I had that fleeting thought about the ridiculous falseness of funerals. Homer would never have been dressed to the nines for sleep, yet here he was supposedly sleeping, complete with necktie and cuff links. He was all dressed up but wore no shoes or spats because nobody could see down there.

I was very uncomfortable because I could feel the many well-meaning eyes upon me. I wanted out of there, but I had to think of Maddy, Mom, Pop, and Aunt Lillian. Meanwhile, I was worried about slobbering in front of all my classmates. If people didn't say anything I was okay; it was when they offered tearful condolences that I couldn't keep a straight face. No matter how I steeled myself, I'd have to look at the floor with my eyes swimming and a huge lump in my throat. Pop, who had sometimes battled with his son, had a big tear rolling down his cheek. He loved Homer. Poor Mom and Pop, what a heck of a "golden years." They sure weren't having fun.

What really tore me was seeing veterinarian Perry Phillips walk toward me with a brand-new black Stetson in his hand. I'd never seen Perry with such a keen hat, and Perry wasn't bald; he had a nice head of hair. It was my first time not to see Perry in Levi's; he was wearing a simple black serge suit tailored with cowboy flourishes and fancy black rodeo boots with sharp looking red leather insets. He came up to me and gripped my shoulder with his hand. "You'll do okay, Hot Shot, don't you worry none," and Perry walked out and down the front steps of the school.

It was as if my throat had closed down. I wanted to yell out, "Wait, Mr. Phillips, I'll go with you." God, how I hated all that had happened.

Aaron and Louise Fischer lent their V-8 to Maddy and me; together with Esther and Virgil Clemans of the Corner drugstore, we drove behind Russell Floyd's hearse to Coffeyville, Kansas. I stared at Homer's casket for a hundred and seventy-five miles. Late that drizzly afternoon, we laid Homer Cable to rest at Fairlawn Cemetery next to my mother Florence. In addition to Grandma and Grandpa Ross and a couple of aunts, there were several shadowy figures in black under dripping black umbrellas, some with black veils across their faces. They must have known Homer when he operated the theater in Coffeyville thirteen years before in 1928. A few had said, "Tom, you won't remember me but . . . ."

As the Coffeyville minister droned a few brief remarks, I recalled Homer's words: "If you ever come to visit my grave, Tom, remember to bring along a little bottle of hundred and ninety proof and dribble it on the dirt. It should soak down to me and I'll be forever grateful." Homer and I had laughed.

Thinking of our shared laughter on that wet gray afternoon made me feel better but then my thoughts turned to Chambers and the anger grew inside me. I shifted my eyes to Homer's metal box, which was ready to be lowered into that yawning Kansas hole, and I made Homer a promise: one day I'll even the score.

THE DOCTOR AND THE CAVE

My plane banked slightly and it brought the great Cimarron River slowly into view. Just beyond it were the gypsum-capped mesas sparkling as if sprinkled with diamond dust. It was wild karstic country, dappled with sagebrush and rocks, and home to Herefords, rattlesnakes, lizards, and coyotes. Among the scattered sinkholes were fetid Stygian caves where millions of bats clung to the walls. They pulsated nervously as they stored energy for their nightly kill. Just at sunset they would erupt into a black squeaking cloud, and by dawn they would cannibalize more than their combined weight in moths and mosquitoes—quite a murderous orgy for one night, wouldn't you say?

To bury Doc Chambers in one of those caves beneath a carpet of bat dung had been the demonic part of my meticulous plan. I figured Doc and the ugly devil critters deserved each other. Also, it was like insurance against discovery—casual snoopers avoid a bat cave's stench. More importantly, the Cable family books would be back in balance, and I would now be able to rest. I shall never forget the euphoria of that moonlit night. Everything had materialized so perfectly. It had been pure titillation.

What had Doc done to deserve the dishonor of being planted in a bat cave outside Winelda? Where in the world was Winelda? Why was I now winging over it in a TWA jet? All those whys and whats have been an important part of my life. I've always known that one day I'd write it all down and present it as a fiction, and I'd call it *Homer's Place*.

PART ONE

THE CABLES

Pop Cable was my entrepreneuring grandfather. If not for him, I probably never would have set foot in Winelda. Pop was a rascal for ferreting out opportunity. Because of him, we Cables went to Winelda and despite the Depression and the nation's malaise, we did remarkably well. To be sure, Winelda had its share of hard times but nothing to compare with what we saw each week on *Movietone News*: New York's hordes of homeless, Detroit's soup kitchens, Philadelphians sleeping in pasteboard boxes. Winelda's Depression was so comparatively benign, they could've called it the Magnificent Depression. Still, by the time I got around to dispatching Doc, fate had reduced our once successful Cable family to shambles. Of course, there had been other contributing factors, but Doc was chiefly to blame.

I remember the family gatherings in our house on Cecil, the sandy unpaved street Wineldans proudly referred to as their silk stocking avenue. It was certainly not a Fifth Avenue or a *Champs-Élysées*. It was, however, charming and there was little traffic to spoil it, and in the early summer the locust trees bordering the curbs were in full bloom and pleasantly fragrant. To me, as a kid, those family gatherings were electrifying—aunt and uncle and father and grandparents all milling around the house; the live music; the ripples of conversation; the bets they made on geographic trivia and the race to the encyclopedia to prove the winner.

Uncle Virgil, my father's younger brother, was a graduate of the Chicago Conservatory of Music, which at that time was Chicago's counterpart of New York's Juilliard. He and Aunt Iris were both fine musicians and attended graduate school at Stillwater. As Uncle Virgil started a rendition with his violin, Iris would accompany on the parlor piano. I'd watch mesmerized as Virgil closed his eyes and played as if in a trance. Then he would suddenly lay aside his violin and switch to the oboe and later to his clarinet and finally to a bassoon. Together, Iris and Virgil played beautifully, and Pop welled with pride. He'd lay far back in his easy chair, his eyes closed and a faint smile brightening his face. Pop had a right. He'd educated his children while he had never attended high school. It was his hard-earned money that had made everything possible.

While Virgil and Iris played, my grandmother—the family had always called her Mom—would be making her final culinary touches in the kitchen. Alongside her, my father, Homer, masterfully mashed a huge pot of potatoes. Only he could whip them until every lump had disappeared. Music, mashed potatoes, and Pop reveling over the fruits of his labor—it was a harmonious house on Cecil.

When I first arrived in Winelda, I was only eight. Pop Cable was already seventy-one and set in his ways. Perhaps I had upset the tranquility he had come to enjoy. Still, when I least expected it, he delighted in collaring me and giving me the giggles with his brush mustache. Shortly after I arrived, Pop and I started having long talks in the shade of the front porch. Pop would tell me about our pioneer family, how in 1859 his father had come to America. Pop's old eyes sparkled when he recounted those stories.

The Beginning

Pop's front porch recitals were not those of an old man incoherently mumbling disjointed family history. Pop was sharp and to make the record even clearer, he'd pencil a family tree as he rattled on about our family skeletons. One day he revealed—almost reluctantly—that his dad, Heinrich Kabel, had been a fugitive from justice. What a surprise! My own great-grandfather, born in 1820 in Hamburg,

Germany, had been a criminal.

Pop said that when Heinrich attended Heidelberg University, he was a hell-raiser. As a student of geopolitical science, he thought the German government was an abomination that demanded correction. After graduation, Heinrich traveled throughout most of Europe, taking odd jobs while he comparatively analyzed Europe's capitals. Finding no single governmental utopia, he reappeared at age twenty-six in Hamburg. And like today's Berkeley malcontents, he and his friends tainted normally peaceful street corners with their tirades for governmental change. When the police drove them underground, they resorted to clandestine midnight meetings. The authorities became so enraged by the subsequent 1849 Baden Insurrection that they put the ringleaders on a hit list. Great-grandfather was high among the wanted.

One night in 1858, the Kulturkampf police finally located Heinrich in far southern Freiberg. Luckily, when he had only scant seconds to spare, a confederate tipped him off. Great-grandfather fled with desperate haste through woods and over moonlit fields to the banks of the Rhine. While being rowed to the French side, he saw police torches coming down to the very spot he had just left. He heard the angry shouting, the yelping dogs. Once on the French side, he hurried through the night toward Cherbourg. He broke into a cold sweat as he booked passage at the crowded dock. He was petrified. Any around him could be secret police waiting to arrest him. Even after setting sail, his runaway paranoia made him maintain a low profile aboard ship. He was sure they were there, watching and waiting for the right moment to pounce.

Old Heinrich was a fairly early immigrant to America, even before Ellis Island's establishment. Unfortunately, he could make no triumphant landing like Myles Standish. At age thirty-eight, his own government had run him out of his homeland. Late in the afternoon his ship tied up near what is now New York City's Fulton Fish Market. He almost feverishly scanned the dock's lengthening shadows for the chancellor's henchmen. They were surely there! They were waiting to drag him back to some dank German prison. Finally, sensing safety, he sneaked ashore and spent a tormented night among crates and boxes. When dawn broke, Heinrich headed straight for Chicago, and as the hours passed, he felt freedom. Incarceration had been so close; he was fully convinced the time for a dramatic change was at hand.

He resolved to restore order and tranquility to his chaotic life.

The story Pop told was over seventy-five years old, but because Pop never lied or embroidered the truth, I'm certain to this day that everything happened just as Pop described. I would also suspect that the circumstance of Heinrich's disgraceful flight to France, like a pathetic fox pursued by bloodthirsty hounds, is why the Cables perpetually forbid speaking German in all Cable households.

Pop Cable was obviously proud of his father. "Just because your great-grandfather was a political hell-raiser," he said, "don't believe for a moment he was tarnished goods. No, sir, he was a goodhearted, principled man. He had integrity, honor, and an excellent character. He was a responsible family man and quite worldly because of his many travels.

"He was also a go-getter because once in Chicago he quickly established two small businesses: Kabel's Photography Studio and the Kabel Smokery. He touted himself as the tobacconist who supplied Chicagoans with superb cigars. I knew him intimately." Pop would say this with a thrust of his jaw. "A fine man, indeed, and, as a new citizen, my father read all the great Americans like Thomas Jefferson, James Madison, Thomas Paine and Benjamin Franklin. Most important of all, he prided himself on being one hundred percent American, and not a German-American." Pop's eyes would blaze when he discussed this favorite family topic. "He avoided German-American organizations, and he worked hard to rid himself of his German accent. He was definitely not among the dreamy-eyed Germans who constantly jabbered about the great fatherland! Also, because he remembered his German downfall, he forever forsook meddling in American politics. That, Tommy my boy, was your great-grandfather."

According to Pop, the Schneiders, farther down Randolph Street, were precisely the brand of new American his father did not wish to emulate. On their stoop they'd clack away in German and read aloud from *Die Abendpost*, a locally printed German-language newspaper.

"Otto, why must you speak always German?" asked Heinrich. "In our new country your kids should talk like Americans already."

Otto Schneider responded icily, "Vell, warum nicht sprechen Deutsch, Heinrich? Vee are Chermans, chust like you!"

"Otto, if Germany was so good why you left it? Huh? You should in America not be a foreigner. Ahead look, not back. Ja?"

Charged by this encounter, the very next day my great-granddad went to the Chicago courthouse to officially change his name from Heinrich Kabel to Henry Cable. And that same year, at age thirty-nine, he did something not considered unusual for the time. He married the good widow Dora, and with her four children, they moved into a Victorian at 26 West Randolph near Canal, very near Chicago's City Hall. Henry proved to be a good provider.

On the Fourth of July, in the year 1861, Henry proudly handed out free cigars. Dora had given birth to Pop. Born on the Fourth of July, he was a real Yankee Doodle Dandy. They named him Gustave Frank. Imagine naming a cute little kid Gustave? It was probably why most everyone would later call him Pop or Mr. Cable. Two girls and two more boys followed Pop's birth. Old Heinrich, who had fled Germany in the night, was now an established Chicagoan with a wife and nine children and an American flag nailed to his parlor wall. And he reveled when called either Henry or Hank Cable.

On our Wineldan front porch Pop told of how when he was only four Henry had held him up one April day to see Abraham Lincoln lying in his casket. He also relived the terror of the Great Chicago Fire of 1871; Pop had been ten. He took me to the front door and showed me the brass doorstop. It was the same blackened flagpole eagle he'd found in the Chicago Post Office ruins. I still have the beautiful brass eagle. It remains blackened as my grandfather and great-grandfather found it.

It was because of this great family history that I've always been proud of my ancestors. I would have treasured meeting my great-granddad Henry but he died in San Diego in 1904 at the age of eighty-four, twenty years before I was born.

BEFORE WINELDA

The year Pop was born, the town of Winelda did not exist. Winelda was the place where the great Cables would unravel. Winelda's future site was in Indian Territory, a western spot with rolling sandy hills covered by sagebrush. It was an area constantly inspected by buzzards—huge black and white birds with ugly red heads that were vultures in every sense. These feathered morticians soared relentlessly, searching for dead or dying things. Then they would swoop down and use their razor-sharp beaks to tear at dead flesh, gorge themselves, and keep the prairie clean.

Most likely, the very day Pop was born in Chicago, far to the southwest some alert buzzard rode the thermals over the sage-covered area that would become Winelda. It spotted a small splinter herd of shaggy buffalos in a wallow cavorting like a pack of mammoth dogs. They were snorting and rolling among the aromatic sagebrush, rooting and throwing sandy soil into the air. With hooves skyward, some wriggled and scratched their blanket-like backs on the roughness of broken sage and sun-baked buffalo chips.

The big bird's sharp eyes then shifted to a band of mounted Kiowa hunters stealthily encroaching upon the wallow. The bird had seen this action play out many times before and it knew exactly what to expect. It soared quietly and patiently to a thousand feet, confident the Indians would leave something, at least the viscera. From this altitude, the buzzard could see to the south where the Cimarron River looped around the jumble of Aeolian-eroded sandstone rocks Wineldans would one day call the Devil's Playground. A few miles beyond and arching from the south to the west were the sparkling gypsum mesas. A huge bat cave was among the mesas but out of view. At that cave, almost ninety years later, I would create my own justice for a miscreant named Doc Chambers. That was the extent of Winelda the day Pop was born in Chicago. Unbeknownst to anyone, thirty years later, the buffalo wallow would become the exact spot where Winelda's Main and Cecil Streets would intersect.

WINELDA'S FIRST SETTLERS

It all began when a hard-drinking bunch of cattlemen from the Keystone Ranch near Archer City, Texas, strayed off the Chisholm Trail. They made camp near a creek in a grove of tall cottonwoods. It was a place their Comanche scout identified as Sweetwater, and very near the spot where the buzzard had seen the Kiowa stalk the buffalo. The trail boss fancied the place. "If we raised these critters up here, we'd be three hundred miles nearer the railhead at Hardtner, Kansas. Why in hell's name do we make this long dusty drive from Texas every year?" And they staked their claim nine years too early in an area later known as the Cherokee Strip. They became the Indian

Territory's very first illegal "Sooners." But because they were peaceful and small in number, and wisely made peace with Cherokee Chief Bushyhead—they occasionally presented him a few beeves—the Washington authorities never noticed the trespass.

And when they built a ranch headquarters, the brawny trail boss arbitrarily nailed a sign over the door proclaiming "Winelda–Pop. 18."

"We're namin' it after my late beloved," he said, and from the gravity of his tone no one dared argue. They were all aware that in Texas, his wife, Winelda, had entered a pigpen where a sow suckled its new litter. With phenomenal speed, the enraged animal had charged and ripped her from limb-to-limb until no semblance was found of her. I sometimes wondered if this could have been an ill omen—the use of a woman's name who had met death in such a bizarre and revolting way.

THE PRAIRIE

When Pop turned nineteen, he excitedly told his father he'd heard of timber claims in Kansas; he wanted to leave Chicago to try his hand. Old Henry was both proud and secretly glad. The departure of the children aroused his secret and latent wanderlust. He'd always dreamed of going west to California. Only days after Pop took the train south to Bloody Kansas, Henry and Dora chugged westward to San Diego, where again they would do well with cigars and photography. I have an 1899 photo of Henry and Dora sitting under a palm tree on their San Diego lawn. He wore a vested swallowtail coat and she was severely dressed in a long black gown that swept the ground. All my pictures of great-grandmother Dora show a stern yet beautiful woman that epitomized the pioneer woman. She had somber, decisive eyes that I'm sure would never have blinked at the challenge of taking a wagon over the Donner Pass.

When Pop headed south to look for life's thrills, he must've been a cocky daredevil. An old photo I have indicated his lean hard physique; he wore a rakish western hat and a vest. Because of his shaggy mustache and sharp eyes, he was a dead ringer for museum pictures I've seen of Wyatt Earp. I would imagine Pop's rangy appearance was a signal to those itching to fight to try elsewhere, especially in violent Kansas of the 1880s—wild with raucous buffalo hunters and the tumultuous Indian wars.

To some, western and central Kansas are flat and boring, but not to Pop. Just as a sailor loves the main, he forever loved the prairie's boundlessness. He marveled at the sheer number of buffalo and the excitement of each day's wild events. When a chocolate sea of buffalo sometimes blocked the tracks, he said the exasperated train crewmen fired their rifles and blasted the locomotive's whistle. The buffalos paid scant attention and grazed as if the world were made of inexhaustible time.

MOM AND POP CABLE

As Pop's train chugged across the Kansas flats, he knew nothing whatever of the Chisholm Trail or of the cowboys naming a spot of ground Winelda. He knew virtually nothing of the Indian Territory that later pioneers would call Oklahoma. His enthusiasm was focused solely on claiming Kansas land for his own. How could Pop Cable have known that, one day, destiny would draw him from Kansas southward to Winelda, just as surely as Doc Chambers's miserable ghost inexorably beckoned me back to Winelda time after time?

Pop staked his timber claim near the village of Ellinwood in Barton County on flat fertile bottomland south of the Arkansas River. And as if in purgatory, he labored like a beast. With a sweat-soaked harness over his shoulder, he spent months and arduous years clearing and plowing the land while gazing interminably at the wrong end of his impassive mule. And all the while his father and mother enjoyed San Diego's golden beaches, sunshine, and palm trees. Fortunately, Pop was young and powerful, had stubborn perseverance, tremendous self-discipline, and hadn't been cast upon the prairie alone.

All around him were plucky pioneers, mostly of German stock, who were also opening fields. None were afraid of work, and with great strength of character, they were unaware of words such as "cope" and "stress." Theirs was the kind of dogged and daring performance that was making America great, and during that early time, many were unknowingly harvesting golden eggs which in their old age would see them comfortably through the Great Depression.

One Saturday in 1892, while visiting the Ellinwood blacksmith,

Pop noticed the Langrehr family recently of Corning, Missouri. Their comely daughter Bertha was physically robust and quick-witted. The set of her jaw suggested uncommon strength. Pop, then thirty-one, yearned for this pretty eighteen-year-old prize. He'd been working hard for eleven years, had developed a fine rich farm, and was a steadfast part of the young community. He'd been alone far beyond what was considered natural, so it was no surprise when a wedding ceremony was soon set for the groom's home.

Pop proudly sent an announcement to his parents. Henry, now an old man of seventy-two, was delighted. He wrote, "Son and Bertha, from beneath our palm tree, we send congratulations for your joyful wedding day."

The elder Cable continued pressuring his favored son to come to his senses and join him and his other two boys in California. "Son," he wrote, "get off the farm. It's backbreaking, and you'll never recover in cash all the toil and sweat you expend. Leave the monotonous Kansas flats to those who enjoy digging in the dirt. Come to the beautiful mountains, the fertile fruit-laden valleys, and the glistening beaches of California." Henry could never comprehend why his Gustave preferred following a mule on a desolate windy field when California held such promise and beauty.

Paradise kept calling, but Pop cherished the very things old Henry abhorred. He loved the flatness, savored the roaring storms of winter and spring, and relished the furnace-like summer heat that made crops virtually pop out of the fertile ground. And in the winter, it was a thrill to skate on the brittle Arkansas River from Ellinwood to Great Bend. Upon return, he'd huff great foggy clouds like a plow horse, stomp on the ice, flail his arms, and proclaim, "Sure as hell can't do this in California." This was the loyal attitude of the true plainsmen, and if not for this intrinsic reason, the whole of Kansas, Nebraska, and the Dakotas might've turned their mules loose, junked their plows, and have run en masse to the Pacific.

MAKING A FAMILY

Once Bertha was on her own with her new husband, she immediately changed her name to Bettie—not Betty like all the others. And, without delay, Bettie bore a daughter named Lillian, and then, come September of 1897, the ill-fated Homer arrived.

Homer was born to a troublesome course. His initial adult life was similar to old Henry's rocky start, except Henry had managed to steer through adversity and get smoothly back on track. Homer's bus, on the other hand, seemed to sink ever deeper into sucking quicksand. Homer had a keen mind and a strong body, and everything went well through high school. It probably went well because on a severe Kansas farm his leash was very short. There was no pickup truck to drive to town. Farm kids spent their idle time taking care of never ending chores, or they read prescribed tomes around the well supervised pot-bellied stove. It was a very austere lifestyle, but good for Homer.

When Homer was six years old, during the Christmas of 1903, Pop received the crushing news his mother Dora had died in San Diego. Pop was not a vindictive person, and he was usually willing to forgive injustices, but in this instance, Pop was miserably resentful that the Lord would take his mother on Christmas Day. Pop normally took everything in stride, but not the death of his mother. It was as if he had expected her to live forever. Thereafter, he refused both church and the celebration of Christmas. Forty years later, Pop would still neither accept nor give Christmas presents. Mom would handle everything. She'd hand me a present and say, "This is from Pop," but Pop was in the backyard with his horseshoes. He'd do anything to shun Christmas. To him, Christmas was the bleakest, blackest day of the year, certainly not a time for joyful celebration, and he carried this wound to his grave. I must say that it was my grandfather's only eccentricity.

Come 1904, old Henry Cable also gave up the ghost to join his beloved Dora. At the age of eighty-four, they interred him beside her in San Diego's Mount Hope Cemetery. It was in an area known as Rancho de la Nacional, a suburb later named National City. Colorful Hank Cable would travel no more. His life had started fretfully but had ended happily and with great fulfillment. The life of his stalwart son, Gus, would be just the reverse. He would start famously, and then, as his children matured, the fizzling would begin. The many unsettling problems were just down the road.

When Virgil was born in 1906, Pop at forty-five heeded a measure of his father's advice. He leased the backbreaking farm and moved into Ellinwood. He opened his own cigar shop, and he banked the standard one-third share of each crop brought in by his tenant farmer. He and Bettie kept their eyes cocked for profitable investments, and together they prospered. Pop was proud of his three kids, and he frequently took the entire family over to Great Bend, to Wilson's or Halladay's, to have yet another family portrait taken.

There is certainly much to be said for having children. Some kids are forever loving joys that never cunningly pit mother against father, that do reasonably as told, perform well in school, and grow up to be bankers, mayors, merchants, and senators. Children can be the source of tremendous pride, the ultimate ego builders: "My son the doctor, my daughter the professor!" And the boys perpetuate the hallowed family name. On the other hand, one misfit child can be like a handful of pernicious sand in the family's gearbox. Think of Billy the Kid; his mother must have doted on him. What about Bonnie and lovable Clyde, or the James or the Dalton brothers, doubtlessly they were someone's darling children. Who would have thought them capable of eventually bringing so much grief to others?

I suppose if Mom and Pop had never had children, they would have quietly brooded and considered themselves unfortunate. But how were they to know that these bundles of joy would eventually bring them a parade of heartbreak?

Their oldest, who I called Lily, was my ambitious Aunt Lillian. An extremely bright youngster, she had been a cut above Ellinwood's High School class of 1911. She had already determined that life in a frame house on a bleak Ellinwood farm was not her idea of living—not in flat Kansas, so redolent of various manures—not among its wheat fields, its dust and sizzling summers, nor its remoteness from a city's cultural advantages. Her most torturing nightmare was that she'd fall in love with some rural swain and live a life of everlasting servitude among the chickens and pigs on a dusty windswept Ellinwood farm. She wanted an education, to walk off with honors, anything to insure that a lifetime in Ellinwood would never materialize. In the fall of 1912 Lily entered Emporia College and immediately set about achieving her goal. Mom and Pop were delighted because their own road to academia had been short lived. They intended that their offspring would enjoy every opportunity.

When Lily went to Emporia, Homer was fifteen, and had grown up partially on the farm and partly as a town kid. Later on he would continually tell me I never read enough. He would often recount to me how he had prepared for life by sprawling in the kitchen during the cheerless winter hours, voraciously reading his way through the town library. Perhaps that's the side everyone hears from his father, but I figured it must be true. The great depth of his astounding vocabulary lent credence to his story. However, even today, it's difficult for me to picture my dapper, cosmopolitan father in a frame farmhouse next to a potbelly stove steadfastly reading by the dimness of a coal-oil lamp, while outside, the howling winter wind swirled a mix of dust, snow, and tumbleweed. However, when Homer graduated from Ellinwood High in 1915, there was no apparent rush to send him off to college.

In the spring of 1916, Aunt Lily, age twenty-three, graduated valedictorian from Emporia College. She had gone to Emporia to excel and she had achieved her goal, and she had already set her sights high for her breadwinner-to-be. Shortly after graduation, she married for upward mobility and not necessarily for love. She wanted a ticket out of drab Kansas, and her business-executive husband seemed to be moving in the right direction. Should he not perform as planned, she was certain she would know how to propel him along. Immediately after their wedding, Lily and he departed for Spokane, Washington, where they paid cash for a nice home and began living happily ever after.

ANTHONY

Losing Lily to distant Spokane was a disappointment to Mom and Pop—all of the neighbors' children had stayed in Ellinwood. They knew this could happen so they faced it and refused to fret. Possibly it was the packing up of Lily for a far-flung place that set Pop's latent wanderlust to bubbling, just as it had in his father. Pop was fifty-six and Mom, forty-three. They wanted something new, but neither would give up the prairie for California.

They sold out of Ellinwood, and in their Model-T, drove Homer and Virgil south to Anthony, a flat Kansas town located only twelve miles from the Oklahoma border. Like most other prairie towns, dogs cavorted in the streets, and there was a huge water tower. The tallest buildings in town were the regionally ubiquitous grain elevator and the three story Morrison Hotel. They paid cash for a two story

Victorian at 424 North Anthony Street and bought the old Opera House at 519 East Main, renaming it the Novelty Theater because of their "novel" plan to present vaudeville followed by a silent movie.

It was a quintessential family operation. Pop took tickets and supervised the floor while Mom manned the box-office and managed the money. During that summer their first picture was *Ten Nights in a Barroom*. Homer, then nineteen, was chief projectionist—a tiring hand-crank operation—and eleven-year-old Virgil sometimes helped coordinate the Victorola sounds with the picture. If the gunshots in the saloon scene went off too soon or too late, it was attributed to little Virgil's lack of synchronization.

Pop invested in a farm west of Anthony and Mom bought one to the east. Pop often said, "Real estate is money in the bank," or "Never sell the land!" They leased the farms, and come harvest, collected their standard one-third. A year later they purchased a large corner building on Main Street, which they rented at fifty dollars per month to their perennial Easch Pharmacy tenant.

HOMER'S KANSAS UNIVERSITY

In the fall of 1918, Mom and Pop sent Homer to the University of Kansas, where he joined the SATC program—a forerunner of the ROTC. It was a hectic time of war and tumultuous excitement. As Homer was arriving on campus, the deadly Spanish swine flu virus plagued the nation as well as virtually every corner of the world; twenty million people were to die of it. For six weeks the university completely shut down. Officials hurriedly established Sunshine Hospital on campus, and nearby Rosedale Medical Center sent its students to assist. Faculty wives and the ladies of Lawrence, Kansas, served as nurses. Hundreds of students fell to the disease, and some died. KU benched Homer's football team. Fortunately, by mid November, the flu began to subside—only to be followed by the uproarious celebrations of Armistice. World War I was over! It was a chaotic time for the students, and serious academic excellence was hard to achieve. Homer's performance was far from desirable.

One of Pop's principles was to never openly discuss other people's shortcomings, particularly family. Consequently, he never gave me a straight account of Homer's first and only year at Kansas University.

I went through most of my life assuming Homer—who in this case never corrected my aberrant imagination—had been a football star and a KU graduate. I also learned, years later, that during this turbulent time Homer had discovered both booze and the titillation of lighthearted vampish flapper girls. I can more clearly visualize that perspective of my father rather than a Homer submerged among stacks of books in a coal-oil lit farm kitchen, or in a university carrel.

Homer and his classmate, Fred Enfield—it was Fred who later told me these details—often danced and caroused over in Kansas City until near dawn. One day, Pop stormed into Lawrence like Bill Quantrill's Raiders to break Homer's festive bubble. Pop told Homer if he didn't start hitting the academic ball, he could pack up his red wagon and come home. Gus Cable certainly didn't expect reckless behavior from any son of his, and because both of them were strong-willed, it forever repressed their rapport. I believe the strained distance that developed between them became a part of Pop's first real unhappiness. He loved his son, but "by God I'm not going to put up with damned foolishness when money is so hard to come by." Pop forever distrusted carouser Enfield, who was also from Anthony.

WWI had come and gone without dispersing the family. Pop had been too old and Virgil too young for service. Homer had been in the Student Army Training Corps uniform with the official Army rank of private. Because he had never been more than a hundred miles from home, he was sorely disappointed. He had missed the exciting challenge of the Great War, and the rare opportunity to explore Europe. I know that Homer would have been a rage in Paris. Unfortunately, never in his lifetime was Homer to visit Europe. Cosmopolitan Homer never once set foot outside America, not even to go to Mexico or Canada. In Homer's time, only missionaries and the very rich traveled abroad.

In the spring of 1919, Homer quit KU and returned to Anthony to help with the family business. But after Lawrence and Kansas City's faster pace, Anthony seemed downright funereal. He subscribed to a business administration mail extension course and began devouring its thirty-eight books from cover to cover. I later thumbed through his well-worn books, saw the copious underlining, and the many marginal notes on each and every page.

This furious study pleased Mom and Pop. They knew Homer had a keen mind, but they also knew he was unhappy in Anthony. In late

1920 they presented him with a grand opportunity. They staked Homer to his own theater, the Columbia, in Coffeyville, Kansas. The theater was a splendid opportunity and Homer was grateful.

Coffeyville, also known as Javatown, was a progressive town in the flint hills of Southeastern Kansas. It had a zinc smelter, a Sinclair and a Skelly oil refinery, a Katy and Missouri Pacific railroad facility, a huge vitrified brick concern, the Oil County Specialties, and an oilfield equipment firm which very soon had its very own Beechcraft executive plane. Everyone in town had been out to see the Beechcraft and Raleigh Inman, its rakish pilot. Javatowners sometimes saw Inman in his convertible touring car, tooling around Coffeyville with a young lion that lounged regally on the back seat.

Homer had come to Coffeyville at age twenty-three. He had "attended" KU, was blessed with exceptional intelligence, was handsome, and a faultless dresser. He was one of Coffeyville's youngest and most successful businessmen as well as the vice president of the newly established Lions Club. He was seen everywhere with Florence Ross, one of the most popular young ladies in town. She was both racy and beautiful, a talented pianist, and none in town could excel her Charleston. At the time they were among Coffeyville's most discussed, most admired young couples. At last, Homer's achievements were a reward to Mom and Pop for enduring the travails of having kids. Despite the initial disappointment at Kansas University, Homer had obviously turned the corner, proved he was Cable "stuff," and had become a glowing success in Coffeyville. It was the absolute zenith of my father's life.

Virgil

In 1923, my Uncle Virgil left Anthony at age seventeen to study music and violin at the Chicago Conservatory of Music. He was the perfect son—gentle, polite, a scholar of music, and the antithesis of roughhouse Homer, who was the family's intellectual athlete. Virgil had made Pop and Mom Cable and his big brother very proud. He played the violin beautifully along with several other instruments. That he would most likely never become a businessman or have money was of no family consequence. He was a sensitive scholar and a talented artist. However, although handsome, he was not as robust as past male Cables had been. He would eventually take his turn at disappointing Mom and Pop.

In Chicago, he married Iris of Waterloo, Iowa, whom Mom immediately distrusted because Iris was almost six years older than little Virgil. Mom was an extremely fair unbigoted person yet she was positive Iris had taken advantage of her darling Virgil, and then there was the smell of tobacco in Iris's clothing and hair. This placed her character in serious contention. Certainly no young lady with breeding would ever smoke.

Their first visit to the folks was palpably tense, but because they came often this soon eased. Iris would always accompany Virgil's violin with her excellent piano renditions. She did this lovingly, and Mom and Pop would beam with pride. In time, they came to accept Iris as having had no ulterior motives, and it was obvious the marriage was sound. Also to Iris's credit, she never once brazenly smoked in their presence. So what had been initial disappointment eventually cured itself.

Iris and Virgil loved academic life and their goal was to do graduate work in music and literature and to eventually become teachers. Mom and Pop were primarily responsible for subsidizing their attendance at nearby Oklahoma A&M's graduate school.

"Well, it won't ever pay them anything," said Pop to Mom, "but they're so happy together." And the idea of having career scholars in the family was certainly appealing. This period during the twenties was probably the crest of my grandparents' lifetime. Unfortunately, their lives were on the threshold of a horrendous roller coaster plunge.

HOMER'S MARRIAGE

One hot night, after two years of ardent dating, and most likely catalyzed by the impassioned heat of July, Homer indiscreetly spirited Florence the fifty-two miles to a justice of the peace in the little town of Columbus, Kansas. It was flawed judgment Homer would live to regret.

Mrs. Ross was matriarchal and a staunch Methodist. News of this elopement provoked her to rage. Behavior much less crass than this could within seconds flash her one-quarter Osage Indian blood to fury. "Homer," she fumed, her black eyes piercing Homer's like a hawk's, "how dare you *sneak* away with my daughter!" The word "sneak" exploded like a whip. "Now you listen to me," she snapped, "don't you ever let on that you and Florence did this marriage thing in Columbus. Am I perfectly clear?" She clenched her jaw and ground her teeth. "You and Florence will be properly married in our home by my Methodist pastor!" Mrs. Ross was just short of grabbing Homer by the ear. "Damn your Columbus marriage!" She literally seethed.

In the *Coffeyville Journal*'s society page, Grandmother Ross announced the "coming" wedding. During the brief ceremony she smiled sweetly. That is, until her eyes fastened onto Homer, and then they reflected anything but love. Because of the elopement, she would never forgive or trust my iconoclastic father-to-be. Grandfather Ross, a kindly, sweet man, liked his successful new son-in-law, yet he seldom foolishly crossed swords with Grandmother Ross.

How did I discover this *contretemps?* Years later, my mother's sister, my Aunt Myrtle, gave me a yellowed newspaper clipping. It announced my parent's wedding at the home of Mr. and Mrs. Ross. It was a creditable piece of treasured family memorabilia for me to file with other genealogical data. However, several years later while piecing together the family tree from Topeka marriage records, I accidentally discovered the Columbus marriage! It even included the Columbus Justice of the Peace's name. Strange, the newspaper clipping my aunt had given me indicated Florence and Homer had been married in Coffeyville! Again I visited Aunt Myrtle, who hesitantly and reluctantly corroborated the spicy details of the Great Family Explosion.

Most kids generally believe their parents are near perfect paradigms of righteousness and cannot imagine adults, especially parents, capable of risqué dance or sex. Later, to positively learn they were human, less than perfect, and that fooling around had indeed taken place was an exciting revelation. "Can you just imagine mother and father . . . ?" The Cables had interesting skeletons. It has always amazed me how tightly locked our family closet has been over the years.

As an example, once, while I was in high school, my Aunt Lily had to have an invasive operation at the Mayo Clinic. I wanted to know why, but because it was a hysterectomy involving hallowed female apparatus, I was simply told some of her insides had grown together, and this promptly terminated the conversation. It was years before I was privy to the true word regarding Aunt Lily's insides.

However, to return to Homer's two weddings with my mother, it must have been that torrid July night in 1923—the first marriage—because exactly nine months to the day of that marriage, Anthony's Dr. Galloway delivered me in April 1924. They named me Thomas. Thomas Cable. I always liked that name because as a kid I was Tommy, as I grew to a man I was Tom, and I suppose when I'm elderly I will be Mr. Thomas G. Cable. It hasn't been a bad name, and it's been easy for people to spell.

My father's triumph by producing a son created much happiness among both the Cable and the Ross families, and everyone, with the exception of Grandmother Ross, figured Homer made a fine husband. After all, Homer and Florence doted on each other; it was clearly a marriage of true love.

Gus and Bettie Cable and Fred and, eventually, Susan Ross were drawn together. Fourteen days after my birth they all joyfully celebrated the occasion in Coffeyville. On subsequent birthdays the grandparents took turns holding the celebration alternately between Coffeyville and Anthony.

Four years later, they scheduled the reunion in Coffeyville. Even Uncle Virgil and Aunt Iris, still purposely childless, announced they'd lay down their postgraduate books to be present. Homer and Florence had driven up to Kansas City in their new Model-A Ford on important business. I had been left in the care of one of my mother's sisters (I later learned most of these details from those doting aunts). Homer had assured everyone he and Florence would return in plenty of time for the family festivities.

I never saw my parents together again!

The Night in Kansas City

The final Kansas City event for Homer and Florence was a huge party at a prominent country club. There was a big-name band, good food, and plenty of bootleg bourbon and bathtub gin. Homer and Florence were terrific with the Charleston, and they danced into the early morning hours.

Because of the occasion's festivities, and the continuously heavy drinking, a KU classmate of Homer's had overindulged. He was nauseous and declared both himself and his wife in no condition to drive. Because Homer had a good tolerance for liquor, he offered to drive them home. At 2:00 A.M., the four of them, singing "My Blue Heaven," set off toward the Meuhlbach Hotel in downtown Kansas City. En route Homer planned to let the couple off at their home.

A light drizzle collected on the windshield; each little droplet created a tiny sparkling light. After ten minutes on the road, Homer saw an arched concrete bridge ahead. A truck was about mid-span, its headlights making a thousand points of dazzle on Homer's windshield.

The truck driver later said that as he was leaving the bridge he thought someone, possibly an animal, jumped onto the road. His natural reflex was to swerve. He sideswiped Homer who was just about to come onto the bridge. It caused Homer to collide squarely with the bridge's massive concrete abutment at thirty-five miles per hour.

Except for Homer's four fractured ribs that he sustained as he hit the steering wheel, and the facial cuts and the broken nose when his head shattered the windshield, he suffered no serious physical injury. His friend's wife had been lying across her husband's lap in the back seat and had fallen asleep. Her limp body had impacted against the front seats, and she sustained minor lacerations and a few sizeable contusions, but nothing that required hospitalization. Unfortunately, the impact threw her twenty-eight-year-old husband into a boulder-strewn ditch twenty feet below. His back was broken, the spinal cord so severely damaged he was destined to spend the rest of his life in a wheelchair. The impact against the windshield broke my mother's neck. The rescue unit pronounced her dead at the scene of the crash. Her facial lacerations were such that the funeral director advised the family to have a closed-casket funeral.

In the following years, all I ever discovered from the closed-mouthed Cables was that there had been a terrible accident. However, much later in life, I researched the complete story in the *Kansas City Star* morgue. Then I confronted my elderly Aunt Myrtle, who made a clean breast of all the horrible family details. Strangely, the revelation relieved me. I had grown up with no mother while every kid in town seemed to have one. Because there had been so many mysteries, I had often wondered as a kid if I were adopted.

Why am I dredging up all this material? It helps explain Homer's subsequent, often-aberrant psyche; it also explains how Winelda and the Doc Chambers incident came about.

BAD DREAMS

Following the terrible crash, my sedated father fuzzily awakened, tried to bring the ceiling into focus, and then suddenly his terrible night crystallized. He remembered Florence's head hanging at such a bizarre angle, and he suddenly went wild. For two difficult hours the doctors feared they might lose him to severe shock. Homer's nightmarish recall recurred over and over, everything so very real, and each time he'd go berserk. The attendants strapped him down as if he were some predatory creature. It became clear to everyone that Homer would never be able to attend my mother's funeral.

Mom and Pop arrived and saw Homer's blackened eyes, the whites partially blood red, supposedly as a result of hematoma and the broken nose. Afterwards, the doctor carefully advised them to commit Homer for psychiatric care.

"Commit, commit!" It was like being struck with a hammer!

That awful word: "commit"—frightening language that implied something grievously awry with Homer's mind. The physician recommended Topeka's already-famous Menninger Clinic, and said he would see to the arrangements.

In the meantime, they would hold Florence's funeral in the same living room where she had been married five years before. Mom and Pop planned to drive down from the Kansas City hospital and stay overnight at the Hotel Dale in Coffeyville. They were certainly not prepared for what happened.

THE OUTBURST

When they arrived, my aunts greeted and hugged them the way kin do at such times. Grandfather Fred Ross just stood there, his head hanging. Mom broke into tears and gently hugged him. At that precise moment, Susan Ross came sweeping out of the bedroom, a wild and demented cast in her eyes. Always meticulously groomed, her raven hair was now unkempt and very unlike her. Standing before Mom, she made no inquiry of Homer, offered no words of comfort, just fumed like a dormant volcano ready to explode.

In the background was Florence's closed casket, engulfed in a mound of Easter lilies and other flowers. Mom, still by the doorway, still wearing her traveling coat and hat, reached out for Susan and hugged her, but my Grandmother Ross stiffened. She gave Mom a hostile look, gritted her teeth, and fairly hissed, "Bettie, your son killed my daughter! I knew nothing good would ever come of it." Because of her crazy eyes, Mom instinctively recoiled!

"Dad gummit," interjected Grandfather Ross, "none of that now!" But Susan Ross was resolute and vented her rage specifically at Mom, possibly because it was she who had brought Homer into the world.

The outburst bitterly wounded Pop. He and Fred Ross turned and walked onto the front porch. "Gus, I'm sorry. It's as if Susan's gone mad. This morning she insisted on having the Skinner Funeral director open the casket. I tried to stop her from seeing Florence that way, but you know how mule-headed she can be. It was terrible."

Grandma Ross announced with finality that she intended keeping me in Coffeyville. "He's the only living thing left of my precious daughter," she wailed. "You cain't have him." Pop and Mom took on their quiet stance. This was obviously not the time to take a stand; custody would eventually sort itself out. They departed for Topeka.

But time mellowed nothing. Regardless of weather, Susan took to making daily visits to Fairlawn Cemetery. The grave obsessed her as if it were a consecrated shrine. Fred—only he could drive—had to make these daily visits to his youngest daughter's grave all the while enduring Susan's spiteful words.

MONTGOMERY COUNTY COURT

When they finally released my father from the Menninger Clinic, everyone said he was different, had lost his spark, and was similar to a person who'd undergone a mild stroke. No longer was he the dashing young businessman who had taken Coffeyville by storm. Even though Menninger described him as a person psychiatrically stabilized, he was an introverted shell of his former self. My family never told me these details. I learned it all years later from Enfield, my father's old university pal.

Dr. Charles Menninger explained that for Homer to be around Coffeyville would be counterproductive. Consequently, Mom and Pop, who held Homer's note on the Columbia Theater in Coffeyville, decided to sell. The prospects for liquidation in late 1928 were excellent, and they turned a neat profit.

When Bettie Cable told the Menninger doctors that Homer must appear in a Coffeyville court to regain custody of his son, they reluctantly approved. I grew up never aware there had been a family storm and that Grandma Ross had refused to hand me over "to the man who murdered my daughter." Mom and Pop again drove across the state to appear in court with Homer. They had a sworn Menninger Clinic deposition that Homer had, to all palpable appearances, recovered completely.

In Judge Barringer's view, Homer's was a shocking ordeal, and he empathized with the young widower while Susan Ross became her own worst enemy. She made frequent fiery outbursts, interrupted the court over and over, and shouted that Homer had been "committed to the institution!" Her hateful, gratuitous remarks infuriated the judge.

Susan Ross lost the case. She wailed and pounded the table like a woman possessed. Eventually they physically restrained her, forcibly sedated her, and then—jerking like a trussed wildcat—they carried her wild-eyed from the courtroom. The judge banged his gavel, sighed, awarded the son to father, and remarked that perhaps sometime in the future the two families could amiably reach some solution to visitations.

On the long day's trip back to Anthony, Homer drove; in the backseat Mom played with me. The ugly episode was over, and despite their love and sympathy for Grandpa Fred, they blotted *Ross* from the Cable vocabulary.

THE FRENCH QUARTER

Homer lazed around Anthony for several weeks and suddenly realized it was time to get his act together, to start his life moving again. While operating the theater at Coffeyville, Homer had made several good contacts with United Artists Films. Consequently, after a few letters and calls—"have Model-A, will travel"—he was soon on the road—at a base salary of twenty dollars per week plus commission—selling United Artists pictures to theaters in Arkansas, Missouri, Mississippi, and Louisiana. If Homer had good sales, he had every opportunity to make as much as two hundred per month, a very good living at the time. He once told me of those traveling salesman days, how he'd pull both the Model-A's ears down and race around the graveled curves of the Ozarks.

At first, the sales were difficult. From his interminable reading and his year at college, Homer had developed a rich vocabulary. However, for all his ability to articulate, he soon discovered that his pleasant personality and a thesaurus-like delivery didn't generate sales. He was not communicating and this stumped him.

Finally, a film exhibitor in Springfield, Missouri, who had taken an instant liking to Homer, told him over lunch one day, "Goddamit, Homer, I love ya, Boy, but half the time I cain't unnerstan' yer highfalutin' words. Why cain't ya jist speak the king's English fer chrissakes . . . maybe you'd start makin' some fuckin' sales. Try some downhome plain English, Boy, and see what it does fer ya, okay? Now," he said as he wiped the grease from around his lips, "hows about givin' me a chance to buy some of yer pitchers." And he bought several blocks of A, B and C-grade pictures.

Homer later said that that lunch was his turning point to success. He began expressing himself in the vernacular and was soon making seventy-five and eighty dollars a week. His sales progressed so phenomenally he soon captured the attention of corporate headquarters. Times had become quite bad. Regardless, Homer was making things move. United Artists promoted him to Southeastern Region Deputy Director of Sales, and my father and I moved to New Orleans. Two months later, they promoted him to Director of Sales.

For Homer, the bachelor-cum-film executive, caring for a five-year-old was not an easy task. Homer hired Orletha Washington as my full-time companion. She lived with us in our modest living quarters which Homer leased in the French Quarter. Weather permitting, Orletha often walked me to the markets near historic Jackson Square and on down to the Mississippi riverboat landing. It was a place that beckoned to any boy my age. We'd feed the pigeons around General Jackson's statue and occasionally peek in on some Bourbon Street bistro where a jazz band played wild, wonderful music. Orletha, a quadroon, was on a first-name basis with many of the musicians and, if it moved her, she sometimes sang. On those occasions I still remember how someone always hauled me up to sit atop the piano. We'd spend an hour or more listening to a parade of impromptu arrangements.

When Homer came home, he always had some prize—a stalk of sugar cane or a baby alligator or a pecan praline. And after dinner I vaguely remember riding on his back as he laughed and bucked and crawled on all fours. Homer tried his level best to make sure I was not a neglected kid. But both the great tragedy and Susan Ross's hateful, damning words were always lurking. Sometimes he'd dwell too long on his memories, get into a funk, backslide, and spend too much time after work at the Old Absinthe House, drinking quietly by himself. He'd grow progressively maudlin until Levy, the bartender, preferred that Homer go home.

The Girl from Bayou LaFourche

Enter Laurence Thibodaux, a beautiful, uncommonly well-educated girl born in the Bayou Lafourche area near New Orleans. Laurence was just short of six feet, had a very pleasing Mediterranean complexion and was blessed with marvelously long Cyd Charisse legs. She always swept her shoulder-length silky black hair back from her sculptured face to accentuate her striking almond eyes. When lissome Laurence entered a restaurant, heads snapped. My recollection of her is hazy at best, but I remember she was strikingly beautiful, always smelled good, and I usually called her "Lawrence."

"It's not Lawrence, Tommy, it's Lah-rawnce," and Homer and I would laugh.

I felt very comfortable with Laurence, and often wondered if Homer would bring her home so I'd have a mom the same as my kindergarten friends.

Laurence's attraction to Homer was understandable. He was obviously bright, was always turned out smartly, stood taller than she, and was an excellent dancer—she taught him the Cajun stomp—and they were always going to Antoine's, Arnaud's or Gallatin's for a delicious *pompano en papier* dinner and a bottle of their favorite—*Pouilly-Fuissé*.

But mixed with the good times were Homer's occasional bouts of depression, and he'd begin to drink too much and speak of Florence.

For Laurence, these phases were difficult; she couldn't compete with a dead person whom Homer had obviously canonized. But Laurence was no fair-weather friend, and she tried, despite his sporadic demand for a succession of drinks. Booze forever made him argumentative.

Society should outlaw liquor to the Homers of the world, those who after a few drinks have a history of predictably turning snarlymean. A clumsy waiter or a meddlesome person at an adjacent table could set him off. However, he never once mistreated Laurence.

When they rose to leave, Homer sometimes stumbled around like the drunken person he was and accidentally pushed into the tables of others. This perplexed Laurence because this slob of a person reflected nothing of the real Homer—a person who was friendly, lovable, and considerate, even gentle. His dual personality was like a weird enactment of Dr. Jekyll and Mr. Hyde, with the sinister Hyde always coming straight from the bottle.

Homer's old university pal once told me that my father had obviously changed. "When we were on our drinking-dancing sprees in Kansas City, your dad was always a pile of fun. Homer never fought with anyone unless someone really worked hard for it." Obviously, the wreck had in some mysterious way altered his body chemistry, which in turn changed his personality. After a few belts—and Homer always belted—he was no longer the same charismatic Homer.

One drizzly night in 1931, when Homer and Laurence were together, he stepped awkwardly off a high curb and snapped his leg. Dressed immaculately in a beautifully tailored white silk suit, he was a pathetic mess as he agonizingly rolled back and forth on the French Quarter's dirty wet bricks. He pitifully cursed and wept until the ambulance arrived.

Laurence stayed by his side in the hospital. It was agreed by her, the medical staff, and Homer that he should stay a few days to dry out. Mom and Pop were informed. Pop was provoked because he looked upon the drinking as Homer's dismal failure to come to terms with real life. Pop's perspective was irrefutable. "He's got a damned fine job down there, why can't he discipline himself? Goddammit to hell, it's unmanly."

Strangely, at the early age of thirty-three, these interludes never affected Homer's work with United Artists. None of Homer's office associates were aware of Homer's nightmares, his depression fits, nor of the bottle battles. Everyone had learned Homer's wife had died and that he had been left to raise a kid, but nothing had ever interfered with his dedication to corporate sales. In New Orleans, only Laurence was aware of the two Homers. Other than lunches, Homer very rarely socialized with his office. They considered the broken leg a freak accident, and everyone in the office signed his cast. They didn't know when he had broken it he'd been bombed out of his skull and had been crazily mumbling about a similar drizzly night in Kansas City.

YET ANOTHER PROBLEM

Two years earlier, when the Great Depression had badly shaken most American households, Mom and Pop's nest had, because of hard and constant work, been well feathered. Their stock portfolio had been inconsequential—fifty shares of Cities Service Oil. I remember when the whole family stopped in front of a Cities Service pumping station and Mom had said, "I own a piece of that company." And Pop had quipped, "Tommy, you see the floodlight over the door? That's about what Momma Bettie owns in Cities Service." And everyone laughed.

Ninety-eight percent of Mom's and Pop's assets were either liquid or in good property. All the kids had been educated; everyone had clothing; the Novelty Theater remained successful; the farms produced wheat; the drugstore paid its rent; and the cupboard was never bare. But then came crushing news from Lily.

The Depression had not been kind to her marriage with Schrepel, the misbegotten marriage which had never grown into love. Schrepel's business unfortunately went on the rocks. They had had to sell their Spokane home at a great loss. That was when fair-weather Lily bailed out of their essentially passionless marriage. To her credit, she did not take advantage. She asked for a few hundred dollars and went south. But, for a woman to become divorced in 1931 was about as unsavory as announcing to the neighborhood she was undergoing treatment for a venereal disease. Divorce just wasn't Christian. It made a farce of vows, it was tawdry, and its blemish was a family embarrassment.

That Lily was now a vivacious thirty-eight-year-old divorcée who had moved from remote Spokane to San Diego to become someone's executive secretary, crushed Mom and Pop Cable and caused them sleepless nights. They thought of her high school senior picture, her long locks of beautiful hair, those large captivating eyes, and the hint of a pout on her pretty mouth. What was she doing right now, a divorced young woman in San Diego? It caused them great heartache as they tossed and turned.

Life's parental lottery is indeed strange. From the very beginning a couple feeds its offspring at ungodly hours when even ignorant chickens have the good sense to sleep. They watch their beloved offspring spit up and throw its Pabulum to the floor. They clean vomit off the new divan, panic when the thermometer soars, and rush to the expensive doctor. They buy the kid new clothes, and eventually worry and consult with teachers over obviously brain-dead grades. They dig deeply into every pocket to send their issue off to college. Finally, when the child passes twenty-one, a parent should have absolution, should feel entitled to some heaven sent bounty, some return.

But nothing had ever come easily for Gus and Bettie Cable. They had struggled for everything and persevered. If during the Depression some poor cousins were jealous of Mom and Pop's desirable position, it can only be said the Cables had earned it honestly. There had been no inheritances, no unearned social register entrées, no silver spoon, or platter. They had made it fair and square. Someone had written somewhere that children would mature like good bonds and bring their parents in their later years one joyous coupon after the other. Yet, in Mom and Pop's autumn, their children seemed hell-bent upon complicating their lives far beyond the trials of Job. My grandparents were very good people, and despite the fact Pop no longer recognized God, they deserved a much better hand from whomever was in charge of dealing.

Mom and Pop were clearly resilient, "can do" people. They had steadfastly refused to become discouraged because Homer had disappointingly acted up at college, and had injudiciously eloped with the Ross's daughter; because Virgil married a smoking woman six years his senior; because Homer couldn't make a go of New Orleans; or because their college valedictorian Lily was now a divorcée running free-spirited and untethered around San Diego. All of this certainly had not made them gloriously happy, but it also had not dampened the indomitable Cable *esprit de famille*.

But regardless of the folks' worry, egotistical Lily was basically a very good person and resourceful. She never once played the swooning female role by running home to camp on Momma's doorstep. In San Diego, she enjoyed life to the fullest. She became an executive secretary for a large corporation and was designated a Life Master Competition bridge player. She referred to herself as Mrs. Lillian Cable Schrepel, and at a distance of fifteen hundred miles from everyone, she gradually evolved into a fully independent person, a veritable Rock of Gibraltar. In Lillian's case, a glimmer of adult promise materialized.

THE DEPRESSION AND WANDERLUST

Whether the culmination of these events was a cause, it is not clear, but Pop grew increasingly restless with Anthony's now predictable routine. He had become tired of playing pinochle with other male seniors at Anthony's musty Metropolitan Club; tired of hearing everyone's passive Great Depression despondency; tired of the interminable recitation of senior physical ailments; tired of seemingly incessant bad news from the children. Pop wanted to break the spell. He wanted to go out and make something happen. That was Pop's way.

In his "club's" magazine rack he came across a Chamber of Commerce handout: "Winelda, the Most Modern Small City in the State of Oklahoma." He took it home, put on his glasses, and used Mom as a sounding board.

Referring to his map he said, "Winelda's not so far, eighty-five miles, mostly west and a little south. Says Winelda's county ranks first in Oklahoma's wheat production, fourth in cattle, ninth in poultry . . . blah blah." Pop liked this brochure because it incessantly plugged progress. There was not a solitary mention of gloom and despair. He looked over the top of his glasses at Mom, who was busily knitting. "Are you hearing what I just said?"

"Yes, Gus, I heard." In recent years, Mom's head had taken to moving a little from side to side, and when she answered it traversed a little more intensely, a condition that lent a new and real emphasis to her words—a takeoff on film star Edward Everett Horton.

"Says Winelda has a Santa Fe Railroad division point and three years ago Lindy went there and built an important T.A.T. air terminal [TWA's forerunner] for those big hundred mile an hour Ford Trimotors. Says, come sunset, twenty or so passengers land at Winelda after flying all day from Columbus, Ohio. They're bussed to the train depot and a Santa Fe Pullman takes them through the night via Amarillo to Clovis, New Mexico. At sunup a waiting plane flies them on to California. Coast to coast . . . always moving . . . by God, isn't that something? It captures the imagination."

Pop put down the article and looked over his glasses. "Who would have ever thought that just in our lifetime we'd progress from wagons to airplanes? I tell ya, it's simply amazing." He scratched his head. "But what I can't figure out is how come, with all the big places like Tulsa and Wichita, how come they pick on little Winelda, Oklahoma, for a railroad center and a big air terminal?"

Mom pursed her lips as she continued knitting and her head began to move a little from side to side as she said, "Probably because it's located at the right spot."

Pop Cable liked the sound of her words. The right spot! Yes, sir. The right spot! Yet, Winelda was really nowhere, the nearest bona fide city, Oklahoma City, was a hundred and thirty-five difficult miles away—Amarillo about two hundred and forty.

He returned to the brochure. "Says here Winelda has two doctors, two lawyers and an undertaker. Hmmph," he said thumbing to the next page, "sure can't get away from those fellas. How about this: 'Newcomers will receive a hearty welcome from Wineldans who are native Americans with negligible foreign elements.'" He put the pamphlet down. "Ha! Now how in hell does that read between the lines?"

Mom kept knitting as she matter-of-factly said, "I would say it means you're welcome if you're white and have no accent. And when they say 'native Americans,' they don't mean Indians, they mean Wineldans."

Pop Cable looked at her adoringly and said, "Momma Bettie, that's why we've always done so well. You get right to the heart of things! Whad'dya say one day we go take a look at Winelda?"

"When?" she said rather noncommittally.

"First thing tomorrow's as good as any. Go early, get back in time for the picture show . . . only sixty-seven miles each way."

ENTERING WINELDA

Mom Cable later told me she always did the driving in their powerful, racing-green Chrysler. Theirs was the venerable model with the classic winged radiator cap, the cap with a see-through thermometer. Ever since Pop crashed the Model-T through the Ellinwood barn in 1916, only Mom drove. And as the de facto captain and chief operator, she had long since vetoed Pop's spitting tobacco out the window. "Gus, now look how you've messed the side of our car? It's disgraceful!" Thereafter, Pop always kept a Maxwell House coffee can half filled with sand between his feet and, as they traveled, he'd read the Burma-Shave signs, check the quality of wheat fields, and complain of the oil fumes that forever seeped through the floorboards—common for that vintage car. He'd also gauge the speed and danger of on-coming cars. He'd caution, "Better watch this one," which often sent a clatter of gravel onto their fenders, and was some-times capable of shattering their non-safety windshield glass.

Mom frequently recalled that initial trip to Winelda. She'd remember how huge lop-eared jackrabbits—"the size of small dogs!"—occasionally dashed in front and whacked against the car. "Oh me, oh my!" she would gasp as a big jack had just splattered its life over the big steel bumpers. There were hordes of them, and like funeral directors, the buzzards forever circled in search of their lifeless remains.

Then far off, in a lovely valley with a purplish cast, Pop spotted Winelda's aluminum-painted standpipe glistening in the sun. It was such a pleasant spot with leafy elms, huge cottonwoods, and locust trees. Off to the west stood stately red mesas capped with sparkling gypsum. Some locals called them the Glass Mountains because chunks of their crystalline gypsum sometimes sparkled in the sun. The pioneers should've called them the Diamond Mountains much like Diamond Head in Hawaii.

THE WINELDA SQUARE

Mom Cable often told how impressive Winelda looked that day. Half a mile from town a sign read: "Entering Winelda. Pop. 1840." And nestled among the cottonwoods on both sides of the road was a helter-skelter village of small unpainted houses that the people of Winelda referred to as Mexican Town. Delightful brown children romped in the sandy dirt, and there was a tiny Catholic Church ornately trimmed with neon tubing. Just beyond was the Mexicans' workplace—the Santa Fe roundhouse and the largest ice house this side of Chicago.

Pop said, "How come the Chamber of Commerce pamphlet prided itself there were no foreigners yet here's a whole town full of Mexicans."

"Because," Mom said matter-of-factly, "this isn't Winelda. Winelda's up ahead. These folks live out here on railroad property."

Entering town, Mom turned right on Cecil and headed toward the Square. "Look, Bettie, they're pitching horseshoes back of that Eason station."

They continued to the heart of Winelda—the intersection of Cecil and Main. It was the very spot where in 1861—the year Pop was born—the Kiowas had come to hunt buffalo. It was the spot where in 1880 the Chisholm cowboys had settled and had named the town Winelda to commemorate a lady killed by a rampaging Texas hog. It had been a part of the 1893 Cherokee Strip Land Run. It had seen its share of celebrities—Charles Lindbergh, Wiley Post, and Will Rogers. Amelia Earhart had twice eaten lunch at Eastman's Restaurant, as had Lindbergh, and she had spent the night at the Santa Fe's Harvey House. And now, come 1932, Winelda had already become a colorful chapter in Oklahoma's aviation and rail history. It was a bustling town teeming with twenties automobiles and "native" Americans named Faurot, McNally, McGurn, Bosley, Bay, Guyer, Clapper, Hutchison, Barker and Nutter. Pop spat in his coffee can, "Depression sure's not hurtin' these folks."

To be sure, Wineldans lived conservatively. Cuffs and collars were regularly turned. The ladies and girls made their own dresses. From their straight or sagging front or rear hemlines, it was easy to spot those handiest with a needle. Boys wore store-bought corduroys, bib-overalls, and Levi's. Some had patches on top of patches but no self-respecting mother ever allowed her son on Winelda's streets with holes in their clothes. Funny that, sixty years later, softer people would pay big bucks to look poor, to wear faded jeans with phony holes in the knees and rear-end—holes not caused by honest work.

Pop continued his commentary on the first leg of the Square.

"Wright's Drugs . . . here's a Doctor Chambers's office. Yes, sir, doctor and drugs side by side . . . real devils. Surprised there's no undertaker shingle amongst 'em. And here's the Commercial Bank and the Commercial Hotel. Lot more action here than in Anthony. My God! Just listen to that commotion! Pull up by the hotel . . . let's see this." Now came the mighty blast of a steam whistle that created an odd harmony with the "ting, ting, ting, ting" of the Broadway grade-crossing bell.

Just as Mom parked, two monstrous locomotives suddenly appeared from behind the Commercial Hotel with white geyser-like steam clouds whooshing from their cylinders. The ground beneath them shuddered while dense ebony smoke boiled two hundred and fifty feet above the doubleheader's stacks. These were immense black steel behemoths majestically bound for California. "My God, would you look at that . . . the two of 'em together must be a city block long!"

They were the mighty 4000-series Baldwin locomotives, commanded by jaunty engineers wearing cocky visored denim caps and flashy red bandannas. These captains kept one gloved hand upon the throttle while the other hung devil-may-care outside the cab. Their eyes were upon the rail as the big shiny connecting rods resolutely turned each engine's eight huge drive wheels. Seemingly infinite power was in the air! No puny clink, clink, clank sound. It was a mighty BOM, bom, bom, bom, BOM, bom, bom, bom played to a background of spewing hissing steam. As the two locomotives made distance, the initial thunder gradually faded to the quieter click-click-clack, click-click-clack of a hundred and ten following freight cars. It was a sound of kinetics and energy occasionally punctuated by the mournful metallic wail of a wheel's flange knifing its way across a switch or a track's frog.

"Simply beautiful," marveled Pop.

They watched the numerous cars pass in review on tracks that divided the commercial part of town from the less prosperous residential area known as "across-the-tracks." After several minutes came the increasing thunder of yet another approaching locomotive. BOM, bom, bom, bom, BOM, bom, bom, bom. It was the chugging pusher engine heralding the end of this Goliath of steel and steam. Neither pastoral Anthony nor Ellinwood, Kansas, had ever seen a train such as this one. "By God, three engines!"

As they were climbing back into the Chrysler, a doubleheader from the opposite direction shook the ground as it, too, whistled and thundered behind the Commercial Hotel. It would stop near the Mexican Town yards, and its refrigerator cars, loaded with precious lettuce from California, would be re-iced for the long trip east. The locomotives would be serviced, and fresh crews would take the train on to the next division point at Wellington, Kansas. The arriving crews would lay over in Winelda, see a movie, spend the night at the Santa Fe Reading Room, or possibly a railroader would stay at the Commercial and enjoy earthy therapy with one of its spirited girls.

Mom and Pop turned south on Missouri Street—even today no one knows why they named it Missouri Street. It was the dead side of the Square, with a few limping businesses and a long-dead theater. They circled around the Square's wide, clean concrete and back to prosperous Main and parked in front of Miller's Bakery. The air was filled with the tantalizing aroma of Mrs. Miller's newly baked bread and cherry pies. Whittling in front of the Post Office was a gaggle of old-timers discussing how Roosevelt might better run the "guvmint." From across the street could be heard the clunk, clunk, clink of the *Enterprise*'s linotype machine and an occasional whiff of hot printer's ink. The weekly paper had gone to press.

Next to the bakery was the Majestic Theater. It was the sole reason for the trip to Winelda. It literally smelled of a failing business: peeling paint, marquee sagging, doors with no bronze kickplates, no brass show cases advertising coming attractions.

"Why is there no smell of popcorn?" said Pop. "Let's go to the confectionery down there and have a cold root beer."

No Deal Busting Attorneys

Nick's Confectionery was primarily a soda fountain with two ceiling fans that harmoniously chanted—whap, whap, whap, whap. It had a marble counter and the usual array of Hamilton Beach malted milk mixers, a line of press pumps for chocolate and cherry syrup, Coca-Cola, and phosphate among others. There were big-handled spigots in the center for carbonated and tap water. Coca-Cola wire chairs lined the counter.

Big Nick was a blimp of a man in a white shirt open at the collar, his sleeves rolled evenly above his thick wrists. A new leather belt circled his girth to hold up his trousers. He had big lips, big meaty fingers, big teeth with gaps between them, and a big belly that jiggled when he made a friendly chuckle. Nick was the size of man that everyone preferred to forever chuckle.

Mom and Pop sat at the counter and asked about local business.

"How about the theater?"

"Well, our picture show—whoee—it could be a heap better, but it's the only one we got. Ha, Ha." He held up a glass to the glare of the front window, wiped it carefully as if it were a surgical instrument, and inspected it again. "Winelda's not big enough for two, just right for one—people like the fillums—but lately Grover's had a lot on his mind and his leg's been ailin' with arthuritis.

"I try to cheer Grover and tell him a little asspern would make it feel better, but he pays no mind . . . gets in the dumps . . . wife died a coupla years back. Sometimes ma wife cheers him with a bouquet of flars. But yeah, he's sure nuf let the movie house run down . . . busted seats, lets the sound get too low, some folks say they see rats. Lands! No excuse fer that. A coupla hungry cats'd cure that in no tahm. Show's just achin' for competition to come open the empty one over on Missouri. Sure don't want that. This here's the good side of the Square and Grover's movie house keeps things lively." Nick mopped the marble counter for the umpteenth time.

"You folks innerstid in Grover's picture show?" He wiped his brow with his big hairy forearm as Pop nodded.

"Well, that's sure good tuh hear." Nick stuck out his big paw of a hand. "I'm Nick Nicholson, mighty glad ta meetcha. You folks go on up to the yella and white cottage at Cecil and Church, justa coupla blocks, knock on the door, talk to Grover. I know he wants to sell out and go live with his sister up in Tuh-peka."

Thirty minutes later, Grover was telling the folks four thousand was his rock bottom. Mom and Pop thought it fair and they made a handshake deal—no realtor to rake off five percent, no deal busting attorneys, no escrow, nothing in writing, just a simple handshake. The shake was as good as oak and the brand of a more ethical society.

MAKE THAT MAJESTIC HUM

As the Chrysler pounded back over the wash boarded gravel, they were relieved to see Anthony's tall grain elevators and its huge silver water tower with "Beat Harper" emblazoned on its side. As they drove by Gillespie's Garage on Main, Pop said, "I hope we didn't make a mistake."

"Your idea was good, Gus; it's a winner. Things are happening in Winelda." Mom set her jaw and her head wiggled a little. "You'll see." While in Winelda she had also signed a thirty-one dollar a month lease for the large Olmstead house opposite the Congregational Church on Cecil.

Mom turned off Main at the Morrison Hotel and drove by the courthouse. A couple of blocks farther she parked alongside their beautiful Victorian at 424 North Anthony.

Pop leaned over and nuzzled her cheek with his mustache, "Such a fine driver." But Mom just sat there, a serious look on her face. "Gus," she said, "I've been thinking of Homer down there in New Orleans. That big house we leased has plenty of room. Why don't we invite Homer to come live with us? Tommy will be starting the fourth grade . . . high time he had a regular home and someone to take the place of his mom." Her determined head began rattling around on her neck. "With Homer we can make that Majestic hum."

Pop stared through the windshield. "Oh, boy," he sighed.

Pop was skeptical. He'd raised three kids, educated them and now they were on their own. He was thoroughly enjoying his Bettie and some well-deserved privacy. Why take on problems? Homer's Kansas City tragedy had overwhelmed him as had Homer's recent broken leg and the drying out in a New Orleans hospital. "Hell, Bettie, the kid's eight. He'll be a ripper. You sure you want to get involved in all that pandemonium?"

"Gus, I think it would be wonderful to have my boy and my grandson home. We'll all run the show in Winelda, and when you and I decide to retire again, Homer can take over. It'll be his fresh start and we can come back here to Anthony."

After a silent moment, Pop spit out the car window. "Well, dammit to hell, if that's what you must have then go with it. But by gol I won't have his drinkin' in the house or any of that New Orleans kind of carryin' on. Winelda's too small for behavior like that, and I'm too damned old to put up with it." Pop Cable slapped the dash with his open hand. "Nuthin's been right with Homer since Kansas City."

"Well, Gus, whatever are parents for if not to help when one of their own is in trouble?"

"There you go making sense," Pop harrumphed as he got out of the car and again spat on the road while snapping his suspenders. "Hell, Bettie. Homer's big city now. You honestly think Winelda's going to appeal to him?"

"Homer needs our affection, and I'm sure everything will be just fine in Winelda."

Pop snorted, "All right, but I won't allow carryin' on."

KANSAS CITY SHADOWS

Homer and Laurence dined at their favorite corner table in the Court of Two Sisters and drank nothing stronger than chicory coffee. It was one of those evenings when she most loved him because he was pure Homer. He told her his parents had recently acquired a theater in Winelda, a small town in Oklahoma, and he was going there to help speed them to retirement. "If the place makes money and you don't mind living in the sticks, it could even work for us." Homer smiled, "Great for kids."

Laurence bit her lower lip as her eyes moistened. She knew it was over and probably heaven sent. Had Homer remained in New Orleans, she could never have broken it off despite her pragmatic side whispering that life with Homer would become a colossal disappointment. Kansas City would forever be there lurking.

It was late spring 1932, when they said goodbye.

Homer locked our apartment and walked me to the waiting taxi. Nearby a Dixieland band made spirited funeral music. Homer looked down the wet, French Quarter street with its clutter of antique shops, bars, and jazz mills. In spite of the usual faint smell of French Quarter sewage, he hated forfeiting this place and his job. He loved it, but it was time to get his life in order. He had to do the correct thing for his folks and for me.

I suppose Orletha Washington had grown used to us because the day we left she bawled and carried on until all of us, including Homer, were dabbing eyes and choking on words. But once the taxi sped away, Orletha was soon eclipsed. My thoughts now focused fully on the Ford Trimotor, the great Tin Goose that was about to fly us to Wichita!

I had a million questions, but I could see Homer was lost in his thoughts. As we turned up Canal for the airport, I saw him clinch his teeth and shake his head a couple of times. He had surrendered his fast-track corporate life, New Orleans, and Laurence to life in rustic Winelda—probably a dull tank town made even duller by the Depression.

It would prove to be anything but dull.

REUNION AND BLAZING WINELDA

When we landed at Wichita, Mom and Pop Cable were waving from the ramp. They had leased their home in Anthony and we were taking the Chrysler to Winelda. The next day, as we rounded the curve by Mexican Town, Mom pointed at Winelda and said, "Well, Tommy, there's your new home. That's Winelda. Look over there, see the red mesas? Real cowboys live out there, and Indians used to hunt in these parts."

Mom knew how to excite a kid. I was at the age where cowboy country thrilled me, but I wondered if Homer was silently comparing this and New Orleans. I couldn't tell by looking at him. Coming into town, he was genuinely sharing the folks' enthusiasm.

After driving completely around the Square, Mom told Homer to pull in at the newspaper, the *Enterprise*. We all got out of the car and stood in a family clump as Pop motioned across the street, "There it is!" Homer saw a tired Majestic shimmering in the blazing June sun. The dry oven heat must have been at least a hundred and one degrees, but there was no siesta. A half dozen trucks brimming with wheat passed en route to the elevator; a huge doubleheader boiling steam and smoke whistled as it thundered from behind the Commercial Hotel. Compared to the pastoral dreariness we'd just driven through, little Winelda was fairly throbbing. I could tell Homer's adrenaline was pumping.

As he studied the shoddy Majestic, I knew big ideas were zipping through his mind. He was visualizing a huge marquee with a hundred lights; he was covering the dismal khaki paint with shiny aluminum lacquer. He was already ordering brass ad cases for coming attractions. To make it look like a theater, the doors needed glistening kickplates. The foyer was filthy. The initial stages of decay were setting in. Pop Cable, aware that Homer was taking inventory, broke the silence. "What it needs, Homer, is a good-smelling popcorn machine that'll draw people from down the street."

"It needs a helluva lot, Pop, but nothing's insurmountable."

As for finding good pictures, Homer knew how the industry worked. No longer would Winelda have stale films. Homer had connections. Winelda's Majestic would become the break-in spot for all the new releases. Homer would have them at least a week ahead of Oklahoma City's big chain theaters. He was determined to pay back some of what he owed Mom and Pop. New Orleans was over. This was the place, and he was determined to do it right.

"Mom," he said, "how about an ice cream soda? Tommy?" And the four of us crossed the street to the Rexall Drug Store, where Hamilton Beach mixing machines whined and ceiling fans were whap, whaping. The smell of chocolate was in the air, and many of the customers wore fancy boots and cowboy hats. Winelda and New Orleans's Bourbon Street were definitely different.

TEUTONIC DISCIPLINE

For the past four years, I had lived an "anything goes" existence. Homer and I rarely spent more than a couple of waking hours a day together. When he came home, I was glad to see him because I genuinely missed him. I also knew he'd bring some little prize, and after dinner we'd have a romp together. But for the long hours of each day, Orletha had been my constant companion, and within reason, she'd usually give me anything I wanted. So there was little wonder I was spoiled rotten.

I had become a little rosy-cheeked beast but no one had yet detected this. Consequently, I was initially lavished with undeserved attention. Mom seemed to never tire of me, was always hugging me, and telling me what a good boy I was. Even Pop, who was seventy-one, occasionally grabbed me up and whiskered me. I'll never forget his trademark—the faint, manly smell of Day's Work chewing tobacco. And, typical of a designing kid, I figured with Mom—almost as permissive as Orletha—I could get away with virtually anything. Pop's limits I had yet to test, but discovery was soon on the way. When adults look at a loveable eight-year-old, there is no ready evidence of the designing machinations already at work in the little monster's head. Even the kid is doubtlessly unaware; it's instinctive.

I believe it was some time during the initial two weeks that Pop warned me his backyard garden patch was off limits. That was all the challenge I needed, and a few days later he caught me fiddling with his new tomato plants. I had no concept of the inherent depth of Pop's Germanic regimentation and orderliness. Nor was I conscious that the innate insubordination lurking just beneath my angelic surface was the antithesis of those Teutonic traits. This tomato episode set off our initial household explosion. Spotting me in the garden, Pop suddenly came after me. Like a rabbit, I tore around the house but was alarmed to discover that Pop, for a skinny old guy, ran amazingly fast. With a switch held high, he charged relentlessly yelling *"Du dummer Esel"*— one of the very few times I ever heard my grandfather speak the funny-sounding language. I was dismayed, and because Mom was my only surefire sanctuary, I ran for her.

When I reached the kitchen with Pop in hot pursuit, she yelled, "Gus, what in the world?" Pop spouted his grave charges. To save me, Mom whisked me up to the bathroom "for a good whupping with Pop's razor strap." I remember her raising her voice so Pop could hear. "Now young man grab the edge of the tub!" Then she laid the strap on my buttocks, but so gently I could hardly believe my good fortune. Yet, I made sure even the neighbors could hear my howls. Pop listened from the kitchen, and more than satisfied he bellowed, "All right, Bettie, all right, enough already." Then Mom, who feared she had struck too hard, burst into tears and grabbed me up in her wonderful arms and we bawled together. "Oh, Mom," I sobbed with absolutely no pain whatsoever.

Very shortly we experienced the roll-top oak desk episode. Pop's roll-top was a veritable honeycomb of tiny drawers and pigeonholes. Each held tantalizing Indian-head pennies or one of Pop's magic gadgets. One tiny drawer had a rock with an obvious speck of real gold. Pop's treasures were like magnets. The day he caught me rummaging through his oaken sanctuary was when I discovered that not even Mom touched the hallowed roll-top. This time I had really upset the household's combined yin and yang and *feng shui*. I was particularly lucky because Homer was always busy downtown.

For the fourth time in recent days, I ritualistically marched to the tub for my strapping, but this one was different. After my usual sobbing charade, Mom grabbed my shoulders and shook me harder than usual. "Tommy," she said, "listen! If you can't behave yourself, you can just pack your duds and get out of here." And tears were coursing down her face, and her head was moving around, and I had never before heard her use a strange, harsh word like "duds"—where had she learned that? If rejected, where would I possibly go? I was fairly certain I couldn't complain to Homer. That they might ban me from the property crushed me. The memory of Mom's crying, and her ultimatum at that final strapping, remains vivid to this day. I never gave her cause for another disciplinary trip to the bathroom.

After the roll-top incident, I realized Pop had locked onto my number like a homing pigeon to its destination, and I knew he was quick to enforce his relentless rules. Early on I learned he hated locks. Consequently, I never again locked him out of the house by hooking the screen door. At breakfast, I made sure to give Pop a sincere smile and a lusty "good morning." It was another of his family rules: "No long faces at breakfast." I made every effort not to cross him, but I was quick to see that with the roll-top incident, I had destroyed our rapport. It had been quite some time since he had last mustached me.

Homer hadn't been present for my initial punishments. Every day he was extremely busy refurbishing the Majestic. But I perceived word was starting to leak to him. There must have been a secret family meeting, because his attitude toward me dramatically changed. I suppose it was a matter of fatherly pride. He didn't want his kid acting like a beast in Mom and Pop's home. But whatever, Homer immediately inducted me into his very own French Foreign Legion, and I began walking the straight and narrow. Hereafter, I was to sit next to him at the dinner table, and my manners were to be impeccable. Very soon I began wishing I was back with Orletha sitting on top of a piano surrounded by her jovial friends who fed me stalks of sugar cane like the house ape I was.

I hadn't yet managed to destroy Mom's fondness for me, but I sensed I was decidedly off Pop's list. This I sorely missed because Pop had a special magnetism that drew me to him. Perhaps it was the respect I had gained for him during his Olympian pursuit of me around the house. Anyway, I tried my best to rekindle the cama-raderie we had once enjoyed, but try as I may, there was no perceptible thaw.

However, I liked to watch Pop pitch horseshoes. I marveled at how his shoe always flipped perfectly just as it came down for yet another ringer. It was as if it were radio controlled. One day, back of Eason's filling station, Pop saw me among the spectators at one of his championship horseshoe games. "Why are you here?" I believe he was grumpy because kids didn't usually hang out there. I told him I had come to see him win. "Humph," he went, spat his tobacco, rubbed his mustache on his sleeve, and didn't give me a second look. I could tell from the conversation that Pop's friends clearly considered him as among the county's very best. Then, when it wasn't his turn, I noticed he started coming over and standing beside me. Eventually he even casually put his hand on my shoulder, and then almost proudly he told everyone, "This is my grandson!"

Slowly, we began to bond, and he even taught me to play chess. Some afternoons after his noon nap, we'd play in the living room. You'd think Pop would have let me win from time to time, but he never dropped a game. He'd always take a couple of minutes to critique the reason for my fatal mistake, and then we'd start another game. One day I challenged Homer. He sat down devil-may-care, and in only eight moves, I had checkmated him. Pop slapped his thigh. He never let Homer forget that the kid had won. Thereafter, Homer was especially careful, and I never won another from him until high school. Mom's game was Parcheesi, which I also enjoyed, and managed to win with more frequency.

All through the summer, the house was full of activity. Uncle Virgil and Aunt Iris often came from nearby Alva, where they took summer courses at Northwestern State Teacher's College. Iris was working on her second masters—in English this time—and Virgil was taking courses prior to commencing his position as Mullhall, Oklahoma's music teacher. Their duet of beautiful music always fasci-nated me. Pop cherished it, and I could tell Homer greatly admired his little brother's discipline for having become such an accomplished musician. Homer certainly loved Virgil. Their bonding was nothing short of extraordinary.

I told Homer I wanted to be a musician like Uncle Virgil, but he said, "One musician in the family is enough." And Mom had laughed, so I knew the subject had come up before. I later learned that, in my father's philosophy, music and teaching careers spelled a life of self-imposed genteel poverty. It meant old tweed jackets with elbows reinforced with leather. But because Homer loved both Iris and Virgil, he would never openly denigrate their aspirations. After all, they had developed great tangible skills, and the two of them were always bubbling with unbridled happiness. Happiness was something Homer had yet to achieve.

That summer on Cecil Street was my first memory of the Fourth of July—Pop's Yankee Doodle birthday. Right after Pop hung out our nation's flag, he casually gave me a huge silver fifty cent piece. "Go whoop it off on firecrackers," he said. It was the most money anyone had ever handed me, and it had come from Pop who counted every solitary penny.

With the Flanders boy and the Holyfield kid, I spent the entire Fourth blowing up tin cans, annihilating red ant dens, and sending neighboring cats scurrying for cover. Later on, we showed off for Juanita Cronkhite and Lucinda Flanders. We let them hang around and watch because we knew that every now and then, they'd light one of their good-smelling sparklers. Then Homer rolled home in the green Chrysler with a sack full of Roman candles and fountains and invited my friends to come back at dark. It was the grandest Fourth of July! It was so grand I don't specifically remember any of those that followed.

HOMER, THE DYNAMO

All during that summer, Homer tirelessly refurbished the theater. He personally painted the front facade with glistening aluminum lacquer, and installed a hundred light marquee. Wineldans loved it because at night it made the Square come alive. And even if it was the Depression, no Wineldan ever reached up to steal a light bulb. Homer recarpeted the lobby and laid new aisle runners. He rented workshop space across the street, and with the help of the theater's projectionist, installed springs in three hundred of the formerly plain wooden seats, and upholstered them with luxurious mohair. The front ten rows remained plain wooden seats. I thought that was discriminatory because that's where we kids sat. Regardless, Pop had set a budget, and it was the Depression, and Homer was right. The kids didn't give a whit if the seats were mohair or knotty planks. Kids came for the Westerns, and they'd sit mesmerized and slop Coke all over themselves and the old wooden seats.

Air conditioning was not yet invented, but Homer set up a miraculous air-conditioning system tailored to Winelda's fierce bone-dry heat. He and his workmen dug a six foot deep mini-pool in the theater's rear basement and lined it with thick concrete. Each day the iceman dumped six hundred pounds of ice in the pool. This was how Homer was able to legitimately advertise "Ice-Cooled Air." A powerful centrifugal pump pulled the frigid water from this reservoir and made a chilled fog of it through a dozen fine-mist nozzles. Two huge squirrel cage fans with big ten-horsepower motors sucked the outside air through this cold mist and blew a veritable gale of chilly wind over the audience. It was so powerful, the kids in the first few rows always appeared as if straight from a Rockwellian picture, their eyes glued to the screen, the blast of air so strong that it blew their hair back as if they were racing on motorcycles. Sometimes droplets of water made it out to the audience, but at a hundred and four degrees outside, there was never a complaint. The Majestic was a place to be entertained, and to blissfully cool off. Outside on the sidewalk, people often stopped and stood in the shade of Homer's marquee and enjoyed the rush of cool air coming from the Majestic's foyer. And to serve them, Pop was there to sell them aromatic bags of his nickel popcorn.

OUR DIFFERENT LIFESTYLE

I was too small to take part in any of the Majestic's renovation. I spent most of each day with my new friends, T.S. Bunting or Holyfield or Flanders, as we vicariously chased imaginary Indians or WWI Kraut across the lawns.

During that first summer Homer always came home around 5:00 P.M. wearing an old paint-splattered shirt wet with sweat. He usually had aluminum or some other color of paint on his hands and around his nostrils. He always said "Hi, everyone" and marched straight for the shower to prepare for dinner.

Dinner was a dependable ritual with everyone congregating in the kitchen. Pop usually set the table while Homer mashed potatoes; Mom always had plenty of potatoes. One of her specialties was franks and sauerkraut cooked with diced onions and a generous splash of caraway seed. Sometimes she'd add little pieces of apple. Our Pavlovian signal was the city hall siren. When it went off at exactly 6:00 P.M., all the Teutons immediately sat down. This was the most ironclad of Pop's rules—not 5:56, not 6:05, always at 6:00 P.M. sharp! How Mom managed to finish everything right on the dot was forever a source of amazement to me.

Despite the Depression, there was plenty of food on the table, food that was never blessed because Pop forbade prayers. And as we passed the food around, the table became the forum for all the Cable family business. I soon discovered that, unless addressed directly, I was to take little part in this family discussion. When it came time for dessert, Mom served up a delicious twenty-five cent pie still warm from Miller's Bakery. Mom had raised her family. Now she was a businesswoman, and she had also become involved with her various civic clubs. She no longer had time for fiddling with cookies, cakes, or pies.

THE MAJESTIC

After dinner, while we males washed and dried the dishes, Mom Cable dressed for the 7:30 show. Together we'd walk the three blocks down Cecil to the Majestic. During show time, Mom ran the box-office, Homer took tickets and managed what we called "the floor," and in the outer lobby Pop ran the Jolly Time Popcorn machine. That's the way the family divided its duties. At that time I contributed little to the family.

And Pop was right. The aroma of his popcorn, which he liberally salted and buttered, captured people from up and down Main Street. He was the Jolly Time Pied Piper, and he sold a ton of popcorn at five cents a bag.

Through the week there were three different "fillums"—twenty cents for adults and ten cents for kids. Saturday was always double-feature day. Railroaders called them doubleheader days while my folks called them the money days. We always had a Hoot Gibson, or Buck Jones, or Hopalong Cassidy Western—Roy Rogers was coming on line—with a companion "C" picture, like a Laurel and Hardy, or a Red Skelton. Added to this was the one-reel adventure serial that sucked in every kid in town week after week.

If there was a heavy "A" picture featuring Paul Muni, or Bette Davis, or George Brent, or the Barrymores, it was scheduled with a *Movietone News* for Sunday and Monday. For those, Homer charged a prohibitive twenty-five cents to cover the extra "A" picture rental, and we usually lost money. Most ranchers and railroaders weren't too keen on the "heavies," and the Wineldan pulpits killed attendance by forever denouncing Sabbath movies as evil.

Every night I went to the Majestic, but as soon as the first show was over, I was told to pack it in and head home for bed. At first, Mom or Homer walked me home, but later that summer, they just summoned me and told me to get to bed. By then, I had come to realize we were different from most people. We were a nighttime business family.

I usually walked up Cecil's sidewalk. This was somewhat forbidding because there were no streetlights beyond the Square. If I had just seen a "scary" picture, I walked in the middle of the sandy street with no fear at all of traffic because there was virtually none. And, like radar, I kept my eyes constantly scanning the curbside shadows. I feared no Wineldan. I only feared the superhuman that Flanders and Holyfield and I sometimes discussed as we chased lizards. Consequently, I was always alert. Like a young feral animal, I kept my body cocked, ready to zing a hasty retreat to the Majestic. Because it was against Cable household law to lock doors, I was well aware that it was possible for any ghost or spirit to take up residence in our home. Regardless, locks were useless because ghosts could have easily passed through closed doors and walls.

To this day, I remember a real horror of a movie shown in late summer of 1932. The murderer was a mad sculptor, an accomplished master at poisoning his victims. Most bizarre, he'd hide a body in his gallery by cleverly plastering it to look like one of his stone sculptures. The movie's alert police inspector knew something was amiss when he saw a lively fly crawl along a statue's leg, and then suddenly fall off stone dead. The audience had audibly gasped. In retrospect, I suppose the rationale was that the lethal fumes from the poisoned body had permeated the plaster and had killed the fly. Anyway, everyone got the point. The inspector definitely knew. I especially remember when he took out his knife and started to cut into the plaster. That's when all the women and kids in the theater screamed in horrified unison—the terrible thought of slicing into the dead person's thigh!

That picture terrified me, particularly the murderer; he was bushy-browed Bela Lugosi who lived in a haunted house. Each shot always showed him at the top of a cob-webby staircase, his geisha-white face highlighted by an eerie light that always made his eyes and cadaverous cheeks look like hollow sockets.

When the movie ended and the lights came up, Homer told me to take off for home. That particular night filled me with chilling trepidation. As far as the Campbell Hotel, everything was okay, but that's where the streetlights ended. Beyond was yawning darkness, and there was no moon, and when I headed into Cecil Street's inky blackness, I was far from jaunty. I whistled cautiously and weakly as I proceeded down the middle of the street. I could hear the Oklahoma wind moaning eerily through the elm and locust trees, and it wasn't difficult to imagine real whispering voices—even words: "T-o-m-m-y." All the way home, I thought of Bela Lugosi and his menacing fang-like teeth. When I reached our darkened front porch, I continued my whistling, but by then my lips had become so dry the air would only whish out. My mind was totally pervaded by that illuminated skull-like face in that hideous movie. I opened the unlocked door and went in.

I suppose when I looked up our staircase, my reaction would come as no great surprise to any professional psychologist. But there, at the top of our staircase, stood Bela Lugosi—lighted face and all. He glared down at me hatefully. I ran screaming out the door, feeling as if ice water were squirting through my youthful veins. I leapt off the porch and sprinted down the middle of Cecil faster than Mercury himself. I was certain the mad sculptor was right behind me, his flapping cape all flared out, and he gripping a trowel loaded with Plaster of Paris. I ran like a springbok, and had my bladder been full, I would surely have peed myself all the way to the Majestic. Only a block to go, the twinkling lights of my sanctuary—Homer, and Pop Cable, and our ever-present marshal and his six-shooter; they would all be there.

Although that very morning Bob Flanders and I had bravely killed several Indians and German soldiers up and down Cecil, that night Bela Lugosi had scared the wits out of me. Unless Homer—not

Mom—personally checked out the stairs and the upper living area, I steadfastly refused to return home, and no adult coercion could change my mind.

THE WINELDA KID

A t that initial time, one of my best pals was T.S. Bunting, a neighborhood kid. T.S. owned a Daisy BB gun with a real compass imbedded in the stock like a jewel. On Saturday mornings, T.S. and I would take turns plinking tin cans and bottles. For a nickel, we could buy a phenomenal number of BBs. Occasionally we stalked birds in the neighbors' trees, but due to poor marksmanship, and housewives shaking their fists from back porches, the wildlife survived. We tried hard to be killers, but we never bagged a bird.

T.S. and I discovered a Concord grapevine in a neighbor's backyard. We became expert in selecting the very best dried pieces that would smoke well. Then we'd light one, and suck in the hot smoke, spew it out into the air, and laugh. "Just like my old man," said T.S. while holding the sprig of vine expertly between his thumb and forefinger. "Does your dad smoke?"

"Yeah," I said. "He smokes Camels."

T.S. and I sometimes puffed away in the privacy of the Cable garage until the tips of our tongues burned from the hot smoke. Then we'd gallop our make-believe horses all over the neighborhood in search of new discoveries. As we ran, we always thrust our left hand out front to hold our imaginary reins, and with our right hand, we'd spank our right buttock to get our horse to top speed. We must've looked absolutely ridiculous. Occasionally, at full gallop, we'd stop whipping the horse long enough to fire nonexistent six-shooters at lurking Indians, "Pow, pow, gotcha." From breakfast to sunset our days were loaded with fantasies that we easily fanned into virtual reality! When shot from our saddles, we'd contrive shrieks and super theatrical crashes, and would roll crazily in the Bermuda grass.

This was also the time of Inspector Post. Send in two box tops from Post Corn Flakes and receive an Inspector Post badge and a simple pamphlet that spoke of clues, how to investigate crimes, and various tricks of the trade. The best trick of all involved using milk to write invisible letters; heat the paper and the writing magically appeared. T.S. and I were both inspectors, and when we weren't into grapevines and WWI Germans, we were out looking for clues. One day we found a gin bottle in a Baptist deacon's trash. We immediately rode our horses down to the Square to find Billy Patton, the town marshal.

Mr. Patton was a kindly man who seemed ancient, but at the time he wasn't more than fifty-five. He always wore a cowboy hat and boots. His indisputable authority was a mammoth six-shooter that hung from his ample waist. By talking to the marshal, it gave us the opportunity to view this awesome weapon up close. We could actually see the real bullets peeking from its cylinder. The great thing about Billy was that we could always find him. He'd be somewhere on the Square talking to a citizen or to a store clerk, or he'd be sitting at the Rexall fountain having a glass of water. He liked his job, and everyone always knew Billy was somewhere near. In Winelda, he certainly maintained law and order. We caught up with him at the corner of Main and Cecil, and he greeted us like confederates. Billy was fully aware that we had become "his" inspectors. We exhibited the gin bottle.

In 1932, there were only three dry states in the Union, and Oklahoma was one of them. Even though Winelda was about as wet as Louisville, anything to do with liquor was unlawful. I remember how painstakingly Billy examined the empty gin bottle and its Arkansas State seal. Ever so carefully he checked its red federal seal, and all the while he made "MMmmm" sounds and would scratch a sideburn. Then he said, "By golly men, this is very important detective work. Where'dja find it?" We whispered to him and he squinted his eyes with great concern. "Oh, is that so?" Because we had nailed the sanctimonious deacon, Billy's innards were probably bursting with laughter, but he made us feel that bringing this gin to justice was his most pressing task of the day. "Well, fellas, I'm much obliged. Thanks a heap and keep your eyes peeled. Tomorrow I'll see this is turned over to the G-Men when they come up from Oklahoma City." Billy always made us feel very important. Then we'd gallop off in search of more important clues.

HELL PERIOD

When school started in the fall of 1932, I noticed another major change in Homer's new strictness. I was in Miss Dorothy Tanner's fourth grade, where none among my Cecil Street friends had a fever to establish scholastic records. Our thoughts centered on pranks, recess, marbles, whispering, spitballs, decimating late summer flies with rubber bands, double-bubble gum, and exploring Winelda's environs. Up to this time, Homer—like most fathers—had always been confident I was one smart kid. I was the youngest in the Winelda fourth grade because I had skipped the second grade in New Orleans. I remember in New Orleans, he had especially applauded my rapid advance, and he doubtlessly thought he'd spawned a gifted son, but somehow in his dual interest with United Artists and courting Laurence, he had overlooked that I had almost flunked the third.

I had made Homer happy when we came to Winelda because I had immediately adjusted and made friends easily. But when I brought home that first six week report card for his signature, he was so shocked he actually slapped me. Suddenly I was a great disappointment. Miss Tanner had written tersely on the card, "Indicates below average interest in Math." Homer had surmounted most of the Majestic's problems, now he turned his full attention to his kid, and this created an ever-increasing turmoil within the Cable household.

After dinner, Homer set up a dartboard in the kitchen with rings valued at +3, +5, -2, et cetera. His novel innovation was supposed to be "Let's have fun with arithmetic." I'd throw a dart, and straight from my head, I'd announce a running score. But as the score mounted, it became less and less accurate, and Homer could see me stalling and counting on my fingers. Like a film director, he'd shout, "Stop dreaming!" If really infuriated, he'd sometimes shake me as if I were a defective alarm clock. For me, the kitchen was no longer a happy place. The darts were such a formidable trial, I looked upon them as the Inquisition, and I was certain Homer was thoroughly convinced he had spawned the village idiot. He seemed almost humiliated that I might even be publicly discovered.

Mom Cable occasionally dropped in, and from her scowl I was never sure if she too disapproved my pathetic arithmetic, or if it was the way Homer was carrying on. Before we left for the theater,

Homer's frustrated loss of temper, and my arithmetical stupidity ruined quite a few family evenings.

One morning in the late fall, this hell period reached its crescendo when my disillusioned father said, "And today don't forget your books!"

I must have been in an exceptionally spacey stage of my life because not ten minutes later I put on my leather aviator cap and took off for school, but without my books. I'd gone perhaps a block when I heard Homer bellow. I turned and there he was, fury written across his face, coming at a fast clip. When he grabbed my arm, he nearly lifted me off the ground. Snatching a locust stick from the ground, he began thrashing me hard. He broke the stick, reached for another, and yelled, *"Get home and get your books!"* As I ran he pursued, and because I was bawling, he swatted me again and again. "Stop that bawling, *stop it!*" But it hurt so much it was hard not to cry, and another swat would whack the back of my legs. It was one of those unforgettable experiences.

Watching our approach, Mom Cable stood stoically on the back porch, a hard look on her face meant for Homer, but I thought for me. Again Homer swatted me hard with the stick, and Mom announced with steely cold, "Homer, I think that's about enough."

As a kid I never once looked upon these disciplinary measures as what today's liberal society considers abuse. All my friends told me they received punishments from time to time. I figured it was the cross all kids had to bear—a part of growing up among a world of adults. That night, as I was putting on my PJs, Mom Cable saw the dried blood caked around the black and blue cuts on my legs. "Is that what happened today?" she said. I nodded, and she hugged me in her fleshy arms and cried. That's when I wondered if she or Pop had ever taken a stick to Homer, but I didn't ask because I knew there would never be a discussion. Neither Mom nor Pop idly gossiped or told tales. In retrospect, I have only this to say about my father's rather severe punishment. Other shortcomings would definitely surface in my life, but I never again forgot my books.

"I'm concerned about him," Homer later said to Mom.

"Homer, you're making too much of it. You're so anxious you make him nervous. He's eight years old. For goodness sake, let Tommy be a boy! Have you forgotten that you were no shining light in the Ellinwood school system or at Kansas University?"

"I used to read ravenously. He reads nothing." My acute ears heard this.

"It's true, Homer, but Tommy's also much more inquisitive than you ever were. He likes to poke around everywhere. We all have our pluses and minuses." I also heard this.

On Cheating the Lord

One Friday after school, T.S. and I stopped traveling over our nonexistent range long enough to plan a conspiracy. We had grown tired of grapevine and wanted real cigarettes, just like our dads'. The problem was how to come by the necessary dime to buy a pack of Wings—the lowest priced ready made on the market. A nickel sack of Bull Durham or Golden Grain would've been even cheaper, but the art of rolling your own was far beyond us. We suddenly remembered our only cash flow was the dime given each of us for Sunday school. Our solution was for each of us to withhold a nickel and then pool our resources. If carefully analyzed, the crime we'd hatched was pretty heinous. It amounted to embezzling funds earmarked for the church, and if our Sunday school teacher, Mr. Wilbur Barnett, ever learned of it, we'd surely burn in Hell.

Come Sunday, T.S. and I flushed our emerging ethics down the drain, and God got only a nickel from each of us. Monday after school, like two sneaky criminals, we headed straight to Ben Taul's general store on the quiet side of the Square. The Rexall was out of the question, because not only did Mr. Curtis know my folks, he was a virtual pillar in my Methodist Church.

We knew we could hoodwink old Mr. Taul. He always looked sleepy, smelled of liniment, and would doubtlessly regard us with scant attention. We were prepared to tell him the Wings were for our dads, which would manifest two serious infractions of honor. Mr. Taul just sat there with a fly swatter in his overstuffed chair, pointed to the cigarettes with his crutch, asked no questions, and when he pocketed the Lord's dime, he didn't seem to even fully open his eyes. There was no tax. The nice thing about the Depression era was that few in contemptible government had discovered tax, and yet every-thing—schools, street cleaning, fire engines, and our law and order—seemed to run swimmingly well for very little money. I suppose scant overhead was the key.

The brown pack of Wings cigarettes in hand, we ran our horses at top speed back to our corral in the Cable garage. I can't describe how truly wicked we felt as we sat in a dark corner and opened that genuine pack of cigarettes.

"Yeah," I told T.S. expertly, "only tear off half the tinfoil and paper at the top so that air doesn't spoil 'em." Homer had once told me this when I'd opened a pack for him. Too bad Homer hadn't just heard me repeat it. It might have gladdened him to discover I wasn't brain dead after all. T.S. took out the first cigarette and held it stiffly in front of him. When I lit it for him, the match almost crossed his eyes, and then T.S. lit mine.

Unlike the puny puff of blue-white smoke from the grapevine, this was a real cottony cloud. We'd suck the smoke in our mouths then blow it grandly toward the ceiling like movie stars—wonderful! We were so fascinated we never heard the approaching Chrysler as it suddenly swept in like a clap of thunder. I flattened myself to the wall like a postage stamp. I'll never forget that moment as Homer looked down into our wide eyes. We stared back mutely, like two goats looking through a hedge, and didn't know exactly how to respond. T.S. foolishly fanned at the smoke and tried to hide his cigarette in his cupped hand, but it kept burning him. "Ouch, ouch," he faintly gasped. I was absolutely frozen. In the vernacular of the theater, I knew this was curtains! It was finito!

Homer fastened his eyes on us and swung out of the Chrysler. From the back seat he pulled a wooden orange crate filled with groceries. He had yet to speak and everything was very awkward; the atmosphere fairly crackled with St. Elmo's fire. I knew Homer's temper, and for some odd reason I was concerned for T.S.; I wondered if Homer would embarrass me by taking a whack at him as well. Instead, he grandly said, "Hello, boys!" and the slamming of the car door seemed to cancel the necessity for responding. Homer checked his watch and said, "T.S., isn't it time for you to be going home, Son?"

"Yes, sir, Mr. Cable, I was just leavin'," and T.S. immediately began sidling out of our corral. He did a peculiar little clumsy bow—T.S. never bowed to anyone—then he said, "Well, goodbye, Mr. Cable." He took off hesitantly with a weird little stiff legged hoppity-walk-run. I'd never seen this gait before. The smoke had obviously crippled T.S.'s horse. I also noticed T.S. never said goodbye to me, never so much as turned to view the impending murder of his pal.

Like a bad dream, I clearly recalled my medicine when I had forgotten my books. What would smoking and stealing the Lord's money amount to? Broken bones? I was surely on the threshold of big, big stuff because there was something eerily ominous about Homer's attitude. No parent in the neighborhood would have reacted similarly. Was Homer going to throttle me in the garage? Bury me in Pop's garden? Whatever my fate, I was certain nothing was going to be okay in the OK Corral.

Then he said, "Tom," not Tommy, "get on in the living room. I want to talk to you." It was all very unsettling.

MISERY

My only remaining hope of salvation was Mom and I hastily cased the grounds. T.S. and I had already spotted Pop playing horse-shoes down by the Eason station. Except for the back screen door slamming behind Homer, the house was deadly quiet. There would be no savior. Mom wasn't calling out; Mom was attending her Monday afternoon Ladies' Aid. I was sure this must be exactly as it had been at the Langtry, Texas, gallows West of the Pecos, and I knew I wasn't going to be brave.

I stood there in the living room waiting for whatever terrible medicine when Homer entered from the kitchen. Homer was neither grave nor smiling. I was further mystified when he said, "Well, sit down and tell me how school went today, what did you learn?"

And as I sat on the forward edge of the overstuffed chair nervously mouthing off about 'rithmetic, and spelling, and penman-ship, Homer started to light up. But suddenly he stopped and interrupted me.

"Oh, I'm sorry, Tom. Here, have a smoke." He shook up a ciga-rette and thrust it toward me.

I was shocked! This was unheard of, and I scrunched my head down between my shoulder blades and shook my head. But he wouldn't be put off, and there was a special commanding tone when he said, "Here! I said have a smoke."

I withdrew it from his pack, dropped it on the floor, jumped down to pick it up, and zap, there was Homer's lighted match. I was mortified. "Come on," he said. "It won't light if you don't suck in on it." I was incredulous. Homer was treating me as if I were an adult. I climbed back up in the chair with the lighted cigarette and sat dumbly on the edge, my legs too short for my feet to touch the floor.

"Well, this is certainly a surprise, Tom"—there it was again—"I didn't know you were smoking already. I'm disappointed you didn't tell me. Remember. This is the Cable family. We don't sneak around. What you do in the garage should be good enough to do in the living room in front of the folks and me. What would Mom say?" Homer had emphasized "sneak" so that it imparted a shameful miscreancy I had seldom felt.

Homer settled back in his chair. "Well, isn't this something? The two of us are sitting here having a smoke, and talking together like men. I thought I'd have to wait years before we could savor this."

Savor? I didn't understand, and I was too stunned to analyze the event. It hadn't yet occurred to me that Homer was being disingenuous. I sat there woodenly with the cigarette between my thumb and forefinger.

Homer said, "Well, hell, Tom. Smoke the damned thing," and this time it was more of a command than a suggestion. I immediately sucked in some smoke and held it in my mouth for a second the way T.S. and I had done with the grapevines, and then I sort of let it burp out of my mouth. The dumb smoke stayed right there curling around my face and smarting my eyes. In retrospect, I'll have to say that Homer remained very cool, and because he wasn't treating me like a harebrained kid, I was becoming increasingly confident he wasn't going to slap me around.

"Now, Son," he said with a friendly smile, "if you're going to smoke, I don't want people down on the Square laughing at you. You have to smoke right. Now look, suck in the smoke like this." He took in a big drag that made his cigarette burn brightly. "Open your mouth like this, and suck the smoke deep into your lungs." He did it. "There, that's called inhaling. That's how smokers get the good from the smoke." As an afterthought, Homer expertly threw in a small smoke ring. "There you go, Tom. Do it that way, and afterward I'll show you how to do the rings."

I sucked in, and the smoke grabbed at my lungs as I went into a coughing-gagging fit, almost dropping my cigarette as tears rolled down my cheeks. But Homer was right there, patting me on the back and saying, "Ah, don't let that worry you, Tom. Beginners often experience that feeling with the smoke." When I recovered he said, "There you go, try it again. It gets easier and easier and more satisfying. Like they say," he laughed softly, "makes you want to walk a mile just to get another Camel." He sat back and casually blew off another remarkably perfect smoke ring.

This experiment went on for about five minutes. In between my coughing fits, Homer would lean forward with an elbow on his knee, and just like an equal, he'd tell me about the progress at the theater, how today they had installed new copper kickplates on the main outside doors. But I wasn't feeling as good as I had, and I just sat there losing my interest for the theater, and tobacco, and anything my father had to say.

Homer said, "Tom, don't just hold the thing like women do, smoke it like Randolph Scott does." Homer knew that among my cowboy heroes, Randolph Scott had recently moved to the forefront—even ahead of Buck Jones. He must've also noticed my forehead was beginning to shine from perspiration, and that I was growing pale and clammy, but if he did notice, he didn't let on.

"You know in the foyer where Pop has his popcorn machine? Well, we painted the floor of that entire area a dark green. It's already dry and looks like glass. Tonight, the first people will walk on it."

At this point, I didn't really give a flying fig about Pop's machine, or the green cement, and just then I jumped off the chair and ran to the half-bath off the living room. Homer quickly followed and lifted the lid just before I threw up. It was awful, and at that point, I would have gladly accepted death, anything to free me of the bilious, smoky misery. Five minutes later I was still on my knees gagging and retching into the toilet, retching for something that refused to materialize. Nothing was left, nothing but smoke, and gasps, and fumes, and "arrrggh" after interminable "arrrggh."

I remember Homer stroked my hair, and patted me on the shoulder, and said, "I'm sorry, Tommy. I shouldn't have let you smoke. Boys just aren't old enough to be men yet. They shouldn't do men's things until they're men. Besides, it's a known fact that cigarettes will stunt your growth. You start smoking now, you'll probably always be a runt, probably won't grow more than an inch or two, will wind up working in a circus." Following Homer's "dwarf" pearl, I heaved one more retching dry heave, and I truly believe Homer was feeling a remorseful twinge that another of his innovative teaching vehicles had gone astray. He came back from the kitchen with a wash-cloth, cleaned up my mouth and nose, and flushed the toilet. "Come on out to the kitchen, Son. I brought you a cold bottle of Coca-Cola," and then Homer did a strange thing. He actually hugged me. A few years later, he would tell me he could definitely smell the smoke coming from my pores.

Homer gave me one last fatherly shot: "Remember, don't do things that you're ashamed to let me, or Mom, or Pop see. You tell me what it is you want to do. If it's proper enough, I certainly won't steer you wrong."

And I said with fervency, "Dad, please don't tell Mom."

"If you want to tell her you can . . . I certainly will not."

And he didn't, and I never smoked again—not because I was such a great temperate kid, but even the distant smell of cigarettes on a Greyhound bus would make me nauseous. Much later, I couldn't stand to date a girl who smoked because I could smell it in her breath, hair, and clothes. I decided Homer would never become a successful math teacher, but I'll say his approach to my premature smoking was a triumph. And I eventually grew to be over six feet tall.

CARNAL KNOWLEDGE

I respected my father's point about family leveling. I knew he must be right. But I also figured there must be a certain entitled privacy, and that some sacrosanct experimentations should be off limits to the folks.

Just a half block north from where I lived, and running parallel to Cecil, was Broadway, and beyond it was a wheat field. Along the fence line there was a dense growth of castor beans and luxuriant, assorted weeds as tall as corn. We kids would go deep into those weeds, and pull enough of them to provide a two or three square yard secret jungle clubhouse—at least that was what it was to us. When we crawled in there, we felt as if we were in a different world. It was our secret sanctuary closed to all adult eyes.

One day, I was in our retreat with my tomboy friend and neighbor, Juanita Cronkhite. She was also eight years old, but a grade behind me. I don't know how our doctor-nurse thing started, but it had progressed to "I'll let you see mine if you'll let me see yours." Sex had not the slightest thing to do with it; there was no kissing, no touching. It was purely a matter of discovery, of intense curiosity, how hers was different from mine. And Juanita was equally curious, and certainly no passive wilting flower. She was giggling and wanted to cut the BS and get on with the revelation.

Then came small arguments over who would take the first step, who would show first, and because there was sufficient distrust, we could come to no ready agreement. Finally, we decided the equitable solution was to flash at the same time. As quick as a wink Juanita pulled up her cotton dress and held its hem under her chin. She had her hands on the top band of her baggy yellow bloomers—a bizarre discovery in itself. With this show of good faith, I immediately dropped my corduroys and made ready to snap down my shorts. Then, with a one-for-the-money and a two-for-the-show, she flicked down her bloomers and I dropped my shorts. We immediately yanked them back up into place, and as we straightened our clothing, Juanita chirped, "You sure are different," and that matched my findings exactly; she had no willie at all. These surprising revelations happen when you've never had a brother or sister.

The Juanita experience was my very first carnal knowledge, and no matter what Homer had said, I couldn't share that with Mom, with anyone. It was Juanita's and my secret. The opportunity for this investigatory situation to develop into something more substantial collapsed two years later when she moved to Pampa, Texas.

MISS TANNER

Report card day came every sixth week, a day that brought reckoning, and a measure of fear. I would hand the card to Homer, which would set him off into spasms of disgust. He would peruse the card, and then announce: "Oh my God! Arithmetic D, spelling C-, even Health Habits is a lousy C!" And he'd resignedly shake his head while saying, "How the hell, Tommy, are you ever going to compete with kids in Oklahoma City when you can't get to first base in Winelda . . . Chriiist!"

And because Homer had frequently—more than any other parent—visited Miss Tanner to discuss my progress, I gradually became one of Miss Tanner's focal points. She began monitoring me ever closer. Frequently looking over my shoulder, I could feel her presence behind me. A few of the kids picked up on this, and began calling me teacher's pet, but if that was the case, my grades certainly didn't reflect it. Miss Tanner was twenty-five and very attractive. Because of Homer's several visits, I once queried him if perhaps Miss Tanner might become my new mother. He snapped, "No, you dummy. I'm just trying to discover what goes on inside your thick head."

It probably hadn't escaped a town the size of Winelda that the recently arrived Homer was smart, and handsome, and at thirty-four, absolutely one of the town's most eligible bachelors. And Homer had certainly reformed—not a single drink, not even a home brew since his arrival. Possibly Homer had come to realize that alcohol offered no solution, and that it was a weak way to bury bad memories. He also knew Pop wouldn't put up with it, and should he begin boozing again, it would surely break Mom's heart.

Winelda offered Homer fine dating possibilities. Besides Dorothy Tanner, Miss Bessie Proffit was another comely member of Winelda's teaching staff. I'm sure Homer had noticed this delightful young lady. Unfortunately, neither teacher had set off a driving eagerness in him. Perhaps the Kansas City memories, or those of Laurence, were still too vivid. I sometimes thought of these possibilities. Also, in whipping the Majestic into shape, he expended considerable time and energy, possibly enough to keep his mind from wandering toward the delights of Dorothy or Bessie et al.

Evidently Dorothy Tanner was pleased there were concerned parents, and I'm sure she enjoyed Homer's visits. In her bubbly, youthful way, she tried to reassure my father that while in lower school, Einstein had also been a poor student—hadn't blossomed until much later. I'm pretty sure this optimistic analogy impressed Homer not a whit.

My next report card, which I still have, had a notation: "Showing marked improvement, esp. in Arith." That evening at the miserable dartboard, I'm sure Homer tried his very best to catch the glimmer of a latent Einstein, but all he saw was my blank face. Homer wasn't fooled. There wasn't a sliver of improvement except for my dart throwing.

SUFFER THE CHILDREN

In my classroom, the handful of Mexican kids mixed together with the white kids, but according to my friend, José Ramírez, it hadn't always been that way. Before my Wineldan arrival, evidently the first grade teacher, Miss Effie Jo Jensen, segregated the Mexicans and relegated them to the seats on the far right of the room. When the Mexican parents heard, they looked uncomfortably at each other. This was probably another brown-white discrimination to endure, yet none would ever militantly protest.

Racial discrimination was not the problem. Miss Jensen had noticed the Mexican kids constantly scratching their heads, and discovered unmistakable gray specks on their scalps and in the hairline of their necks. Unfortunately, neither she nor the principal had ever explained that it was because of head lice. According to José, the separation mystery remained for three years until Roberta Jackson came along.

Roberta Jackson was a student of the Bible, and she played the piano for the choir at the Congregational church. Between hymns, and as Reverend Treat droned, she would study the large picture on the nearby wall. It depicted children of the world of every stripe and color, and among them were many little lambs. Looking upon them with a glow on his consecrated face was Christ with his staff, the true Good Shepherd. One day, as Roberta played "Suffer the Children to Come to Me," the clear message rang out to her—Christ loves all the little children the same!

Roberta, a member of the Winelda School Board, made a decision then and there to terminate the despicable segregation of little children. At the next meeting, she bellowed, "Our Lord wouldn't have had that," and no one wished to run afoul of Roberta's fire and brimstone. She and the board motored out to Mexican Town to meet with its community leaders. It was the very first time the Mexican parentage had heard of the lice problem.

To add presence, Roberta had taken Doc Clapper with them, the man who had brought into the world virtually every child in Winelda. His word was like incorruptible gold. He was an altruist who was only centimeters away from sainthood. There were Wineldans who would actually swear they had seen a halo around Doc's silvery head.

Only recently, the Winelda Town Council had proclaimed him Winelda's Most Useful Citizen. He was, without question, a community pillar of the highest rank.

Anyway, with Roberta's leadership, and Doc's disclosure of how lice spread typhus and other possible diseases, they launched a spirited campaign. Doc told the Mexicans about cleaning up bedding, and the best ways to exterminate the head lice, and the mothers and fathers of Mexican Town immediately rid themselves of this pestilence. By the time I arrived in Winelda, thanks to Roberta's energy, little brown and white kids commingled in the classrooms. It remained that way forever.

LIKE CHICKENS IN ASIA

Winelda's goings-on were pretty amazing. If the *Enterprise* recorded all the community's daily gossip, the paper's appeal could have far outstripped the *New York Times*. As it was, the paper reported whose horse had kicked whom, who had dropped in on whom for Sunday dinner, and who had been stung by an outhouse Black Widow Spider. Where the spider had stung was immaterial because everyone knew. But the paper rarely printed the really good stuff. The "hey-didja-hear?" dirt was kept from eavesdropping kids. And while all this good back-channel information was chewed over, and circulated over clotheslines and at the feed store, Wineldans pleasured themselves by saying they "strictly minded their own business . . . we keep thaings tuh are-selves."

Very little escaped Winelda's view. As an example, if someone saw Elmo's dog trotting down the street alone, he'd be moved to remark, "Ain't that there Elmo's dog? Wonder where Elmo's at? They're usually together." And Wineldans took a special pride in knowing how everyone in the community genealogically interlocked; how this Mixon boy had married a Kendall; how a Kendall girl had married a McBride; and a Bay had married a Barker. "Don't never talk about them Bixlers to anyone, Son, 'cause they're related to jist 'bout everyone in town." This was the reason why a newcomer had better be very careful with remarks until he discovered just how everyone interlocked. "Hey! You talkin' about Billy Louise? She's my niece."

Winelda's thirst for information certainly invaded privacy, but it was beneficial. Point one: Almost no one locked his house because so many eyes were perpetually scanning the street for news; it was the quintessential neighborhood watch. Point two: Winelda's constant surveillance made it an ideal place to raise children. It was as if it were one huge child care center.

We kids were like chickens in an Asian village. Every adult knew who owned us, and where we lived, and we were aware the entire town indirectly observed and controlled us. It was as if we were everyone's responsibility, and this was sometimes annoying. But even without the services of a town psychiatrist, or the expensive present day counselors, this community situation made us feel very secure. No one ever snatched us off the street.

As an example of how it worked, one day when I was in the fifth grade, I was in the large, vacant lot directly behind the Commercial Bank. I sailed a coffee can lid high into the air, immediately lost sight of it in a flash of sun, and like a boomerang, the tin lid came back and struck me squarely on top the head. It was nothing serious, but head wounds do bleed profusely, and very shortly I looked like attempted murder. Blood streamed down my forehead and into my eyes. Before I could panic, the observant bank cashier, Tom Perry, ran from behind the cage to the lot, grabbed my hand, rushed me the half block to Doc Clapper's office, and then quickly returned to cashiering at the bank.

There were no forms to complete—abominable health insurance was not even in the imagination stage. Doc shaved the wound, used three metal clamps to hold the wound together, and then personally walked me around the corner to the Majestic. He told Homer of Tom Perry's quick action. My dad thanked Doc, promptly paid his four dollar fee, and invited Tom to a game of dominoes at the Snooker Parlor. Good Samaritan deeds worked smoothly in 1933 without insurance or fear of lawsuits. It was a matter of looking out for "one anuther."

RESPECT THY WINELDA TEACHER

Another Winelda code or standard was that every kid in town clearly understood, that under no circumstances, was he to be disrespectful toward any adult. To do so would have been a gross miscarriage of courtesy, and Homer and other fathers would have been super quick to correct such crass manners. I don't recollect how those lessons evolved—certainly not from counselors, because parents neither wanted nor needed them—but it seemed the families all taught ethics from the same book. No matter what the adult's station in life, we were always to say "Mister" Patton and "Mrs." Miller and thank you ma'am, thank you sir—yes sir and no sir. When speaking with adults, the word "Yeah" was never a part of a kid's vocabulary. A donkey-like "Uh huh" was a close step toward a perilous precipice. The business of saying yes sir and no sir had absolutely no military connotation whatsoever nor did it imply subservience. They were simply the unwritten rules of behavior everyone expected between juniors and seniors. It was a pleasant departure from today's some-times crass egalitarianism. The grownups liked or loved us, but we were not to consider ourselves their buddies unless some special rapport permitted it.

Teachers were even more sacrosanct. What a teacher directed was open to absolutely no debate of any kind. The teacher represented absolute law. The grand wizards of this celestial group were the grade school principal, Mr. Ruff, and the high school superintendent, Mr. Pennington. In the eyes of kids, these two were in essence supreme beings, and every kid made an effort to avoid coming to their atten-tion.

The closest I ever saw to classroom disrespect was by Lee Hales in the sixth grade. Lee had flunked the fourth grade once and the sixth grade twice and should've been a high school freshman. Six feet tall, he was one big kid for his age, and a little bit of a playground bully. He soared over Mr. Oxley, our bespectacled little teacher. One day, Oxley caught Lee shooting paper wads, stood him up, and told Lee he would be staying after school to clean erasers. Lee said nothing, but he shrugged his shoulders to indicate he didn't give a damn. Every kid in the room gasped at this obvious insubordination.

Mr. Oxley immediately shot over to Lee, grabbed him by the shoulders, and shook him so hard a piece of hidden gum fell from Lee's mouth. Lee's head rolled around, and the vibration made his face look funny. The shaking made Lee lose his balance, and he acci-dentally banged against the windows of a little bookcase. A small pane of glass tinkled to the floor. Such an ominous sound! It struck us dumb. Then Mr. Oxley pushed Lee back to his seat, ordered him to sit, and to place his hands on top his desk. Order restored, the class continued. Not a shoe scraped the floor, not an eye gazed out the window, or at the repentant Lee. Justice had been swift. Mr. Oxley, the little hundred and thirty-five pound bulldog, was in full control. Ever mindful of his explosiveness and quick justice, he had our undivided attention for days to come—no counselors, no memo notes, just prompt action.

Homer and the other parents had much to do with the respect given teachers because they backed them solidly. Had Homer ever received a note that I had been disrespectful to a teacher, he would have quickly nailed my hide to the kitchen wall. This was a depression, and taxpaying Wineldans looked upon school as a place for learning, and not for sparing the rod. For their hard-earned money, they expected results and good education. Occasionally Miss Clapper slapped palms with rulers, and she ordered some miscreants to stand dumbly in the corner, others stayed after school to clean blackboards. Everyone knew school was a no-nonsense operation, and the teacher had the capability to enforce immediate punishment. To test them was unwise. During my Winelda schooling, Lee Hales's punishment was the most impressive I ever saw. There was none in high school.

So, because the community bonded together when it came to kids, Wineldans were able to turn their offspring loose to figuratively graze from one end of town to the other, and into the surrounding hills. I recall no kid that was killed or maimed, and none ran away or disappeared. If there were some few that were molested, it was the deepest kind of secret. Such a detestable act might well have spawned unmanageable Wineldan vigilantes.

Kids were never told they could not go in Mrs. Dutweiler's house or to Mr. Wentworth's barn because Winelda had no real strangers living among them. Everyone was a known quantity. But even in Winelda there were a few cautions.

"I don't want you riding around the Square in Haywire Dwyer's car."

Haywire was different from most, and somewhat strange for the times. He was a happy-go-lucky, twenty-eight-year-old who drove a bright yellow Model-A roadster with a rumble seat, chromium plated wire wheels, mud flaps, a coon tail, and an Ah-oo-gaw horn. On weekends he especially liked to drive slowly around the Square with a couple of his boy friends who some might very well have called "sissy." As they cruised the Square, one of them occasionally yelled to a curbside gawker, "Hey, you wanta ride with us." They were always tickled pink when some young kid frothing for a chance to ride in Haywire's rumble seat would join them. That insignificant act would energize Winelda's all-seeing community eye. Word would swiftly pass to the dad, "Hey, Emory, yer kid was a ridin' with Haywire's bunch Sattiday aftuhnoon." And Emory would seek out little Marvin and make his instructions crystal clear, "Don't you ever again git in Haywire's car. You unnerstand, Boy?"

THE HOUSE IS ON FIRE

Thank Governor "Alfalfa Bill" Murray for pushing through State Question 183 on 11 July 1933. No longer would Oklahomans have to put up with making home-brew. No longer on hot afternoons would they have to defend against an invasion of ants because bottles of the sticky stuff commenced blowing up all over their back porches. Now Oklahomans could enjoy a cool refresher of legal 3.2 Old King Beer from an Oklahoma City brewery.

And it couldn't have come at a better time. The summer of 1933 was a scorcher with scant rain. It was commonplace to see people sleeping under dampened sheets in their yards. And from far-off— four hundred and fifty miles—Colorado Springs came reports that well-heeled city folks, who had spent fifteen dollars a night vacationing at the Broadmoor Hotel, were themselves also sleeping on that hotel's lawn. "Hell, I kin sleep on the lawn in Winelda just as easy as I kin up in Calla-rada Springs, and it won't cost no damn fool fifteen dollar fortune."

Wineldans rigged air coolers—cubical boxes that measured three feet each way—in their windows. Around the top backside of the box a pipe with small holes spurted fine streams of water onto excelsior, and a squirrel cage fan mounted inside sucked the hot dry air through the cool damp excelsior and out into the room. In the thirties, such a contraption—later sometimes called a swamp box—was the only known home air conditioner, and because of the generally low humidity, it worked phenomenally well.

Outside the window, where the water dripped from the cooler onto the ground, people planted mint for their tall iced teas. People sat on front porches in loose cotton clothes, sipped iced tea, nuzzled the mint, and grumbled about the broiling weather. "Yeah, they say it gets hotter every year, and I sure don't doubt that none. Bible says one of these days we'll all burn up, and we're danged near there." And with all those people observing from their porches, they overlooked no Wineldan detail. "Well, I'll be darned, lookit there, that's the third time this afternoon Luther's driven down to the Square. What the hale's got his interest?"

Homer came home late one night after the theater had closed. He missed a step as he slipped up the stairs to his bedroom. Pop heard the misstep, and alarm bells rang in his head. Pop lay there, and for a moment he stared at the dim outline of the ceiling. It was midnight, and his thoughts weren't good, but he willed himself back to sleep.

Homer had had several 3.2 beers—"just to cool off." He sat for a moment on the edge of his bed, and clumsily removed everything but his shorts and undershirt. The alcohol made his heart beat a little faster, and his brain seemed to whirl a little. "Been a long time." He lit a cigarette. God, but it was hot. It must've been ninety-one degrees in the bedroom and no breeze. Homer's bed abutted the open window. He placed his pillow on the sill, and dropped on it with his head half out the window, the lighted cigarette in his extended right hand.

The tenseness soon left Homer's body, and as he fell asleep, the cigarette slipped from his fingers and dropped a foot to the dry shingles of the back porch roof. The cigarette bounced and danced three feet down the roof's slope before coming to rest on some rotted leaves between the old shingles. A tiny spiral of smoke rose, and then a fleeting rogue breeze fanned it to redness and popped it into a small flame. Soon there was a patch a yard square burning vigorously, and smoke sucked back into the house past the unconscious Homer.

"Gus," shouted Bettie, "wake up! I smell smoke. The house's on fire." Mom ran to my room and shook me awake. Pop wearing only his shorts ran downstairs and out the back door. There was the fire over the back porch, and Homer's head was hanging out the back window. "Goddamn, smoking cigarettes in bed. *Homer! Homer! Wake up dammit!*" Homer didn't stir. Pop grabbed his garden hose and turned it on full. He shot the cold water the short distance to the roof, and beyond to Homer. Homer jumped up and smashed his head into the underside of the raised window.

"Shit!"

Half awake, I stood out back listening to this electric language.

"Goddamit, Homer. Get in yer bathroom and throw a bucket of water onto the roof." The flames were gone now, but there was a small cloud of white smoke which Pop continued to hose down. Homer pitched a bucket of water from his bedroom window. Only the neighbor on the east side awakened, but by then the commotion had subsided.

Pop was angry as he returned upstairs. "What kind of damned foolish business is that to come home, smoke in bed, and damned near burn the house down? We turned in at 11:30 . . . where were you?"

"Pop, for God's sakes, I'm thirty-six years old."

"Sometimes I wonder. What's to do in Winelda after 11:30?"

"There was a dance at Harmon Hall. I took a few turns after the show, and I shouldn't have to explain that."

Harmon Hall, located just off the Square on East Santa Fe, was a two-story brick building with a danceable wooden floor upstairs. About once a month a band came through town for the dance.

"Yeah, I hope a few turns was all you took." Mom and Homer both knew what Pop meant, but only Homer really knew about the Old King Beer.

"Oh, Gus! That's enough," said Mom. "Come to bed. Come on, Tommy. Let's all get back to bed."

I watched Mom go over to Homer. Pop had doused him good, and Homer was drying his hair with a towel. With a surge of love, she looked into her son's eyes, and remembered that early morning on the Ellinwood farm when she had brought him into the world, her first son. She took the towel, and as she rubbed Homer's head, she thought of him here in this small town—no wife, and no special interests except the family, and the Majestic. It wasn't natural. Homer had been an executive in New Orleans; had been on the road selling pictures; had met so many people. He seemed much more cosmopolitan than most Wineldans. He belonged but then he didn't.

"Are you ail right, Son?" She sat beside him, ran her fingers through his hair, and hugged him. She smelled the sour beer.

"I'm fine, Mom. Sorry I got Pop riled up."

"He'll get over it, Son," she said to ease the moment, but she fervently hoped Homer wasn't slipping. She kissed him and went to bed.

The next day, a handyman carpenter replaced a dozen shingles. It created a bright patch among the other grayed shingles.

A DIFFERENT KIND OF AFFECTION

The years from 1932 to 1934 were especially good for Mom and Pop Cable. Homer totally involved himself in the development of both the Majestic and me. On weekends and holidays, Virgil and Iris often came from Mullhall. We'd have the music in the parlor, and Mom and Iris would cook something special. One time Mom served everyone his own individual quail, each was like a little turkey on its back, a tablespoon of sage stuffing inside, and all the trimmings. A center platter held extra unstuffed quail. I particularly enjoyed these festive occasions, because when Virgil was there to take Homer's time, I had a temporary reprieve from learning another valuable lesson in life. To spare me, I sometimes wished Virgil and Iris would come live with us.

During those visits, I noticed Homer demonstrated real affection only to Mom, or to Uncle Virgil. I was certain Pop and Homer loved each other, but I often wondered if there had been father and son warmth between them as Homer had grown. Obviously not. Was that a Cable family edict? Fathers and sons were not supposed to show affection? Was it considered unmanly? I knew Pop was capable of emotion because he was always grabbing and whiskering me with his brush mustache. But Homer and Pop rarely backslapped, rarely shook hands, or hugged, seldom demonstrated real warmth.

There were those very few occasions when Homer would say to me, "I'm proud of you, Son," or "That's terrific." Still, I always felt there was an arm's length between us. To be sure, he was a fully involved father as Pop had been with him. Perhaps neither felt his role was to be his kid's pal.

Yet, sometimes he'd amaze me. Out of the blue he'd say, "Go get a bunch of your friends. We're going on a picnic." We'd all pile into the Chrysler and head due west on a little sandy road, cross the new Cimarron River bridge, and immediately be in the red mesa country. About six miles west of Winelda was Three Step, a huge gypsum-capped mesa that beckoned to any kid willing to climb a few hundred steep feet to view from topside the wondrous beauty of the Cimarron River Valley.

Like a scoutmaster, Homer would tell us to be alert for the deadly and prevalent diamondback rattlers—some as long as eighty inches. Then he'd lead us single file to the top of Three Step. During the climb I'd hear some of my friends say, "Mr. Cable why . . ." and "Mr. Cable how about that . . ." and he always answered with their names, "Well, Leslie, that's because . . . ." When he took on this role, he made me very proud to be Homer's son—not to mention the modest boost I received in peer status.

After being more or less confined to Winelda, conquering Three Step was to us kids what Everest must have been to Sir Edmund Hillary and Tenzing Norgay. This aerie overlooking the painted Cimarron River Valley could do magic for boyhood fantasies. Off to the south we could see Chimney Rock, a thin pinnacle that reached dizzily upward. Beyond was a shimmering volcano shaped butte called Mount Heman. Just to the left of Heman, the well traveled Santa Fe rails glinted in the sun, and it was never long before we would hear a doubleheader's distant wail. Soon it would roar and whistle across the railroad bridge as it headed past Heman for mystical California, the place where walnuts, and oranges, and almonds, and avocados supposedly grew on trees.

Homer would leave us alone and return to the car. Eventually he'd honk the Chrysler's horn several times and wave his arms. He looked so small down there. By the time we returned to the car, Homer had a mesquite fire going, and he had ice cold grape Kool-Aid, and from Coury's grocery some jumbo five cent franks, buns, a jar of mustard, piccalilli, and a couple of big packages of marshmallows. After the roast, we'd search and poke for arrowheads. Often enough, someone would find one, its flint shining in the red dirt. This mesa wonderland was only twenty minutes west of the corner of Main and Cecil. It was among many reasons why Winelda was a great place for a kid, and finding a real Indian arrowhead sure beat the hell out of looking for four-leaf clovers.

Another place Homer had taken the gang was only a scant ten minutes south toward the South River Bridge. This was Devil's Playground, a federal land of some eight hundred acres of salmon colored sandstone formations sculpted by centuries of wind. It had little sandstone knobs, and pinnacles, and beautifully grained flat sandstone tables, and a couple of complete arches whose pictures had appeared in some ancient National Geographic edition. The high school library had a copy on display. The land was still available for free homesteading, but hardly worthwhile farm country. Just a mile away, the South River Bridge spanned the Cimarron, which had looped around from the West River Bridge.

It seemed wasted, this piece of God's beautiful untouched land, because other than occasional Wineldans, outsiders seldom visited. This was probably just as well because its ecology was indeed fragile. Nervous coyotes enjoyed its peace and quiet. They'd spend an afternoon trying to waylay the long-tailed packrats that suddenly scampered from one sanctuary to the next. The wily packrats managed to survive by keeping one eye on the coyotes, and the other on the sharp eyed chicken hawks that always circled for a warm meal. In the Saharan-like sand dunes around the Devil's Playground perimeter were sandhill plum bushes, and shrubby hackberry trees that produced wild fruit in May and June. Wineldans used the plums to make great sandhill plum jelly.

When we kids were at Devil's Playground, we looked for coyote tracks, or had shoot-outs and ambushes among the rock formations. Later on, Homer would call, and he'd have the Kool-Aid—much cheaper during the Depression than bottled drinks—the usual franks, and marshmallows. Afterwards, we'd pillage the wild area of its sweet to tart plums, and its crusty hackberries, and before we left, Homer insisted we clean up the place. "Leave it as if we were never here," he'd say, and we'd bury the embers, and our tiny amount of trash. "Okay, Men, mount the green stagecoach. We'll head on back to town." Such corn; I'm surprised my dad ever said it. But now and then a kid would come up beside me and say, "Gosh, you're lucky, Tom. Your dad's really swell." As if his dad wasn't. This was apparently the mule-looking-at-the-grass-in-the-next-valley syndrome; everyone thinking others had better grass. They should have been around to observe Homer's congeniality on my report card days.

Report card days were when I imagined Homer wished I'd never been born. That's when I'd secretly hanker to be somebody else's kid over in the next valley. Yet, in my memories of Winelda, I recall several mothers who gave me cookies, and a few who even invited me for Sunday lunch, but not one of my friend's fathers ever once invited us all to big mesa country or to Devil's Playground for a picnic.

BEING YELLED AT

Being late to a Cable dinner was a major offense. I'd be off with T.S. Bunting or Holyfield, and I'd suddenly hear the whine of the six o'clock siren, and numbing fear would seize me. Like a greyhound after a jackrabbit, I'd sprint for the house. Sweating and panting, I'd crash into the chair next to my father and wait for the explosion. This was such egregious conduct Homer would use his big, open paws to box me around a little, and then order me to the bathroom to clean up. The interrogation that followed generally made the meal a miserable experience for everyone. I could sometimes tell that Mom thought Homer made too much of it, but unfortunately my chair, not hers, was right next to his. In his ordered way, Pop thought discipline was just fine, but he resented it spoiling the tranquility of dinner. Dinner was for discussing the wheat market, the lack of rain, horseshoes, and something that had happened twenty years ago. It seemed as if everything with Mom and Pop was always twenty years ago, a time frame entirely beyond my comprehension.

Like Homer's depression, my tardiness was seasonal. Most predictably it occurred during the spring and summer, when there was always bright daylight at evening siren time. There were a couple of times when they shut the siren down for repairs. Those were truly major calamities because by the time I got home everyone had finished dinner, and there would be real hell to pay. Even sweet old Mom would be mad. But even though I knew I'd see my share of stars upon reporting in, I always knew that eventually I could eat my fill. Homer would surely inflict some pain, but he never sent me away without a meal. I'm certain he was constantly mindful that both my skinny frame and my brain were malnourished.

For my ninth birthday, Pop Cable, who was tired of the loss of familial order at dinnertime, bought me a dollar Westclock pocket watch. He also counseled me that if I waited for the six o'clock siren, I was already late. I've since wondered why the folks never scheduled dinner for 6:05 so I'd at least have the benefit of the siren warning. Adults always exacerbated troublesome situations. Regardless, the watch was a godsend. I spent a lot of time showing it off, and because it came at springtime, I was never late through that summer. Unfortunately, a few months later, it died when I fell into Dog Creek.

But by then I was in the clear. Fall had come, and early darkness with it, and I was always home by 5:30. I figured if my family were Indians, I'd never have had a problem because the Indians timed everything with the sun and the moon.

Never again did I suffer skin breaking thrashings like the black day when I forgot my books. But because Homer was quick to lose his temper, I got my ample share of being yelled at and boxed around. Perhaps this will sound strange in this day of abuse issues, but I seldom felt like some poor, mistreated kid. I figured Homer's punishments were probably no more severe than what any other kid endured. This was a big people world; consequently, in my kid's world, I always strived to avoid wrongdoing that would enrage big people. In my view, Homer wasn't so bad. A few neighborhood girls had confided in me that on a number of occasions their parents had ordered them to bed without dinner. To me that was indeed bestial; that was abuse of the first order. Mild beatings were decidedly better.

EVEN THE KIDS HAD A WORK ETHIC

In launching the Majestic, Homer had certainly done his part for Mom and Pop. Outside, it gleamed. Inside there were new seats and plush carpet, and Homer's management was flawless. True to his word, he pampered Winelda by obtaining the most recently released pictures in the state. The Majestic exhibited them even before Enid or Oklahoma City. Unfortunately, this efficiency initially backfired. Homer would feature a hot new picture still unknown to the public, and attendance would be fair to middling. Two or three weeks later, the same picture would begin showing in Oklahoma City, and Wineldans would start noticing all the promotional jazz in the *Daily Oklahoman* and *Life*. Then they'd realize it was a Hollywood blockbuster, one that had already played at the Majestic, and they had missed it. They began paying attention. "Hell, this feller, Homer, he gets them pictures way before Tulsa or Oke City." So the reputation of the Majestic grew, and during those depressed years, it eventually drew people from as distant as Carmen, Cherokee, Fairview, Wood'ard, and Alva. We had consistently good business in the middle of the Great Depression.

Today, I wish I had a collection of Homer's breezy handbills that he always used to sparkplug business. Many Wineldans thumb tacked Homer's handbills to their kitchen walls just because of Homer's colorful writing style. He'd sometimes labor over a handbill for an hour, and then have the *Enterprise* run off a stack. Homer would tell me to round up some boys. "Tell them they get a free Saturday matinée ticket if they do the door to door delivery." One girl, Virginia Clemans, accused me of discrimination. She wanted an equal opportunity to earn a free ticket. And because she could spit between her teeth, beat up boys, and run faster than most, I'd let her go.

I'd show up with Leroy, Morris, Julius, Jack, and Virginia, and Homer would tell us to get on the Chrysler's running boards and up on the fenders by the headlights and to hold on like firemen. The running boards were wide and the handholds good. He'd drive to the first street and dispatch two of us, one up each side of the street. We'd run from door to door throwing a bill inside each screen door. Homer would rush a block ahead, dispatch two more runners and then move on to the third block. Then he'd circle back for a pick up. With three leapfrogging groups, no kid was winded, and in a little over an hour, we covered the entire town. It was a fun time of yelling, running, and riding on the old Chrysler. When finished, Homer handed out the freebie tickets and praised us as only he could. Each kid could proudly tell his folks of his accomplishment—he had earned his very own ten cent ticket to the Saturday movie.

Homer was careful. He always cautioned us never to jump off the running board until he had stopped, and even though a few eager ones had jumped and fallen, no one was ever injured. Young kids were delighted for a chance to earn their own ticket to Saturday's packed program. And Homer, like all the other businessmen, always had odd jobs for kids because there was no Workmen's Compensation Insurance or minimum wage to kill off a kid's opportunity. No one spoke of Medicare deductions, liability insurance, or disability insurance, or social security, or income tax withholding, or W-2 forms, or the countless other directives that started with FDR.

Had a kid fallen down and skinned his knee, no Wineldan would have been waiting with bated breath to sue Homer. It wasn't that kind of society. This was proved by the fact that no attorney even hung his shingle in Winelda. The two we had, had long since departed. The very last one had shot-gunned himself in his own office—legal business was that bad. Most regional lawyers squirreled themselves away at the Alva county seat in musty second floor offices surrounding Courthouse Square. There they roosted like ravens overlooking a cemetery. There they patiently waited for a rare divorce, or a death to probate, or for some other predatory juridical opportunity. Most Wineldans abhorred lawyers almost as much as Shakespeare's Dick the Butcher, who said, "The first thing we do is kill all the lawyers." Wineldans didn't kill them. They ignored them to death.

Young kids did a lot of work in Winelda. And by earning their own money, they gained a world of self-esteem, and no rational person, even an ultra liberal, could vaguely attempt a sweatshop correlation. Some oversized high school kids could even heft ice from the ice truck and carry it to household iceboxes. Home refrigerators with the compressor on top didn't come to Winelda until around 1936. Kids mowed lawns the hard way, with cantankerous, ever-jamming push mowers. They washed windows, and chopped kindling with a real ax, just as did every kid out on the farm. Teenagers pumped gas, delivered papers, and jerked sodas. Grocers hired kids to sweep, bag, and restock shelves. Restocking did not require Superman's genetics. Moving a case of canned peaches from the storeroom to an empty shelf was dumb work any kid could handle. In high school, I worked summers for Coury's and my thrill—just imagine, a thrill to work— came in the afternoon when I made deliveries in the store pickup truck. Mr. John Coury would counsel me, "And listen carefully, Tom." I was fifteen then. "If anybuddy reports you been speedin' aroun' town, it's the end of yer job." It was a wonderful, simpler time when there were no driver's licenses, and no niggling sales taxes. Many of the other socialistic taxes were slyly generated to be paid by those who worked, and then handed out to those who didn't work.

Out on the farms and ranches, kids milked cows, slopped hogs, and fed chickens, while teenagers plowed, and drilled, and harvested behind the wheel of Johnny Pop tractors. They rode horses, fell off horses, roped calves, and learned how to castrate pigs.

Girls learned to cook and bake, market, make clothes, produce well-made quilts, and care for infants and old alike. They learned that to relegate a shirt with a frayed collar or cuff to the ragbag was pure folly, especially when it could be "turned" to last months longer. Most girls desired a career of marriage and children, and they prided them-selves on developing homemaking talents. If a husband and children were not paramount in their plans, then they were free to become professors, actresses, opera stars, or executive secretaries.

And, yes, many girls eventually became executives. Women like Mom Cable were initially homemakers, but after they raised their children, they became entrepreneurs, self-made business executives. Many women operated large family ranches, held the purse strings, and kept the books. Others operated hardware, grocery, and drug stores, or a half-section farm, or edited the local newspaper. But before their business career, they first raised their children, if they wanted children, and most did. This made it possible for a mom to always be in close proximity to her home. She welded her family together.

Seldom were kids bored. In addition to the plethora of money earning jobs—even during the Depression—everyone had assigned household chores with plenty of time afterward for study. This hint of family regimentation had absolutely nothing to do with the Depression or with austerity. It was merely a matter of everyone under a family roof pulling his own weight. Kids started contributing at an early age. It taught them what it cost to live, how to take responsibility, and that they weren't always getting something for nothing.

Most of today's thoroughly modern mothers would quail at the thought of their offspring dangerously axing wood, stocking canned goods, delivering groceries, and driving tractors or trucks loaded with wheat. I don't recall a single kid in the Winelda school system with a missing eye, thumb, or foot, or who required psychiatric care for stress, or who lost his life because of working. And there were no counselors in the Winelda school system to mother other people's children, or to purvey career or behavioral guidance. Helping a kid overcome grief, or stress, or to plan his future career was the parents' job! These were solemn events too important to delegate to young strangers.

We weren't choir kids, but neither were we hooligans. Other than a few pranks, none of us ever found ourselves in serious trouble. Come graduation day, Winelda's kids were well prepared to face either college or the world. We learned to earn our own money, and by doing so we had acquired a work ethic. This gave us all an inner feeling of competency and self-reliance, and we had the basic manners needed for getting along in everyday life. Not one of my forty-three Winelda classmates was a failure as an adult. All could read, all could write an acceptable letter, and none went to prison. Something must've been very right with Winelda's simple lifestyle in the thirties and forties. Unfortunately, American families in the fifties and sixties allowed the government to systematically destroy what some later called the Greatest Generation.

BACK TO KANSAS CITY

By the time I started the fifth grade in the fall of 1933, Mom was very proud of Homer's accomplishments. She began talking about retiring to Anthony, and visiting old friends scattered from Kansas to Appleton, Wisconsin. She wanted to vacation in Florida, and Pop wanted to see if the family Victorian at Chicago's 26 West Randolph still existed. Both spoke of taking Route 66 across the Mojave Desert to see Aunt Lillian in San Diego, and visit the graves of my great-grandparents—Henry and Dora. Mom and Pop deserved this overdue travel and leisure.

But nothing came to easy fruition.

Only a couple of months after the fire incident, Homer and I were playing catch in the backyard when Hale's Lincoln-Zephyr Ambulance rolled in behind their adjacent funeral home. Hale's Funeral was on the big lot west of us, and because of the huge leafy elms, we rarely noticed what went on over there. Felix Hale walked over and said, "Homer, sorry to interrupt you and Tommy, but could you give me a hand? Don't bring the boy."

"Stay here, Tom," Homer said, and I figured it must have something to do with funeral business. It chilled me when I saw the large bloody handprint smeared on the side of the white ambulance.

As they walked away, I barely heard him say, "Bad car wreck other side uh Mexican Town. Leland had to take the man to Doc Clapper for some cracked ribs. This young girl's not heavy, but it's awkward."

As they placed the stretcher on a long table in Hale's basement mortuary, Homer listened to Felix's recital, and his mind began wandering.

"Her folks' car went plum outta control, crashed hard into the ditch. This here girl was stuck half through the windshield, and her neck is broke. See here." Felix matter-of-factly pulled down the sheet, and there was a beautiful, dark-headed fourteen-year-old, her eyes nearly closed. "Yuh see the funny angle . . . neck's clean broken, musta killed . . . Bam! . . . just like that. Terrible ain't it? Purdy liddle thaing." Felix Hale carefully covered her face as if he were tucking her in. "Her folks er drivin' from Missourah to New Mexico . . . tsk tsk, sure enough spoilt their trip."

Homer's mind was right back in Kansas City, and Felix noticed he had paled. "You all right, Homer? I know this's a sight. I had not oughta put you through this. I sometimes fergit cause I see death alla time."

"Glad I could help," said Homer, but Homer was undone. He went directly to the Chrysler and on to Lottie and Jimmy's. Lottie and Jimmy were the local bootleggers located just across the Santa Fe tracks on Broadway.

LOTTIE AND JIMMY

Lottie was a pleasant person with big fleshy arms and a black leather patch over her left eye. As a girl she had dangerously left a screwdriver on the top rung of a ladder. When she returned to climb the ladder, she jarred the tool off and it stabbed her eye. Her other distinction was her tattoos. Her upper left arm had three—a horse's head with a flowing mane, a Christian cross with a crown of thorns resting on its crosspiece, and beneath the cross a single word— "Mother." No one ever asked Lottie about the tattoos because they were plainly too personal, and she never volunteered. Lottie was the kind of person who was sweet and tolerant if you were worth it, but if you were a suspicious stranger, her one perceptive eye would turn grayer and a tad cooler. Her distinct signal translated: I'm being congenial, but don't screw around with Lottie Beaman.

Jimmy, her husband, was tall and slim with a weather-beaten look. He always wore a curled up old cowboy hat, continually had a plug of tobacco in his jaw, and was forever at Lottie's beck and call. His gait was strange because long ago a horse had kicked and permanently damaged his knee. So, on any day, he could be seen running around their place with his little hippity hoppity run. He'd run out to the garage, around the house with a hose, out to the wash line, and off to the grocery. Lottie, who was heavy, rarely ventured outside. She stayed home and attended to business. Lottie and Jimmy never hugged, or pecked, or said endearing words in front of other people, but everyone knew there was a powerfully binding chemistry between them.

Lottie and Jimmy were Winelda's premier bootleggers.

Later, I came to know Jimmy and Lottie Beaman intimately because I'd sometimes spend the night with their son Jack. I probably knew them as well as anyone, but I knew few of their family details because neither Jimmy nor Lottie spoke much of the past. A few times Lottie mentioned Cody, Wyoming—how it had been too gawd-awful cold to spend another winter there. Other than that smidgen, I never learned more, and if I were to probe Cody—a Wild West place that interested me—they'd quickly change the subject.

While at Lottie's, I discovered Homer wasn't the only disciplinarian in town. More than once I'd seen Jimmy hoppity across the yard in hot pursuit of Jack. Jimmy would grab him by the ear, and then rapidly hustle him back to the porch and into the house. I don't know what happened inside, but I was aware that such an abrupt action marked the end of our fun time.

Together, Jack and I got into considerable mischief—nothing very serious, but niggling things that tended to provoke adults to rage. In most cases I figured we probably deserved it—like the day we were using Jimmy's garden hose as our space ship telephone. For realism we wrapped it halfway around Jimmy's garage so Jack and I couldn't see each other, and then we'd speak through the magic hose. It was an unreal experience to hear Jack's voice come from the hose like wizardry, and with him not even in sight.

One day, after we had run out of things to communicate, Jack suggested we fill the hose with sand. We figured it would be hilarious to see Jimmy come to water in mid afternoon and to have sand shoot out instead of water. We unscientifically figured that that should produce a truly hilarious reaction. For several minutes we knocked ourselves out just thinking about it. Then, with a funnel from the garage, we took sand from the street and eventually filled the hose. We then screwed it back onto the bibcock the way Jimmy had left it.

We hid in the bushes until finally the kitchen screen door slammed. Jimmy was right on schedule, and the tension was almost more than we could bear! When Jimmy turned on the water, the sand didn't stream out as we had expected. Nothing happened! The water just made the sand hard, and a big bulge formed in the hose. Jimmy unscrewed the hose, saw the sand, saw us peeking and grabbing our sides, and he was tremendously pissed off! With his lips curled back baring his tobacco teeth, he charged after Jack. And as he charged, he yelled at me, "You get lost, Tommy," and like T.S. Bunting, I made tracks eastward leaving my pal Jack to suffer alone. Our sand-in-the-hose shenanigan had been the most miserable fizzle.

Jimmy never once touched me, but there were times when I was sure he was ready to spring. I suppose it was an unwritten Wineldan law. Adults were free to yell at other people's kids but they weren't to punish. Only teachers had that preternatural power.

Only once did I ever have a non-family adult lay a hand on me, and that was the afternoon Jack and I broke a window at the derelict Dew Drop Inn—Amelia Earhart had once spent the night there. The splintering glass had hardly touched the ground when like a Jack-in-the-Box, up popped Ferd Layton, our school custodian. It was phenomenal how quickly Ferd materialized. He had each of us by the ear as he yelled and carried on about Marshal Patton and Paul's Valley until my blood ran cold.

Paul's Valley was the dreaded location of the boy's reformatory in southern Oklahoma—a truly awesome place. Like a snapping turtle, Ferd gripped our ears, and all the while he ranted about privacy and destruction of property, and trespass as if they were hanging offenses. The wild raving went on for three or four minutes and then just as quickly, he turned us loose without calling Billy Patton.

We thought, *Good Mr. Layton. Good old man only warning us, only scaring us a little, teaching us a lesson—good guy, Mr. Layton.* Although we figured we were scot-free, within two hours both Homer and Jimmy knew. That was kid justice in Winelda. In those situations there was no arraignment, no hearing, no trial, just immediate corporal punishment. We never again visited the old cobwebby Dew Drop Inn, and it wasn't until I was in high school that I could be comfortable around Ferd Layton. It was then that I discovered he was one of Winelda's kindest men, and that he loved young people.

Most of Winelda's "genuine" church folk looked down on Lottie Beaman because they considered bootlegging dissolute, truly low-down. On the totem pole of goodness, her peers regarded her to be barely above the madam at the Commercial Hotel. Also, it was widely known that neither Lottie nor Jimmy had ever once darkened the doorway of any Wineldan church. This made it abundantly clear that these wayward heathens were far past saving, and obviously deserved heaps of scorn.

Lottie was childless, but she had taken in an orphaned tad of a boy, Milburn, and had cared for him as if he were her own flesh and blood. A couple of years later, they found Jack in a basket on their back kitchen steps. He would become my very best marble-playing Winelda friend. Because Milburn was six years older than Jack, he was far outside our world. Jack was the hellion; Milburn was gentle and refined. I doubt if Milburn ever played a game of "keeps" in his life, which was probably why he was clearly the apple of Lottie's remaining eye. She often said to Jack, "Why can't you be like Milburn?"

I'd hear Lottie say that to Jack, and I'd figure life would never be fair, and that pleasing elders was next to impossible. Milburn compared to Jack? Shoot!

But the origin of the Beaman kids was a deep dark secret known only to Jimmy and Lottie. Not a kid in town ever knew they were fosterlings. I never knew until I was an adult, and then it was Jack who told me. If any Wineldan knew the secret, they certainly never let on, nor did they tell their kids. Jimmy and Lottie raised those orphan kids, gave them love, and the Beaman name, decently clothed them, and sent Milburn off to college. Had not the war intervened, they would have also sent Jack. This meant that during the Great Depression, they sacrificed considerably for two kids that were not their own, and regardless of what some church folks thought, they were warm-hearted humanitarians dedicated to those two abandoned boys. Lottie and Jimmy certainly deserved no scorn. I thought they were among Winelda's finest, and I knew everyone.

THE BOOTLEGGERS

Lottie and Jimmy sold only top-brand booze, the very best to be found in Winelda, and they sold it by the shot or bottle. If a patron wanted a nip of bottled-in-bond, he tapped on Lottie's back door and was let in and served in her kitchen. Many times, after I practically became Lottie's child, I stumbled unannounced into the kitchen and would be flabbergasted. The soulful-looking gent having a shot at the table was the same grave man who took up Sunday collection at the Baptist Church, practically a deacon. After months of running in and out of Lottie's kitchen, I could identify ninety percent of her clientele. Adults often believe kids are slobbering rattleheads who won't remember anything. Not true; I remembered them all; still do to this day.

One day Jimmy took Jack and me back of the garage and swore us to what was like a blood oath. We were never to speak of the kitchen activities, the names of customers, and the unlawful bottles of booze. All the while Jimmy spoke, he fastened his piercing, almost hateful ice-blue eyes directly on mine. His lip curled back in a sneer. He told me how important this trust was. He never threatened, but I was fairly certain that default might very well lead to the ultimate sacrifice. I don't think any CIA agent was ever sworn in with any more solemnity than what took place back of Jimmy's garage. And it was effective because I never spoke of Lottie and Jimmy's operation to anyone, even to Homer, or to Mom, or to Pop. Gone were my Inspector Post badge and my book of clues, and no longer was I Marshal Patton's special agent. I had crossed the line.

My most electrifying sighting at Lottie's was around dusk one chilly evening, when I saw Mr. Ruff, the school principal, come to the back door with his coat collar turned up and his hat snapped down.

What a momentous discovery! Yet, I'd taken an oath to tell absolutely no one.

Mr. Ruff could've been a stand-in for James Cagney, which was why it had been so easy to spot him. He'd come for a carryout bottle of Old Crow. I don't believe that witnessing a genuine Biblical miracle could have been any more stupefying. This was the principal! He ranked right in there with the Lord and the apostles. Consequently, I wanted to give Mr. Ruff every benefit of the doubt. I figured that his grandmother must've had a sickness, and he was there to save her. But more than likely, we of the school were driving him bonkers, and he was seeking eighty-six proof solace.

In any event, during the Depression, and the terrible dust storms, Lottie's kitchen provided a therapeutic haven for a passel of troubled souls. It was a hidden spot, a refuge for relaxation and good idle talk: "God, but that was good sour mash, Lottie. Better give me anuther tot."

Lottie and Jimmy made additional income by renting the top-floor apartment and two smaller ones on the ground floor. Because the Santa Fe tracks were practically in the front yard—it was indeed the nearest house in all of Winelda to the tracks—they aptly named it the Railroad Inn. Everyone else called it Lottie's Place. It was a fairly tranquil spot until a hundred car doubleheader approached with steam geysering from every cylinder, the engineer blasting away at the Broadway crossing with his ear-splitting whistle, and everything would rumble and shake, rattle and roll like a 5.5 on the Richter Scale.

A passing train affected Lottie's occupants in different ways. Hod Phillips was one of the regulars whose nerve ends had long been frayed by sour mash. A sharp whistle could sometimes reflex Hod right up out of his chair. "Gol dang that thaing," he'd say as he sloshed his starched front with stinking whiskey. But the trains lent special atmosphere to the place, especially because Winelda was a railroad town. This was the main line of the Santa Fe, and it was, after all, the Railroad Inn.

Not more than three blocks farther west was Lottie and Jimmy's only viable competition—Jake German. Jake and his wife and three kids lived in an unpainted small frame house on a low hump of a hill west of Dog Creek and Elm Park. They had a dirt yard, not a blade of grass, and their simple box of a frame house was set up off the ground on a few concrete blocks. Jake sold only corn moonshine by the pint bottle. It was much cheaper and less wholesome than the named stuff at Lottie's Place. German's was also less convivial. Mr. German only opened his door five or six inches. He'd peer outside, ask what was wanted, and then close the door in the customer's face. In a few moments he'd return with a small package wrapped with Montgomery Ward catalog paper and a simple rubber band—no frills, no Lottie-Jimmy hospitality, strictly cash and carry.

All the kids interested in earning money knew where Mr. German lived because his was the only market in Winelda for pint-sized moonshine bottles. Unwritten federal rules required that moonshine be sold in a smooth whiskey shaped bottle with no raised writing on the glass. To find such a bottle was the same as winning a free Fudgsicle. Hand it through the crack of Jake German's door, and he'd immediately pay five cents cash. Afterwards, we'd head for Nick's Confectionery with Sam's nickel, buy a Fudgsicle, and suck the good stuff with alternate peeks to see if the buried part of the stick had "free" stamped on it. Finding a freebie was probably as exhilarating to us as when the miners discovered ore at Sutter's Mill. We considered getting two "free" sticks in a row was about as rare as walking on water, but it had indeed happened to Ernie Lord.

COME STAY IN MA JAIL

Bootleggers, like German and Lottie, had a cautious yet strange respect for the law. They took their chances outfoxing the local "dry-state" law but were very careful not to annoy the Feds. That's why Jake never dared use a federal-type bottle marked "forbidden to refill;" he would pay only for the smooth. And that's why the bootleggers always made sure to tack up a federal license on their premises yet took their chances with Oklahoma and the county, where there were no licenses to be had.

And the authorities sometimes came! One day, Jack and I were playing out back when Jimmy drove into the garage in a cloud of dust yelling to Lottie: "Ken Greer's over on the Square, and he's uh headin' this uhway." Everyone knew Ken Greer, the county sheriff from nearby Alva. To have Ken drop into Winelda always meant trouble. Today, he was raiding Jimmy and Lottie's, and at such times Jack and I knew we were supposed to get lost. It was always a mystery what triggered the raids because Lottie's Place and Jake German's had long been open secrets.

As Ken and his deputy guh-lunk, guh-lunked their car across the roughness of the Broadway rail crossing, Jack and I heard pure bedlam inside the house. Jimmy and Lottie were smashing whole bottles of good booze in their bathtub. Ken and his deputy braked in a cloud of dust, bailed out of their car, almost tore the screen door off its hinges, and stormed into the house. All they found was a lot of broken glass in the bathtub, and good whiskey trickling down its drain. Jimmy curled his lip and grinned, "Sorry, Ken. No evydense." Jimmy's expressions and looks often made him a dead ringer for Walter Brennan in MGM's *A Bad Day at Black Rock*.

Ken sighed and flexed his jaw, "Nuther day, nuther day. Sooner or later I'll gitcha, Jimmy. Then you can come stay in ma jail." And the grungy Alva twosome climbed back into their car, its squalid windshield a mass of smashed grasshoppers, and rattled and clanged back across the tracks. They headed northward to Alva, where most local folks figured they should've stayed in the first place. And out in the side yard, Hod had hidden himself next to the inn between the snowball bush and Lottie's roses. There he was nervously fighting to free his red suspenders which had become entwined in the thorny branches.

Jack and I could never fathom why all that glass and the stink of raw booze weren't evidence. Had we broken a bottle, the mess of shards would have been plenty of evidence for the adults to have nailed us without a second's delay. The ways of the law were virtually unfathomable.

News of Ken's forays always spread like wildfire around the Square, especially among the post office whittlers. They figured how strange it was that in these difficult times some humans "worked so hard to make life so miserable for one another." On the other hand, the WCTU ladies thought it high time Ken had showed his face.

In Winelda there was a strange alliance between its bootleggers and the ladies of the Woman's Christian Temperance Union. The WCTU wanted the state dry for Christians. The bootleggers wanted it dry for bootlegging. So the WCTU and the bootleggers became strange bedfellows who worked hard to keep Oklahoma dry.

I told Jack I was sorry the sheriff had wiped out his folks, and he grandly said it was nothing. They'd lost only the five partly filled bottles, the ones they kept on the kitchen counter. Regardless, five bottles were a meaningful loss, but according to Jack, five were a mere blip on Jimmy's inventory. And because I was practically a member of the family, Jack figured it was time I knew everything. It was hot that day, and after cleaning up her stinking bathtub, Lottie was deep in sleep. Jimmy was running errands on the Square—he literally ran—and that was when Jack revealed to me the deepest of family secrets.

RUNNIN' BOOZE AT NIGHT

He went over to the parlor bookcase and pulled out Lottie's white leather Bible. Behind it was a ring. Jack pulled it, and it released a catch enabling him to rotate the bookcase. Back of the case there must have been eight or nine cases—a hundred bottles!— with labels that read: Four Roses, Old Crow, Old Quaker, Old Granddad, Old Forrester, Old Fitzgerald, everything was old something. Jack stood beatifically, just as if he had revealed Moses's lost tablets, put his finger to his lips, and slowly closed the bookcase. There was a distinct click, and then Jack replaced Lottie's Holy Bible. Oh what some of the Wineldan deacons might have said for using the Bible in such a blasphemous way.

Jack took me out the back door to the garage. It was empty because Jimmy had the V-8. "Gotta hurry," said Jack as he pushed the floor drip pan aside. Underneath was a round cement plug similar to one on a sidewalk that covers a gas turnoff valve. Jack pulled on the iron ring, hefted the lid, and I could see a small cavern underneath which held yet another hidden reserve of twenty or so bottles.

Like a kid, I said, "Gaaaw-leee!" It was a veritable gold mine because bootleg whiskey cost three and a half times more than in wet states. I was impressed with this wealth and said, "How does it git here?"

"At night," he whispered, "a runner comes in a car from Arkansas. I come out wunst and seen 'em. Dad gets a Coleman lantern, and they remove the car's inside door covers and take out the back seat. You wouldn't believe the bottles uh whiskey everywhere. Car's equipped with extra heavy springs so it doesn't look overloaded."

Just then we heard the sudden "guh-lunk, guh-lunk, guh-lunk" of a car crossing the tracks. In a flash, Jack deftly replaced the lid and drip pan. The car turned out to be Mr. Red Ritter zooming by for home. Red sold cars at Bixler's Ford. Regardless, Jack, quite pleased with his quick reactions, stood tall.

Seeing both the Bible and the garage caches was pure exhilaration, and our friendship bonded even more tightly because of the profound trust he'd placed in me.

HOMER CRASHES

When Homer arrived at Jimmy and Lottie's after his ordeal at Hale's Funeral Home, he tapped on Lottie's kitchen screen. As usual, Hod "Cowboy" Phillips was at the kitchen table, neat as a pin, and nursing a shot of bottled-in-bond Old Granddad. Hod never over consumed, he just wanted a little every day, and he treasured Lottie's and Jimmy's hospitality. You might say Hod, and the passage of Santa Fe freights, lent atmosphere to Lottie's.

"Well, hello, Homer," everyone said.

"What brings you here at dinnertime?" put in Lottie.

"Not dinner, Lottie. I could use a drink." And Lottie served him, and he had another, and Homer missed the sacred Cable dinner bell as well as the evening movie. Unlike Hod's sipping, Homer slugged down over half a fifth on an empty stomach. He drank until he fell out of his chair, which was something Lottie rarely allowed. Hod Phillips had watched Homer, and knew Homer had not come for conversation. Therefore, he sidled out of the back door and left. Lottie was unhappy because Homer's style of drinking was what gave drinking a bad name. She finally urged him to leave.

On the way home, down deserted and sandy Broadway, Homer clumsily missed a gear, couldn't get it to fall into any slot, and kept searching and grinding the gears until the Chrysler slowed to only four or five miles per hour. Homer cursed and kept trying to shift, looking down at the gearshift to determine what was wrong, and as he continued to mumble and clash gears, the Chrysler veered and rolled dead center into a huge utility pole behind City Hall. The collision only slightly bent the Chrysler's thick steel bumper, but Homer slammed into the steering wheel, and the crash temporarily winded him. Broadway was dark, and because it was a deserted, unpaved side street that served the rear entrances of the Square's stores, no one noticed Homer's predicament. "Ah, hell," slurred Homer, and he fell asleep hugging the inert wheel.

But nothing in Winelda escaped the phenomenal Marshal Billy Patton. Just then he came around Thorne's Hardware toward City Hall and noticed a headlight strangely burning on each side of the utility pole. He saw the wreck, hurried over, helped Homer out of the car, and turned off the Chrysler's lights. It didn't take Billy long to smell Homer, and to know he was in no condition to walk, much less drive. Homer quickly demonstrated his ugly, straight-from-the-bottle demeanor, and tried to push Billy. "Meddling old fart," growled Homer. While trying to wrestle with Billy, Homer stumbled and crashed cursing to the City Hall lawn. With Homer slobbering and stumbling, it wasn't easy for Billy to get him to his feet. He got under Homer's arm, grabbed Homer's side, and managed to get him moving.

"For chrissakes, Billy. Will ya quitcher goddam weavin' around?"

And then there was another block up the Cecil Street gentle hill to the empty Cable house. After arriving at the front door, Billy stood there like a persistent horse fly, "Go on Homer, you hear, get upstairs to bed."

"Yeah, yeah, yeah, get in bed, get in . . . ." Clomp, clomp, clomp.

When Homer had cleared the top of the stairs, Marshal Patton walked down to the Majestic. He told Mom and Pop what had happened, and gave them the keys to the Chrysler. Unfortunately, the Chrysler had to spend the night at the telephone pole, but there was no worry because no one around Winelda would stoop to strip or steal a person's automobile.

That night at dinner, when Mom wondered about Homer, I told Mom and Pop that he had gone to help Mr. Hale with a body. Right after dinner, Mom and Pop walked over and checked with Felix Hale, who told them about the girl with the broken neck, and how Homer had acted strangely. Felix didn't understand, but without consulting each other, Mom and Pop understood. It was no surprise to them that Homer never appeared at the theater. When flustered Marshall Patton clutched at his Stetson, and reported the bad news to my respected grandparents, it was more a relief than an unwanted surprise, but it was still a heartbreaker for Mom and Pop.

The next morning, Homer was both hung over and remorseful and could hardly wait to get his shaky hands on his cobalt blue Bromo Seltzer bottle. He knew he was a disappointment, and he cursed himself for his weakness. At breakfast, Pop was far from cheerful, but said nothing. Pop eventually put down his paper and tossed the Chrysler keys on the table. "The car's back of City Hall. Better bring it home," and without further word, Pop cleaned his coffee cup, and went to Eason's to pitch horseshoes.

As for Winelda, this wasn't the first time someone had over indulged, but because Homer wasn't a known drinker, it was news. Only one couple had seen Billy Patton leading Homer home but this was the kind of information that kept Winelda alive. "Hey, Willard, didja hear 'bout Homer the other night, the pitcher show man?" The word buzzed its way slowly around the Square.

HOMER BEGINS TO RAMPAGE

The crash of the Chrysler marked a new chapter for Homer, for his relationship with me, and for his attitude toward Mom and Pop.

Now that he'd crashed the Chrysler, everything seemed to be out in the open. Charades were no longer necessary. Homer seemed to say, "This is the way I am, this is your Homer, and I'll try my best, but sometimes you'll have to expect the worst." He respected Pop, and he loved his mother, but if he occasionally fell off the wagon and into the gutter, they would have to accept his frailty. He was thirty-seven years old, and he was tired of playing games.

As for me, I am sure he loved me in his way, but he was dedicated to the proposition that strong discipline was what I needed regardless of his inability to control himself. The upshot was that nothing seemed right when he was drunk, and it was unfortunately then that he was most apt to want to take corrective action. I had always accepted discipline as a kid's cross to bear, but I had come to resent being slapped around while Homer was drunk. I was pretty sure the other kids were being disciplined, but not by drunken fathers. When Homer was drunk, it brought out viciousness foreign to sober Homer. I am sure the next day he was always inwardly sorry, but he certainly did nothing to mend his ways, and there were never apologies. It was this newly emerged trait—his poor example as a father—that put him on a collision course with Mom, and when that happened, Pop could lose his temper.

One day I came home from school and I heard loud conversation in the kitchen. Mom was telling drunken Homer he had to straighten up and be a proper father. I saw him leaning slump-shouldered against the stove, and wiping drool with his sleeve; his hair hung in front of his eyes. I knew he would never touch Mom nor would he ever raise his voice to her. But Pop began ranting words like "shame" and "disgusting," and was so angry he pushed my father up against the wall.

Homer eyed me blearily and snarled, "Well, what are you looking at?"

Mom, unaware I was there, ushered me out of the kitchen. "You go on," she said. "We're having a talk." And I ran up to my room, but even up there I could hear Pop and Homer yelling at each other. "You're a disgrace," Pop repeated, and I heard a crock or something in the kitchen break. Later, when I came down to the kitchen, I was flabbergasted when I saw Pop had a streak of blood that ran from his left nostril through his mustache. Homer was sitting at the table weeping. I had never seen my dad cry, and I was on the verge of bawling because Pop was seventy-three, and I couldn't believe Homer would lay a hand on him. I hugged Pop. "Go on," he said.

For a kid ten years old starting the sixth grade, this was very upsetting. I told Mom I was going to Jack's, and thankfully Mom didn't argue. I was out of there. I clearly remember that night at Jack's. I had a terrible nightmare where there were loud angry voices and a mob of people chasing me down a narrow street. It was like the running of Pamplona bulls with no side exits. As the mob drew nearer, their wrathful voices grew so loud the sounds all ran together in a terrifying roar. When I awakened, Lottie was holding my shoulders and saying, "Now, now, Tommy, you've had a bad dream," and I remember I was drenched with sweat. Jack was resonantly sawing logs, so I hadn't disturbed him. Then big old Lottie covered me, and hugged me as if I were her kid. "There, there," she said. I was surprised, but Lottie's rare tenderness was something I really needed.

Exactly the same nightmare must've reoccurred a couple of dozen times before I entered high school—always with the sweats, always the snarling anger of the enraged pursuers. I've never known to this day if I had some strange bug that caused the sweating, but whatever the reason, the dream faded, and after the eighth grade never returned.

HARVE BERRYHILL, THE WRESTLER

Harve Berryhill was a keen-minded man who lived very frugally in a shack-like house near Dog Creek. He was basically a good person, the father of six fine sons and one lovely daughter. Hard times had befallen Harve when his wife had regrettably died during her final childbirth. Harve was distraught at the loss, and began consuming increasing amounts of alcohol. He'd once been Oklahoma City's premier sign painter, not small signs, but the huge Coca-Cola and G.E. and Ford signs at key city and highway locations. He was so talented he created their time honored logos freehand. But after his beloved wife died, he would draw his paycheck, drink until the money was gone, paint another sign, and repeat the cycle. On one occasion he fell off a scaffold and had to spend some time recovering. Eventually he became so undependable, he lost his job, and there were the seven kids. Instead of looking for virtually non-existent welfare, the family bonded even more tightly. A brother in Enid gave him his Winelda Dog Creek property and took the two youngest sons off Harve's hands.

Harve was a genial, likable person, but he was a little like Homer in that after tragedy struck he could never quite pull himself together. And, like Homer, he would live a pure life for a time before falling off the wagon. He would then become a completely different person.

I often saw Mr. Berryhill in denim bibbed overalls loafing around the Square, his hands in his pockets. I always said, "Good afternoon, Mr. Berryhill." His face never failed to light up, and he would call me by name. I often wondered why a nice person like him didn't do something with his life. His two oldest sons must have provided support because they both had good jobs at the ice plant and the Santa Fe roundhouse. Still, there were two others in the fourth and seventh grades and the daughter.

Berryhill's daughter Madeline—everyone called her Maddy—was eighteen, very attractive, but conservative in dress and manner. She was a quiet, almost withdrawn girl. I would imagine this demureness made her seem even more mature and engaging. In high school she had excelled in secretarial and bookkeeping skills, and probably could have found a good job with the Santa Fe. Unfortunately, she was stuck out on Dog Creek as a surrogate homemaker to her father and four brothers. Mending, cooking, and making beds for that crew occupied all of her time.

With Homer in his present state of turmoil, it wasn't long before the old birds-of-a-feather adage proved correct, and Homer and Harve came together like parasitic mistletoe on the tree of life. Homer delighted in vitalizing Harve Berryhill's remarkable wit and intellect. Harve was an aficionado of Edgar Allen Poe, and when he wanted, he had the theatrical power to spellbind small audiences. Without a catalyst, he generally preferred masquerading around the Square as an abject ex-sign painter in patched denim. Homer enjoyed Harve's engrossing philosophy, and at Harve's Dog Creek shack, they often shared a bottle, and incessantly argued intellectual points of view.

The two of them exhibited further similarities in that, after a few drinks, they enjoyed a kind of cavorting belligerence—very much like two dogs playing grab tail on a courthouse lawn. In their case, they delighted in wrestling. They ripped each other's ears with headlocks, and rolled around roaring drunk on the bare wooden floor. They would knock Maddy's Spartan furniture helter-skelter, and cut their faces and elbows. Sometimes a couple of other boozers would be at Harve's, and I'm sure Homer enthusiastically took on all comers. When he'd eventually show up at home, blood was sometimes on his face, his trousers often torn, or a pocket ripped clean from his shirt.

This didn't happen on a daily basis, but after the funeral home episode it began happening every third or fourth week. Homer would fall off the wagon and go to Harve's place. There they'd sit together enjoying both bottle and their fascinating yarns. Eventually they'd become maudlin over their respective plights and turn to wrestling. It's a wonder Maddy ever stayed. When matters got out of hand, her older brothers occasionally interceded, but everyone had learned never to reason with or to push Harve or Homer too far when they were drunk and unreasonable.

KEEPING OUT OF HOMER'S SIGHT

If I saw Homer weaving up the walk, I'd lay low. Sometimes he'd note my absence and bellow for me to report to the kitchen. And now that I was in the sixth grade, he had taken on a new style of combativeness. I can only suppose he was harking back to his very brief WWI tenure as an on-campus private in the Army. He'd have me stand at attention while he criticized my pathetic scholastics, and with bleary eyes, he'd say, "Suck up that gut, Cable." If I didn't respond quickly enough, he'd flat hand my belly. "Don't look at me. Look straight at that wall, shoulders back . . . come on, Cable!" Then he'd light a cigarette, dribble a few others on the floor, momentarily go into a brief coughing fit, and then say, "At least do that right for chrissakes, even if you do nothing right in school."

This sort of thing usually continued until Mom and Pop came home to find me standing at attention. "Homer," she'd say, "stop that. Tommy, go dump the trash," and the heat would shift from me, and I'd never return. Mom would survey Homer's latest wrestling wounds, and with her head slightly turning from side to side, she'd begin applying Mercurochrome. "Oh, Homer," she'd say, "why in the world don't you straighten up?"

At such times Pop made every effort to keep his nose in his newspaper. Back in early Kansas, they hadn't mistaken him for Wyatt Earp for nothing. Regardless of his age, he was quite fit, and capable of losing his temper and slugging Homer. Later on, he would philosophize to Mom that the Berryhill influence had caused Homer's decline, which was a simple explanation, but not entirely true.

The next day, Homer could be the perfect son, attentive to his parents, fatherly to me, friendly with everyone around the Square, and filled with innovative ideas as to how to promote the next picture. On those days, he could have easily been elected the mayor of Winelda, except that he had no personal political ambitions.

In the meantime, the proud old Chrysler accumulated ever more dings and bruises. But during this hectic year of 1934, particularly during the winter—always the winter, never the summer—Homer made his frequent Berryhill visits. It finally registered on him that although Maddy was only eighteen, she had Harve's unusual intelligence, and was tantalizingly beautiful. When Homer could get away from the Majestic, he'd take Maddy—with Harve's permission—to a dance at Harmon's. Sometimes, after the show on Saturday night, he'd take her to Goods's Dance Hall located in a barn several miles to the south.

Mom and Pop Cable were sure nothing good would come from the Berryhill connection, and now that they'd heard about the Maddy attraction, they were certain Homer was headed straight for hell. In their wildest misgivings, they would have never imagined what was to eventually happen.

PART TWO

POP GOES TO JAIL

The year 1934 was awesome for Winelda. Not only was there the Depression but something equally as ominous had raised its ugly head.

Back of the Eason Gas Station Pop Cable and his horseshoe cronies spit and cursed. They complained about the Roosevelt government's recent ruling that forbade a farmer to plant his entire farm to wheat. A farmer who failed to keep a prescribed amount of acreage fallow would receive a stiff penalty. But if obeyed, the government would pay a modest subsidy for the unused land. Possibly Washington economists were regulating the national grain market, but throughout the wheat belt this unheard of governmental intrusion rankled the old order, such as Pop and his friends.

It was the beginning of the big spend programs. Eventually, this one alone would cost eleven billion dollars annually. It would give birth to a new bureau, a new regiment of governmental sinecures, gofers, and sparkling new federal office buildings. Washington D.C. began growing so phenomenally that some murmured it may one day become a city-state—a nugatory sovereign state that would blot up taxes with the same fervent sucking sound of an espresso machine.

"What the hell," said Pop, spitting tobacco juice into the dust, "it's my damned land, ain't it? They don't plow it; they don't plant it; they don't make the payments; how do they come off telling me what to plant and how much? Such tomfoolery isn't what made our nation great!"

One afternoon, Pop and his cronies hitched a ride up to the Alva Courthouse and Pop, the most vocal, went ranting down the hallways proclaiming, "I know not what course others may take but as for me, give me liberty, or give me death." So Sheriff Ken Greer told defiant Pop which course to take, and popped him into jail to cool off. Mom and Homer drove up and claimed custody, and Ken told Mom that the new farm subsidy had absolutely nothing to do with the county. "Calm him, Ma'am. It's one of them federal things."

BOILING MEAN BLACKNESS

For four hundred miles in every direction—Colorado, Kansas, and Oklahoma—speculators who had never farmed a day in their lives couldn't pass up such a lunatic windfall where the government would pay something for producing absolutely nothing. The speculators included out of work barbers, musicians, attorneys, and the like. They began buying cheap grazing land, land that was too marginal to be profitably farmed, and because the government had said it had to be a "working farm," they plowed natural prairie cover that had taken centuries of biological interactions to establish. They accomplished this feat in a matter of days. And some well established ranchers got in on the act by plowing virgin pasture.

If they planted enough acreage to qualify, then the speculators could wait for their governmental windfall check. It was this legal rape of the ecology that laid the groundwork for a natural disaster, and considering the ongoing depression, it certainly wasn't what the country needed. Most of those speculating around Winelda secured their loans from the First National Bank at the corner of Cecil and Main. It was the very same bank that had advertised in the Winelda Chamber of Commerce publication: "a safe bank, making good loans, and avoiding speculative dealings."

The summer of 1934 was blistering. Across the Cimarron in Major County the red earth was so parched that cracks two inches wide began zigzagging among the mesquite; its surface looked like a giant jigsaw puzzle. Old timers on both sides of the river said they'd "never seen nuthin' like it before, so gol-danged dry, so burnin' hot, land's baked to powder, wheat's so poor we'll have to harvest with a lawn-mower." It seemed as if farmers repeated those same words every year. This year, however, was especially torrid. Too bad the great global warming debate wasn't in vogue, some might have believed it. There were many days when the *Daily Oklahoman* reported Winelda as the nation's hottest town, even hotter than Needles, California, or Yuma, Arizona, or even Presidio, Texas. It was a dubious claim to fame but it was fame of sorts.

Late in the fall, while Homer and Harve Berryhill were wrestling for another Dog Creek championship, the first stirrings of a strong "blue norther" came down from Liberal, Kansas. But this windy cold wave was different; it had a new twist that staggered even the old timers.

Somebody yelled out, "Gol-danged, wouldja lookit! Biggest gol-danged tornaduh I ever did see." Off in the distance came a boiling mean blackness, like an ominous line squall at sea. Strangely, it didn't go high in the sky—no more than four or five hundred feet—but it stretched to the right and left as far as the eye could see. It boiled angrily, and rolled swiftly forward even though in Winelda there was absolutely no wind.

Everett observed with his squinty blue eyes and spat, "Got no funnel. Ain't no twister."

"Yeah, but it's sure movin', comin' rot at us, or is it goin' side-ways?" People always asked judgments of Everett because Everett Rose was a steady Rock of Gibraltar not given to panic.

"Well, Henry, see Perry Phillips's place way out there? 'Bout three miles wouldn't ya figger?"

"Yeah, Everett, that's about rot."

"Well, thet storm 'pears to be almost there. Lookit, Henry, only a second ago you could see Perry's barn in the bright sunlight, now you cain't. Lookit, his windmill is phasing out . . . disappearin' . . . now it's gone. There goes the house jist like it was swept away but it ain't, it's a hidin' in thet black storm cloud." They wanted to run, but their awe of it fastened them to the ground.

"Spose it could be rhine?"

"Nope, don't smell sagebrushy like rain."

They could see the ominous churning as if the evil black thing had an animal temper and coldness crept into their spines.

"Henry, ah figger it's gonna be here in three or four minutes." Because Everett worked at the wheat elevator, he was a phenomenal whiz at figures. If he said four minutes, you could put mortgage money on it.

Then a light breeze commenced and grew steadily stronger. In minutes the "norther" temperatures dropped from seventy-five degrees to fifty, and then to a chilly thirty-five, and like a great unseen flood, the High Plains wind grew from zero to a moaning thirty miles per hour. It buffeted and wickedly churned the recently plowed soil no longer held together by a network of hundreds of tiny grass roots. Tumbleweeds, like scouts before the storm, bounded along crazily and stuck in fences. It was now only three blocks away. The darkness passed over the small sun-lit hill where German sold bootleg whiskey. His once clearly outlined frame house grew fuzzier as if it were in fog. Except the fog was dark brown, and although it was three o'clock in the afternoon, the bright sunlight vanished. Birds settled noisily in the trees, milk cows headed home, and moronic chickens went dutifully to their roosts. All that was missing were the distant notes of Gabriel's horn.

It was a *dust storm!* The very first in memory, and it was unreal!

By half past six, the real darkness had come, and when we all walked to the Majestic for the evening show, the Square's lights glowed dimly in the brown gloom. Our eyes were gravelly, nostrils stuffy, and our throats phlegmy—everything felt dirty. The fine loess-like dust sifted through cracks and under doors. Some swore that it actually came through the plaster. Everyone stayed home, shut their windows, and stuffed damp towels around their sills. That night Pop didn't sell a single bag of popcorn. Only twenty adults came to the show for a miserable take of four dollars.

The next morning a perfectly white oval was on the pillow where my head had rested. The remainder was a dirty dark brown. Although the windows were all closed, dust was everywhere: on the kitchen table, in the sink, on the linoleum. At school, runny noses were muddy, and because boys at the time used Vaseline, their hair was a sticky, gritty mess.

The awesome Great Dust Storms, akin to those of North China, occurred all through that winter of 1934 and into the spring of 1935. The *Daily Oklahoman* printed pictures of five feet high fence posts, now poking only six to twelve inches above the fine silty dust banks.

Movietone News featured farms around Dodge and Liberal with valuable topsoil gusting thickly across the fields. Dust drifts three and four feet deep closed highways. Instead of snowplows, they used road graders to keep the roads open.

The huge doubleheader freights eerily passed through Winelda at mid-day with their powerful headlights knifing through the dirty darkness. Many pulled a hundred flat cars of nothing but Bethlehem Steel I-beams. People said the steel was en route to sunny San Francisco where they were building a bridge called the Golden Gate.

GETTING OLDER EVERY MINUTE

One miserable dirty day Mom said, "Gus, this isn't living. I want to drive out to San Diego and see Lillian. You're seventy-four and I'm sixty-one, this is supposed to be our good times. We were going to get Homer settled here and then take some trips."

Pop looked up from the market report, "What is this you're saying? I can't believe you'd leave all this to Homer and that good for nothing Berryhill. Now just what the hell do you think would happen?"

"Well, I'm reconciled to Homer. He'll never heal the scar he carries . . . it'll keep festering and breaking open. But I feel we've become his crutch; he knows we're here to rescue things. I say the time has come to pitch Homer in. He either sinks or he swims; this will be his test."

Pop was agreeably pleased. He could see motherhood wasn't standing in the way of good sense. "But who'll watch out for Tommy with all this carrying on?"

"Homer loves Tommy or he wouldn't care so much about what he does. Who knows how Homer will adjust. Homer likes that fourth grade teacher. What if he'd marry her? That would surely change things around."

"Hmm. I'd feel real sorry for the girl that gets tangled up with Homer."

"Oh, Gus! What a terrible thing to say."

"Spade's a spade, Bettie. Homer's undependable. One morning he's as stable as a battleship, but by the time the sun sets he's tossing around like a canoe on a wild river."

Mom continued her crocheting at the dining table, her head turning from right to left, her lips pursed. Pop went back to reading his *Pathfinder* paper. Mom knew Pop was probably right, but like any mother, she hoped for a turning point. Mom was thinking: *Homer is so intelligent, so handsome, such a lovable and loving son. Why can't something good happen in his life to take him away from the booze and those 1928 Kansas City flashes?*

Pop looked over the top of the *Pathfinder*, "Well?"

Mom peered over her glasses, "Well, what?"

"You want to turn it all over to Homer and get the hell out to California?" Pop smiled.

"Yes," her eyes twinkled, "we're getting older every minute."

That evening, as Mom stirred the peas and Homer mashed potatoes, she suddenly said, "Homer, Pop and I are moving out."

Homer was as surprised as I. Mom's words gave me a great sinking feeling. I couldn't imagine the household without Mom's or Pop's steadying influence. Homer had been a loose cannon ever since Felix Hale had interrupted our game of catch.

"We're going back to Anthony," Mom said. "Going to get our house in order, and then leave for California to visit Lily. A couple of years ago you said you were coming up from New Orleans to retire us. Well, Homer, make good your promise. Pop and I are going to get out of this dust and go sit under a palm tree somewhere, have a swim in the ocean, and see the great San Diego Exposition. At this time of our lives we feel entitled."

Mom's head, with its slight nervous affliction, jiggled for emphasis, and her impassive business stance had displaced any semblance of fawning motherhood. Pop remained prudently silent, and passed everything to Mom's superior judgment. "We'll charge you eighty-five dollars a month for the rental of the theater. If it starts to fail, we'll sell it, and you'll be on your own to find whatever it is in life that interests you. On the other hand, if you make a go of the theater, one day the place will be yours." It was a fair deal, and certainly not a give-away. It was the time honored Cable way; things had to be earned.

Homer was both sad and glad. With the folks gone, he'd be out from under; he'd have total control. It also meant he'd have to knuckle down to business, pay more attention to me, and certainly not continue his relentless slide to nothingness. It would be another opportunity to make amends for his behavior to Mom whom he worshipped, and to Pop whom he respected highly. And it cheered him that the folks were going to put their dream into action.

"I'll have to let this place go," said Homer.

"I would hope so," said Pop matter-of-factly. "It's much too large for just you and Tommy. Where will you live?"

Being off on his own was nothing new to Homer, "Well, this is some surprise . . . I don't know, perhaps the Campbell Apartments or the Railroad Inn. Right now Lottie has the upstairs vacant. We could camp there until something more appropriate shows up." My ears perked up. Lottie's Place would be terrific because I'd be just upstairs from Jack.

However, the mention of the Railroad Inn also made Pop's ears perk up. I saw Mom look hard at Pop because she was almost certain he was about to make some unnecessary remark about "moving in with the bootleggers," but Pop said nothing. Possibly he thought, *What the hell, there's nothing to be done.* In the past, Pop and Homer had had some heated arguments because Pop hated what booze did to his otherwise fine son. Unfortunately, Pop had always made the major mistake of counseling Homer when Homer was ugly and brimming with alcohol.

CALIFORNIA

A week later in Anthony, Mom and Pop traded the battle-scarred Chrysler for a new, five hundred and eighty-five dollar Plymouth sedan, a two door, all steel job except for the inset canvas roof. Unlike the Chrysler's mighty winged radiator cap, a cheap looking little schooner with no function had replaced it. The new cars hid their real radiator caps under streamlined hoods. Because cars in the thirties were infamous for boiling over—even new ones—the dealer had thrown in two canvas Desert Bags filled with water. It was not uncommon to see these tied to the front bumpers of cars. The folks would need these to cross the scorching Mojave Desert. Even the trusty Ford V-8s were notorious for vapor locking, and refusing to move until cooled. Homer had read of the Mojave, and he advised the folks to negotiate the broiling desert by night.

With Mom gone, I realized there would be no buffer between

Homer and me. I loved Homer, but when drunk he could become a wild man. Thankfully, spring was not far off. With spring, Homer always took a turn for the better. Perhaps by next winter he would have turned a new leaf.

The folks headed west in May 1935 and flooded us with postcards from everywhere: Carlsbad Caverns, the Grand Canyon, and the almost-completed Boulder Dam. Beyond San Bernardino, they marveled at trees full of lemons, oranges, walnuts, and avocados. From what had been written, I could tell the beauty and the change of agriculture overjoyed Pop the farmer. But as a plainsman, he still preferred flatness from horizon to horizon, and seeing the wind blow the ripening wheat like ocean waves. He wasn't too keen on "good for nothing mountains." On the other hand, Mom loved the geography's ruggedness, and she quickly blotted the memory of Winelda's dust and wind.

Their journey ended at Lillian's elegant Haleiwa Apartments on San Diego's hilly Front Street. She was elated to see Mom and Pop, and to make it enjoyable for everyone, she had leased an extra apartment in the building for a few months.

FOREVER LOST IN ARIZONA

Shortly after Mom and Pop left, I received a great surprise. Homer had made a secret deal with Mom while she had been straightening up her affairs in Anthony: "While I get our things moved to Lottie's Place, let me send Tommy out to San Diego for a couple of weeks." He also mentioned vague possibilities of marriage. The idea delighted Mom. Perhaps this was Homer's necessary medicine.

I was ecstatic! I had seen countless trains bound for California and now it was my turn. Homer took me to the depot, put me aboard the Santa Fe Scout headed for San Diego, and handed me a ticket two yards long. He told me exactly how to behave. He showed me how to raise the window, how my seat could be made to recline, and how, together with the footrest, I could lie horizontally. Then Homer detrained, and as the Scout slowly left Winelda, he waved from the platform. I was on my own for sixteen hundred miles.

All through the day the Fred Harvey man came down the aisle selling sandwiches, apples, candy, grapes, or magazines. At the major service stops, everyone would get off and walk up and down the station platform to gawk at the locals, at each other, and to be gawked at. After several minutes the conductor would yell, "Alla Bort," and shortly the locomotive would ring its bell followed by a slight lurch and the famous train would begin its stately and almost imperceptible departure. Although I was soon familiar with the interesting routine, I'll never forget the Flagstaff stop.

At the station platform there was a profusion of real Navajo Indians wearing beaded moccasins, feathers, bells, and loincloths. With paint on their faces, they danced, and pounded their drums, and collected coins tossed by the travelers. Over in the shade several Indians were selling Indian folk art displayed on tarpaulins. The dancing, the hoo-ah-ah singing, and all the Indian crafts engrossed me so completely I never heard the conductor's "alla bort;" never heard the locomotive's ding-dong bell; never heard the silent wheels of the Scout commence their westward roll to California.

I turned just in time to see my car go by. The kindly old lady who sat in the seat behind mine had her hands pressed to the glass with a look of shock on her face that probably reflected the horror on mine. I ran down the red brick platform fervently yelling up at her, "Stop, Stop!" I clearly remember coming within an ace of wetting my pants. Jumping aboard was impossible because all the stairways to the vestibules were up and locked.

The train disappeared around a gentle curve, then all was quiet, and the magnitude of this thundering calamity unnerved me! My seat to San Diego, my little suitcase with ten or twelve dollars and my ticket, the small clot of people I had come to know—these were all leaving me in the middle of Arizona. A bunch of Navajo strangers with war paint surrounded me, and I had only five dimes in my pocket!

I remember looking down those empty tracks, and try as I may, I couldn't stiffen my quivering lip or chin. Worse still, I became aware a number of people were looking at me. I immediately clenched my lips. I wanted to appear experienced, a traveling man, not an eleven-year-old goofball with a tingling in both his bladder and his bum.

Then, miracle of miracles! The train reappeared; it was slowly backing around the curve. The old lady waving at her window finally reappeared, and the conductor opened the vestibule door. He sternly yelled down, "You aimin' to stay in Flagstaff, young feller?" He escorted me to my seat, sat down next to me, and began speaking of passenger responsibility and schedules. I could see the disapproving glances of some of the other passengers, and with another grumbled caution, the conductor left me.

I was never so deflated. Instead of looking at the grandeur of snow-capped Humphreys Peak, a mountain twelve thousand feet high, I just hunched my shoulders and contemplated my shoes. And then the little old lady leaned over my chair. "I told him," she smiled, "that you weren't supposed to get off until you changed trains at Los Angeles, so he stopped the train."

I wanted to jump on her lap and hug her. She had certainly saved my life. Instead, like an abashed clunk, I shook her hand woodenly, and mumbled some words of thanks for what she'd done. I still remember her saintly face and later wished I had asked her name and address.

THE WONDER OF 1935 SAN DIEGO

In San Diego I discovered Pop's venturesome side. He and I walked everywhere and poked into everything. He was a real piece of work. Very rarely did he say, "No, we can't do that." Anytime I expressed awe—which was often—it fueled him for even further exploration. Pop always said, "Never hurts to ask; they just might let us do it." Shortly after the U.S. Fleet came in for the San Diego Exposition, I remember Pop asked a sailor if we could board his launch and ride out to his battleship in the bay. "Come aboard, Sir."

"See!" he whispered. Pop really took to the launches, and because he was such a can-do guy, we boarded virtually every major ship in the Pacific Fleet: the battleships *Pennsylvania, Oklahoma, Wyoming, Utah, Arizona,* and the huge heavy cruiser *Indianapolis,* and at North Island we boarded the aircraft carrier *Ranger.*

On one of the piers, we happened on something destined for historical significance. Stacked for loading were tons and tons—a city block long—of tin cans pressed by some mammoth compression machine into footlocker sized blocks. Easily identifiable were Folger Coffee, Carnation Milk, and Del Monte cans. A stevedore told Pop, "These bales are being shipped to Japan where they need the metal." Only six more years down the road those same spinach and tomato cans would sink most of this very same fleet at Pearl Harbor!

One day Lily drove us down a two lane dirt road to Tijuana, my first trip to a real foreign country. En route we stopped at Agua Caliente, a huge racetrack. It was the same kind of track I had seen in the movies except this one was covered with tall weeds, and there were no horses or people. It was the only ruins we saw in San Diego to remind us of the Depression.

In Tijuana, we went to the Longest Bar in the World and Pop ordered a huge pitcher of Corona beer, my first time to see the folks drink beer. Pop also had a Mexican photographer take a picture of me wearing a sombrero and a serape over my shoulder. I sat on a little burro that stood asleep in the sun.

A few days later, Aunt Lily took us to lunch at the famous Hotel del Coronado. I had to wear a necktie. Afterwards we visited the beach called the Strand. This was my first time to visit the ocean, and Pop took full advantage of this fact. "Now," he said, "if you're quick like a fox, you can chase the water out, and then scamper back here before you're caught by a wave. When I tell you, put yer head down and run like the wind." I remember that the pull of the outgoing water actually helped my stubby legs gain speed. And then I looked up just in time to see a huge wave cascading over my head. I quickly reversed direction, but it crashed on me and rolled me end over end right up to Pop's feet.

Pop was wild with laughter, and he kept repeating, "You forgot to run back. You forgot to run back!" This exasperated Mom. My new corduroys and tie were soaked, and I had sticky sand in my hair and ears. She gave Pop a few words on the side.

Over the next two days we returned to the Strand. Pop wore his old black woolen trunks with a tiny moth hole in one bun. Mom and Aunt Lily were in their one piece suits and rubber bathing caps. On another day we went to LaJolla's beach which was by far the most beautiful but scary—for me the water deepened too quickly.

"Pop," I asked, "why do they call it LaHoya when it's spelt Law Joe-la?"

I remember he looked at Mom and said, "I hear this all day long. How do you answer such questions?"

These were my very best days with Mom and Pop. If the folks had had some disappointments with Homer and Kansas City, and Lillian's divorce, and Virgil's marriage to an older woman who smoked, and my disruptive scholastics, they were making up for lost time in San Diego. We all had fun in California, and I never once heard either of them say, "No, that costs too much."

Mom bought a beautiful seashell and told me to put it to my ear and I'd hear the ocean. I remember later when we were back in Kansas, I'd put this same shell to my ear and I could hear the LaJolla ocean and remember the good time we'd had there.

One day we made a rather dreary trip to the Mount Hope Cemetery in National City. Pop wanted to see his mother's and father's graves. My great-grandfather Henry Cable, who had fled from Germany to America, had been buried there in 1904. I saw silent tears creep down Pop's cheeks as he puttered between the two graves. I was glad when it was time to leave. Pop's silent tears could be very moving.

Pop and I sat on the curb together and watched a parade in down-town San Diego. A half block away, I could see a couple of dozen cowboys approaching on high-stepping quarter horses. I jumped up, "Look, Pop," I shouted, "Leo Carillo!" Leo was a long-time famous Western star with a thin mustache and an always happy face. And then, I spotted Buck Jones riding on Silver! Buck was indisputably my Saturday afternoon idol, and here he was! I blurted out to the throngs around us, "Hey, everybody, there's Buck Jones . . . the *real* Buck Jones!" It embarrassed me when the people burst into laughter.

Buck Jones also heard.

I'll never forget him leaning down from the saddle and handing me the little American flag he had been carrying in his shirt pocket. He said, "Here ya go pardner." There was applause. I was stunned to silence, and for the rest of the day I felt as if I'd met the Lord Himself. I treasured the little flag, and kept it until I went off to the Army seven years later.

My two week stay extended to a month because there was the exposition to see. I saw things I'd never seen before. Two men in white coveralls took a Ford V-8 engine apart in record time, displayed all its mysterious innards, and then put everything back together again, turned the key, and started it running. Applause. Then they'd take it apart again. It was a demonstration never seen in Winelda.

I stood there like a bumpkin for three demonstrations. I would have remained, but Mom dragged me away to the Lionel electric train exhibit. I could've lived with the trains a week and was sorry I had spent so much time at the Ford pavilion. Lionel had a huge double track layout in an extravagant desert setting covering at least a quarter of a football field. Some six different trains were all going at once. The layout had automatic block signals, and switches, and a thousand tiny twinkling green and red signal lights. I said to Mom, "Where's Pop? He's got to see this."

"He's watching Sally Rand dance," she said. "We'll see him later."

Sally Rand? We went to the Sally Rand exhibit just as Pop was coming out beneath a colorful sign featuring a woman wearing a big hat with plumes and dancing behind a huge balloon. One of her bare legs was stuck out in a high kick. I wondered how my pal Pop could possibly prefer this sort of thing to the trains. Mom chided Pop and asked him how he'd liked it. He just grinned and looked sheepish. As I grew older I better understood what a wonderful rapport the two of them had together.

And, like any kid, I was beginning to think California with its mountains, and ocean, and battleships was a helluva place. I asked, "Mom, can I stay here and go to school?"

"No," she said, quickly eradicating my daydreams. "Your father wants you home. Besides, Winelda's school is very good."

HOMER GETS A NEW EVERYTHING

I remember I was on the back steps fiddling with my soapbox racer when the mailman came. I heard the drone of Mom, Pop and Lily's conversation turn to hushed voices. I strained to hear; it was my first time to hear our family clan discuss one of their own. From what I gathered, Homer had married, but they weren't celebrating. Pop boomed, "Well, that does it! He'll practically live with that Harve Berryhill." Evidently Homer hadn't married the fourth grade teacher; he had married Madeleine Berryhill! Mom immediately shushed everyone, "Shhhhh. Let's see how things work out."

A little later, Mom said to me, "Well, your dad is very happy. He married Madeleine, and for awhile you're going to live at the Railroad Inn near your friend Jack."

Pop chimed in, "Yup, living right there with the bootleggers," and this immediately met with Mom's scowl.

To me it was terrific news. I had met Maddy a few times when she had come to the show. I had seen Homer dance with her at Harmon's when we kids sometimes sneaked up there early in the evening to see how adults carried on. I always thought Maddy was pretty keen and beautiful. I was glad my dad had married Maddy.

In two weeks I was back on the Santa Fe train. Again I watched the Indians at Flagstaff, but this time I stayed right next to my chair car. All the way back to Oklahoma, I fantasized going to the San Diego school I'd seen with the red tile Spanish roof and palm trees scattered over what they called "the campus." I thought California kids had it made.

But when the train began sweeping up the Cimarron River Valley past Heman, and then crossed the trestle bridge, my heart quickened. At the stockyards, I heard the faint braking sound commence, and I knew we were coming into Winelda, and California skittered far from my mind. It was the kid syndrome, where one extravagant notion is quickly rejected for another.

I saw Homer and Maddy standing on the platform, anxiously looking in the windows of the train. And when I came down the steps, the three of us went into a huddle-like hug. I still remember how good Maddy smelled, and it was another of those rare occasions when Homer hugged me.

"Come on," he said, "before the show we'll get over to Eastman's Restaurant and celebrate." He grabbed my bag, "By the way, now that you're a sixth grader, you've just been elected the Majestic's new usher. You're now on the staff, and pulling your weight at three bucks a week." At last, I was finally ready to participate in the family business. Maddy was to man the box-office as Mom had done. Homer would take tickets and supervise both the lobby and me. During dinner I took a few side looks at Maddy, and once I caught her watching me. She sure was pretty. I was glad for Homer's and my good luck.

As we walked back to the Majestic, Homer stopped in front of the First National Bank. "Whad'dya think of this building, Sport?"

"Best building in town, Dad. It's the bank."

"Was the bank. It went bankrupt and I just bought it at a receiver's sale. It's now the Cable Building. Except for the dentist's office, we're going to make the entire upstairs our apartment. But don't get too excited; it'll take a while."

Together we looked through one of the big ground floor windows.

We could see the teller's cage and the safe. Strewn all over the floor were deposit slips, counter checks, and other forms. "How about the downstairs?" I asked.

"I'll have the safe moved to the Majestic, and a new business called the Corner Drug Store will rent from us . . . Esther and Virgil Clemans."

I remember how much I had looked forward to living at Lottie's but to live at Winelda's epicenter, right at the corner of Cecil and Main, with no lawn to mow, with all the action; it was terrific! It was the very heart of Winelda.

That Homer had bought Winelda's most important building was difficult to believe. It was my very first time to think Homer and I had risen above the poor side. No longer would we rent, and pack all our possessions into a single suitcase. Now the Cables were people of property, the same as the ranchers, and farmers, and all the other kids in my school.

The bank had been an unfortunate sign of the times. When the land speculators failed to pay their loans, the bank had foreclosed on worthless, blown-out land that should have never been plowed. Homer Cable was the only one to win. He had bought the best building in town for only thirty-six hundred dollars. No longer was it the bank building. Hereafter when someone asked whose building it was they'd say, "That's *Homer's Place*."

SUMMER AT THE RAILROAD INN

During the remainder of that scorching 1935 summer, Winelda set national heat records—hotter than Yuma. "By gol, we made the news again; we're the hottest town in the whole danged country!" It was certainly a dubious honor, but at least it put Winelda in national contention for having the most of something.

Living above Lottie's Place was a new experience. With Maddy and Homer cooking dinner, the three of us around the kitchen table in family conversation, it was an entirely new experience, a new start.

I was well aware Lottie's booze surrounded us. Every time I climbed the stairs to the apartment, I knew Jimmy and Lottie's alcoholic Bible cache was only inches beneath the stair treads and my feet. But Homer only visited Lottie to pay the rent.

One hot afternoon, I bounded up the stairs to report something, and I opened Maddy and Homer's bedroom door. They were in bed, and I detected some movement under the covers. Embarrassed, I immediately retreated down the stairs. I'd heard about honeymoons. I never again barged into their bedroom.

I liked the change in our home, and I wanted the summer to last forever, especially because it was the season when Homer was always in charge of himself. I didn't want to think of winter when Homer, like an old renegade wolf, might possibly revert to his howling, almost feral, ways.

Since my San Diego journey, I'd acquired a new interest in trains. My apartment window was like a railroad signal tower that overlooked the Broadway railroad crossing. Every train on the Santa Fe's southern system had to pass my view. I'd wave at the engineers, and in return they'd blast their whistles. In a little notebook I'd write down the locomotive's tender number. It wasn't long before the engines returned and a pattern developed. I could almost forecast when I'd see 4052 or 4038 again.

In the big house up on Cecil Street, my bedroom had been quiet; at Lottie's it was different. The very first night I turned in, a hundred and ten car train thundered by Lottie's, whistling and spouting smoke and steam, shaking the windows, the entire building—I thought sleep would be impossible. But trains had become magical to me. They were headed in the night for mystical places: Mountainair, Flagstaff and Barstow. I'd check the tender numbers, jump back into bed, and listen to the rhythmic click and clack of the wheels over the Broadway crossing. Occasionally I'd hear a wheel flange knife cross a switch and it would mournfully wail. This, to me, was music. Then I'd hear the brake shoes commence their grinding against nine hundred wheels. I could detect the train slowing, and from the stockyards a mile away, I would hear the faint whistle of the lead locomotive. This signaled the brake test had been okay, and all systems were a go. These events would produce thoughts of the Mojave, and the ocean, and battleships. It was seldom that I heard the pusher engine come by; I'd already be in a deep sleep.

I've recently seen sleep machines advertise their recordings of surf or Beethoven, and I've wondered why none of them have thought to tape a hundred and ten car doubleheader at the Broadway crossing; it'd be a sure fire success for sleep . . . click, clack, click, clack.

HOMER'S PLACE

Just before school commenced, we moved our belongings into our new three room apartment at Homer's Place. From the upstairs hallway our entryway opened directly into our kitchen. The kitchen table in the middle of the room was where we took all our meals. Left or west of the kitchen was Homer and Maddy's bedroom and bath. To the east was my room. From my window, the magical heart of Winelda was just below—the intersection of Main and Cecil. Across the street was the twenty-four hour action of Etta's Café.

I don't know what Homer and Maddy thought of our digs, but for me to be living at the corner of Main and Cecil was the zenith. Not once did I feel deprived because we didn't live on an acre or so of ground in a huge rambling house surrounded by elm trees adjacent to similar neighborhood houses. It is possible that some of my classmates felt being cooped up in a downtown flat with no porch swing or yard left me disadvantaged. Nevertheless, I felt lavishly fortunate. This was the locus of Winelda's activity. The corner of Main and Cecil was the ultimate, especially after I learned I was living only thirty feet from the site of the wallow where in 1860 the Kiowas had killed buffalo; the spot where real Chisholm Trail cowboys from Texas had decided to establish a town; the town reportedly named for a woman who had been devoured by a Texas hog. What fantastic lore, and I was right there at the center of it all!

Just below my window was the streetlight where they chained the Saturday drawing barrel. Right there! That streetlight was Winelda's prime meeting spot: "Meetcha at the barrel 'bout noon." It was the hot corner! Everything and everybody in Winelda passed my corner. And as if that wasn't sufficient magnetism, Virgil and Esther Clemans, two people who would become almost like surrogate aunt and uncle, opened the Corner Drugstore just below. The Corner was an instant success and attracted even more people. I marveled at Homer's business acumen for having seized upon such great property.

Of course there were a few disadvantages. Separated from my bedroom by the thinnest of walls was the office of Glen McCollum, the dentist who rented his space from Homer. Glen's office offered no problem at night when it was always closed. Only on Saturdays was it a bother because that was the only morning I could ever sleep in.

But when Glen began extracting some poor sod's tooth, the painful howling would cause me to bolt upright in bed. I'd visualize the dentist standing on the man's chest, yanking away, and I wondered if Glen had yet discovered Novocain. If Glen had no Saturday morning patient, it was no panacea because that would leave him free to make dentures. His high speed grinder, only inches from my head, would whine and rumble incessantly. This was probably just as well, because before the matinée I had to shine the Majestic's brass.

Another minor problem: around the Square I had heard the tale of Winelda's last attorney, a despondent man who for reasons unknown had aced himself in his office with his own shotgun. I hadn't learned exactly where this ghastly demise had taken place, but it became shockingly personal when I later discovered that right there in my bedroom was where the deed had been done. I carefully checked the walls, but they had long since been cleaned and repainted. Still, I knew his unhappy, litigious ghost must still be hovering. I will candidly admit that this knowledge created some initial problems, but after two or three weeks the gossamer attorney and I got along just fine. I owed this rapport to the nightly blaring of the jukebox in Etta's Café. I'm sure the "Beer Barrel Polka" and others helped to take my mind off my silent roommate. Had we lived out on some country road with moaning wind, my adjustment to the attorney would probably have taken much more time.

A very inconsequential problem: to get ready for school I had to pass through Homer and Maddy's bedroom to use their bathroom. I always tiptoed by their bed with averted eyes because having closed the theater after midnight, they slept late every morning. This wasn't great privacy for them, but at least the apartment was all ours. It was a give and take situation. They had to put up with me, and I had to inure myself to Glen's miserable clientele howling through my Saturday morning plaster.

One morning, only a couple of days after our arrival, I crept by their bed, closed the bathroom door, and stood in there relieving myself. I heard Maddy giggle, and then Homer boomed out, "Sounds just like Niagara Falls." God but that was embarrassing! After that, I'd use the hallway toilet reserved for Glen's patients, then I'd go into their bathroom to wash—shaving was not yet a problem—brush my teeth and comb my hair.

And just as Mom and Pop divided the family duties, so did Homer and Maddy.

Maddy bought the groceries, sent out the laundry, cleaned the kitchen and master bedroom, sold tickets at the theater, did the theater bookkeeping, and banked the money.

Homer contracted for the pictures, took tickets, planned advertising, handled the theater maintenance projects, and did everything else along with preparing most of the evening meals.

I was to work at the theater seven nights a week plus Saturday and Sunday matinées. I was also to shine all the brass fixtures in front of the theater every Saturday morning. That may sound heavy for a kid, but my shifts were only two and a half hours, and my work rarely exceeded twenty-five hours a week, brass shining included. These were business related duties, and I received the substantial salary of three dollars per week. My daily household duties were to make my bed, leave my room in reasonably good order, prepare my oatmeal, take the trash down to the alley incinerator, and then perform certain janitorial services.

Janitorial services? Homer had made a deal with Glen McCollum, the dentist, that his patients would always have a clean stairway, hallway, and toilet. Homer immediately delegated this janitorial responsibility to me. That's the way it was. There was no platoon of people in white smocks that miraculously appeared each morning to do this work. Salary for this janitorial work was never mentioned because, in Homer's view, this wasn't "business." Instead of a lawn to mow, this was to be my dutiful household contribution for being provided with food, books, shelter, and clothing. There was no plausible way to argue with Homer's logic. This constituted our symbiotic relationship over the Corner Drug at Main and Cecil.

Thirty-Two Miserable Steps

I thought the custodial work would be a gas, much easier than lawn mowing, but then Homer's German heritage got in the way. Homer demonstrated precisely how he wanted the six days a week hallway maintenance organized. First, pour a splash of Clorox into Glen's toilet bowl—which I also used—and brush it around. Second, sift a full coffee can of the oil impregnated sawdust along the hallway and throw some down the stairs. This sanitary chemical stuff made the place smell like a Greyhound bus station, but it was excellent for picking up the ever-present dust, and for superimposing its odor over any unseemly redolence. Once scattered, I was to push broom this sawdust from Glen's office door the full length of the hallway to the steps. Homer clearly emphasized he never wanted to find little pieces of sawdust left behind, and he made certain there would always be sufficient cleaning material—he bought a gargantuan barrel of the stuff.

Once I reached the steps, I was to switch to a regular broom and begin sweeping the sawdust down each of the thirty-two steps. Homer was specific, "You sweep from the right to the left and down to the next step, then from left to the right and down to the lower step, then right to left, et cetera, et cetera, ad infinitum." Every morning after I had gone to school, Homer, the first sergeant, punctiliously inspected the toilet, and the route from Glen's office door to the bottom of the thirty-two steps. Sometimes there were critiques together with the aphorism: "Nothing perfunctory. If it's worth doing, it's worth doing correctly."

NIGHTLY TERROR IN THE HALLWAY

I loved our pivotal and centrally located domicile. I'm not sure if the term is correct, but I suppose our home could be loosely described as Winelda's only penthouse. However, I came to detest the long hallway, and those thirty-two steps. At least a lawn would have hung over me only every couple of weeks or so, and only during the summer. The gnawing hallway was out there every day, and Homer wanted it to look and smell nice.

Homer took pride in his hallway, and I soon discovered the bats appreciated it as well. The bats became a contentious force. I knew when I came home at night—around ten o'clock—I had an eighty percent chance of being ambushed by lurking bats. Every night, at least two or three of the furry little devils reconnoitered like F-16s up and down my hallway as they murdered various flying insects. I suppose some would say this was commendable—the animal kingdom at work.

There are people who detest centipedes, leeches, snakes, sharks, or spiders. I loathe bats and still do to this day. I examined dead bats, observed their hideous Transylvanian ears, their ugly skin-like wings equipped with claws, their hateful gleaming eyes set in repulsive little monkey-like faces, and their mouthful of surgically sharp teeth. Even in the dark, when I could only hear their devilish wings, I could clearly visualize how grisly they must look, their mouths gaping, how their radar saw virtually everything while I was helplessly blind.

I'd bound up the dark stairs, and when nearly at the top, I'd stop, hunker, and quietly peer through the balusters down the dark hallway. Acquiring my night vision, I'd make my preparations for the battle I seldom won. Wily little devils, the bats never divulged their location until I started my run for the kitchen door. Then they'd suddenly swoop down the hallway, and barely graze my head. I felt the wind from their beating wings, heard their diabolical "squeak, squeak" and clearly remembered the gruesome tales of how bats purposefully entangled themselves in people's hair. This thought always sent chills down my spine, not unlike my Bela Lugosi experience of prior years.

In a crouched position, like a Fort Benning soldier, I would zig and zag down the hallway. I'd hear the squeaks and fluttering wings, and uncontrollably yell—I hated it when I involuntarily yelled out. Unfazed by my odd mobility, the cunning little night fighters would return and attack me from the rear, and metaphorically part my hair. I could never reach the kitchen sanctuary without their making at least three passes. Once, a resolute bat followed me right into the kitchen. Horrified, I fought the sucker valiantly from room to room—swinging the broom and yelling—and just before I was ready to abandon the apartment and flee onto Cecil Street, I finally knocked it senseless, threw it out the window to the street below, and furiously scrubbed my hands.

It made no difference to me that these critters ate their weight in insects every night. I only remembered they forced me to cower, and to run, and to involuntarily yell in my own hallway—my domain— and I resented this intrusive humiliation.

ETTA'S CAFÉ AND THUNKETY SLEEP

Humans are adaptable creatures. As I had learned to sleep next to Lottie's railroad tracks, I immediately adjusted to Etta's twenty-four hour café and its booming jukebox. For a nickel or six for a quarter, the music machine played endlessly. Every night I was sung to sleep by "Ma, She's Makin' Eyes at Me," or "The Hut Sut Song," or "Funny Old Hills," or "Deep Purple," or "The Beer Barrel Polka." All were popular at the time. During the winter, when Etta's door had to be closed, the melodies were muffled. All I could hear were the deep tribal thunk, thunk, thunks of the accompanying bass fiddle or bass drum: thunk-thunk-thunk-boom, thunkety-thunk-boom-boom. But eventually these jungle sounds served to send me off into a deep sleep. Quite oddly, it was when the jukebox occasionally didn't play that I sometimes tossed and turned until somebody down at Etta's sprang with another nickel and sent both me and the attorney's ghost off to never-land.

PERRY—LATE SUMMER 1935

That summer, by being a fixture around the Square, I saw everyone in town, everyone except Mr. Berryhill. Since Maddy and Homer's marriage, he rarely came downtown, and I knew Homer no longer went over there to wrestle. Possibly Mr. Berryhill resented the loss of Maddy. I never asked, and not seeing him for months, he gradually left my thoughts.

Winelda had a number of fine people. One of my idols was Perry Phillips, the only "vet" for miles around. If Winelda considered Doc Clapper saintly, then Perry could sit on the same dais. Around Winelda, a man's family was first priority, followed by his "place," and then his livestock. In times of trouble, Doc Clapper took care of the families while Perry attended to the cattle, the hogs, the valuable quarter horse, or the prize purebred breeding bull. These two men locally occupied a plateau slightly higher than even schoolteachers or clergymen.

Perry was a real western cowboy, but he was not a part of rangy Gary Cooper's awesome looking genre. Perry was short and skinny and wore a permanent squint from spending too many years in the sun. He always wore faded but clean Levi's, complete with denim jacket, a tad of a kerchief around his neck so dust wouldn't get down his front, and a pair of utterly exhausted Justin boots. Put in rustic terms, if Perry were a chicken, nobody would ever choose him for a

Sunday dinner.

Only his brother Hod, the same Hod of Lottie's Place, knew whether Perry had hair because Perry forever covered his head with a disreputable Stetson. Its sweatband, crown, and brim were mottled with dirt, sweat, and dried calving mess. When birthing an upside down calf, Perry had often rammed his head and hat right into a cow's rear end. Consequently, neither a Buck Jones nor a fancy Gene Autry would have ever touched Perry's veteran Stetson. I'd give anything to have Perry's priceless Stetson hanging on my living room wall. It had such remarkable character. Just one look at that old hat spoke volumes: the rigors of ranching and animals, the Dust Bowl, and the Great Depression.

Perry was the epitome of a Marlboro Man, except the truly rugged types in the thirties smoked Bull Durham or Golden Grain, seldom splurging on ready-mades. One day, in front of the post office, I studied Perry as he sifted some tobacco on the paper, squinted his eyes as if scientifically measuring the correctness of the tobacco's distribution, licked the paper, and with a blurred Houdini flick of his fingers, it was rolled. That was pure artistry. Then he'd poke it in his mouth, give the end a twist, produce a huge kitchen match, and whip it up the backside of his Levi's. It always left a black streak with tiny particles of sparking sulfur. Perry would drag in, smile warmly at me, and say, "How'm I doin', Hot Shot?" I'm sure he could see hero worship written all over my face. I figured Winelda was lucky to have Perry walking its streets.

One evening at dusk, Perry came into the theater, a cigarette hanging from his lip, "Where's yer dad, Hot Shot?" I showed him to the office door, and I heard him say, "Homer, I gotta drive out north uh town tuh Cobb's place. He gotta special mare that's about tuh foal, and Cobb wants me there. I thought your boy might learn somethin' from the whole thaing. City kids jist go to the liberry . . . don't git to see nuthin' real."

Homer was happy with the idea. He came out of the office to take my place and told me not to devil Mr. Phillips and to do as told.

In minutes we were headed northward on Cedar in Perry's Ford V-8. It was brand new, but it always seemed to have a big piece of tumbleweed stuck under the bumper, and grasshoppers plastered to its windshield. "Ain't no use to clean 'em off, jist come rot back." The right fender had a big bloody dent with dried rabbit entrails and fur still clinging to it, and the back roads' blowing sand had already pitted the car's gray paint job.

"'Fore it gets dark . . . you like to take the wheel to Cobb's?"

"Sure!" I said, and he pulled over to the shoulder. Mom had let me drive the Chrysler a few times. I remember touching the chrome starter button on the dash, hearing the growl, and feeling the new V-8's special power.

"Don't take 'er over thirty-five cause these here sandy ruts can sometimes throw a car plumb outta control." I must've satisfied Perry because he let me drive the whole eight miles to Cobb's.

The situation was as Perry had suspected. The mare had a troublesome history, and Perry figured the unborn needed turning. The Cobb family was standing around the stall with Coleman lanterns, their eyes following Perry's every move. When Perry patted the mare, she rolled her eyes toward him and whinnied softly. Then Perry lifted the horse's tail with his left hand, and began working his right hand slowly up her business, clean past his elbow. I couldn't believe it, and with all those Cobb girls watching. Perry went all the way to his shoulder grunting and grimacing as he worked, "There we go, there we go, ya little devil. Hold on, old girl; be over in just a jiff." And as sweat streamed down Perry's face, the foal gradually appeared. Perry stood, picked up a handful of clean hay to wipe the blood and yucky mucous stuff from his hairy arm, and then buttoned his sleeve. "Right pretty little filly," he said. And, as always, some of the mess had managed to splatter Perry's trademark Stetson. Then the mare stood and began licking her foal, and everyone gave a soft "Yaaaayyy."

One of the Cobb kids took me over to a cow's stall. "Wanta see something?" and he showed off by arching a stream of milk to a waiting barn cat. The cat loved it as it eagerly flicked its tongue in and out while splatters of milk beaded all over its face. We both laughed. "Wanta try milkin', Tom? It's easy." But I couldn't make the thing work, and the cow commenced stamping, mooing, and slapping the side of my head with her tail.

Up till then, I thought I was the only kid in Winelda involved in a family business. At Cobb's, the entire family was every bit as occupied, and had acquired skills entirely foreign to town kids.

Perry drove back to town while I asked questions about the foaling. He could answer anything, and I figured Perry was a pretty keen guy. Thereafter, I often chauffeured Perry to the country. We gave hogs cholera shots, and treated horses for sleeping sickness or infected hooves. We'd castrate a bunch of pigs, or help a cow at calving time, or one with a broken horn. Perry and I had bonded from that first event at Cobb's. Anytime he saw me around the Square, he'd wave and shout, "Hi there, Hot Shot!"

While recounting these fascinating experiences, I must've mentioned Perry's name frequently at our table. I believe Homer was secretly proud that Perry kept inviting me. Homer told me he'd spring me loose whenever possible because he considered it a valuable part of my education.

To this point of my life, I had fantasized about being the rear driver of a hook-and-ladder fire truck, a Ford Trimotor pilot, a Santa Fe engineer, and a cowboy movie star. Now I wanted to some day take Perry's place.

DOCTOR JEKYLL AND MR. HYDE

The dust storms of the 1935 to 1936 winter were even worse than 1934 to 1935. To me they were more dreadful than those Chinese famines described in Pearl Buck's books. Worse still, they eventually brought on the cicada-like cycle that allowed Homer's Kansas City syndrome to slither quietly into the forefront of his thoughts. They were thoughts that zinged in and out of his brain like little blue and silver rockets. Was he going too fast in Kansas City? What if he had not been drinking? At Menninger's these bouts had been referred to as "full-blown clinical depressions." Homer's therapy was to grab a bottle, and like Dr. Jekyll's shocking creature, he'd gradually become Mr. Hyde. This was an extraordinary transmogrification. Our Hyde had Homer's face and physique, but everything else was out of character. No one wanted to be in Homer Hyde's company.

Homer fell off the wagon in November, the first time since my return from San Diego. Maddy was very young, but very intuitive. In early November she quickly detected the commencement of Homer's slide. She effectively squelched his thoughts, and successfully brought him back to normal. But once winter was full blown, and the dust was upon us, she eventually failed. I felt particularly bad for Maddy. But of course, it was no surprise to her; she'd witnessed many Dog Creek wrestling matches. Homer would yell at us for any imagined reason. Sometimes he'd disappear for two or three drunken days. Sometimes he didn't disappear, but we wished he would.

When his internal storm was over, the dynamic Homer would return as surely as Mr. Hyde reverted to Dr. Jekyll, and he would be as loving and considerate, and as interesting and as imaginative as he had ever been. Yet he would never sit down and disclose what torment he had just experienced. Even had he sought professional help, there was no one within a hundred and thirty-five miles of Winelda with the competency to clinically treat him.

Our Fathers, the Painters

Only once do I remember Homer plastered and funny at the same time. Harry Perry, a local railroader who lived on Missouri street, had seen Homer spray paint the front of the Majestic. He asked Homer if he could borrow the spray equipment because it was perfect for painting his kitchen. Harry was a good customer, and his son Frank was only a year ahead of me in school. Homer agreed, but because the compressor and paint gun were Homer's pride and joy, and not inexpensive, he volunteered to show Mr. Perry how to spray paint.

Frank and his dad drove to the back of the theater, and we loaded the gear. The two dads put on brand new Sherwin Williams painter's caps, and tied bandit-like kerchiefs over their noses. Frank and I left them mixing Mrs. Perry's selection of pea-green paint. She had gone to her lady's club, and because our teachers were attending a conference, we had a free day. The kids next door invited Frank and me to play a new game called Monopoly. After three hours of Monopoly, Frank had captured all the hotels, and we decided to check on our fathers the painters.

When we entered the kitchen, we discovered they had obviously been mixing pleasure with artistry. They had apparently ambushed each other repeatedly with the spray gun. Our fathers were painted pea-green from their Sherwin-Williams caps to their shoes. There they were debating world affairs at the kitchen table with a paint smeared bottle of Three Feathers blend standing between them like a referee.

When Frank and I entered, they stopped momentarily to perfunctorily focus on us with lizard-like eyeballs peeking from their weird avocado faces. Then, without missing a breath, they continued arguing the merits of the NRA. Should it survive? I remember Homer said, "Hell, Harry, I'll drink to that." And they laughed, slugged some Three Feathers, and banged their glasses on the table. Frank and I weren't sure who was for what. We could only stare in disbelief at the kitchen disaster. Everything was pea-green: the floor, the overhead light fixture, the ceiling, the windowpanes . . . Mrs. Perry's stove! Everything was uniformly green.

Frank and I protected the Perry car with a drop cloth, and got Jolly Green Homer and equipment home without any Wineldan seeing us. Maddy spent most of the afternoon cleaning Homer's face, sideburns and hands, and all the while, thirty-nine-year-old Homer was telling Maddy how he'd shot down Harry Perry with the paint gun. For several days our apartment reeked of turpentine.

Frank told me his father and mother didn't speak for two weeks. Mr. Perry hired a handyman to restore order to his wife's kitchen, and to his life.

As long as Homer had to tie one on, I preferred that happy approach, but this modus operandi was a rarity.

1936 RABBIT DRIVES

As if cold blue northers and dust were not enough, huge jackrabbits plagued the land around Winelda. These animals nibbled away at the winter wheat and what little range grass that remained. At night they'd sit along the highway, taking turns jumping through the expensive grilles of hard-to-come-by automobiles. They were a furry menace—armies of them—and the ranchers were out to annihilate them by announcing rabbit drives.

When some beleaguered farmer or rancher proclaimed a rabbit drive, he'd put a little y'all-come ad in the *Winelda Enterprise,* and every kid and most adults for miles around turned out for the free chili and crackers, and the grisly event. Rabbit drives were free, social, and actually served to dispel some of the dreariness of the Great Depression.

I arrived at my first drive to find three or four hundred people milling around with baseball bats, clubs, and ax handles. All together we looked like a militant labor union and I wondered how this mob would go about finding rabbits. But the "committee" was surprisingly well organized, and they soon had our rabble deployed into a long irregular line stretching across the pasture. They had temporarily reinforced the opposite corner of the "bobbed war fance" with chicken wire. This would prevent the egress of most small animals. When the drive director gave the signal, our line of clubbers began moving the quarter mile toward the reinforced corner. In a phalanx behind us, armed with shotguns loaded with short distance birdshot, were a dozen or so adult marksmen on horses. As a credit to their attention to safety, I never heard of a single soul around Winelda who, during a rabbit drive, ever collected birdshot in his hind-side.

A "scared up" rabbit would run crazily along the line with everyone shouting and throwing clubs. At times there were four or five rabbits zigzagging and biting the dust under a blur of hurled clubs. No one was foolish enough to jut ahead of the line. If a rabbit suddenly scampered through the line of clubs, the mounted guns quickly brought them down. And as we neared the chicken wired corner, sometimes a hundred rabbits were running in circles, leaping at the chicken wire while demonic kids clubbed them right and left; blood splattered otherwise cherubic faces and clothing.

In retrospect, the rabbit drives were cruel, ugly, almost savage rites, but at that particular time even ardent churchgoers felt justified. It was a case of survival. The horrid little beasts were multiplying as rabbits will and they were systematically stripping what little the drought hadn't already destroyed. Cattle had to survive, and buying hay was an expensive proposition.

For the most part, it wasn't wasteful, wanton killing. No rabbits rotted in the field; the tender cottontails would soon grace Wineldan tables. The tough old jackrabbits were tossed to the hogs, which ravenously ate them, fur and all. "Yes, sir. Them rabbits are sure enough good fer hogs, even better than store bought tankage. Makes 'em grow, too."

Not until a person has seen a hog with fur and blood drooling down one side of its snout, and entrails down the other, does he decide a pig is no longer cute and cuddly and should not be allowed to share the front porch. Any hog farmer can attest that, like people, many hogs can be sweet while others may react weirdly. Hogs can move phenomenally fast, and they have long sharp teeth, and I could never forget that they named Winelda for a woman who a hog had eaten right down to her shoes. "Mabel, yer little kid's 'bout to get inta thet pigpen. You hadn't oughta let 'im."

EARL ARNOLD—MARCH 1936

Very few Wineldans can truthfully recall the Great Depression as devastating or cruel. But bound to surface are a few heart-wrenching, time distorted stories about hunger, no clothing, no money for the doctor, or a grievous burial of a little kid or two in simple wooden boxes. But the truth of the matter is that no one ever looked gaunt or threadbare in Winelda, and everyone had a place to sleep. Every month they sold new cars, new rifles, and new boots around the Square. If not against their religion, most families went to the movies at least every other week. Thanks to the Santa Fe, Winelda's depression was quite mild. And had it ever come to Doc Clapper's attention, he would never have allowed a fee to stand in the way of saving a life, particularly some sick little kid's.

South of town, near the Devil's Playground, lived a Winelda family that had probably fared the least well of all. Their plight was not from the lack of trying, or sheer rawboned courage; theirs was from a flawed decision exacerbated by drought, wind, and dust. The land around the Devil's Playground was federal land that could be legally homesteaded, but before a homesteader could gain title, the family had to live on it for at least a year, make improvements, and work it. If these conditions were met, then the land was theirs forever, and absolutely free.

Barney Arnold, his wife, and their son Earl staked a claim, and not a stone's throw away were the salmon colored rocks of Devil's Playground. They lived in a one room makeshift hut snuggled on the lee side of a sagebrush covered sandy hill. Nobody was certain where the Arnolds had come from, Missouri or Arkansas—somewhere over east. Their hut was part red sod from across the river, part orange crates, part tarpaper, and anything else Barney could come by. The floor was nothing but tamped dirt. They had no creature comforts, not even a privy. Digging a sump for a privy in the ornery sand was a losing proposition. If anyone had to go, they grabbed a shovel and last year's Montgomery Ward catalog, and poked off through the redolent sagebrush.

If any family around Winelda was poor, it was indeed the Arnolds, but they had hope, and they trusted in the land and in seven months or so it would be theirs. They received no welfare, and if such a thing was available, they asked for none. They were good people, but Barney had mistakenly put his faith in land so marginal that no amount of hard work would have made it pay. According to regional historians, even the vagabond Indians had always avoided the Devil's Playground area. This is why, thirty years after statehood, it was still up for grabs. But Barney Arnold had hope, and no Wineldan ever poked fun at what he was trying to accomplish.

I met Earl at school, and on one of my hunting forays I visited Earl's hogan-like hut. His mother and father, very nice people, invited me in for a chili and crackers lunch, and because of it, Homer made a very rare exception by permitting me to invite the Arnold family to a free movie.

Homer met the Arnolds in the lobby, and he too immediately liked them. Just seeing them made Homer recall his days on the Ellinwood farm when Pop would bring the mule to the barn after a hard day's plowing. Homer's job had been to unharness the grateful critter, and while it ate, to clean the clay and pebbles from its frogs, and currycomb and brush it dry. That had been a Homer hardship on a relatively rich farm, and I'm sure he respected Barney working his heart out in mostly sand and little loam, as well as an area plagued with rabbits.

Later on, Earl invited me to hunt rabbits and spend the night. I quickly discovered no self-respecting cottontail lived near them, only a few tough sinewy jackrabbits. That night Mrs. Arnold made a nice dinner. I noticed that no two of her plates matched. Later, we sat around a coal oil lamp and ate popcorn. There was no Amos and Andy program because there was no Philco radio, no electricity. So we told stories, and Earl spoke of awakening one time to find a four foot diamondback rattler snuggled next to him in the warmth of his pallet.

Mr. Arnold backed up the story, "Yep, Earl, he done said, 'Daddy, I gotta snake in bed with me, what kin I do?' He had a kinda whimper in his voice, and I tolt Earl to lay still as a rock. He'd awready pulled the covers back, and I seen this here snake lying stretched out lenth-ways next to Earl's lag agittin' warmth. I reached over and fetched that forked stick yonder,"—Mr. Arnold pointed to a stick by the door—"I take it with me when I walk around here. Well, I clamped that snake's head fast inta the pallet, and it a wrigglin' and thrashin' aroun', and Earl, he jumped out right smart. Then Ma come over with the shovel and clipped his head clean off right at the fork of my stick . . . seven rattles. Happened jist thet wunst." As Mr. Arnold spoke, I furtively scanned the single room's shadowy corners.

Later on, Mr. Arnold played a good guitar and sang real cowboy songs. Then, when Earl and I had snuggled down into our pallets, and the wind had stopped sighing through the sagebrush, we could hear coyotes—loads of them—calling to each other from all around Devil's Playground. The place had real Western atmosphere.

When school started that fall, Earl didn't show up. Billy Patton and a couple of Wineldans went out to check around. The Arnold hut was just a shell, and the old Dodge truck was gone. "Don't 'pear to be no foul play," said Billy. "I reckon they up and follered the Okies to California."

I always hoped Earl would drop a card, but he never did, and to this day the Arnold family remains a Wineldan mystery. But given tenacious Barney Arnold and his family's true grit, I knew they'd make the most of California's greater opportunities. Somewhere out there, in Fresno, or Lodi, or Modesto, or Salinas, there's undoubtedly a prosperous Arnold family. Anyway, that's how I have always wanted to think of them.

THAT'S BUSINESS—SUMMER 1936

Even though Homer did pretty well, I couldn't wait for that winter to be over, and for mid May to come. I wanted the gruesome seventh grade buried forever. Each year I hoped the next grade would present a surprising improvement. But it never seemed to happen and the verve for academia continued to elude me. I had just about concluded that scholarship wasn't for me and perhaps I was better suited to manual training. Perhaps I was better suited for bicycle repair, welding, or the skills needed to be a plumber's helper. Homer had not yet given up on improving my mind, although it was not with the same robust obsessiveness he had demonstrated back in the fourth and fifth grades.

Still, report card day was always the exception. I don't think many treaties in the world were ever battled over as painstakingly as those smudged little report cards. The only thing missing were tiny drops of my blood. Homer would take one aggravated look and gasp, "Oh, for God's sake!" and then he'd pause while he theatrically held his head in his hands. He'd continue with "Heaven have mercy," or "By God, this kid is doomed," or "Sweet Jesus," then he'd go through his usual spiel: "Son, how do you ever expect to compete with kids from Tulsa and San Diego?" There was always some new piece of geography where I was to eventually wear my colors in competitive battle. He'd rant and rave, and I'd go through a little shoving and knocking around. If he were drinking, the treatment was more prolonged and severe. Ultimately my Thespian father would sign the detestable report card, and it would be "out, damned spot," and I'd be pretty much off the hook for another six weeks. Once I asked Maddy to sign, and she smiled the most radiant, unbelieving smile, "Tommy, have you lost your marbles? That's your father's sole domain . . . I wouldn't think of trespassing."

I was especially anxious for May because Austin Cue, who owned the filling station catty-corner from Sharp's Lumberyard, had offered me a summer job pumping gas. Homer deplored my scholastics, but he obviously admired this industrious side of me, and that I never planned to sit on my backsides through summer. He liked the idea of my working for Austin. It was a job where I'd have to talk to people, perform service, and collect cash. "Now that's business," he'd proudly say. He would give his okay, but only so long as I performed my nightly stints at the Majestic as well as the Saturday and Sunday matinées. He'd always declare with finality, "Nothing pre-empts the Majestic! It's the family's bread and butter."

Earlier, he had dealt me a truly crushing blow by refusing to let me take a paperboy opening. It paid a phenomenal fifty dollars a month! Now that was real money, and to me it was real business, but Homer imperiously scratched it; gave it a fat Nero's thumbs down. "It's dumb work. Terrible job! I won't have it. You see no one, you make no sale, and you just run around in the dark of early morning and throw papers at people's front porches. And it's cold, and you miss valuable sleep, and it's just dumb, dumb work. Forget it. Besides, you don't have a bike, and I'm not buying one."

I had discovered long before that Homer brooked no whining. Once Homer had made a decision, there was no further appeal, no higher court. If I witlessly pursued, Homer would laser me an unmistakable look that indicated I was venturing onto very thin ice. After such a distinct tip-off, if I foolishly pursued this imprudent route, then it virtually amounted to self-immolation. I suppose this system had merit, because it eliminated needless plaintive yowling around Homer's Place. Although I continued to hanker for the paper job's dumb twelve dollars per week, I was mindful never to bring it up again. The decision was final. It was what Homer loved to categorize as his peremptory ultimatum. "You don't know what that means?" he'd resignedly say. "Go look it up."

Without further demonstration, I silently reviewed Homer's viewpoint, and I personally thought pumping gas was itself pretty dumb work. Yet, Mr. Cue paid well—eighty cents a day was a bona fide gold mine. Compare for example ushering at the Majestic, where Homer paid thirty-four cents each weekday, and sixty-eight cents for each Saturday and Sunday—a weekly wage of about three dollars, and I had absolutely no bargaining power with management.

While considering dumb labor, I thought the dumbest of all dumb labor was the hour and a half I spent each Saturday morning shining the Majestic's dumb brass. Homer never broached additional pay for this truly heinous work. In his view the brass was a part of my Saturday matinée salary. Like that! Possibly in his tabulated reasoning the brass was an additional defrayment for clothing, food, and shelter. In any event, a brass shining stipend, much like the thirty-two steps, never appeared on any agenda.

Homer was a taskmaster, and without question the brass became my heaviest cross to bear. He was even more critical of the brass than he was of my janitorial duties. He'd meticulously inspect it and announce those parts that required additional effort. I learned to hate fingerprints, and hoped for the passing public to keep its hands in its pockets. Most of all, I hated the dry cleaner's dog, which is another saga.

From the theater and the gas station combined, I would make seven dollars a week. This represented considerable buying power for a twelve-year-old kid. Bear in mind that, in 1936, a quarter would buy a haircut or a plate lunch at Etta's. Plate lunch? Etta's plate included a roll, a pat of butter, a glass of milk, slices of pork or beef, a big glob of mashed potatoes deliciously covered with gravy, and succotash or okra, finished off with a choice of apricot, apple, or cherry pie—all for twenty-five cents! If a person wanted to go absolutely crazy with money, he could buy a super sixteen ounce T-bone steak at Eastman's with potatoes and trimmings, salad, dessert, and milk, and starched linen at seventy-five cents. But to go to Eastman's was really running wild with money! Equate it in these terms. After all, a dollar would take a kid to the picture show ten times. Many correlated their buying power in such ways. As for my daily lunches at Etta's, Homer always paid. I only use Etta's and Eastman's prices to illustrate what twenty-five cents would buy, and how to measure my gainful earnings.

Meanwhile, back to dumb work: to make eighty cents a day pumping gas, I had only to ask the customer if he wanted white or high-test gas; this involved no real salesmanship. To make him feel good, I'd jerk the pump handle a couple of times just so there was no doubt that I had topped off the pump's twenty gallon glass container; we're speaking of ounces here. Everything at Austin Cue's station always worked because it was manual, and the customer could actually see each gallon as it came down to his tank. The process was not quite as rapid as the twenty-first century, but you really knew what you were getting. White gas was fifteen cents a gallon, but white had a tendency to "ping" (pre-ignite) on hills. High-test ethyl sold for eighteen cents, had a bronzy color, and because of its higher octane, seldom pinged. Experts said it was better for the engine. Most didn't care and saved the three cents because in the main we had only rolling low hills, few steep hills.

"Hey, son, gimme six gallons uh white gaaas." Unlike today, no one ever said to give them two dollars worth because arriving at 13.333 gallons would've taken some attendants days to calculate. Besides, the glass container atop the pump was marked only by gallons. And, dissimilar to today, I couldn't just put the nozzle in the tank and walk away; I had to stand there and watch the gas flow down from gallon line to gallon line, and be prepared to stop at the exact amount requested. When I finished refueling, Mr. Cue's unwritten law was to pump her back up to the top. Then I'd put water in the "raddy-ater," because cars of that vintage always needed a refill. I'd wash the grasshoppers off the windshield, check the dipstick, and lastly I did the "tars." This dumb work, this truly unskilled service, was well within the capabilities of any normal twelve-year-old boy.

Austin Cue was not permissive, but he was a leader. He was fair and rightfully demanded good work and service for the wage he offered. For the station's heavier and sometimes imperiling task, he hired Grover, the experienced older employee who repaired flats— truly dangerous work—changed oil and batteries, and greased and performed the station's arcane mechanical repairs.

STEINBECK'S OKIES

That summer at Cue's I saw my first Okies and Arkies. Whole families sporadically filed through Winelda in ancient jalopies piled high with blankets, pots, tin pie pans they used for dinner plates, boxes of clothes, and four or five threadbare spare tires. They pointed their motorized covered wagons westward across mountains and deserts toward the golden hills of California, toward the Promised Land where they hoped to pick fruit, do anything to support their families. Weird climate had parched their fields, making it impossible for them to make their payments. Backs and spirits broken, they, like the Barney Arnolds, headed West with the hope of finding something better.

When they drove into Austin's station, the head of the family would order six gallons of white, and then inquire about "old tars." Our station always had several down and out tires at fifty cents apiece. With care and a boot, they might last four hundred miles on graveled roads. Another query: "Boy, ya got any used all?"

Austin Cue had briefed me, "Don't waste no time gittin' these paypull free used all. You tell 'em 'Yes sir, come on, I'll show ya some roun' in back.' Ya hear me, Tom? Thet's all you do. Then ya come back up front and help them thet pays." And Austin would smile his mouthful of brown cracked teeth framed by red whiskers. It was the business way, yet considerate.

Austin dumped the oil drained from Winelda's cars into an open topped barrel around back. The Okie or Arkie would dip a can into the black stuff and drip oil back to their jalopy. "I gotta gallon jug, Boy. D'ya mind if we fill 'er up?" And I'd tell him it was okay. And because the jalopies were no longer precision machines, they could digest used oil.

When the service was completed, there was never any argument about money. They always carefully counted the coins, started their engine, and drove away in a dense cloud of white smoke. Austin Cue would grunt, "Reckon that one burns 'bout a quarta all every twenty-five miles. They's sure down 'n out fokes." If I learned nothing else that summer with Austin Cue, I learned Austin Cue's tolerance for those who were down and out, and just how rough life can become.

Those hardy Okies were probably the last vestige of America's breed of covered wagon pioneers. No matter what perils lie ahead, they had the grit to survive. Those who made it to California faced yet another obstacle: California redneck sheriffs and ruffians who turned fire hoses on fellow Americans, on their lean-to camps, on their mothers and sisters, and when Okies finally landed a picking job, they were ofttimes virtually robbed of their pittance. Yet, the hearty ones persevered, and infused courageous new blood into a California that had grown smug for no good reason. No Californian had made the climate good nor had he made the mountains and valleys more beautiful; he had only lucked out by having arrived there years earlier.

One night at dinner, when I told Homer how pathetic the Okies and their vehicles were, it visibly moved him. It provoked him sufficiently to give me some disquieting fatherly advice, so disturbing that I remember it to this day. "Tom," he said, "if you ever have to go it alone, there are a few survival tricks. Go to a bakery and buy a sack of old oatmeal cookies, or buy a loaf of old bread. Every bakery has these, and they'll give you sustenance and will cost very little." And just as quickly, he changed the subject.

I wasn't sure what bee I had put in Homer's bonnet. Despite the fact we sometimes ate stew for three successive days, I thought the Majestic was doing pretty well, and we certainly weren't blowing money. But Homer's strange advice sobered me. I visualized myself standing alone on the shoulder of a road with a sack of old oatmeal cookies in my knapsack.

THE WEEPING BARBER—FALL 1936

Homer was intent upon increasing his net worth. Toward the end of summer, while I was with Austin, he bought a dilapidated one story building at the intersection of Main and Cecil kitty corner to Homer's Place. It was the dead end of Main, a superb location. Homer never told me what he had paid, but the frame structure was not near the quality or size of the bank building that had cost him thirty-six hundred dollars.

Homer made immediate cosmetic improvements. He used his paint gun to cover the front a bright red trimmed in white, had a carpenter re-cover its shabby interior walls and ceiling with brand-new unpainted Celotex, and left the concrete floor hosed clean but untouched. The interior was clean, and neat, and smelled of new construction, and before the front had dried, an out of towner named Hank leased it for fifty dollars a month and opened Hank's Place. It was to be Winelda's very first beer joint. Hank installed a cheap bar, and several tables and chairs, and to help serenade me at bedtime, another jukebox created lively music for Winelda's key intersection.

This Hank had made a deal with Oklahoma City's Old King Beer Company, which emblazoned its logo on the building's big red front. In the upper left boldly painted in white was "Hank's Place." Below that, holding a frosty foamy beer, was a grinning cherubic-looking guy wearing a kingly crown. To the right of him were the huge flowing words "Old King Beer," and in smaller letters was written "Oklahoma's Finest!"

Winelda's churches certainly didn't like it one iota even though many who attended church also sipped a cold foamy Old King at Hank's.

Even Homer received a few bad words because Hank sold beer from Homer's property. I seldom ventured into Hank's Place because Homer said none of the patrons wanted twelve year olds gawking while they salted and sipped Old King and noshed on hardboiled eggs and pig cracklings.

Wineldans didn't take to Hank for several reasons; he was unknown, unfriendly, and mysterious, and a number of people thought he was about as shifty as a ferret. All they knew of him was what he'd already hinted, that he'd come up from Texas. Most Wineldans didn't hold that against him.

But one day a knot of people collected at Seaman's Barbershop. They were all buzzing, and occasionally they'd dart looks at Hank's Place. It wasn't long before most everyone on the Square came to Seaman's. They were eager to make discovery of all the commotion.

On page four of Seaman's *Police Gazette* was the feature story: "Jake, The Weeping Barber." There were pictures of this Jake with clippers in hand standing by his barber chair. There was also a grisly shot of a strangled woman, her eyes rolled back to the whites, the barely visible tongue poking darkly and unnaturally between her lips. The article also displayed Jake in a courtroom with his face twisted in tears and captioned: "Jake, The Weeping Barber." But it wasn't Jake.

"Well, I'll be gol-danged, that's Hank! Well, gol danged, whatta ya know?"—voice going to a soft whisper—"a strangler right here in our Winelda."

Norman Rockwell missed a terrific opportunity: the bespectacled Mr. Seaman holding up the *Gazette*, his right hand still clutching his clippers, while five or six wide eyed men crowded around to look over his shoulders.

For two weeks that particular *Police Gazette* received considerably more attention around Winelda than did the Bible, and that says a lot. Xerox machines had not yet been invented; consequently, the *Gazette* passed through so many hands that it was virtually reduced to shreds.

According to the article, Hank had been a barber in some little town near Dallas—Mesquite or Garland—and had strangled his wife so savagely he had dislocated a vertebra in her neck. Months later, at trial, he was a nervous wreck, and each time he took the stand, he'd fall into jerking sobs. Hence, they named him the weeping barber. According to the article, people weren't sure if this remorse was for real or for show. But because his wife had cuckolded him, Texans took pity, and only sent him off to Huntsville for a few years of character building.

Another of the *Gazette*'s pictures depicted a fierce looking Jake in prison with a skinhead haircut, prison fatigues, and a big number emblazoned across his chest. No longer a bereft whimpering man, he was now an ominously angry somber man. Everyone in the barbershop agreed this picture most resembled Hank today. "Gol-danged and right here in Winelda, gol-danged!" But because the article hadn't emphasized adultery, but had instead focused on the loathsome murder, the grapevine cautioned all Wineldan women and girls to never associate with Hank, never to be caught with him in any quiet place. "He obviously don't respeck wimmen."

Hank became instantly famous, and men from Avard, and Carmen, and Belva, and Capron, and Freedom drove to Winelda just to drink an Old King at Hank's Place, and to see a real *Police Gazette* celebrity—a "gen-u-ine" prison convict. And no one, not even the rednecks, got cute with Hank. That is, no one created situations by standing around eyeballing him. They remembered, "This dude, he put his bare hands around her throat and squeezed out her gurgling life! Can you imagine thet?"

Because the damnable *Gazette* had uncovered him, Jake became even more sullen—like the convict he had been. No doubt about it, Hank was a celebrity, and his business boomed. And despite the Depression, he took money to the bank every day, and always paid his rent to Homer on time.

ANOTHER REAL TRAGEDY

During the winter Homer was unpredictable and in February of 1937 he did an unprecedented thing. One cold, dusty morning after I had gone to school, Homer, on the spur of the moment, told Maddy he was going to spend a few days in New Orleans; just like that! Homer put on his new double breasted suit, his immaculate camel hair overcoat, his spats, and said he'd take the bus to Oklahoma City then fly to New Orleans via Houston. Maddy told me he was sober, and there had been no quarrel.

Homer hadn't been gone twelve hours when a long distance call came from Mom Cable. That summer she and Pop had been in Appleton, Wisconsin, and were now back in San Diego for their second time. Mom's voice was tearful and halting. Virgil's high school band was having a concert over in Mulhall when Virgil stepped up to the podium, tapped the lectern with his baton, and then fell over in a faint. Iris said that only three hours prior to the concert Virgil had complained of an unusual neck and backache. He never regained consciousness. Within the hour, thirty-one-year-old Virgil died of the dreaded and mysterious spinal meningitis. Iris was taking the body to Anthony for the funeral. She'd assumed the folks would want Virgil interred in the Cable plot at Ellinwood. To add to the misery, the health authorities had ordered a closed casket because no one was yet positive how lethally contagious meningitis might be.

Mom had told Iris to wait for them in Anthony. She, Pop, and Aunt Lily would leave San Diego immediately by car. Now Mom, who was crying because Virgil was such a tremendous loss, wanted to speak to Homer. I said, "Mom, he went out of town. We'll try our best to get in touch with him."

"Out of town? Where?" she asked. There was nothing to do but to tell her New Orleans. "Well," she said hesitantly, "is he all right?" And I knew what she meant, and I said my father was okay, but the ensuing silence told me what was riffling through Mom's head. "Well, all right, Tommy. Tell Maddy we'll come through Winelda to pick up Homer. Lily will come with us and help drive. We think we can do it in three or four days. In the meantime, get in touch with Homer."

Maddy was distraught. She was aware Homer idolized his little brother, but Homer had irresponsibly mentioned no travel details. After all, he was the head of the family. Any number of things could happen during his absence. We should've known exactly how to reach him. It was another indication of how a winter of hard drinking could fuzz his normally fine judgment. In the past, Homer had spoken to Maddy of the Hotel Roosevelt as being New Orleans's finest. "Some day," he said, "I'll take you there." Having no better lead, she immediately placed an emergency call to the Roosevelt.

In 1937, placing a long-distance phone call was enough to drive a teetotaler to drink. Sitting next to Maddy, I could hear the Winelda operator talking to the Enid long distance operator seventy-five miles away. Enid was ringing the Oklahoma City operator, and after several minutes and some beeps and bops, we heard Dallas, and then, very faintly, the Houston operator as if she were off in Nome or Rome. There was a roar of popping and crackling and Houston said she'd try another line. Unfortunately, everything went dead, and then Enid came back on the line trying to raise Oklahoma City. Sometimes as the operators slowly linked their communication chain, the next trunk line might very well be busy. This was why operators asked callers to hang up; they'd ring back when the call was set up. A place as distant as New Orleans could take fifteen minutes, or even two hours to reach, and it was expensive. When a caller in the thirties said, "I am calling long distance" people paid attention. It represented great expense, and inordinate effort.

At one time, we actually had the New Orleans operator, and she was just connecting us with the Roosevelt operator when we were cut off, and the entire connection process had to be restarted through Enid. The Winelda operator asked Maddy to hang up, but Maddy wanted to hear the call go through. I was very proud of Maddy's untiring persistence.

Finally, the Hotel Roosevelt's reception came on the line, and Maddy asked for Homer. After a brief silence, reception said, "Sorry, no Mr. Homer Cable is registered." Because everyone from Winelda to New Orleans was listening, and had known it was an emergency, there must have been sighs of disappointment. In desperation Maddy even called Antoine's, because Homer had said he enjoyed dining there. In the background we heard the clinking of glassware, the pop of a champagne cork, but there was no Homer. This calling went on for three days, and Maddy ate very little, and her temper became short, and her face paled. I felt sorry for her. Maddy and the tireless Winelda operator both deserved medals.

That night, just after the first show, Mom, Pop, and Lily arrived. It was one of those "blue norther" nights with the temperature at a brittle ten degrees, and the Rexall Drug Store sign squeaking and squawking in the moaning wind. The tumbleweeds were bounding along the sidewalk, and a thin river of dusty sand snaked its way down the middle of Main Street. To make everything even more dismal, we'd just turned off the marquee lights.

Maddy wrung her hands and broke into tears. "Oh Mrs. Cable," she cried, "I've tried everything."

"Well, we've no alternative," said Mom. "We'll just have to go along without Homer. Tomorrow I'll call from Anthony and let you know the final arrangements." She turned to me, "Tommy you stay with Maddy. She needs your help. Besides, you wouldn't be able to see your Uncle Virgil anyway." Mom was a cool one when the chips were down. Pop couldn't bring himself to speak. He kept patting me on the shoulder and fighting back tears. With Lily behind the wheel, the three of them headed north in the dark to Kansas.

Two days later they buried Virgil in Ellinwood, Kansas.

A couple of days after Virgil was in the ground, Homer rolled into Winelda shortly after sundown. He came up the stairs sober and carrying a box with a ten inch alligator for me. He was happy, and looking better than I had thought he'd look. He handed me the box, "Give this guy some raw hamburger and some water." In addition he fished out a large can of pecan pralines, and a bag of fresh sugar cane joints. For Maddy, he had brought some I. Miller high heels, and a jacket with what looked like a white rabbit fur collar. I asked what kind of fur. He said it was lapin. I asked what lapin was and he said it was the fur from a very rare Egyptian pigeon. He was clearly in a good mood, and he squeezed my head in a gentle headlock. But suddenly he became aware of Maddy's attitude, and he said, "Well, what the hell's the matter with you. Homer's home! This is supposed to be festive?"

Then she told him.

It was as if she had hit Homer with an ax. Homer had proven he wasn't a great one for family pressures. When he heard about Virgil, the little brother he doted on, it was as if bolts of electricity convulsed his body. He immediately poured a glass of hundred and ninety proof grain alcohol, sucked down a third of it, and coughed. He became the accuser. "How could you let them bury my little brother without me being here?"

For such a basically good person, Homer could sometimes be very unfair. Homer went after Maddy with a shower of abusive language; like a cheap district attorney he never permitted her to respond. Once I thought he would strike her—she cringed, but the blow never came. I could only sit there thinking how unreasonable Homer was.

Suddenly, Maddy's eyes blazed. "Homer, you bastard! I tried my damnedest for you. Now that you've made a complete ass of yourself, I suggest you start thinking what you're going to say to your mother, and your father, and to your sister. There's the phone! Come on Tommy, we have to open the Majestic." Homer was slack jawed. I believe this jarred him to his senses. He realized he had to phone. As Maddy tore out the door with me following, he seemed almost stunned, and showed real remorse for his behavior.

I'd never ever confronted Homer, but as I was going out the door I said, "That wasn't fair, Dad; for days Maddy tried everything." It was one of the very few times I spoke up to Homer, and I expected the worst, but he never responded. I left him slumped at the kitchen table. Everything was so very sad.

On the phone Mom said to Homer, "I missed you, Son. I so counted on you being there."

Homer hated himself for failing Mom and Pop when they had most needed him. He crashed miserably. He ate virtually nothing, drank consistently, and became gaunt, malnourished, and unwashed. One day I saw him stumble over to the fridge, remove a quarter-pound stick of butter, bring it to the kitchen table, and shakily bite into it as if it were a candy bar. He ate it all. His degenerative condition eventuated to a coma of sorts. One day after school, Maddy told me that she and Doc Chambers had taken Homer up to the Alva Hospital, where he was being fed intravenously. The hospital ordeal was a first for Homer since New Orleans. And because elderly Doc Clapper was phasing out, it was our first time to use Doc Chambers's services. He was the very same Chambers that I would eventually set out to kill.

With Virgil fresh in her mind, Maddy felt she should inform Mom Cable that Homer had been admitted. She didn't care if Homer would later excoriate her for having done so. Because Aunt Lily had already taken the Santa Fe to San Diego, Mom drove the sixty-seven miles alone. Pop was too distraught from the funeral to make the trip. Besides, he wasn't keen on seeing Homer, especially now. Mom, on the other hand, was both aggravated and worried. She had just buried one son; she didn't want to bury her last one.

Maddy told me that Homer was not a pretty sight. He was sometimes a wild man. Neither Mom nor Maddy wanted me there; my presence would add nothing. I began fervently yearning for spring. I knew with spring things were bound to improve.

AMERICAN LEGION

That spring of 1937 I turned thirteen. The week before I graduated from the eighth grade, the Winelda Chamber of Commerce invited me to lunch at the Campbell Hotel. As a kid I was very self-conscious and uncomfortable to be the guest of Winelda's Chamber. I was very glad to see Mr. Fischer of the *Winelda Enterprise* because I knew both him and his wife, Louise, very well. He was the chamber president, and they seated me to his right. Just before the lunch was served, he called Monroe Hastings to the lectern. Monroe was secretary and treasurer of Winelda's American Legion organization. Monroe immediately called me to stand beside him, and it was only then that I discovered why the chamber had invited a kid to their lunch.

Mr. Hastings began reading from a big certificate about leadership, and character, and scholarship, and then he presented me with the Legion's annual bronze medal award. Every spring the Legion bestowed this honor to Winelda's most promising eighth-grade boy. I was virtually thunderstruck, and wondered how it could be—my scholarship was a fiction. And the Chamber hadn't done it to please Homer, because Homer for some reason had never been a member. And while they later droned about Chamber business, I figured they had needed a name and the picture show kid's was the easiest to remember. Other than Billy Patton, I was probably the most notice-able fixture around the Square. As for scholarship, none of the boys in grade school had been scholars, only the girls were real scholars, and the Legion had struck no medals for girls.

But it was my very first time to win anything, and Homer and Maddy were obviously very proud. Homer even thundered, "Hot possum-a-la!," a bucolic victory cry that I figured emanated from Ellinwood's wheat fields. Homer gave me a special look, one I hadn't seen before, then he hugged my shoulders and said, "Go to the head of the class, Cable. I'm very proud of you." After fingering the beau-tiful bronze medal for a few moments, he went on to be pure Homer. "It was fortunate," he said, "that this award was not heavily weighted toward scholarship." Even so, he had the parchment certificate and the bronze medal framed, and then he hung it on his office wall. It was probably one of my grandest days. Even more important: the school had promoted me from grade school to high school.

Later that afternoon, Perry Phillips saw me and yelled from Etta's Café, "Congratulations, Hot Shot. I heard you got the medal!" And he bought me a ten cent chocolate ice-cream soda at the Corner Drug.

Also that May of 1937, I began to grow, but I was still a skinny kid. When the traveling photographer came to town to take the annual class pictures, I weighed a hundred and four pounds and strained to stand tall, but he still stuck me on the front row with the shorties. I looked behind me at the thyroid specimens on the fifth tier. Some were already shaving and were as much as six feet and a hundred and seventy-five pounds. I doubted if I'd ever make it up there.

Goods's Barn—Summer 1937

I believe everyone in and around Winelda lived for Saturday. If Homer was in a funk, Saturday would do wonders because he knew the Majestic would be bursting at the seams. When Homer fell off the wagon, he'd sometimes miss several days at the Majestic, but he seldom missed a Saturday. It was a day for non-stop business, busi-ness that paid for some of the weekdays that actually lost money. It was because Saturday was so busy that most Winelda businesses reserved Friday night for any celebration.

One grand Friday event was the Winelda Volunteer Fire

Department's annual benefit dance, which the firefighters held for their own benefit. The firefighters were a close knit organization. They'd store the dance proceeds in the bank to use in the event some fireman became sick or was possibly injured in the line of duty.

Winelda's Volunteers were on call twenty-four hours a day and at no salary. When the City Hall siren wailed, it meant either six o'clock or a fire. A fry cook at Etta's would rip off his apron, a clerk at the hardware would grab his hat, and Austin Cue, the gas station man, would leap into his pickup truck, and they all headed for City Hall. No matter if they were in the middle of making love, the wailing siren ordered a rush to the station.

The ancient Dodge fire engine rarely started, it was coerced. The firemen had to push it from the City Hall garage while the driver pulled at the choke, pumped the foot feed, and waited for the key moment to release the clutch. And in half a block or so the engine kicked in and the firemen grabbed at handholds, put on fire gear and leaned forward.

As they roared down Main the honorary fire chief cranked the siren and waved at Wineldans. The people in front of the post office knew the firemen were en route to ax down some poor sod's front door. It was the old whittlers who eventually spread their sage advice around the Square—first report a fire and then run like hell to open your front door.

The Fireman's Annual usually took place across the Cimarron at Goods, a fancied-up barn with a slick maple floor. Fun makers from miles around paid their dollar to stomp with Carl Cole's Flint Hill Cowboys. Because Goods was thirteen miles from town, there was an unwritten city ordinance forbidding fires during the Fireman's Annual Benefit, and there never were.

Little nips of hidden corn whiskey always livened up the dancing at Goods. But this corn also undid a few misfits. They were never sure if they were where they were supposed to be, and doing what they were supposed to be doing. Some of the younger corn gurglers were also a menace to innocent folk on the highway.

Fortunately the dirt road exiting from Goods dropped down a steep red hill with a sharp curve near its bottom. It was a built-in safety valve that demanded sensible speed. Through the years, a great many Goods stompers who had also filled themselves with corn obviously hadn't made that curve. Off in the shrubby pasture one could readily see ripped up sage, and skinned mesquite, and ruts deeper than those along the trace of the Oregon Trail. A driver who ignored these vivid reminders obviously had no business on the highway endangering others.

I suppose the corn made some drivers feel invincible, and they'd sneer at fate until the unforgivable curve was upon them. It was a real moment of truth! Their pickup would shoot off the road in a low trajectory, and wild eyed rabbits, which had seen this happen before, would run for their furry lives. And shattering the stillness would be cries of "Gol Dangs," and tinkling glass, and fenders clanging against immovable mesquite. Finally, the deepening sandy furrows would grab at the tires and make the engine chug and die. Only then did solace return to the little valley, and the numb revelers just sat there dumbly and peered through the windshield, as if waiting for a divine revelation or the apostle John.

Way up on the hill none of the retiring folks heard the whine of the pickup's wheels hopelessly spinning in the sand. And as the moon disappeared in the west, the thick tongued remarks coming from the cab gradually dwindled to snores. The rabbits, by now neurotic, began cautiously hopping back to their ill sited homesteads which inevitably lay near the revelers, just as if it were one big peaceable kingdom—fauna, and dissolute man, and his dead machine. Because of Homer's zest for vicarious thrills, and the decrepit look of Mom's Chrysler before she left Winelda, I'm almost sure at least one set of those ruts was a Homer creation.

Come the hazy dawn, the Goods would look down over their coffee, spot the inert vehicle far below, and remark, "By gol, there's yet anuther." Eventually they'd drive down a tractor to drag their humbled, and hung over customers back onto the road. It was the humanitarian thing for the Goods to do, because it was Saturday, and on Saturday everyone had to get to Winelda.

TEN-GALLON—SUMMER 1937

In and around Winelda's trade territory, everyone but preachers lived for Saturday. Winelda came to double life because everybody came to town. "Going to Wy-neldee!"—a pronunciation citified Wineldans deplored. For ranch and farm folks it was a time of great expectation, a time to buy a new shirt, new shoes, ammo, groceries—a time to see the picture show.

Ten-Gallon Harris, one of the Majestic's best customers, lived south of the Cimarron. Folks had called him "Ten-Gallon" for so many years, everyone had long since forgotten the given name of this six foot six inch string bean of a cowboy. On Saturday morning while carefully checking the V-8's dipstick, he'd check out his hat by peering into the windshield. He was damned proud of the hat, the biggest whitest cowboy hat in all of Major County, and with an extra high crown roomy enough for twice the volume of Ten-Gallon's head. Nobody knew where he'd bought it; perhaps at Oke City or Amarillo, but no local store had one. While looking at his reflection, he'd smile, cock the hat just a gnat's ass, and smile bigger. "Yessiree . . . motty fine."

No matter if Ten-Gallon were checking the radiator, the fan belt, or opening the door to the privy, he wore a perpetual smile. Even when changing a flat he'd grin, which sometimes made folks worry, because a flat was nothing to grin at.

Myrtle—everyone called her Myrnie—was Ten-Gallon's scrappy dynamo of a wife. Myrnie was out of the Lauderdale family, a rough, tough clan that lived near Quinlan, and who prided themselves on being able to endure anyone and any condition. It was this indomitable spirit that probably made Myrnie so completely happy, even during the Depression. She adored Ten-Gallon, and although she stood only five feet, they struck a handsome couple on the sidewalks around Winelda's square. Some slyly speculated that it was Myrnie, the little pistol, who accounted for Ten-Gallon's perpetual grin.

And why not? Myrnie had given him five fine boys and two pretty daughters—all born at home—and together they lived raucously on their big spread of thirty-two hundred windswept acres—five square miles of solitude with the nearest neighbors four miles south. Imagine that kind of room.

The Harris clan could play their radio as loudly as they wanted, shoot a rifle in the air, or race the V-8's engine, and there was not a single neighbor to complain. Imagine a family like Ten-Gallon's trying to adapt to San Francisco's or Baltimore's style of scrunched-up living?

Still, all that land would only marginally support six hundred or so head of whiteface cattle. Ten-Gallon also kept four quarter horses, a passel of chickens, four or five hogs, three hound-like dogs, and three of the brawniest and meanest barn cats in all of Northwestern Oklahoma. Some thought they were the amorous results between Myrnie's twenty-two pound tabby and some passing bobcat. Whatever, these big pawed felines dominated the barnyard with such intensity that no coyote ever dared to touch Myrnie's chickens.

The Harris's well used two story frame house would most likely never appear in *Better Homes and Gardens.* It had three bedrooms: one for Ten-Gallon and Myrnie, one extra large one equipped with bunks for the five boys, and a bedroom for the two girls. There was no swimming pool, no yard, no manicured grass; the thirty-two hundred acres of ranch was the yard. Directly in front of the house was a tumble of huge gyp rocks, and growing from them were two scrawny mesquites, and a large prickly pear cactus with its numerous flowers. It was God's own rustic *Ikebana* arrangement; no accomplished Japanese gardener could have bested its simple beauty. Ten-Gallon often stood in his doorway, grinned at the rocks and wildflowers, and considered the good luck that had blessed his life. He was thankful, and he loved it all. It made no difference to him that dust blanketed everything, and the temperature was nudging a hundred and four degrees— everything in view was paid for.

Near the barn was a double walled smokehouse with a slow fire hickory pit where Ten-Gallon cured delicious ham and bacon. In the barnyard was a galvanized steel watering tank that measured three feet deep and twenty feet across. Not only did it serve as a cattle watering hole, but most of the kids in Northwestern Oklahoma learned to swim in tanks like Ten-Gallon's. This one sat next to a complaining Aermotor windmill, and the kids would cannonball from its tower into the tank. Near the house was the Snappy Windcharger's steel tower, its bank of series-wired wet batteries on a platform beneath. They powered Myrnie's real electric lights in her huge kitchen/dining room. Rural Electricity would not reach the Wineldan hinterland until 1943. Coal oil lamps with clear glass chimneys lit the other rooms, and because of the lamps, the aroma of coal oil had pervaded everyone's clothing and hair. Also powered by coal oil was the Coolerator fridge, which always provided well chilled Old King Beer.

Out back was Ten-Gallon's pride and joy—the two holer privy.

He'd cut a sliver of a moon and two small stars in the door, and on each side near the roof was a heart. Ten-Gallon often said, "A privy's a poor man's paradise, and everythin' about it oughta be jist raht."

Ten-Gallon and Myrnie had normal kids except perhaps for Billy. Billy was a nutty little guy who liked to eat the red dirt. Most any day he could be found at his favorite dirt fingering spot, putting some in his mouth. Before long, red mud streaks would run down both sides of his face to the jawbone. Some suggested it was a vitamin deficiency, but more than likely he was straining to get attention. Billy would walk around looking like a vermilion streaked Indian yet nobody so much as said, "Oh, Billy, for gosh sakes, you've been eatin' dirt again." Myrnie's other kids didn't purposely ignore Billy; it was just that they had begun to think their brother was supposed to look that way.

Every night Billy stalked around the kitchen furtively drinking the remaining slosh from any beer bottle left by Ten-Gallon or Myrnie. Sometimes he got lucky and found a whole quarter of beer in a forgotten bottle on a windowsill. A generous slug of Old King and some lively radio music could move Billy to do his version of a jig. At such times, it was plain to see who his father was; he'd be grinning exactly like Ten-Gallon.

Myrnie's sister Rowena lived only nineteen miles west, and she visited from time to time. She told her sister she was sure Billy would grow up to become an alcoholic. And Myrnie would say, "Why? Because he eats mud?" Rowena never understood why Myrnie let Billy drain off what was left in the bottles, never understood Myrnie's inane logic—"Because it pleasures him, Rowena." Sometimes Rowena would sit there in stunned amazement as she watched her sister, brother-in-law, and all the kids squirming or rolling around on the floor among the patient tail wagging dogs.

Rowena was a perfectionist and childless, and there was a lot she didn't understand about Myrnie's household. To her, it was a miracle such families survived. "For God's sake, Rowena," said Myrnie, "you're makin' me nervous. Relax and have another beer."

When "Inner Sanctum," or "Amos and Andy" finished on the Philco, Ten-Gallon often broke out his guitar. For three or four minutes, he'd grin at it, and fiddle with it until he'd plucked it into his idea of tune. Very shortly the whole gaggle would be kye, yigh, yippee yippee-yayin'. Ten-Gallon would stomp his booted foot and an inspired dog would occasionally lift his head to moan or howl. If by then Billy had found a good slosh, he'd probably be dancing around with a glazed look on his face while his skeptical Aunt Rowena looked on with dismay.

"When he's growed, Rowena, he's gonna be a raht good dancer," said Ten-Gallon. And Rowena wondered. She wondered about all of them because they were contrary to the norm. Still, she had to allow that few families were as happy as Ten-Gallon's. What belonged to one of them belonged to all, except that Billy did have a lock on the beer dregs.

To watch the Harris family load into the V-8 on Saturday morning was an exercise in logistics. Ten-Gallon had installed an oversized luggage rack on top. Myrnie's "agg" crate rode up there along with the four or five crates of returnable Old King bottles and, there was usually a side of freshly butchered beef to trade at McBride's. On the homeward trip, the same rack would carry their loot from Winelda's stores.

Ten-Gallon covered the rack, and all the stuff on top with an old piece of unevenly cut tarp, which he'd expertly tie down with reverse Baker bowline knots. It was impossible for anything to leap off. When they began zooming along there was something about the flapping tarp that gave the gray V-8 a stagecoach aura—particularly with Ten-Gallon grinning back of the wheel, Myrnie's hair flying razzle-dazzle, and the other seven faces peering out the rolled down windows. To complete the rusticity of the Harris presentation, they never seemed to get off their property without a tumbleweed becoming entangled behind the V-8's front bumper.

Ten-Gallon had the front seat pushed way back so he could get uncoiling room for his uncommonly long legs. And because his torso was abnormally short, he could sit comfortably behind the wheel and have room to spare for his Ten-Gallon hat. Wearing his hat, he looked very good in the V-8—very Western and devil may care.

On a horse, Ten-Gallon looked as strange as Ichabod Crane. His short upper body rose out of the saddle not much higher than a boy's, and then there was that huge hat resting on his ears and bending them outward. But even when astride the tallest quarter horse in Major County, his long long legs unreeled so far it seemed his spur rowels would start spinning in the dirt. This was probably why no horse was ever obstreperous with Ten-Gallon. I'm sure they instinctively sensed that those legs were easily capable of snapping like scissors and crushing their rib cage. However, on rodeo day, when all the Winelda area cowboys were on parade to show off their best boots, saddles, and bridles, Ten-Gallon looked far better in the V-8.

By half past nine, families were converging on Winelda from every direction. Once on the scene, they would scatter around the Square. Myrnie had material she wanted to buy from Frank's Dry Goods; one of the boys needed a new pair of Buster Browns; and Ten-Gallon went to Hough's for some leather work gloves, and to Frank's long underwear sale. For candy, most kids went to McBride's, where Mrs. McBride put penny candies in little brown paper sacks—big red or black jawbreakers at six for a nickel—the ones with little hot seeds in the center, good candy. Fleer's bubble gum was six for a nickel; standard-sized Butterfingers and Baby Ruths were a nickel; and miniature ones with the same style wrappers sold for a penny. For five cents, she'd fill the little paper bag with a scoop of red hots.

When country families went to the grocers, they didn't fool around. They went out the doors toting big cotton bags full of flour, whole sides of bacon, a case of fruit cocktail, and a case of pork and beans. Cohlmia's favorite leader was a hundred pounds of potatoes for a dollar and twenty-five cents. Ranch families looked like U.S. Army purchasing agents. While witnessing this in the dead of the Depression, how could I possibly visualize the necessity for the soup lines shown in the weekly *Movietone News*?

THE BARREL DRAWING

When Mr. Charley Hink, one of Winelda's oldest citizens, came putt-putting down the main drag around one o'clock in his 1905 International flatbed truck, everyone knew the major Saturday attraction was underway—it was the "drawing," and only a coin's toss from my bedroom window. Charley's was the first and last truck I ever saw with chain drive and solid rubber tires. He'd carefully back through the crowd to the streetlight at Main and Cecil. The "drawing" barrel was always chained there, and Marshal Billy Patton would unlock it with a flourish and then command some brawny men to heft it onto Charley's flatbed.

The merchants bought the drawing tickets from the Chamber of Commerce, and this provided the funds for cash prizes. The drawing was a boon to business because customers only traded at stores that gave tickets as bonuses for purchases. The customer wrote his name on each ticket and placed them in the barrel slots.

"Awright, awright," boomed the marshal, and the crowd's hum quieted in anticipation. "I need a young man up here," and he'd eye the crowd. "Tommy Cable, come on up here, Son," and the big guys would grab my hands and haul me up like a sack of flour. Billy always chose a merchant's kid, because the crowd knew we were inel-igible to deposit tickets, and it made everyone feel better.

"Awright, Tommy. First show everbuddy yer hans," and I'd go through the raise the hands ritual, and look goofy so everyone could see there were no palmed tickets. "Now reach in and fetch us a dollar ticket." The first ten draws were for a dollar each; then three draws at three dollars each; and finally the five-dollar bonanza. When a dollar and twenty-five cents would buy one hundred pounds of potatoes at Cohlmia's Grocery, five dollars was considered a real prize. I handed a ticket to Billy and he boomed, "If she's here, I have one dollar for Lela Mae Vanderhocken."

"Oh, oh," and all heads would turn, and everyone applauded as Lela Mae struggled toward the flatbed.

"Mighty good luck, Lela Mae. Go ahead, Tommy, draw another," and so it went with the tempo rising as the grand five dollar prize neared.

"Oh, no," the crowd roared as Marshal Patton called Miles Olson's name. "Oh, yes," Miles responded enthusiastically, and there was good hearted laughter. "Miles, you lucky sonuvagun, where you gonna spend alla thet?"

"Reckon I'll take a trip tuh Rome." More laughter.

Then the crowd dispersed, and the barrel with all its remaining tickets was again chained to the streetlight. Charley Hink putt-putted his chain drive away in a cloud of white smoke, and a flood of kids headed for the Majestic's doubleheader, where they'd spend the entire afternoon.

SATURDAY NIGHT AT THE MAJESTIC

A packed Majestic on Saturday night was in itself a Wineldan spec-tacle—twenty cents for adults and ten cents for kids. Because I was thirteen and in high school, Homer made a big deal of promoting me to ticket taker with a raise to five dollars a week. Now I was in charge of both the floor and the usher, but Homer sometimes hovered nearby to see how I handled things. He wouldn't put up with a deadpan "thanks." He wanted a name and a heartfelt greeting, "Thank you Mr. Nutter," with gusto, "good to see you again." Anything congenial was fine with Homer.

"Hello, Mr. Janney."

Mr. Janney, an octogenarian from across the river, stuck his ancient horn device in his ear, "How's that yuh say?"

"I said, 'Thank you, Mr. Janney.'"

"Yes, yes, yer quite welcome," and he'd smile and wonder how in tarnation I knew his name. That's the way Homer wanted it. It wasn't long before I had memorized everyone's name for several miles around. Had I been older, I could've run for office. Even Homer began marveling at my phenomenal recall and name filled database. "You're the best," he'd say.

As the house filled, there was always the telltale coal oil aroma from the crowd's clothing. Occasionally, someone arrived with Levi's smelling faintly of skunk, but after several minutes all the odors blended, and eventually nothing was especially offensive. Every seat filled. Down front, where the kids' hair was blown back by the powerful air cooling fans, many kids sat two to a seat for mutual protection from the scalping Indians or stampeding cattle. At times, great sounds emanated from the Majestic. Once, when Red Skelton pantomimed a woman getting into her girdle, Myrtle Harris shouted, "He surely knows!" and the house roared. Ten-Gallon placidly grinned—his Adam's apple going up and down—because any attention to Myrnie's enthusiasm always pleased him.

The Majestic had no possible place to install restrooms, and no other businesses had a restroom except for small ones at Eastman's Restaurant, Etta's Café, and at the filling stations. Directly across Main Street from the Majestic was a vacant lot. During the show, male patrons, and even a few desperate women would ask for me to remember them as they hustled between the two buildings to relieve themselves. On scorching afternoons, that weedy lot could get pretty ripe, and everyone working around the Square would yearn for a real soaker to flush the sand.

OUT LIKE LOTTIE'S EYE

On Saturdays, there was usually a W.C. Fields comedy feature, or the Marx Brothers, or a Laurel and Hardy coupled with a first rate cowboy show. Also thrown in was a hair-raising one reel serial.

Not only did the Majestic exhibit good pictures with good sound and ice cooled air flowing over the crowd, Homer also had his own Saturday evening drawing. The box office tickets had the same stub numbers on each end. As an adult entered the theater, I'd tear his ticket, putting half in the drawing box and returning him the necessary other half to prove ownership of that number. Tickets began going into the box on Sunday, and by the following Saturday there would be quite an accumulation of stubs. Every time an adult bought a ticket, it was one more chance for the ten dollar pot. If a stub were drawn and unclaimed the pot was sweetened another ten dollars. When a winner was drawn, all the stubs were dumped.

At the end of the first show, the lights came up, and Homer marched down the aisle followed by Mean Dean, our new usher. Mean Dean carried the box of stubs to center stage, a duty he loved because he would smile broadly on the crowd, which was exactly what Homer wanted. Homer then pointed to some kid down front to come up on stage, always a proud moment for the kid and his parents. "Oh look, there's our little Herbert."

And as the little kid handed Homer a stub, the crowd became tense, and the Majestic became quieter than church. Homer would hold the stub high in the air for all to see, and then he'd base his voice and say, "I have a stub." Well, everyone knew Homer had a stub but Homer did that for added suspense and the slightest sound could be heard. "The number is"—another planned pause—"four, eight, nine, two, nine, repeat," but before Homer could repeat, there would usually be a scream or "I got it Homer, Gol danged, I got it!" The person would hustle down front with his stub, and Homer would compare it with the number and color of the one just drawn.

One time the prize soared to eighty dollars, which was almost enough money to kill for. Through natural flukes—a railroader out of town, a rancher absent because of illness, someone losing his stub— the drawing had gone winnerless for seven consecutive weeks. There were even dark mumblings of possible rigging and tampering. I sometimes heard a few "Homer-the-Bummer" epithets which was ridiculous, because Homer had to fork over ten more dollars each week, winner or not.

In the *Winelda Enterprise*, Homer announced he was raising the eighty dollar pot to an unprecedented one hundred dollars! Enough to buy four tons of Cohlmia's potatoes! Even the most popular national radio contest went no higher than sixty-four dollars.

The *Enid Morning News* picked up the story, which caused a few people from as far afield as Fairview, Cherokee, and Seiling to participate. During the week, people were coming to each change of feature so they'd have additional stubs in the box. Some speculators even went so far as to buy at a premium the stubs of others. The one hundred dollar Saturday was on everyone's lips. Needless to say, come Saturday night every seat in the Majestic was filled. Even people who detested westerns showed up for standing room only. This was now truly big money.

The night of the one hundred dollar drawing, Homer was uncomfortable because of testy foul play murmurs. Homer looked out onto a sea of vigilant sometimes glinty eyes—the lobby and both aisles were lined with standees. What reaction could we expect if yet another "no-show" ticket were drawn? Homer carefully chose a country boy from a well known family to make the selection. No sooner had Homer read off the last number when Boyd McGurn, married only two months, yelled out, *"I got it. I got it. Oh! I got it!"*

His wife Leona fainted dead away—clunked her forehead hard on the seat in front. The audience turned toward her young, collapsed body, and everyone was very careful as they passed her limpness from the center of the theater to the aisle. Leland Curtis, a Winelda volunteer fireman, had an aisle seat, and as he was big and strong it naturally fell to him to carry her up the aisle and next door to the Rexall. This was an era well before 911 emergency service—no paramedics, no ambulance. It was a time when prescription druggists were often called "Doc," and were literally viewed as if they were indeed doctors. Drug store first aid was free and saved many needless ambulance fees. In no one's memory was any life ever lost in the drugstore.

Boyd, trailing Leland, was in a quandary as to whether to look jubilant like a winning gladiator or mournful because of his unconscious beloved. On the one hand, he'd be all triumphant smiles and then switch to abject, face-twisting agony—great actor. To be sure, he worried about his love, but he also kept thinking, "Golly, golly a hunert dollars!" At the Rexall, two wire Coca-Cola tables were slid together and pale Leona laid out on top. All kinds of people crowded around; three or four grabbed *Liberty* magazines from the rack and fanned her. Leona wasn't acting; she was out like Lottie's eye. For just these occasions, Doc Lloyd Curtis, the Rexall owner, was ready. He immediately brought forth the strong ammonia forever stashed on the shelf beneath the cash register.

Aaron Fischer of the *Winelda Enterprise* snapped a picture of happy Boyd stroking the hand of his unconscious bride. Also in the picture was hovering Doc Curtis. This was a ripe moment for a ton of Evening in Paris perfume to be ripped off from the Rexall's display counter, but it never happened. It was a less affluent time, but it was also a basically honest one.

Leona's eyelashes flickered. "Boyd, Boyd, where's Boyd?" she mumbled as she re-entered the real world.

"Right here, hawney," he said. "We done won us a hunert dollars! You hear?" and again her eyelashes commenced fluttering as if she might fade off to her other world. Everybody allowed that as long as someone had to win the hundred, it couldn't have gone to a more deserving couple.

THE ERLENKOTTER BOY

Crowds are rife with latent problems. As an example, Homer cautioned Mean Dean and me to be particularly alert for the Erlenkotter boy. If Maddy gave me a quick high sign from the box-office, it meant, "The Erlenkotters are here." It was important that Mean Dean and I watch exactly where their ten-year-old boy sat. Months earlier we had discovered that when there were exciting scenes—for example, Buck Jones fighting rustlers on the edge of a high cliff, his spurs hanging out into thin air—that's when the Erlenkotter kid would yell, throw up his hands, and crash to the floor. There he'd writhe and sometimes froth. Thinking he was dying, or having a hydrophobic fit, the little kids around him would flee up the aisles howling *Ma, Ma, Ma!*

Homer would run down, pick up the boy, and quickly carry him back to his office. He had long since stopped notifying the disinterested parents, who had grown immune to their son's many seizures.

"It's okay, Homer," Mr. Erlenkotter would say, "he'll come 'round dreckly."

Homer always laid the unconscious boy on his office desk, and in five or ten minutes his taut little body would relax, and he'd blink his eyes, and sure enough come around. Homer'd give him a glass of water, and he'd be up and tugging to go back to see how Buck Jones had made out. With the Erlenkotter boy, this happened only every other month or so, probably five times a year, but we were ready. In my ten years of experience at the Majestic, no patron ever died or was hurt there.

SATURDAY'S STRANGE PEOPLE

Saturday was a time for curiosity. All the townies liked to watch what flowed in from the countryside, and all the country folk took in the idiosyncrasies of town folk. Vanilla Will, for example, never went without notice—his small bottle of highly alcoholic vanilla extract always poking from his hip pocket. He'd come weaving up Cecil and around Main in his own cloud of vanilla dreams. If not there, he'd be back of Seaman's Barbershop examining its pile of cast off Bay Rum bottles—tapping leftovers much the same as little Billy Harris polished off Old King dregs.

Everyone in town knew Vanilla Will, a gentle, soft spoken bachelor who always needed a shave, and was usually a few shades beyond normal. He never asked for handouts because his family fed and clothed him. Most annoying was when his befuddled mind recognized someone. He'd run up, shake their hand as if they'd been gone for years, and bear hug them closely. Then, still holding them at a range too close, he'd sputter a little tale that was on his mind. The only thing in Vanilla Will's favor was that his breath always smelled vanilla good.

BLACKY BRONSON

A real fixture of the Square was thirty-five-year-old Blacky Bronson, a tough hundred and ninety-five pounder from

Winelda's south end. He was probably the most cantankerous of Winelda's men. They called him Blacky because he had raven black hair, and black eyes that flashed and were surrounded by a dark cast that gave him a vaguely raccoonish look. Blacky was normally well behaved, but never when booze clouded his judgment. It was then he became fractious, a real hellcat of a man. Unfortunately, Blacky was a skilled fighter and relentless; consequently, everyone with good sense gave him a wide berth.

Blacky's blackest Saturday was at Eastman's Restaurant at around nine o'clock. He had come in noisily, reeking of booze, and obviously aching for a confrontation. Swearing, he seated himself at the counter. When Blacky was drunk, he imagined all sorts of slights and insults, which was why most patrons quietly moved to booths across the restaurant. He could be murderous. He'd take on the skinny, the mean, the old, or even women; fairness meant absolutely nothing to a drunk Blacky.

Many secretly fantasized how nice it would be if Lord, the burly blacksmith, were to walk through the door and have Blacky challenge him. That would be something to see. Lord cuddling Blacky on Cecil Street with his thigh-like arms squeezing until Blacky's eyeballs bulged from their sockets. Unfortunately, Lord was usually working or at home, and a Lord-Blacky confrontation seemed never destined to materialize.

Lily was Eastman's head waitress. She was Irish, sassy, and herself pretty short tempered. Her man-like arms matched her ample hundred and eighty-five pound hunk of a body. On this particular hot and June-buggish Saturday, she had been on duty six hours, and was in no frame of mind to put up with the likes of Blacky, who yelled, "How's about some service you worn out old whore." Lily blanched. A Christian, she had never been a scarlet woman, and she had had it with Blacky's nasty remarks, past and present.

She took a quick estimate of the situation, and was aware that whatever she did to protect her honor, it had best be good. She seized a heavy, clear glass pitcher half filled with water and fist sized chunks of ice, and before Blacky knew what had hit him, she whomped it hard against the side of his thick bony head. Glass and ice flew everywhere. It did not cut Blacky, but it did send him sprawling starry eyed to the floor. Had his head not been phenomenally thick, he might have lain unconscious for several minutes. But he sprang up and yelled, "Lily, you bitch, I'm gonna kill you for that!" There were gasps, because Blacky wasn't known for idle threats.

In Winelda, womenfolk were never publicly addressed in such a way even should tempers be high. Deputy Frank Clemans, a former Kansas lawman who was also the dad of Virgil Clemans, the owner of the Corner Drug, sometimes assisted on Saturdays as Billy's deputy. Frank was in booth number three, finishing one of Eastman's seventy-five cent sixteen ounce T-bones. He heard the pitcher crash, heard Blacky's threat of murder, and saw Blacky climbing over the counter to get at Lily. At that moment, Lily was coolly selecting yet another pitcher. For a sixty-year-old guy, cool hand Frank, at six feet four inches, was fit and well constructed—didn't drink, chew, or smoke.

"Hold it right there, Blacky!" said Frank rising, wiping the grease from his lips and adjusting his black Stetson. "You settle down, Boy, or I'll kick your ass 'tween yer shoulder blades."

Blacky, who couldn't believe he was being challenged, turned and saw Frank. "Keep outta ma way you old fart, this one's fixin' to die," and Blacky foolishly turned his back on Deputy Marshal Frank Clemans.

Ever present Billy Patton came through the door just in time to see Blacky hoisting himself over the counter and in time to see Frank bring the extra long barrel of his .45 crashing down on Blacky's head. Blacky slumped to the counter momentarily stunned. Blood coursed down the sides of his head, making him look even wilder, and more demented than usual.

Patton chugged forward and grabbed at Blacky, who with surprising recovery and agility gave the portly marshal a glancing left hook to the jaw. Billy, goggle eyed, crashed hard against the counter and knocked a shower of toothpicks into the air.

Having neutralized Billy, Blacky quickly turned all his attention to Frank. But again Frank brought him to his knees. And although Blacky remained kneeling in a servile position, Frank mercilessly brought the weapon down two or three more times. The sound was disgusting, as if the barrel were striking a mossy old log—thunk, thunk. It was a bludgeoning that would have either killed or rendered most men brainless. Finally, Blacky slid to the floor bonking his thick head on the brass foot rail as Frank roughly cuffed him.

"Emerson," he yelled to one of the diners, "ain't that yer pickup out front?"

"Yessir, Marshal, 'tis."

"Give me a han' then. I wanta load this sumbitch in the back and tek 'im down to the jell." Emerson took this as a peremptory command. He abandoned his hamburger and sprang off the stool. Billy, who had been momentarily stunned, shook the fog from his head, wiped his face with his bandanna, and assisted in carrying Blacky's limp body out to the truckbed. The three of them tossed Blacky in and didn't even close the tailgate, letting Blacky's bleeding head loll over the back.

"Lily," yelled Frank, "call Doc Clapper. Tell 'im to come down tuh the jell for some head sewin'."

The jail was in the City Hall garage, tucked in the corner behind the Dodge fire engine. It was nothing more than a large steel cage made of welded strap steel, hardly high enough for the average man to fully stand. It wasn't too different from the cages circuses use to ship lions and tigers, except this one had a narrow upper and lower bunk for human animals.

Quite a crowd of Saturday evening people followed Emerson's pickup the block and a half to City Hall. It wasn't long before Blacky, who should've been dead, was on his feet, gripping the tiny hand-holds of the jail's latticework of steel. Once the blood began surging through his body, he began shouting how he was going to kill those chickenshit marshals. Stoic Frank stood there listening, but remained as quiet as a statue.

I had just finished my work at the Majestic, and was going upstairs for my nightly bat fight, when I joined the procession en route to the jail. It was only a half block from Homer's Place. Blacky's incarceration had become quite an event, with over a hundred folks crowded around the fire engine. Like a kid, I crawled up onto the seat, walked over the fire hose to the back, and perched myself on the rear only six or seven feet above Blacky. A few other kids joined me up there.

Most of the country folk were awed and glad this crazy townie was under lock and key. Blacky snarled and kicked at the inch wide metal straps of the cage, rattled the door as if he'd rip it from its hinges, and all the while spewed his foul language.

Blacky's bellicose snarling escalated proportionally to the increase of the jailhouse crowd. He became quite theatrical. He even grabbed his mattress, such as it was, threw it onto the floor, and stomped it like a kid having a tantrum, except Blacky's deranged tantrum was wild and menacing. He smashed his fists into the cage's steel latticed door until all his knuckles were bleeding.

"Asshole Clemans, you'll get yores one night when fatso Patton ain't follerin' yer ass around, you goddam coward. *You hear me?*" Blacky would've put the fear of God into any ordinary man, but Frank Clemans remained as expressionless as a cigar store Indian. He was no coward. Sometimes I saw the muscles working around Mr. Clemans's jaw like he was grinding points on his teeth, but with his poker face it was nigh impossible to read his thoughts.

While waiting for Doc, Frank took out his big revolver to examine the barrel and noticed it had been bent upwards. "By gol, Frank," said a nearby friend, "if you was to aim thet at a wild bull, you'd shoot the squirrels outta the trees," and everyone laughed. It eased the tension. Frank shook his head in disgust. His fine old Remington revolver was forever ruined. He angrily plunged it into its holster.

Finally Doc Clapper arrived with his satchel and immediately looked through the steel latticework. "How're you, Blacky? I've come to attend to ya." Everyone in town loved Doc Clapper. He had delivered most everyone standing around the fire truck who was less than forty-five, including Blacky.

Frank came forward, "Git back from the door, Blacky!" Surprisingly Blacky stepped back against the other side of the cage. And as the huge padlock came off, everyone nervously sucked air through their teeth. Sending Doc Clapper in with that wild man was pure lunacy.

"Hey, Doc," someone cautioned, "you hadn't oughta."

FRANK AND THE FIRST AMENDMENT

It was as if Doc Clapper were stepping into a cage with a wounded mountain lion. Doc said, "Blacky, put your mattress back on the bed. I want you to sit there while I examine your head," and, as docile as a lamb, Blacky did this. Doc walked in without hesitation and placed his case on the upper bunk.

While Doc Clapper used surgical soap to shave Blacky's hard head, and commenced sewing up the long cuts, the crowd grew to two hundred. They were piled all over the fire engine, and in every available space as they marveled at the fearlessness of Winelda's treasure. "Gol danged if I'd ever git in there with thet lunatic." It's probably safe to say that if Blacky had disturbed even a hair of the saintly Doc's head, he would have been lynched from the City Hall's elm tree, and Frank Clemans would've tied the knot.

Blacky spent the night in the cage.

Sunday morning Frank came down alone. He wanted no witnesses, except he overlooked Merton Wright, the city electrician, who was in the far corner quietly studying a burned armature. Had it not been for Mert, this eyewitness account would never have made its way around the Square.

Frank unlocked the cage, threw the door open, and fixed eyes as dead as a rattlesnake's on the now sober Blacky. Blacky stood and tucked his shirttail into his trousers while Frank put his boot on the fire truck's bumper. "Blacky," he spoke quietly, "now you listen rill careful and take everythin' I say as fair warnin'. Next time you threaten murder on me er anyone else in Winelda, or if ya ever again come after Billy, or me, I'm gonna blow yer goddam hard head clean off'n yer shoulders. I'm gonna shootcha, Boy, till you do the chicken, and I'll keep on shootin' you 'til there's not a jerk left in yer damn fool lags." Like a metronome, Frank tapped his shot loaded blackjack in the palm of his hand and continued talking just above a whisper, "You unnerstan' thet, Blacky? I'm tired of yer carryin' on in this here town. Now yer probly gonna fret cuz you cain't remember everything and you'll blame alcohol as your excuse. But jist remember: I don't care if you're sober or skunk drunk, I'll fix yer wagon so's it'll never run agin. Damned tired uh you, Blacky. Plumb fed up cuz you cain't handle booze. Now wash out yer slop bucket and git fer home, and as long as I'm alive yer never to enter Eastman's again. You hear?"

Blacky kept his mouth shut and actually looked repentant. Blacky was sober, and as a sober person he was well mannered, agreeable, and almost humble. Sadly, he recalled very little of what had happened, his partly shaved head a muddle of hangover and hurt. And there was remorse, "Is it worth it when you cain't remember not a damned thaing?"

It's curious, the tricks alcohol and other chemicals sometimes play on people's minds. Vanilla Will, Baleful Blacky, Harve Berryhill, and Homer all loved those dear to them, but they obviously cared not enough. They preferred the weaker route of obscene drunkeness, embarrassment, grief, and finally degeneration. It was a strange brand of unrequited love.

In this instance, Blacky wasn't charged with intent to kill or for assaulting Marshal Billy Patton. Order had been restored. Blacky's severe beating mollified Lily; she pressed no charges. Winelda did not wish to call County Sheriff Ken Greer to carry Winelda boys up to an Alva jail. If at all possible, Winelda washed its own dirty laundry right there in Winelda.

PART THREE

THE NEW LEAF

When I started freshman year of high school in 1937, the dust storms had lessened. More rain was falling, and the county aggie agents were strongly advising never again to carve virgin pasture with a plow. And Washington did something surprisingly positive: "You people set aside strips of your land, and your government will provide saplings for shelterbelts. These belts will help block the wind, eventually provide a source of firewood, beautify the stark land, and create a haven for quail and pheasants and other game." And it was true. The shelterbelts grew to thirty and forty feet, and helped stanch the howling winter winds.

On matriculation day, I soon discovered that at thirteen, I was the youngest in a class of fifty. This wasn't based on any remarkable intelligence because Homer was already secretly aware his kid was only a step and a jerk away from being declared academically brain dead. Possibly I was the youngest because I had skipped the second grade in New Orleans; perhaps it was just the quirky result of having an April birthday. But I soon discovered being the youngest had both good and bad features. Good: I figured I'd finish high school sooner than any of the others. Younger, perhaps, but not sooner. It was possibly because of this basic illogic that they never seriously considered me for class valedictorian. Bad: Because I was among the class' shortest and scrawniest males. Any girl drawn to me was primarily interested in playing a big sister role.

Book Day was the beginning of the school year, and every kid went downtown en masse to buy textbooks prescribed by the State. I greatly respect that era when Oklahoma made parents responsible for their children's books. It certainly beat today's system where the state and not the family is the provider. Kid's today sometimes go without books due to poor administration, but even during the heart of the Depression, no Winelda kid was ever without books. No one ever said, "My fokes can't afford to buy the books." If a budget was tight, one could buy last year's used books for thirty to fifty cents each. There was a ready market for used books. Even Barney Arnold had seen that Earl had all of the required books.

Homer could be very tight with a penny, but when it came to books, his largesse knew no bounds. As a matter of record, I preferred the used books because I figured if I dropped one in the mud or lost one, there'd be no pressing reason for a family inquisition. But Homer insisted I buy new books. "Every kid should have a clean book, and be able to mark it up any way he wants." I once looked through Homer's extension course business books and found he'd underlined a good twenty percent of each chapter. And the marginal notes were all his, and not someone else's. I'm sure Homer had adopted Pop's book premise.

Pop told me when he was a kid in Chicago his parents always bought his books, and sent him to school with a lunch box. Pop constantly said it was the duty of parents to buy schoolbooks, and to feed and clothe their own kids. "If they want to have twelve kids, then they should be prepared to afford them. They shouldn't unfairly pass the costs to others who may have but one kid or none." Pop's prized 1874 copy of his arithmetic book has always been in our family bookcase. Had it been state owned, he would have had to turn it in, and today I wouldn't have this family treasure. On its blank pages are many of Pop's doodlings and drawings. Most of them consisted of powerful eagles and flowing American flags.

FOOTBALL

Homer insisted I go out for football. He said it built character and would make me grow. At the same time he forbade basketball and baseball. He believed super jocks often degenerated to a worthless clan that skipped class to play pool and smoke. "We don't want a super jock in the family," he'd say. "One major sport done well is enough." Cosmopolitan Homer used impressive words, had "attended" Kansas University, had lived for a time in Little Rock, and for years had been a denizen in New Orleans, but he still carried a large measure of his rural Ellinwood dogma. Central "wheat field" Kansas had stuck tenaciously to his bones.

When I put on my football gear, I was thirteen and weighed a hundred and four pounds. I was probably the only kid to report who sported only feeble chin fuzz, and not a single dark hair on his chest. Four seniors on the team shaved regularly, had curly hair on their chests, and were six to seven years older than I. One weighed a hundred and eighty-two pounds! That was only five pounds lighter than Homer, who to me was bigger than life itself.

Coach Claunch was trying to forge the Winelda Railroaders into a bestial gridiron force, one that would intimidate every team in our conference. But with only eighty-five boys in the entire school to choose from—and many of those with no proclivity to play football— coach had his work cut out for him. Coach surveyed my scrawny frame, and, as hungry as he was for combatants, he could not visualize me as the beast he searched for. He sighed, "Go home, Son, and grow a little. Come back next year."

This was crushing news to a runt always relegated to the bottom row for class pictures. I had really wanted to prove something to both Homer, and myself. Instead, I had become an instant reject. And to think, Homer had actually been fearful I might become a super jock. Ha! The coach had emasculated me, had sent me back with the girls. This must have been a shock to Homer. Suddenly he had to come to grips with the realization that his hundred and four pound offspring was possibly not All-American material after all. I'm sure my rejection must've stolen some of the parental curl from Homer's macho tail.

SEX LECTURE—OCTOBER 1937

We were only in high school a couple of weeks when an important lecture was announced, an innovative talk never before tested at Winelda. *Sex!* A matter so innately delicate our Baptist superintendent wisely deleted "sex" and substituted the word "hygiene." Even so, the WHS hallways bubbled like a geyser ready to erupt. "Wow, a real doctor from Oke City is gonna speak about reproduction. No animal husbandry stuff; this's the straight word on how people do it." It promised to be pretty awesome material!

When the superintendent's office announced that all girls were to go to the gym bleachers, and all boys to the auditorium, the speculation reached a buzzing crescendo. In the hallways clots of girls whispered while they constantly checked over their shoulder for boys with big ears. I always wondered how our prim girls would discuss this. Would they be as straightforward as boys, or would they talk in circles?

On a warm early October afternoon, a doctor and a grizzled uniformed nurse parked their car in front of our high school. The time was at hand. The special bell rang for assembly. "Boy howdy, now we get the unvarnished truth." And all boys silently filed into the auditorium; the titillated girls went beyond our view to the bleachers.

The doctor galvanized our attention when he casually mentioned sperm. Much whispering followed. "Golly, did'ja hear that? He said it right on the stage." Then ovaries and the uterus were discussed, which he explained with clinical detachment. At the mention of fertilization, everyone again leaned forward. Very soon the good part, the *how*, was bound to come. He mentioned the magic nine months, which we already referred to when making weak unscientific jokes. I sat there slack jawed, absorbing every word.

But then we realized he was skirting exigencies like "missed periods," or when a girl was most likely to conceive, or how did one go about getting to first base! Were there magic erogenous spots? We should know this. The doctor avoided the harsh word "pregnant" and replaced it with a softly spoken "with child," and the "gender" of the individual was referred to rather than the person's sex. In Winelda High School, a word like "sex" was pretty much akin to the F-word, definitely unsuitable for either auditorium or hallways. Also unmen-

tioned was protection. He carefully avoided referring to prophylac-
tics, or really ugly words like condoms, or rubbers, or Merry Widows.
I was certain he viewed condoms as wicked. They were things only to
be found in the restrooms of big city bus stations for so-called "good
health." In all of Winelda there was not a single such machine.

Unfortunately, the doctor maintained his lofty spiritual plane and
obviously had no intention of outlining "safe sex." His message was
clear: "Unless you're married, *never* be intimate with girls." For the
boys, the crux of the lecture was "keep your fly buttoned," and I
suppose the wizened nurse was cautioning the girls not to lose their
pants, or to let a boy get handy.

We never got the straightforward talk for which we hungered; yet,
we became wide eyed when he mentioned scary words like gonorrhea, syphilis and yucko lymphogranuloma inguinalis. Boys and girls
caught these horrible diseases if they "fooled around." What "fooling
around" encompassed was hazy territory, but I was growing confident
it entailed action more intimately complex than mere post office or
spin the bottle.

"Yes, students," he preached. "Some of these diseases can kill a
person or turn him into a raving mad dog!" The doctor's fire and
brimstone words reverberated throughout the auditorium. Syphilis,
he called it "Big S," could only be cured with arsenic compounds.
"Young men," he said, "the very cure itself oftentimes *killlls* the
patient. But without it, you will have insanity and an agonizingly
painful death!" He might very well have continued with, "and you'll
surely roast in hell." We were all squirming in our seats.

If in anticipation of this juicy subject there had initially been a stirring in some loins, perhaps even a few secret erections, by the time the
doctor had finished with "Big S," every willie in the auditorium must
have surely shriveled to mere nubs. Most of us sat there with wide,
vacant eyes. We had looked forward to learning about sex, perhaps to
be better prepared to quest and conquer, to learn if it were true that
too much sex would actually damage our brains. The doctor had
seeded such fear. Our collective thoughts of having a little "hygiene"
with a Wineldan beauty had grown remote indeed. When the doctor
left the lectern, the when and how to do continued to be dark
mysteries.

During the question-answer period, I kept quiet. I didn't want
everyone to know I was virtually a blank sheet of paper when it came

to "hygiene." Afterwards, I quietly cornered the doctor down front of the stage. He had said that "Big S" came from bad girls so I asked, "Sir, how do you know when a girl's bad?" I remember how uncomfortable he became as he struggled for some innocuous and sinless euphemism. And I became especially disquieted when I saw a nearby senior grinning at my ignorance.

"Well, Son," the doctor said, "you have to sense those things. For example, if she wears a lot of lipstick, and rouge, and perfume, and walks suggestively, she might very well be bad."

I responded quite honestly, "None of the girls at WHS fits that description, Sir, so I suppose they're all okay?"

Again I had unintentionally cornered the fidgety doctor. To be politic he couldn't very well say, "Oh, you can be sure there are bad WHS girls;" yet, if he agreed they were all pristine, then he'd be giving carte blanche approval to whatever nefarious plan we collectively had in mind. It was a genuine Pandora's box for the doctor, and I'm sure he must've wished he could've swatted me like an annoying horsefly. Finally, he gave me a smile and said, "Young man, you can never be too sure."

I had a load of questions. I wanted to know exactly what "walking suggestively" meant, but I noticed the doctor's uneasiness. I decided to take it up with Homer because Homer knew everything.

So, what did we learn? We learned that any of us who had "hygiene" before marriage would most likely either be dead or locked up in the attic before we got to college. I got the distinct impression he had classified all females as Black Widow spiders. Touch 'em and you die. I wondered if the old nurse with the bayonet scars had told the girls that we scrubbed boys were also instant death.

At this stage of my life, I had begun discovering mysterious new yearnings inside me, and that girls were decidedly different. By contrast, we freshmen boys were still running around with our shirt-tails hanging out while the girls were neat and had bows in their hair; some were even manifesting flirtatiousness. They had become young ladies, and I had begun noticing that most of them smelled good. But I must admit that the doctor's fearsome lecture had devastated most of my then emerging enthusiasm. Still, some sixth sense told me this girl business was leading to something pretty special, and in the hall-ways I began making a better presentation of myself.

Although the doctor had spoken for over half an hour, he never touched the information I thirsted for. I had heard that the sex thing came after a lot of kissing, but I could never find anyone who could describe exactly how the actual mating was done. Jack Beaman, Lottie's son, had once warned me that sometimes girls become scared, and lock on "the same as happens to dogs." The mention of dogs made me secretly wonder if that was the preferred position. Jack continued effusively, saying that in lock-on cases, there was nothing to do but to yell for help, and have the doctor come and pry you apart with special tools, "perhaps forever losing your dick!"

I tried to imagine such a scenario with Homer, or the girl's father, or both standing just outside the door with both of us yowling, and me possibly sacrificing my willie. I had also been told about shotguns and having to get married. Of these substantial perils, losing one's dick was not the least of our fears. There was also the chilling knowledge of insanity and agonizing death at the hands of "Big S." I seriously began to wonder if the many disadvantages of "hygiene" with girls far outweighed any fun that might be achieved.

Homer was my ace in the hole. I was sure he would dispel the many mysteries left unanswered by the medic. After all, I was born to Homer. This in itself was positive proof he obviously knew every answer. Additionally, Homer was a world wise person, about as well informed as could be found. Now I wondered how I would go about broaching this subject with Homer. Finally, I decided the easiest entry was to tell Homer about the doctor's speech, tell him about the bad girl thing, and see if he'd grab the ball and run with it. I was fully aware that discussing this with my own dad would be embarrassing, but the invaluable revelations would far outweigh any discomposure. It was going to be my first grown-up talk with Homer. It would be a bountiful harvest of information that the other guys would never have because, in my personal view, few of the dads around town were as sophisticated or as well informed as mine.

I brought up the matter in the kitchen, but because Maddy was in the bedroom, Homer said, "Come on, Son. Let's walk over to Elm Park."

In retrospect, I would imagine Homer must have been grinning inwardly while sweating at the same time. This was his initial birds and bees effort with his son, and he must have been thinking, "I knew my day would someday come; now the kid wants to know." And with his arm across my shoulder we shuffled down Cecil and over the tracks toward Elm Park. Now the grand and unvarnished disclosures would come spewing forth.

At Elm Park, Homer and I casually sat down on one of the merry-go-rounds. "Well, Son," he finally said, "I didn't realize the time had passed so fast, and you were suddenly growing up. I s'pose this talk's long overdue." Homer's preamble set me ablaze with anticipation.

I wanted to hear it all, how a boy and a girl got it on; how the diddling actually took place. I wanted to know all about rubbers, how to steer clear of "Big S" and arsenic, how not to lose my dick, what not to do, what to do; I wanted it all. But Homer did not immediately open the informational floodgate. He kept droning about a lot of water under the bridge and over the dam, and his maundering eventually became as uncomfortable as the doctor behind the lectern. I was surprised to find Homer not in charge. I even detected sweat on his forehead. Finally, Homer said, "You know, Tom, in a town like Winelda, there's one thing you don't ever want to do. Don't fool around. You can find yourself in a lot of trouble."

There it was again—fool around—which I immediately concluded was a euphemism that definitely meant to "fuck around." Why in heaven's name would no one come forth and spell out "fool around."

"For example," he said, "to get Delores Twiller in trouble and have old Clint Twiller banging on our door? No sir, that would not be the kind of situation we would ever want."

In trouble? What kind of trouble? Also, if a guy wasn't supposed to fool around in Winelda, Homer must've meant Alva. Homer kept rambling, but not about the good stuff. "If you ever get the urge," he ultimately said, "you get on down to Oklahoma City. You come ask me, but whatever, don't fool around in Winelda. The word would get around, and then imagine what they'd say in your church? There's Lloyd Curtis right next door at the Rexall, he's one of your deacons. No sir, this town's too small."

And before I knew it, Homer had skirted the subject entirely, and had veered off onto football. He sat there and declared profoundly that I'd be a lot bigger my sophomore year, and would definitely make the team. After that stunning disclosure, he talked about the secret cabin he and his Ellinwood, Kansas pals had had on a little island in the middle of the Arkansas River, and how—I'd heard these yarns so many times—they had ice skated down to Great Bend and back. "One thing you boys here might do is build a raft, and some summer go on a trip down the Cimarron. The Cimarron flows into the Arkansas at Tulsa, and then you could go all the way to the Mississippi."

If Homer's riverine geography was a clever design to get me off the initial topic, then it certainly worked. I completely forgot my further questions. The fresh idea of floating down to the Mississippi was a helluva lot more exciting, and certainly less deadly than sex.

That night, as I lay in bed listening to "Ma, She's Makin' Eyes at Me," I reviewed my enlightenment from Homer and I wondered: What are my options in far-off Oklahoma City? I don't know anyone down there, don't have a car, and haven't any place to stay. I can just see myself going up to Homer and saying, "Well, Dad, I'm ready to go sparking around in Oklahoma City. You told me to report in before I went, so here I am, your ever-lovin' son." Fat chance!

Homer's talk had been as disappointing as the dud doctor's had been. It was the very first time I ever saw Homer actually afraid to tackle a topic. Religion, business, academics, ice skating to Great Bend, he was an unimpeachable, unstoppable gold mine of unfettered information. When it came to discussing sex, he was a total, screaming bust.

How the high school "hygiene" talk fared in other families was another of Winelda's secrets. I can imagine there were some strained conversations between Winelda's clear eyed daughters and their quaking mothers, and between uncomfortable fathers and eager sons. What I am sure of is there had never before been a sex talk at Winelda High School, and during my four years of high school, there was never another. Either from private asides or at PTA, the school board had most likely received the message—those are very personal family matters. Don't bring them up in school.

MEAN DEAN AND HAMMERHEAD—FALL 1937

Mean Dean, the usher at the Majestic, was known simply as Dean. I'll tell you why, in 1937, he became known as Mean Dean. He was a great kid, even scrawnier than I, and a year or so younger. He loved poking fun, and in 1937 he began poking most of it at what he considered to be the obtuse flaws of country folk. If we passed by Etta's Café and he saw a rancher wearing his cowboy hat and having supper at the same time, he'd most likely say, "Wonder if he wears that damned thing in church," or "Surprised they don't bury 'em wearing those ridiculous hats." If Mean Dean wished to show utter disdain, he was apt to say, "I'll swear, you act as dumb as a farmer." To him that was the epitome of castigation, the utter of utters.

His new hostile attitude toward non-city folk only manifested itself the year before. Hammerhead Hammer, Mean Dean's classmate, kindled it. Hammerhead had invited him out to the farm to ride horses, and from that day forward, Dean became known as Mean Dean. I know all this because I was at Mean Dean's house the morning Hammerhead rolled around in his pickup. I asked if I, too, could watch Dean ride. "Sure, Tom," said Hammerhead, and as I sat by the window of Hammerhead's International pickup truck, I thought how fortunate for Hammerhead that he could drive to town at age twelve while our family had no vehicle at all.

"Whatcha fixin' to do with thet chestnut stallion?" Muley asked. Muley was Hammerhead's father and well known around Winelda's square. He enjoyed holding court around the drawing barrel, at the barbershop, or at Hank's Place or anyplace he could find people to bore. Once Muley took center stage, he was an obdurate cuss who made it difficult for anyone to get a word in edgewise. That's how he came by the Muley moniker, which had been intended for derision. Nevertheless, Muley liked it; he thought it sounded macho.

"I'm gonna show Dean here how to ride, Pa," said Hammerhead as he tightened the cinch. "He never been on no horse before." I caught the conspiratorial wink Hammerhead gave his dad. Mean Dean didn't see it. At the time, I didn't believe the winking was important, but then I had no way of knowing the Hammers had schemed to have sport at Dean's expense. Besides, I was more interested in the sleek beauty of the valuable chestnut stallion. In retrospect, the Hammers must've had great faith in the animal's intelligence, or else their little stunt might've been a tragic loss.

Dean, the city dude, was pure putty in their hands, trusting and artless, like an innocent fledgling ready for its first leap from the nest.

"Here, let me hep ya get up inta the saddle," said Hammerhead as he and his daddy, Muley, each grabbed a handful of Mean Dean's little buns and plopped him high up in the saddle. So high! I sure as hell knew I didn't want to be way up there, and when I saw Dean pale, I knew he didn't either. But he was a game little critter, and it was too late for second thoughts.

"Now, you holt the reins in your left han' and when you wanta go ya just say 'giddup,' and when ya want 'im to stop just say 'whoa,' like thet." Then they laughed their good old boy har-de-har laughs, and that was the verbal extent of Dean's introduction to equitation. Dean had noticed neither the hackamore curb bit nor the martingale harness. Even had he noticed these restrainers, they would never have registered on a city dude like Dean. Yes sir, the Hammers had a mean streak because any "hard hand" would have known that the gentle old mare in the barn would have been a better beginner selection than a spirited, snorting, tail switching chestnut stallion.

The stallion flared its nostrils, whinnied, beautifully arched its tail and neck, commenced raking the turf with its right hoof, yanked at the martingale, and sounded yet another impatient whinny. The animal could hardly contain itself. "Now, Dean, you git on yonder in the flat and enjoy yerself, ya hear?" Dean had initially been a little pale, but the excited antics of the horse caused Dean to grow quite pasty. Hammerhead then patted the horse on the rump, and it commenced prancing across the lawn, tossing its head as it regally headed toward the wide open southeast quarter.

We all heard Dean softly command "Giddup" and the anxious stallion obliged at a trot. And because the bouncy gait caused Dean's feet to whack at the stallion's sides, it was all the encouragement that that spirited animal needed. It immediately surged into a gallop, and in very short order escalated its gait to an all out Kentucky Derby run. Such miraculous speed! And sparrow-like Dean weighed so little. All across that vast acreage he could be heard plaintively wailing a useless "Whoa." The beautiful quarter horse was running as swiftly as any I'd ever seen in the very best of Western movies.

Little guys like Dean who have been able to survive are seldom dopes. He saw the ground whizzing by, felt the powerful action of the horse surging beneath his own bony little buttocks, and he immediately opted for survival. He dropped the reins and fused both hands to the saddle horn—probably his brightest move since before he had climbed into the pickup truck with Hammerhead. He was going so fast that I was certain a fall would break most of his bird-like bones.

"Lookit 'im go," cried Muley.

I felt very sorry for my friend as I listened to the pitiful redundancy of his cries of "whoa," the thundering hoof beats, and watched the sheer velocity of boy and animal.

Muley and Hammerhead were doubled up with guffaws. "Oh shit, Son, you really done a good un. The kid's paralyzed! Ha, ha, he, ho, ha, ha, Gol-damned but this is goo-ud." Muley squinted at the speeding stallion, "By gar, ya gotta give the town critter credit. He's sure uh hangin' on."

Then the stallion did a frightening thing. He began a gradual turn to the right and headed straight for a barbed wire fence seventy-five yards distant. I was sure Mean Dean's mind had as many terrible things shooting through it as I had in mine. I visualized the beautiful horse torn in a tangle of barbed wire, covered with blood and entrails, and kicking his last of life. Next to him lay a crumpled little Dean glistening with a flood of blood. In another flash of fantasy, I visualized the snorting stallion leaping the fence as in a steeplechase, Dean flying unhorsed and impaled on the deadly wire. No matter which vision, everything pointed to imminent catastrophe.

Through teary eyes Dean also saw the impending fence, and the blur of the ground. He gripped fiercely with his hands while his scrawny chicken legs correctly grabbed the horse like a vise. When the horse was no more than fifteen feet from the fence, it suddenly veered right, an abrupt turn intended for murder, one that might very well have thrown even the best of unsuspecting equestrians into the fence. But Dean held fast, and in spite of the terror, his thought wave was, "Sonuvabitch wanted to kill me, tried to throw me into the wire, wanted to kill me."

Then the stallion came around one hundred and eighty degrees and headed back toward the house, headed straight toward the yawning black hole of the barn's open doors. Dean had been in the barn and remembered the chickens roosting on the low rafters. He envisioned the horse galloping through and emerging from the other side, his own headless body still gripping the saddle horn.

Carrying only ninety-one pounds, the stallion resumed an all out run. Dean later told me his side vision picked up Hammerhead and Muley slapping their sides and waving their big hats rodeo fashion. With the barn only twenty yards away, there was little doubt where the horse was going. Dean ducked his head. The stallion clattered through the large opening and out the other side in a cloud of dust, feathers, and terrified chickens. Then, in the Hammer's front yard, the spirited animal applied its own brakes under the sprawling elm tree, whinnied triumphantly, and began casually nibbling buffalo grass.

Dean remained aboard, still frozen to the horn, and shaking as if beset by St. Vitus's dance.

The joke was a bad one, a truly irresponsible shenanigan that could've resulted in serious injury. Obviously the two Hammers were confident their horse was as smart as it was wily and would not hurt itself, but apparently little thought had been given to Dean. Perhaps they never figured Dean would make it as far as the "bobbed" wire.

Muley Hammer grabbed the horse's reins, "Come on down, Boy. Did'ja like yer ride? Heh, heh, heh, ha, ha, haaah." He slapped his thigh with his big cowboy hat. "Shi-it, Son. Now thet was somethin' else."

Dean wore a peculiar startled or was it a wild look? And as he slid down the side of the horse, he still shook. When he reached the ground his shaky legs gave way, and he collapsed in a heap. Seeing Dean fold up like rubber caused Hammerhead to follow his dad's lead and he, too, began laughing, and father and son slapped each other's backs.

Then Dean slowly got to his feet, his chin and lower lip jerking, and quivering, and flicking like a kid's will do when he's about to cry. That is when little Dean erupted with a choked cry of rage and charged Hammerhead. Fast as lightning, Dean's haymaker landed hard on Hammerhead's mouth. Muley was aghast. Before father or son had time to think about it, Dean maniacally smashed again. This time his fist landed on Hammerhead's nose. Blood spurted, and Hammerhead's eyes were crossed as he wailed, "Dad, Dad, lookit whut he done, lookit whut he done!"

Dean was still bawling with rage, and like a little maddened tomcat, was about to deliver yet a third blow. Muley yelled, "Hey, hey, kid, ya done that twict, now you *stop* thet! That's *mean*, that's no way tuh ack." Muley Hammer restrained Dean as Hammerhead ran bawling to the kitchen with his nosebleed. "I figure ya won't be a stayin' tuh our dinner, don't have decent manners, yer a *mean* kid. I'll drive ya back in tuh Winelda."

Once again, Dean surprised everyone. He stood tall and yelled, "Fuck you, Mr. Hammer! Fuck Hammerhead too! I don't wanta git in yer fuckin' truck, don't want yer fuckin' food either, I'll walk tuh town." Without further comment, Dean turned toward the gate. Muley just stood there in disbelief, his big jaw hanging open. It was one of the few times Muley was ever at a loss for words. Just as I began to follow, Dean turned, "Go fuck yer fuckin' horse, Mr. Hammer." That was the last comment Muley heard as Dean and I closed the gate and headed for Winelda.

Even when he was yelling profanities, Dean was true to the Wineldan kid-adult courtesy code and called Muley Mister Hammer. I was awed at the way Dean had cleaned up on Hammerhead, who was twenty pounds heavier; awed at the way he had addressed Mr. Hammer with unmentionable words. We walked along in silence with Dean occasionally kicking up a puff of surface sand. After ten minutes of hush, he turned and smiled a mouthful of sparkling teeth. "Boy, that fucker could really run!" and we laughed. Several times on our way to town he repeated, "How about that? Sonuvabitch said I was *mean*." And that was when I started calling him Mean Dean, and it was a tale that couldn't be withheld from Winelda.

I was proud of my friend, proud that he was the Majestic's usher. Little Mean Dean's nose was straight and untouched, and he seemed quite satisfied with what he had done to Hammerhead, what he had said to Mr. Hammer, and the fact he had survived such a fantastic ride. Those were the first palpable punches Mean Dean had ever thrown in his life, and he had never before sassed an adult. Thereafter he was never the same. That single horse ride matured him. Unfortunately, that incident caused him to temporarily lose respect for anything and anybody living in the country.

THE FUTURE FARMER AND RED HOGS

Homer was full of lessons. He was aware that I had once aspired to be a fireman, later, a pilot, and then a passenger train engineer. Of late I wanted to be a veterinarian like Perry Phillips. Homer never pooh-poohed my ephemeral aspirations. But one thing Homer was sure of, he did not want his kid to become a farmer or a rancher. He had tasted that life. It was his fixed opinion that such a life broke both hearts and backs, and was fiscally unrewarding. He was glad I never expressed a desire to farm, but in Anthony I once saw a letter he'd written Mom Cable: "I notice Tom likes to dig in the dirt, and it bothers me. I hope it isn't a harbinger of things to come." Thereafter it became his clandestine objective to dispel forever any developing desire that might possibly push me in that direction.

So when the time came for me to enroll for my freshman classes, it was a stunning surprise when he strongly suggested I take agriculture, and become a member of the FFA, the Future Farmers of America. His overt rationale was that everything around Winelda was agriculturally oriented, and I should learn something about that industry. Covertly, he wanted me to discover for myself that it was damned hard work, and only marginally profitable. The agriculture teacher, Harold Dedrick, was one of WHS's very best personalities, so I thought Homer's suggestion was sensational.

Because of animal husbandry's sometimes earthy reproduction subjects, Dedrick permitted no girls in his class. I, the picture show kid, was the only townie taking the course, and this naturally raised a few eyebrows. I think it must've even concerned Dedrick because every student had to have an agricultural project. For farm kids, this was no problem because their fathers would give them the responsibility of forty acres of wheat land, or a flock of show chickens, or four or five fine calves. I elected to raise two red Duroc-Jersey pigs. I'm sure the instructor wondered where Tom Cable, who lived at Homer's Place in the heart of Winelda, was going to raise hogs.

I went over to old Mr. Jim McGurn, who lived a couple of blocks north of the Square. He had a ramshackle shed about the size of a one car garage on three acres bordering the diagonal railroad tracks. I asked him if I could use a small piece of his land. "Why not?" he said amiably, and there was no mention of rent. It was another mark of how senior Wineldans lent a hand where they could see a flicker of promise.

There were plenty of old boards scattered around the place, and because Mr. McGurn did not care, I borrowed a posthole digger and made a pigpen, a big one so the pigs could run. I made a good trough, and the pigs had shelter in the shed. All this stuff I learned in class from farm guys and Harold Dedrick. My friend Perry came out to my pen and told me to put up a couple of scratching poles wrapped with burlap sacks soaked in used motor oil. He said the pigs would rub against them and the oil would forever kill their lice.

I immersed myself in hog lore, almost rabidly, and I sent away for virtually every hog related pamphlet printed by the agricultural colleges. I collected a pile of them, which I read voraciously, and I became a walking encyclopedia of anything related to all breeds of hogs. I talked about hogs with such frequency it must have alarmed

Homer. He must've feared that his secret plan had possibly backfired.

I am sure he derived some solace when he learned the agriculture teacher was requiring each student to keep accurate records on his project, what was spent in time and money. The teacher pounded home that time was money, that hogs were not dogs, or cats, or pigeons; this was strictly business. Homer loved that aspect, often reminded me of it, and asked to see my books.

I'd already spent considerable spare time constructing the pigpen, but to me that time was fun and not business. Then came the big day—I bought two fine little pigs—cute little rascals—and Dedrick insisted I have Perry drop by to give them cholera shots.

I loved the company of my two pigs. When they saw me coming across the field to feed them, they'd look through the fence and commence grunting and squealing. I liked that. Twice a day—early every morning before going to school, and every evening after school—seven days a week, I was with my pigs. The pigs always needed something—water, a fence repaired, or poop shoveled.

One day when I came to feed them after school, I found a board knocked loose in my fence, and both pigs gone. I searched for them until sunset, and returned home devastated. I was late for dinner, but for once Homer relented. He was quick to detect that his distraught son was ready to lay his head on the Santa Fe railroad tracks. Billy Patton sent word over the Winelda grapevine that the Cable kid had lost his pigs. The next day, someone spotted them in a pasture north of town.

"Are you having fun?" Homer casually asked. I answered honestly that raising the pigs was a terrific experience. He visited the pigpen a few times, saw garbage, and asked where I'd gotten it. Every morning after sweeping the hallway and steps, I went to Etta's Café and picked up a couple of buckets of the stinking free stuff. It was too expensive to always feed my pigs sacked corn and alfalfa, and tankage—dried blood, etc. Both Homer and the agriculture teacher kept stressing how profit played the largest part in the project's success or failure.

For thirty days of each month of my freshman year, even on Christmas day, I was bonded to those pigs. I couldn't be lax because every three to five weeks Harold Dedrick would make a surprise visit and ask me about feeding, and carefully review my expense records. Raising pigs took energy, and I had plenty.

THE RUBBERS

W hen not with pigs, one of my most enjoyable pastimes was occasional hunting forays with Mean Dean a mile or so north of
town. Homer allowed me to buy an ancient second-hand Remington
pump .22, and Mean Dean had a new bolt action single shot. It was
during those hunting jaunts that I discovered he was the consummate
baseball fan. Mel Ott was his hero. He ranked Ott somewhere
between God and his father—closer to God.

To become a baseball fan in 1937 in Northwest Oklahoma was of
itself noteworthy. I don't recall a single Wineldan soul who had ever
attended a major league baseball game. It was simply a matter of
space and time. The nearest team was the St. Louis Cardinals, and by
train it was a thousand miles round trip. A time or two I'd heard a
game crackle over the radio, but with no faces or runs to see, I thought
radio baseball was about as engrossing as watching cow chips turn
hard in the sun.

But not for Mean Dean! He soaked up baseball. He was one of
those phenomenal characters who could prodigiously spew out the
names of baseball players, and their positions, and what they had
done back in 1928 and 1933. When he started feverishly reciting those
ridiculous baseball statistics, it was the only times I remember him as
boring. Who really gave a flying fig who was second baseman for the
Brooklyn Dodgers in 1934? To me it was both a waste of brain cells
and good time. Like a machine gun, Mean Dean could accurately
ratty-tat-tat baseball dates and names, yet he could not be positively
certain when the Declaration of Independence was signed.

One day, as we scanned the sagebrush for rabbits from the high
ground, we began reviewing what the Oke City doctor had said about
dying from diddling. I said, "I hadn't known you could die. I thought
it was supposed to be fun. What I really wanted to know was how to
avoid a shotgun, how you did it, and how not to have babies, how not
to take a trip to the cemetery, and most importantly, how not to lose
my willy."

Without hesitation Mean Dean said importantly, "You use a
rubber. You put the thing right on your prick. It keeps you from
having a baby, or the clap, or the blue balls. We sell 'em down at the
Corner." When he was not ushering at the Majestic, Mean Dean

jerked sodas at Virgil Clemans's Corner Drug Store.

"What's the clap?" I said.

"Clap? It's somethin' you catch when you hop on a girl that's got it. Same with blue balls."

"Blue balls?"

"Yeah, blue balls," he said with authority, and he strutted ahead with his shoulders back. I noticed he stood a tad taller. "Blue balls comes from girls. Catch blue balls and your balls turn bright blue like a baboon's ass, and they hurt to holy hell. Hurts so bad you wanna die." Mean Dean chewed his bubble gum faster, and tried to look bored and important as his eyes expertly roved the sagebrush for stealthy rabbits.

I was embarrassed. He was younger than I, yet he knew much more about this mystery. I wondered where I'd been. How could this kid know more than I? The doctor had covered "Big S" and gonorrhea, but never alluded to the horrors of manifesting bright blue aching balls. How did Mean Dean know these things? During one lull in our animated conversation, I seriously considered the advantages of the priesthood. I also cautioned myself not to let Mean Dean discover I was so miserably uninformed. But then I wondered if Mean Dean was fabricating. I looked at him directly, "And you've actually put one of these rubber things on your dick?" I noticed he made a point of not looking me in the eye.

"Certainly," he huffed as if it were one of the dumbest of questions.

"Well, how do ya tie the thing on?"

"Don't tie nuthin' on. They hang on there like rubber gloves do on your hands. Wear one, and you can't catch nuthin'. And remember, if your stuff gets loose in there, *bang*, that's all she wrote—you gotta baby."

Mean Dean sounded very authoritative, and to me it was a real boon to at last get some straight dope. I wanted to get around to technique and the like, and I finally said, "Have you ever done that, Mean Dean? Have you diddled with a girl?"

"Maybe I have and mebbe I haven't. That's not fer tellin', Tom. If you tell it around, then that's the end of all your pussy 'cause no girl will dare have anything to do with ya." Dean importantly based his voice when he said "pussy."

I watched his eyes. They had grown somewhat shifty, and were looking more and more like those of a used car salesman. I was pretty sure Mean Dean was a virgin, so I kept nudging him.

"Have you seen the rubbers down at the Corner?"

"Nope. Haven't a clue. I asked, but Virgil says the customers don't want to buy 'em from no kid." Mean Dean kicked at the sandy ground. "That's what pisses me off. How long are these suckers gonna be callin' us kids?" Mean Dean's self-esteem had grown considerably after walloping Hammerhead. He had taken to talking and walking as if he were six feet four and weighed two hundred pounds.

The next day I was on the way to the theater with Maddy and Homer, when just as I was turning past the drawing barrel, Mean Dean caught my attention. I darted over. "Hey, Tom," he hissed, "I found where Virgil and Esther hide the rubbers. Early Saturday, when you go down to the theater to shine brass, drop in and I'll show ya a real Merry Widuh."

This was an exciting development because I wanted to see one close at hand, feel of it, see its size, how it was packaged, and how much it cost.

The next morning, Virgil had just gone to the Commercial Bank, and Esther hadn't yet come from the house. Mean Dean was sweeping when I entered. He quickly set aside the broom and said, "Get back to the Whitman Sampler counter." Mean Dean ran to the side door to check if Virgil was returning from the bank, then he hustled back to me. "Yeah, I found the suckers the other day while I was dusting." Mean Dean reached under the counter and brought up a little paper box full of the rubber devices. Each was about as big around as an average little finger; they looked like tiny balloons that hadn't been blown up.

I picked up three or four and looked at them skeptically. "You mean you put this thing on yer dick?" I asked. "I thought they were supposed to be individually packaged, a special package."

"Well," snapped Mean Dean, "very plain to see that they aren't."

I fumbled with them some more, felt the soft rubber. "How could you ever get this on?"

"They stretch."

That was when Virgil shot in through the side door, "What you boy's doing over there?"

Virgil had a full view of us. I was holding the little box of rubber things. I'm sure my mouth dropped open, but like a jackrabbit crossing the road, Mean Dean charged ahead. "Mr. Clemans," he said, "I was dusting in here and found these, what're they for?" Dean put his hands on his hips, and looked at me with abundant satisfaction written across his face. He'd set up Virgil to be his corroboration.

"Oh, those?" said Virgil. "They came in yesterday . . . they call 'em finger cots. You cut your finger bad, and don't want dirt, or vinegar, or salt in the cut, you just put on a finger cot." Mean Dean's mouth dropped open. "Pretty handy and cheap, only a nickel apiece. Dean, you put a little five cent each sticker on the box while I check out our ice cream," and Virgil went behind the counter.

Dean avoided looking in my direction, but I wasn't about to let him off the hook. Finally, I said in a voice too low for Virgil to hear, "Dean, you bullshitter, those are so small you couldn't put one on a monkey's dick!" And we cracked up together. I was relieved to know that when it came to sex and rubbers, little Mean Dean talked a good game, but he was just another fountain of gross misinformation.

AMZY CRISWELL

It was freshman year that I started palling around with Amzy Criswell. Of all my friendships, Homer liked this one the best because Amzy was three years older than I. Homer liked Mean Dean's spirit and intelligence, but because Dean was two classes below me, he was afraid I would always be getting my way. He liked Jack Beaman because of Lottie's and Jimmy's strict standards. But because we were of the same age, he doubted that I'd learn much from Jack. In Homer's eyes, Amzy was perfect because if I needed some knocking around, Amzy could do it, and I could learn from Amzy because he was older and wiser. That's the practical way Homer viewed these things.

When I was a freshman, Amzy was a junior—which was awesome because people that old rarely associated with freshmen. I had always looked up to Amzy, and considered it a compliment that he spent as much time with me as he did. Our common and fervent interest in Indians, hunting, and tracking provided the entrée for our friendship. He was quite knowledgeable in tracking animals, and he knew where to find the best dogwood for bows and arrows. We began hunting together. Among our major goals was a daytime shot at a raccoon, or a coyote, or to possibly come across a big blue heron. We'd also heard that a real white owl hung out near Dog Creek's confluence with the Cimarron.

Something else bonded us—Amzy was the only kid in town besides me who lived on the Winelda Square. He lived with his elderly grandmother only half a block away on the upstairs backside of the Winelda Snooker Parlor. Each time I went to Amzy's Spartan apartment I noticed he always talked gently with his grandmother, and loved the old lady as if she were his own national treasure. He was always asking "Grandma" what he could fetch. "Fetch" was one of Amzy's favorite words, that and "pack." Amzy never carried anything, he always packed it. He also never mentioned his mysteriously absent father or mother, and no one ever pried.

Amzy, more intelligent than most, and having great natural ability, was an innate leader, a real free spirit who loved the outdoors with the same intensity that he abhorred books. He had a lean taut body and sinewy arms that reminded me of Mr. Lord's trip hammers at the blacksmith. Staying pretty much to himself, Amzy pestered no one, and he in turn didn't expect for others to pester him. I don't recall anyone around town ever messing with Amzy Criswell.

During September of my freshman year, we were looking for things to do before winter settled in. Not far from Lottie's Place on the banks of Dog Creek was a huge cottonwood tree. Amzy said it was the perfect place for a super bag swing, the kind that could sail Tarzan fashion, way out over the creek. The idea immediately captured our imaginations, and we enlisted nearby Jack Beaman.

First we had to build a platform in an adjacent tree, a place where we could grab the swing and launch ourselves for the great ride. Probably because of his leadership, and the fact he owned the rope, Amzy became the project foreman. "Jack, pack this lumber up that tree to me and I'll start building the platform," and "Tom, you shinny up that cottonwood and on out over that limb yonder. When you're up there, I'll get the rope to you." It was a swing that would soon become known far and wide.

Amzy tied a stuffed and weighted burlap bag to the end of the rope. We planned to use it to swing far from our high platform much the same as trapeze artists do in a circus act. When the bag returned, one of us would leap for the rope, grip the bag with our legs, and take a thrilling ride into what seemed like space. I remember how the wind whistled by my ears, and how the sisal rope always made ominous popping sounds like it would break but never did. At the highest point, we were at least twenty-five to thirty feet off the ground with Dog Creek gurgling beneath. The creek made it exciting, and its muddy bottom served as a safety net in case of a failed jump.

Amzy soon invented the manly game of "chicken." The platform would accommodate four kids, and we'd each take our turn while others lined up on the ground ten feet below. The rule was for the rider to bring the bag to his nose and then, with no push, release it like a pendulum. On the first swing the bag would almost come back to our high platform for an easy leap. We'd ride a couple of oscillations and then go to the rear of the line to work up. We called a simple first swing grab "Firsts." It was so easy, even girls could do it. More sporting was "seconds" because we had to wait for the second full swing of the bag, the creek beckoning far below. I remember Amzy used to say, "Makes your bung tingle don't it?"

Naturally, as with everything, a code of honor developed. It was honorable to leap and miss, but to chicken out—like a kid refusing on a high diving board—was dishonor. A chicken was hooted and razzed, "ah, you pantywaist!," and he'd be sent to the rear of the line. If it happened two or three times, the chickens usually quietly withdrew to seek more humane sport.

Everyone could do "seconds," but the third swing became hairy. Fourths required a really bold long leap, and to miss was to plunge ignominiously into the soft bottomed creek. Fifty percent of our crowd could usually do "fourths," which is why we never wore good clothing. Jack and I were four swing men, a couple of bigger boys around town could do fives, but only Amzy had the nerve and strength for Big Six.

Amzy engineered his own secret advantage. Because no other ever tried for "six," Amzy would be on the platform alone, and before the bag started its sixth swing, he'd begin violently pumping his legs. He'd have everything, including the limbs the platform was attached to, springing up and down. Then, in perfect coordination with the wildly springing platform, Amzy would catapult himself like a jungle monkey far out over the creek. He always just made a fingernail grab, and we'd cheer his feat. One day Amzy tried valiantly for "sevens," until he looked so much like a drowned rat, he never again tried "sevens." We all figured if Amzy couldn't do "sevens," it must be a physical impossibility.

This placed Amzy in hero status, and I suppose Jack and I followed him around as if he was the chief and we were his loyal braves. Everyone heard of "the bag," and on weekends kids bolted their breakfasts in their haste for Dog Creek. It was a wonderful time to be alive in Winelda.

THE GRAND AWAKENING—OCTOBER 1937

Homer accepted Mom Cable's advice about my scholastic prowess, and pretty well laid off me through the remainder of grade school. To be sure, when I brought a report card home, he would grumble, but he no longer went into rampages, or became overly physical. I believe he reached the conclusion that once I reached high school there would be an epiphany, and everything would miraculously repair itself.

Unfortunately, after the first six weeks of school punctuated by bag swings and becoming an owner of pigs, my very first report card in high school was lackluster. Homer ignored my A in agriculture and the B+ in geography; he saw only the D's in both algebra and English, and the C- in something else. I remember I stood silently by the kitchen table for quite a number of minutes while Homer perused the card. It was if he were auditing the Majestic's financial statement. A couple of times he broke the silence with aversive grunts. All in all, I thought he contained himself pretty well. It was also still warm weather, and he felt good, and was completely sober, all of which boded especially well for me.

Then with a low somewhat faint voice he said, "Let me tell you something, Son," and I quickly detected suppressed rage in Homer's voice. It was his I-am-straining-to-be-civil posture, and I knew my position was rapidly deteriorating. It was like standing on very thin ice, listening to faint cracking and popping sounds. As Homer's eyes shifted up and down the report card, they were no longer tranquil. Then suddenly his flashing eyes were riveted on mine—very angry eyes. This was my biological father, but he was exhibiting not the slightest hint of paternal love or friendship. In my peripheral vision, I could see Maddy shifting her eyes uncomfortably between Homer and me.

Homer tapped the report card with a stubby finger of indictment. "What is indicated by 'Does not pay attention in class?' Does it mean you sit there tra-la-la gawking out the window, or that you're goofing around with one of your friends?" These were in essence indictments and not real questions. "How do you think you can possibly compete," oh, here we go, "with boys from Oklahoma City, and Tulsa, or Houston when you can't even match wits with your class here in Winelda?" I had learned not to appear bored at such times, even though Homer had often repeated this same litany over the years, except this time I noticed he had substituted Houston for San Diego. I wore my most soulful blank expression, which I intended to suggest unremarkable intelligence yet, a fervent plea for leniency. "*Well?*" he shouted. "What the *hell* does it *mean*?" Now Homer's engine was fully revved, and he was outraged.

I tried my level best to appear very distressed, which I was. I knitted my eyebrows to indicate concern and contriteness. I was unaware of it at the time, but a few years later Aaron Fischer told me my contrived facial expressions were very close to making Homer burst into laughter. But because the moment was serious, Homer could scarcely afford laughter.

"I'm not going to waste my time telling you how important your high school record will be when you eventually attempt to gain admittance to a university. To you that probably seems a distant four years, but believe me, it's only just around the corner." Homer lit a cigarette and bullishly snorted the smoke. "Tom," he said quietly and deliberately, "how can I climb inside your thick skull to convey to you that no self-respecting university will ever permit you inside its main gate. For God's sake, wouldn't you rather have them clamoring for you instead of *bolting their doors?*" I thought that analogy funny until he banged the table with his fist.

I responded with a very weak, "Yes."

"*What?*" snapped Homer.

I said, "*Yes, sir!*" The situation had suddenly turned formal.

"Your grades have been a matter of contention since our arrival in Winelda, but like Mom said, I decided to let it ride until high school, let you enjoy boyhood. By now I figured you'd have grown up, and would have sufficient sense to come in out of the rain without having to be hauled in like some moronic sheep." Homer's stare knifed into my eyes until I shifted my own down to the tabletop. *"Look at me! Now let me make something crystal clear to you. Next six weeks . . .* that's a month and a half from now . . . you'll be walking in here with your second report card of the semester. Now you listen very carefully because this is what is known as a peremptory ultimatum . . . if you don't know what that means you'd best look it up." Homer commenced rapping the tabletop with his fist. "When you walk back in here six weeks from now I want you to be on the *honor roll*! Nothing below a B. Repeat . . . ." He punctuated each word in an eerie breathy whisper, "Nothing - below - a - B." He finished with, *"you got that?"*

This death sentence was stunning, and my eyes widened in disbelief. Homer's demand was ridiculously impossible, absurd.

"I had once thought," he continued, "the night job at the theater might interfere, but you obviously don't even use class time to advantage. After the show starts, and after most of the people are seated, you can, if you apply yourself, study in the lobby. There are few interruptions then. You can also get in another hour of study when you go home at half past nine instead of hanging out in front of the Corner talking to your cronies. Organize your time. But remember what I said," and he pointed his accusing finger at me. "Anything less than the honor roll and you, my boy, will experience a truly grand awakening. It'll be curtains for you, Tommy boy. *Curtains!* I'm sick to death of this perpetual academic conundrum. By God I deserve better!" He banged the table so hard the place settings jumped a couple of inches from the cloth.

Homer was caught up by his words and he rolled on, "I'm bigger than you, Tom, a helluva lot bigger, and you aren't too old to spank or to push around . . . if that's what it takes then prepare yourself. Six weeks from today, if I gotta kick ass, then by God that's the course we'll take. My liberal approach to gain some detectable cooperation from you has obviously failed abjectly . . . completely! If you were incapable of the honor roll my demands would be cruel and unreasonable. But you *are* capable . . . of that I'm sure."

Homer flipped over the card, and with a John Hancock flourish he scrawled a strong "Homer Cable" on the back, which indicated to the principal he had read the card. Homer dated it, snapped it up off the table, and handed it to me. "Now get into your room and look at your books until dinner. We have over an hour before the show."

Very shortly Maddy tapped on the door. Somehow I knew it

would be Maddy. She came into my room and surprised me by putting her arms around me. She hugged me ever so lightly. This made me feel very sorry for myself. "Tom, now you listen," she said in hushed tones. "You're in high school now, and you must do better. Homer's very disappointed. He's also angry, and I'm afraid he means business. Remember that grasshopper story, 'Oh the world owes me a living teedle, daddle, teedle, daddle, dum?' Well, let me tell you something, Tom. No one out there owes you anything. You must make it for yourself. You can be proud you have such a fine dad that cares. Some dads would just let you skate right into oblivion, and you'd eventually wind up in a shack on the banks of Dog Creek. He's got big plans for you." She looked at my hair and casually rubbed her hand through it and arranged it. "He doesn't want you spending your life on the railroad's section gang shoveling gravel and pounding spikes. He wants you to attend college as a student and not as one of the janitors." It was Maddy's first time to ever speak to me in such a way.

"Ah, Maddy," I said. "What am I gonna do? The honor roll! I've never come close."

"You'll make it, Tom. You've got to start studying, and if you pay close attention in class, you can sometimes learn as much as by reading your books." She pushed me out at arm's length, and like a kid I was working hard not to bawl. "So," she said, "how about making me proud of you. Also, I've got a prize if next time around you make the honor roll."

"What prize?"

"Don't tell your dad because he wouldn't approve of paying for grades, but if you make the honor roll, I'm slipping you a five dollar bill for your bank account." This was a substantial sum of money. "Remember," she said, "it's our secret." Then she kissed me on the forehead, and as she closed the door behind her she said, "By the way, tomorrow morning wash your hair."

I sat on the windowsill and looked forlornly down at Etta's Café. I thought how unreasonable life was. God! The honor roll was really for girls. Like his aspirations for me in football, Homer may have also had dreams that overreached my intellect. He was patently wrong because the honor roll was well beyond my grasp. I suddenly remembered "peremptory" and looked it up—final, dictatorial, no denial, no refusal. The word "final" had special significance. It seemed to shimmer on the page.

Like salvation beckoning to me, a large freight whistled at the Broadway crossing. I could find an empty boxcar and ride to California. But California was so far. I could run to Mom's sanctuary in Anthony, but I knew Homer would appear, and like a hooked fish, he'd chuck me in his creel and trot me back to Winelda. I thought seriously of Father Flanagan's Boy's Town in Omaha. I could show up there as Majenski from Ohio and be lost forever to the Cable family. But what about Mom and Pop? What about the pigs? I couldn't just run off to wherever.

I had no viable alternative other than to give the books my best shot. If that wasn't good enough, then come next six weeks I'd go down just like a ship at Trafalgar, with all my sails on fire. Rather than return home, I'd just jump off the Cimarron River Bridge, and as a spirit I could wing around the Methodist Church and savor watching everyone mourn at my own funeral. They wouldn't have Tom Cable to kick around any more.

Down at Etta's they were playing a new record, a plaintive cowboy ballad that matched my own mood. At that very moment, I decided high school was a complete bust. In only six weeks the coach had rejected me from football, and now the riot act had been read. I made my peremptory decision; if I tried my best and then got banged around, I was determined to take the freight. I'd go west. Like the last movie I had seen, I'd feign amnesia, change my name, and possibly some nice California family would adopt me.

NOT SOMEONE TO TRIFLE WITH

As the Thanksgiving festivities approached, I knew the second cursed report card was only days away. I will be the first to admit that some good had evolved from Homer's edict. I had opened the books and discovered interesting things on their pages. In geography, I learned that Maine's Aroostook County and Idaho's Boise Project produced the most potatoes in America. That evening, as we cut into our baked potato, I said, "Does anyone know where our potatoes come from?"

Maddy said, "Idaho."

"And another place?" I asked, and after some lengthy thought,

Homer came up with Maine. "You know which county?" Ha! Only I knew about Aroostook County.

All my life I had heard these trivia battles in the Cable kitchen: "What's the highest mountain in the forty-eight states; what's the world's biggest lake; what's the third largest island in the world?" I had never had a clue, but Mom, Pop, Uncle Virgil, or Aunt Lily would come up with the answers. Sometimes Mom would say, "You want to bet on that, Homer?" and Homer would answer, "A dollar says I'm sure." And if the bet was called, there'd come the riffling through the pages of the encyclopedia or the dictionary. This had always been exciting, and I had always wanted to participate, but I had never known the answers. Now I was discovering.

I really liked geography, and even began second guessing the teacher for the next day's test questions. Instead of drudgery, I began looking upon schoolwork as a mental competition with my classmates. It was a little like the bag swing, and I wanted to win. By the time the second six weeks ended, I was one of three in the class to make an A in geography. I squeaked through Algebra with a weak B and an A- in Agriculture.

My real failing was English. Miss Strickland had launched us into diagramming sentences, which to me was an enigmatic jumble of predicate adjectives, gerunds, dependent clauses, and objects of prepositional phrases. During the first six weeks, I had unfortunately missed much of the basic work because of my lack of interest, but I was catching up. I believe Miss Strickland could see the filament in my light bulb beginning to glow where before there had not been a glimmer. No longer was I looking out the window, no more paper wads, and no more chuckles with Jack. This business of education had taken a deadly serious turn. I hadn't done so badly in English so Miss Strickland was happy to give me a C+ for effort.

When handed my report card that afternoon, it suddenly dawned on me it was my best ever: two A's, two B's and a C+. Then I remembered Homer's peremptory ultimatum. Nothing below a B! A C+ was not honor roll caliber. Homer's terms had been as clear as crystal, and regardless of the great improvement, this was not within Homer's parameters. I knew he would not relent. I'd come so close but come that evening, I was quite sure there would be no happiness at Homer's Place.

I went from euphoria to numbness, and although school was out and the hallways empty, I sat in the basketball bleachers looking at the dumb card, and I knew how the condemned felt. In deep thought, I sauntered through the darkened hallways of WHS. After a few circuits, I noticed that every time I completed a full circle of the hallways, I was standing in front of Miss Strickland's homeroom that was also her office. From time to time I could see her shadow move through the frosted glass of her door. She was in there, sitting at her desk going over papers.

Miss Strickland was awesome, a lady from the rough and tumble and severe panhandle of Oklahoma, a stern disciplinarian, indubitably WHS's best educated, and certainly not a person to trifle with. Yet everyone in our class knew her to be very fair. I had little doubt my C+ was exactly what I had earned. The thought of altering the report card actually entered my troubled mind, but all the Cables had constantly hammered into me that crime did not pay, and with my luck, it would be a memorable disaster. Suddenly, I found myself cautiously opening Miss Strickland's door.

"Why, hello, Tom," she said, peering over the top of her granny glasses. She was friendly, but there was no special rapport between us. She glanced at her watch, curious as to why I was there a full thirty minutes after the final bell. "What brings you to see me?" she said, and I wanted to run like Hammerhead's stallion.

But I found myself laying my report card in front of her, and like an automaton saying, "I wanted you to see my report card."

And as she picked it up, I could see her eyes flicking from the first six weeks to this one. "Yes, Tom," she said, "I wanted to tell you how pleased I've been this past six weeks with your attention in my class." She scanned the card, "Yes, compared to your first six weeks this is indeed excellent progress," and she removed her glasses and handed me the card.

"Miss Strickland, you'll notice I would have made the honor roll if you hadn't given me the C+." God, but I didn't want this to sound accusatory in any way. It was just a factual statement.

Slightly on guard, she took the card, and glanced at it again. "Yes, that's true, Tom, but it's what you earned. I'm sure next period, if you continue this improvement, you should easily earn a B."

I uttered, "Miss Strickland," and then I let all the words tumble out about how important this particular card was. I added, "And if you'll change my grade from C+ to a B-, just that very small change, I

promise you during the next six weeks, I'll earn an A in your class."
There. I had presented my plea bargain. I literally gritted my teeth.

I had no way of knowing that Ila Strickland had never in her
career had a student ask to have a grade changed, and to do so was
not her way. Her premise was, "you get what you earn." As she
viewed me stonily, I felt like the dissected frog in biology. I had
mentioned nothing about my impending punishment, but to break the
silence I said, "It'll really make my dad happy, and if I can make it this
time, I promise to stay on the Honor Roll." I re-emphasized, "You can
count on it, Miss Strickland, next time I will make an A in your class."

I'll never know, but I believe my final fervent plea is what sold Ila
Strickland. I had asked her to excuse those two or three points just
that one time. I had possibly made her feel she might actually become
responsible for unveiling a potentially good student, that she might
spark me to greater academic achievement. At least that's the way I
had it figured.

Finally she said, "Tom, I'm taking you at your word, and I know
you know what that means? If you go back on your word, it would be
a great disappointment to me." She looked sternly over her glasses
and let it hang there for what seemed an eternity. It was so quiet, I
could hear the flooring creak and the ticking of the Seth Thomas in the
hall. "Tom, I'll do it with two provisos; you'll tell no one I've changed
your grade—it's between you and me—and number two," she emphasized by pointing her index finger toward the ceiling, "this next six
weeks you'll *earn* the A you promised me." She tucked her chin in a
little tighter, and I was on notice. Now I had to contend with both
Homer and Ila Strickland—neither were to be trifled with.

I stood up straight, "I'll do that, Miss Strickland. You can count on
it." For just an instant I thought I could see a Mona Lisa smile, but it
quickly faded to the obdurate face of the Pioneer Woman statue at
Ponca City—very determined, very cold and bronzy, not a glimmer of
warmth.

Ila Strickland raised her chin so high I thought she was trying to
view me from under her glasses. Was she reconsidering? Suddenly,
she took some chlorine ink remover and very thoroughly blotted the
C+.

"I want you to know, Tom," she said as she carefully inked in a B-
. "I've never done this before," and she handed me the card. "Now,
run along and don't become a disappointment." And there was still

Homer's Place

no smile. I later wondered if I had made her feel dirty.

I wasn't sure whether to hug Ila Strickland, shake her hand, or to bow. I simply said, "Thanks, Miss Strickland, you won't be disappointed." She only gazed at me as if I were an insect, said nothing, and didn't so much as nod. I closed her door and ran down the empty hallway to the front door of the building. Normally I would've been off to play until our six o'clock dinner siren, but I ran the three blocks to the Winelda Square, and into the office of the theater where I knew I'd find Homer and probably Maddy.

I flung the door open, and there was Homer with a little cloud of cigarette smoke around his head. He gave me a slight look of exasperation because in mid-sentence I had interrupted Mac Holstein, a representative of Warner Brothers out of Oklahoma City. The two of them were jousting over a contract for next spring's films.

"I'm busy, Tom," he said sternly. "Mac, this is my son, Tom."

"Nice to meet you, Son," he put out his hand. "I have a boy about your age."

"It'll keep, Dad. Here's my report card. I'll see you at dinner."

I turned to leave, but Homer commanded, "Hold it! Just a second there, Hot Shot, hold your horses." He opened the report card and scanned it quickly, and his eyes lit up. "Well, by God, you made it! We even have some A's here." After a moment, he said to Mac Holstein, "Mac, I'm sorry as hell to interrupt this. Let me see you here after dinner, and we'll finish this. I've got to take my son down to the Corner for an ice cream soda." Homer put his arm around my shoulders, and we started to leave. "Sorry, Mac. Hope you'll understand. I'll make it up to you with the contract." Mac Holstein not only understood but he was quite touched by Homer's reaction.

I was nine feet tall as we walked the half block to the Corner, particularly when Homer stopped and said, "Tom you've made me real proud of you. You just won't understand how very happy you've made me." Again, he stopped in front of McBride's Grocery, "Put her there, Pardner," and Homer put out his hand and we shook hands.

Homer's response floored me. It was better than the American Legion Award. It was worth much more than all the extra study. To myself, I vowed to keep on doing it, if for nothing else than to see Homer's tremendous satisfaction. Suddenly, there was a solid new relationship between us. And this new rapport never faltered unless Homer was hitting the bottle, and when that happened, I didn't look upon him as being Homer.

From that day forward, I was never again off the Honor Roll—a whole new world. I found it relatively easy to stay on, and I began working to turn B's into A's. I had also gained a new silent friend in Miss Strickland. Later on, in senior year, she told me she felt partly responsible for my new turn, and she was right. I would have never let her down. And, yes, Maddy did slip me the five dollars; it was our secret.

TURKEY TOSS—THANKSGIVING 1937

Fall was a good time in Winelda, and with it came the great annual Thanksgiving Turkey Toss. According to the Chamber of Commerce, and the *Winelda Enterprise*, there was nothing like it in all of Northwest Oklahoma.

Just opposite Homer's Place and the drawing barrel, the Bird Committee took thirty birds—turkeys, some fat chickens, and a few guinea hens—to the roof of the two story Thorne's Hardware. The moment the drawing's five dollar ticket was announced, a loudspeaker behind the crowd boomed, "The Annual Turkey Toss is about to git started!" and the curb to curb crowd filling the intersection of Main and Cecil collectively about faced and looked toward the roof of Thorne's.

"Now look what I have here," boomed the speaker. And there on the ledge was a huge, copper colored Tom turkey alertly surveying the crowd below as if it were a politician about to speak. Then they shoved the turkey, and it flapped its huge wings and soared over the crowd. It came down very soon to the clutches of a man standing in front of Etta's Café. "I got 'im. I got 'im." And because there were so many witnesses at hand, no one was ever gauche enough to go clawing after someone else's bird.

"And ladies and gentlemen . . . another!" This beautiful Tom flew high across Main toward Homer's Place and banked steeply left. Possibly its sharp turn created excessive G's which manifested the release of the bowels. "Aw shit!" some one below yelled. It was an unusual word for a Wineldan family crowd. He continued, "Now wouldja jist look at this here new shirt, gol-dang it to hale!" Several new and old Stetsons were also liberally splashed, which was an even worse offense.

Half a block down in front of the Majestic stood Ten-Gallon, grinning from ear to ear, with Myrnie beside him. He rose above the crowd like a pylon and easily saw the bird strafing down Main Street directly for him. Ten-Gallon reached out, clamped his vise-like hand around the turkey's leg, and immediately canceled its flight plan.

"Lookit, Myrnie. Lookit what I done," he said with his Adam's apple bumping up and down.

Little Myrnie, standing on her toes, could barely see the action, but she saw the big Tom turkey and hugged Ten-Gallon fiercely. "Yer sure the provider, Hawney," she said as she hugged him tightly. She never failed to turn giddy with excitement and Ten-Gallon grinned.

After the toss, Ten-Gallon secured his bird to the rack atop the V-8, went to see a movie and had no concern at all that anyone would steal his bird. In spite of the Depression, Winelda's society was good. I must admit, however, that, when in season, there was an occasional watermelon stolen from the Johnson patch east of town. But, in all my years in Winelda, no one ever tried to steal the drawing barrel, or a car, no one ever stole one of the one hundred from Homer's marquee. And except for some idiotic prose on Etta's restroom wall, graffiti was virtually unknown.

But to return to the toss, one intrepid guinea hen proved disappointing. The heavy bird went off the roof, turned left and by the time it reached the post office it was flying at an unnerving, feather whistling speed. Hands grabbed wildly, and some said they felt the flick of feathers, but this only catalyzed the hen to push all its engines to full throttle. It rose over Freddy Dad's Produce like a Pan American China Clipper. Three blocks south, next to the phone company, it landed in the crown of Winelda's tallest Elm. By dusk it was still there, its head tucked under a wing; by dawn it had literally flown the coop.

Another disappointment was a very fat capon, a miserable flyer that never once flapped its wings. It crashed resoundingly on the corrugated tin roof that sheltered the sidewalk, bounced off in a fluff of feathers and into the hands of a surprised man, who because of his poor location, thought nothing could possibly come his way. The bird was temporarily unconscious, but just fine for Sunday's dinner.

Because many birds behaved miserably, and could possibly give the Winelda Toss a bad name, they counseled the Bird Committee not to use chickens, or guineas, and to never again feed turkeys the morning of the toss.

NO FAMILY CAR, NO BICYCLE

Another Christmas was coming and I knew the gloom period of the winter's blue northers was nearby. Unlike the High Sierras, Colorado's Rockies, or New England's Green Mountains, Winelda was certainly not a winter wonderland in which to enjoy snow. To be sure, there was snow, but no one could ever ski or sled on it like at New York's Lake Placid or Bear Mountain. The snow never seemed to land anywhere, it just howled horizontally to the ground. Oh, there were isolated drifts ten feet deep, yet vast areas were windswept to the dirt. Kids in Winelda saw sleds in the Montgomery Ward catalog, but no one owned one. They or skis would've been utterly ridiculous in Winelda. Winter in Northwest Oklahoma was a relentless, rawboned, finger and ear numbing ten or twenty degrees, usually blasted along by a twenty to twenty-five mile per hour wind. How does the song go, "Oklahoma where the wind goes sweeping down the plain" or some such? Less romantically, it indeed swept gritty sand to pelt the face, and it sent tumbleweeds bounding down Main Street.

Heralded by the bitter winter would come Homer's splenetic funks—the concomitant drinking—and his health again would generally deteriorate. Homer's meteorological pattern had grown ever predictable. Also predictable, I knew with the first freezing weather Homer would again let me know how he used to ice skate from Ellinwood up the Arkansas River to Great Bend and back. This old story was still exciting, but few in Winelda related to ice skating. Neither the Cimarron nor Dog Creek was skateable. In the spring, Dog Creek could become a raging torrent a quarter of a mile wide, but come winter, it was nothing but a trickle connecting little intermittent crawdad holes. It had too many brush snags poking up and not enough ice for any serious skating. Also, the Cimarron was oddly salty and never froze, and there wasn't a single lake close to town worthy of mention. These were the reasons why no Wineldan owned a pair of ice skates, or snowshoes, or other snow gear.

And bicycles! Homer avoided any mention of bicycles. I had

begun to believe he had something against bikes. To this day, I'm not sure if he ever owned one. Yet ever since the fourth grade, I had strongly hinted for a bike, an issue that was starting to annoy me. I even wondered if perhaps some of my Wineldan friends thought we were disadvantaged.

We had no car. Almost all Wineldan families in both town and country had a car. Only the thrifty Mexican, the very poor, and the Cables had no car. I assumed that Homer covertly imposed this self-denial because he and cars had had their careless, reckless moments. I had to give Homer credit for this deferred judgment, especially when I recall how often we fretted when Homer took off roaring drunk in Mom's Chrysler, and how upon return, it had more dings than ever before. Tired of broaching the subject of a bicycle, one day I went directly to the car issue. Homer shot right back, "Why on earth a car? Every store in town is within a block of us; the theater's two hundred feet away. Cars cost money to operate." All of these propositions were grounded in such obvious good sense, I had no worthwhile counter.

When it came to Depression investments, Homer's acumen was more than impressive. I knew for a fact that the people over at the Ford Agency had offered Homer a brand new V-8 if he would only trade them the big "timed" bank safe Homer now had in the office of the Majestic. A terrific safe, it had a big crank to open its threaded, foot thick door of gleaming nickel steel. Inside its door were three impressive and expensive Longines time clocks. These could be set for the next opening time. Even so, how could Homer refuse a brand new Ford V-8? Yet, he flat turned it down. He said the safe was a useful place to store money, and the V-8 was like a hole that would gobble it up. In this regard, I had to admire Homer for his self-discipline. Now, if Homer could only abstain from alcohol and tobacco as effectively as he had the V-8 and my bicycle, I figured he'd be ready to preach on Sundays.

As to the bike situation, it is true my older friend, Amzy, did not own a bike. However, it seemed every other Winelda kid my age had one; even girls were tooling around the Square on bicycles. Were we really poor folks? After all, Homer owned outright two buildings in the heart of Winelda, and was collecting rent from three businesses.

Yet, Christmas would come and go and there would be no bicycle. I was beginning to wonder if Homer would think I'd be ready for one by the time college rolled around. Perhaps he planned it as my wedding present.

THE PIGS

Come the first week in April, my pigs Porky and Bessie were fat, but now that the big marketing moment was upon me, I had mixed emotions. The pigs had become both friends and pets. The thought of someone knocking them in the head to harvest a few pork chops started weighing heavily on my mind.

My agriculture teacher told me how much the pigs should bring. Therefore, when the butcher at Hutchison's Grocery bettered the estimate by four extra dollars, I was more than happy to get out from under. Calculating my profit was easy because careful records had comprised a good part of our grade. After caring for them twice a day, seven days a week, for almost eight months, I sold the friendship of Porky and Bessie for a pure profit of seven dollars and eighty-five cents, a signal fiscal achievement.

I reported this to Homer, and he shrugged.

"What?" I complained. "That's not bad for a towny. Some of the farm kids actually lost money on their projects."

Homer conceded it hadn't been a total waste of time; after all, I had become a walking encyclopedia of pig lore. But I was quick to perceive that this was the opportunity Homer had long awaited. He grabbed pencil and paper and soon calculated that I had spent four hundred and fifty-three hours carrying slop et cetera and had earned about two cents per hour. He triumphantly threw down the pencil, "You worked for peanuts, Cable. If you think that's good business, then I pass. If you're willing to work for two cents an hour then never again suggest to me your five bucks a week at the Majestic is insufficient." Homer was on a roll. "One of these days soon," he said, "I'll show you how to do even better, better than your work at the Majestic, better than delivering newspapers," and he rested his case.

I banked my pig money, but I experienced no joy in delivering my porcine friends to the slaughterhouse. I knew they'd be butchered for local consumption, so I asked Maddy not to buy a pork roast or chops from Hutchison's during the next month. I couldn't have handled the possibility of dining on Porky and Bessie.

NEVER ENOUGH TIME

Homer always placed heavy demands on my time. I am sure he was well aware I worked both the Saturday and Sunday matinées and every night show, and that I spent a good part of Saturday morning shining the brass on the Majestic's front. I also knew better than to remind him. After all, I was getting paid. Homer was no ogre, but he never once let me miss my evening work at the Majestic unless there was a rare school play or an overnight camp out. Possibly he figured if I had time on my hands, I'd start girling around, and then the trouble would start. If he was actually fretting about girls and me, it was a waste of his time. At that stage of my life, girls were only mysteries to be fathomed; none had yet become heavy on my mind.

Quite frankly, I savored my job at the theater. Other than church socials, Winelda had virtually no organized evening events. Once the sun went down, the Majestic was the hottest item in town—it, and the soda fountains, and Eastman's, and Etta's Café. I liked greeting our customers, and as Homer said, I genuinely tried to "Make 'em glad they had come to the Majestic."

Another big plus was the opportunity to see every picture. Except for the heavies starring George Brent, Paul Muni, Bette Davis, or Joan Crawford, all were appealing, even after two or three showings. The heavies I categorized as dull "love pictures." Regardless, I saw them all, and I could immediately identify every actor in Hollywood, even those with lowly supporting roles—those who constantly played the same type butler, thug, or maid role. From the director's name, I could predict the type of picture it would be. I even knew the names of costume designers like Edith Head. Gowns by Edith Head. Gowns by Irene. I wondered why it was always gowns instead of dresses or clothes. The only gowns in Winelda were women's nightgowns.

I'm sure Homer was aware that during school months I had little time to call my own. The few hours between school and our six o'clock dinner were all I could claim. Next fall, if I made the team, even those hours would be gone. I always assumed Homer never worked me any harder than Pop had probably worked him. Like Pop, he wanted me to appreciate the effort it took to come by money. This made outright handouts as rare as birthdays.

Consequently, being bored was definitely not one of my problems.

Even during the summer there never seemed to be sufficient time. I believe Homer took that into account. He'd remember his skating on the Arkansas River, and the secret island clubhouse he and his Ellinwood friends built back in 1910. I believe that was why he let me off at least one Saturday afternoon a month after the brass had been shined. He let me take off with Jack or Amzy to explore caves, catch snakes and horned toads, or to search along Dog Creek for dogwood, or for the ever elusive white owl. To be able to find dogwood suitable for bows and arrows, or the perfect Y-stick for a super "bean" shooter was to us an art few of our peers had mastered. When it came to trail-craft, we sensed we were the very best.

THE CIMARRON—APRIL 1938

In late April, at the close of my freshman year, Amzy planned a trip "to the mountains"—our appellation for the fascinating flat top mesas across the Cimarron. This was the exciting area where Homer had taken my little friends and me on a picnic four years earlier.

Initially, we asked Jack Beaman to go, but he would never accompany us. "Walk ten miles for fun?" he'd say. "You guys gotta be nuts!" So, when WWII came, it was a grave injustice when the U.S. Army made Jack an infantryman, and he wound up as a rifleman in General Gill's famous 32nd Red Arrow Division. Jack fought the Japanese foot by foot across New Guinea's rugged and steaming Owen Stanley Mountains. It was, without contest, the ultimate cruelty to a guy who abhorred an afternoon's hike to the hills.

Outbound, Amzy and I always followed the Santa Fe mainline tracks. After a couple or so miles we'd reach the railroad bridge that spanned the mighty Cimarron. It was a lengthy—just short of a mile—trestle bent structure with no side rails. Since the collapse of the West River Bridge, it was the only westerly way to cross the Cimarron. Had Homer cautioned us about the bridge, it would have meant he condoned the trespass. So, he opted never to discuss it. Perhaps he took solace in knowing Wineldan kids were railroad savvy. After all, we lived on the Santa Fe's principal southern route. We should certainly have enough sense not to get caught in the middle of a long bridge with a high speed freight bearing down. In any event, my training wheels were off, and Homer had unofficially passed the baton to Amzy. "Pay attention to Amzy," he would say. "And remember, there's quicksand along the Cimarron."

When we reached the bridge, we listened for a train by sticking our noses in the air like wild animals searching prey. After all, we were indeed animal trackers with keen senses. To our front, the west, there was no danger because we could see three or four miles of track. Our rear was the problem because in only three quarters of a mile the track curved out of sight. It hid the possibility of a doubleheader, of two roaring 4000 engines coming hell for leather. Just as portrayed in numerous movies, we expertly knelt and placed an ear to the rails.

Hearing absolutely nothing, we commenced our rhythmic lope. Rhythmic because we had to time our steps to the ties and not hit into the deep graveled chasms in between. We also had to be very careful not to dart glances at the river on our left and right. We'd already discovered that, with no side rails, it was a surefire way to lose balance and plunge fifty feet to the Cimarron's swirling waters. We had sprung along quite rapidly—over a third of the distance—when suddenly, like a rifle shot from our rear, we heard the unnerving shrillness of a whistle! It was the engineer's brake test whistle signifying all was okay and full speed ahead. At that very moment, Amzy and I forever concluded that pressing an ear to a rail was pure Hollywood bullshit.

The sight of two huge locomotives bearing down was benumbing!

They were belching tornadic clouds of smoke. From their cylinders white steam shot forty to fifty feet horizontally, and there was absolutely no indication of braking. It was all resolute power and tons of speeding steel, and the timing was perfect; it caught us at a point of no return.

A hundred feet ahead we spotted one of the escape ladders built for workmen. We raced to it and looked below at the angry Cimarron in spring flood—boiling and whirlpooling, an ominous mist created by its own violent moiling. The creosoted short ladder looked so fragile. Could it be rotten? Then came another murderous bung puckering whistle, and the decision was easy. It was fortunate that we had both peed just before going onto the bridge. Over the side we went. Descending its four or five rungs, we stood on the last rung gripping and hugging the wood, and each other. I suppose we both prayed the thing would hold us.

The steel behemoths came onto the bridge, and the massive bridge began shaking ominously—about a 7.5 Richter—and as the train raced nearer, the intensity magnified. The pandemonium was cataclysmic. The intense Doppler shift of sound waves came—*Bam*—along with the concussive shock of wind from those massive 4000s. The scream of eight hundred steel wheels turned our blood to ice. Amzy and I were in a nether world—a maniacal freight above and the crazy river beckoning us from below. Each was reaching out, each hell bent to have us, neither impressed with how expert we were.

As a possible alternative, I peered below at the scary, eddying water just in time to see a bloated steer swirl by—a clear reminder that eager death skulked there. I actually visualized the hollow eyed guy in the black cape with the huge scythe. Reality returned when a handful of tomato sized ballast rocks jiggled down and clunked my collarbone. Again, the noise steadily built to yet another thunderous crescendo. How was it possible? Louder and louder it became until another shock wave clapped our ears. The pusher locomotive blasted by us gushing steam.

Suddenly there remained only the sound of the rushing water. The big bridge again felt as immovable as Gibraltar, and the train's distant whistle was like its laugh at the perfect trick it had just played on us.

Had our luck been good or bad? We weren't sure how to view it. I remember Amzy said, "Well, I hope that weren't no ill omen."

Back atop the bridge, I looked down at the ladder, and some of my fear returned. Everything normal, I would never have gone down that frail little ladder made of creosote blackened two by fours. I suddenly thought of movies where the hero escaped capture by jumping off a high cliff into a river far below. Now I better understood how such an event was possible. Had there been no escape ladder, jumping was certainly an unwanted alternative.

In unison, Amzy and I quickly looked to the rear, and without further discussion, we hustled onward.

AMZY—YOU KILLED ME!

Once across the bridge, the geological change was magical. We had just come from the sandy sagebrush knolls, but once across the river, it might just as well have been the Sonoran Desert—red clay and alkali flats salted lightly with mesquite and big clumps of prickly pear cactus. Overlooking the torrid flats like huge sentinels were the majestic mesas capped with alabaster that sparkled and shimmered in the bright Oklahoma sun. This had indeed once been real Indian country, a place where Coronado may have walked, and for just an afternoon, it certainly made us feel as if we were Lewis and Clark.

We went two miles farther west toward a mesa no one ever visited. Amzy and I called it No-Name Mesa. We always avoided Three-Step Mesa, the next one to the north, because its aura had been sullied. Before the West River Bridge collapsed, even girls had climbed it. And because a dirt road passed near its base, people had once picnicked at Three-Step, thus eclipsing any claim as pristine territory. Many had climbed its steep slopes to view the marvelous Cimarron Valley. By contrast, No-Name Mesa was our definition of Shangri-la because there was no road and there were no ranch houses in view—no people. Also, at its feet were the enigmatic remains of the two melted sod houses we had previously discovered.

In search of local history, we always poked around this fascinating sod house site, obviously inhabited by long gone settlers. In past excursions, we had found Indian head pennies and a few flint arrowheads. We'd finger those artifacts, pass them back and forth, and fantasize. It did not take great imagination to visualize the pioneer firing his Philo Remington rifle from the doorway with Indians circling this sod house. In the background of our minds, we could even hear the hooting and the hoof beats and see the red dust. Amzy never failed to say, "Happened right here, Tom. Right here on this spot, and nobuddy knows."

We tracked around the sod mounds in ever greater circles, hoping to discover poking from the dirt a grave marker, something with a date or name that might unlock secrets. Back in Winelda we had checked but neither books nor teachers could substantiate any Indian warring, or even the existence of sod house settlers west of town. Yet, here had been a couple of sod houses. How could you justify old pennies from the nineteenth century corroded by alkali, or the randomly scattered arrowheads? Obviously academicians hadn't recorded everything.

En route was a lively prairie dog town, a network of deep interconnecting holes. The dog towns constitute a real menace to the legs of valuable steers and horses. The state even offered a five cent per head bounty to eradicate the varmints. And, as if the cunning little dogs knew humans scurrilously called them vermin, on their mounds they'd stand on their hind legs and commence yapping in their effort to make fools of us. Sometimes we'd waste a half box—twenty-five cartridges—of valuable ammunition on some cute little prairie dog.

Amzy was an excellent shot, but he never brought one down. Neither of us did. We were certain they had special magic, which caused them to plunge for cover a nanosecond before the bullet arrived. We would immediately check for blood at the lip of the hole, but never got satisfaction. We never dared check deeper because everyone knew rattlers, tiny owls, and the mocking little dogs all lived communally.

After firing at a dog, we'd walk ahead several yards, and the same little furry animal would pop up behind us, stand on its hind legs and begin scolding us, taunting us to blow off more ammo. Quite frankly, I'm glad today that there's no scrappy little prairie dog ghost to haunt me. If anything, I suppose I provided them with great entertainment.

At that particular time in our lives, Amzy and I weren't good guys when it came to critters. We were always trying to wing one of the huge turkey vultures that provoked us by cocking their heads as they made their magnificent flybys. Wiser citizens protected them by law; they said they performed a valuable service by eating the prairie's carrion. To kill one was a hefty five dollar fine—enough to buy four hundred pounds of potatoes! But, like a death wish, they would soar tauntingly over our heads. We could never refuse a dare. Amzy and I rationalized they deserved to die because they were known to vomit partly digested meat on people's heads.

On this particular day, Amzy's bullet ripped two feathers from a high flying buzzard's tail. Out of countless missed shots, this had been our nearest score. Because each of us had often brought down jackrabbits on the run, we thought it strange we could never touch a sitting prairie dog, or an almost wholly stationary buzzard. However, on that particular day, all the little animals were safe from me. My rifle was home awaiting a replacement firing pin from Utica, New York.

Homer liked fried rabbit—it was indeed delicious—and he did not mind my side business of selling dressed cottontails to Etta's Café at twenty cents a head. Still, he never approved of my murder of small animals. When it came to God's little creatures, gruff Homer was softhearted.

Wineldans had often invited Homer to go squirrel hunting. He would beg off with some logical excuse, but he'd never spoil their fun by criticizing their sport. And while he would never forbid me to hunt, he sometimes tried to touch my conscience. He'd ask if I'd stalk rabbits and squirrels if they too had guns. Through his superior reasoning process, he could make me feel much less than wholesome.

I think most boys lose their primitive desire to kill defenseless critters when they become men. One morning in Korea, at the age of twenty-six, I killed twenty-five mallard ducks and five pheasant, almost enough to feed my infantry company. Call it a heavenly message, but on that day in Korea something went out of me when I looked at all those beautiful animals dumped together on the ground. My desire to kill animals suddenly vanished. Other than some rattlers, Doc Chambers, and a few Asian warriors who themselves had tried desperately to kill me, I've killed nothing since.

Amzy and I made our slow climb up the steep slope of No-Name Mesa. It was every bit as thrilling to us as Pike's Peak must have been to Zebulon or to Colorado climbers. To the south we could see the slender, ancient pinnacle known as Chimney Rock. Even it was special. Historians opined that a hundred years previously, westward bound pioneers and Indians had used it as a navigational checkpoint. Soaring just above it was an entire squadron of turkey vultures majestically riding the warm thermals. From a mesa top, everything in the Cimarron Valley looked very Western.

Near the top of No-Name we always visited what we called our crystal cave; clear alabaster crystals grew from its ceiling like shiny stalactite jewels. We inspected everything and assured ourselves no one had discovered "our" cave since last summer. Then we stepped out onto the narrow ledge at the base of the mesa's twenty foot thick gypsum cap and began looking for foot and handholds to climb the remaining, almost vertical ascent, to the flat top.

That's when we heard the rattler!

He was on our ledge and only ten feet to our front. A healthy irate whopper, it coiled and weaved its big flat head, its dead eyes fixed on us, its tongue lashing in and out menacingly. I was behind Amzy, but I could see its unusual fury, provoked because we'd interrupted its bathing in the warm spring sun. It was the biggest, angriest rattler I'd ever seen.

We should have backed off, gone another way. Unfortunately, the immense snake was a challenge. Amzy and I had long claimed that flies, cockroaches, mosquitoes, and rattlesnakes were of no use to man. There were plenty of bull snakes and other non-poisonous varieties to rid the earth of rodents, and maintain the ecological balance.

I had every confidence in Amzy who was calmly, but too slowly, taking a bead on the weaving snake. He took up his trigger slack, slowly applied pressure. "*Click!*" It was probably the most deafening click I've ever heard a small bore rifle make.

"*Shi-it,*" said Amzy, reaching for a round in his watch pocket. "Forgot to reload after that last buzzard shot." And the snake's *zzzz's* grew ever more ominous as it weaved and bobbed its business end. From our ledge it was a dangerous jump to the steep slope below. Above us was a near vertical fifteen to twenty feet to the top. But Amzy was cool. He reloaded and took careful aim. *Cccrack* went the .22, and the snake flew backward, its white underside momentarily flashing as it writhed. Amzy quickly reloaded. *Cccrack.* Both bullets struck home, one had hit the snake's head dead center.

That's when I did my foolish showoff thing. I hopped around Amzy, grabbed the writhing snake by the tail to pop its head as I had seen Amzy do before. But I quickly discovered this was no garter snake. This sucker was almost seven feet long, thick, and heavy. I managed a feeble bullwhip pop that did absolutely nothing. It still writhed crazily as I made ready to do it a second time. That's when the snake's fang snagged in the loose skin of my free hand. This scared the hell out of me! Its white mouth opened wide, its fang hooked solidly in my knuckle like a fishhook. I must have given Amzy a strange look as I stood there—literally riding a tiger's back— holding the snake's tail and it still twisting.

"Sweet Jesus!" he gasped, and he dropped his beloved rifle in the dirt. More than anything, this truly alarmed me. Amzy would never mistreat his rifle in such a way. Amzy gripped the snake solidly at the neck. That's when I saw Amzy's neat bullet hole right through the flat top of its head, and another a half an inch farther down at the neck. Amzy twisted and lifted slightly until the curved fang slipped from my hand. A drop of blood oozed out behind it.

Amzy tossed the rattler aside where it continued its death writhing. He took his old faded bandanna from his neck, and with no conversation, hurriedly tied it just above my elbow. Then as fast as lightning, his razor sharp pocketknife glinted in the sun as he cut an inch and a half slash across my knuckle. Amzy did this so fast: one, two, three! I had no opportunity to object. Unfortunately, when Amzy cut my hand, the blood spurted six to eight inches into the air, and it repeated the spurt every time my heart beat. I had never seen so much of my own blood, and with it went my macho. Just like a kid I said, "Amzy, Jesus, you killed me! I'm bleedin' to death."

"You ain't bleedin' tuh death fer chrissakes," said Amzy. And he tightened the bandanna with a cedar stick. I thought sure he'd cut through my scrawny arm. The spurting eased off shortly. When Amzy let off on the tourniquet, it spurted again like bleeding I had never seen before.

I felt myself grow faint, and Amzy said, "Come on, we gotta hot foot it back to town. You shouldn't oughta let the snake's head hit yer hand."

I couldn't believe Amzy would say something that ridiculous.

He stuffed six inches of the snake's tail end under the back of his belt and tightened it. "Better take it to town. Doc might wanta see it."

All the way back to the Cimarron, and over the bridge, and down the railroad tracks, Amzy opened and closed the tourniquet. Each time the wound intermittently spurted and oozed, and I was beginning to experience genuine faintness. A lot of blood had run off my fingertips to bathe my trousers. It must have made a strange sight with me stumbling along and Amzy with six and a half feet of snake trailing behind him, its head dragging and clunking each of the railroad ties we passed. By the time we rounded the curve at the stockyards, and could see the distant Winelda passenger station, I had convinced myself I was near death. I even fantasized my own funeral—piles of carnations—in the Winelda Methodist Church. I visualized my bereaved father in the front pew for his very first time. Surrounding him was a large number of my weeping classmates. Nice words were being said. To be able to view this was almost worth dying for.

Amzy and I walked off the passenger station platform, and took the dead side of the Square past Ben Taul's general store and the creamery. Everything was abuzz because it was Saturday. We made quite a picture turning the Commercial Bank corner—me with plenty of shiny blood squirted over my shirt and trousers, and Amzy with his rifle and the big rattler dragging behind him on the sidewalk. Amzy was headed for Doc Chambers's office. Winelda being the kind of town it was, the news was preceding us.

"Hey, Amzy, what in hell's far? You shoot the Cable kid?"

"Rattler done bit 'im."

"I declare … hey is thet it?" The man ran over along with a half dozen others. "Wilson, would'ja lookit thet whopper. Eighty inches if it's an inch. Big lump in 'is belly, some animal in there, or mebbe a mess uh baby snakes."

"Hey, how come all the blood? Oh my Gawd! Oscar, lookit the bite the snake took outta Tom's hand."

Amzy was cool and offhand. "Snake didn't do alla thet. I cut 'im to dryne the venom."

Feeling really sorry for myself, I said nothing. I felt even sorrier when I had forgotten the fine funeral and began thinking of Homer's reaction to my foolish act.

Someone yelled from a pickup truck, "Amzy, you better git him to Doc Chambers, ya hear?" As if that wasn't where we had been heading for the past hour and a half.

"That's a derned good idea," yelled Amzy. "Now why in heck didn't I think uh thet?" Amzy abhorred attention, and I knew he was hot, tired, and exasperated.

Doc Chambers was having a quiet Bromo Quinine at the Corner when someone ran in and told him, "The Cable kid been shot." Doc slurped down the foamy stuff, which left a white mustache of fizz residue on his lip, and ran outside. Chambers could see our procession marching from the alley toward his office.

Doc Chambers was never my favorite, possibly because he had a little of the W. C. Fields in him; he didn't particularly take to kids. He was a tall skinny guy, and he always had a toothpick stuck in the side of his mouth. He looked more like a card shark than a doctor; sometimes he even wore a black garter on one sleeve. I always wished old Doc Clapper hadn't retired, not that I visited a doctor more than once in two or three years, but kindly Doc Clapper looked and acted like a family doctor. It had always been Doc Clapper who, in his kindly way, had checked and swabbed my sore throat. By contrast, Chambers would grab my hair with his left hand, and with the right he seemed to swab all the way to my stomach. He would leave me gagging and gurgling, and with a self-satisfied look on his face, he'd say, "Gotcha!" I suppose he thought it was funny and relaxing. Adult folks were sometimes strange.

When Doc bolted out the door, Virgil Clemans saw and heard the crowd and yelled back to Esther, his wife, "It's Tommy Cable. Get down to the Majestic and tell Homer he's been shot."

Esther dropped this on Homer, who came sprinting around the drawing barrel and saw the knot of twenty-five or thirty people peering through Doc Chambers's office window. "Ah my God!" And everyone made way for Homer the father.

Doc's examining room had a full plate glass window facing the sidewalk. Because his Venetian blind was pulled all the way to the top, faces were glued all over the window. Because the door was open, people had spilled in and around the examining table. It was a public gallery for Winelda's Saturday afternoon crowd, and Doc made no objections. "Gawd awmighty. Jew see alla the blood, enough to make a person sick."

The bloody clothes also flustered Homer, but Doc immediately said, "Hi, Homer. Not to worry. He's okay."

"Where's he shot?"

"Not shot, he's bit. Rattler's under the table. Not to worry. I awready gave Tommy some anti-venom, now I'm fixin' to tie off this here cantankerous artery."

I was sitting in the middle of the examination table with my legs dangling over the side. Doc was standing before me with Amzy at my side holding the tourniquet stick.

Perry Phillips appeared from somewhere and laid a firm reassuring hand on my shoulder. I was glad he was there, and wished he would take over from Doc because I figured he probably knew more.

Perry looked at the snake lying under Doc's examining table and said, "You shoot 'em, Amzy?"

"Yes, sir."

"I reckon with that bullet hole where it is you plumb blew his venom works clean outta his head, but what you done here to Tom was right smart thinkin'."

And everyone within earshot heard Perry the oracle, and they immediately looked upon Amzy as a young hero.

"Perry's rot," went the word through the growing crowd. "Thet Amzy probly saved Tommy's lahf." And this was followed by "yeahs," and "uh huhs," and "you better bleeve its." And all through the babbling, Doc sucked on his toothpick and worked. Someone said,

"Tommy done earned hisself into the White Fang Society." The Society was a dubious distinction for those dumb enough to let a rattler bite them, and to be sure, there was no medal or certificate.

Homer stood next to Doc, and I noticed he had grown both quiet and a little ashen. His confusion was unusual because Homer was always the "take charge" man.

Doc said to Amzy, "Now, let off on the tourniquet a mite," and again the blood squirted into the air and splashed on Homer's seersucker pants. The crowd of men gasped, and Esther and other women gave out "ooohs." A man said, "I gotta get the hale outta here," and people made way. Doc quickly tightened the tourniquet and told Amzy to hold the stick. I wasn't reassured. I must have grown extra pale because Doc suddenly handed me a tiny glass capsule of ammonia covered with cheesecloth. "Here," he said, "sniff this thaing while I do my work."

With commendable equanimity, Homer watched Doc's every move. I don't know why I thought about it at that frantic moment, but it was the second time of my life—the first was my honor roll report card—that Homer evinced real feeling for me. Over the years I suppose I had developed some doubt as to whether Homer really cared for me. While drunk he had made many remarks, things most fathers would never say to a son under any circumstance. But seeing him now, genuinely contrite, erased all those doubts. Homer obviously cared. Besides, of the two Homers, the drunken one's words were, in my view, essentially meaningless.

Doc Chambers took a small forceps from a glass case, located the severed end of the artery, and clamped on with the forceps, tied a suture around the end of the clamped forceps, and then pushed it down over the artery and tied it off. There were some gasps from the crowd, "Jew see thet, jew look at the way he done thet?" Doc got another rise of "oooh ooohs" out of the crowd when he ran a hypo needle into my hand in three different places.

"Don't worry about all that ooohing you're hearing," said Doc Chambers. "I'm numbing this so the stitching won't hurt."

In spite of the turmoil, and my blood all over the floor and me, I remember thinking that Doc sure had bad onion breath.

There were near fifty people either in the office or with their noses smashed up against the window. Neither Doc Chambers nor Marshal Billy Patton made an effort to clear them. Why? Because it was a spontaneous Wineldan event on Saturday, a community thing around the Square that was free and added zest and a purpose to living. Consequently, the marshal saw no reason to deny the townsmen and ranch folk whatever made life more interesting.

"Land's sake, what the hell happened to 'im?"

"Big rattler bit 'im."

"You don't say. Well, I'll be. Is thet the snake under the table?" And there, under the sterile examination table, lay the obviously dead snake. "And how come he's under the table?"

"Well, Elmo," someone finally said with exasperation. "What the hell diffurnce it make, he din't just crawl in here."

Doc pulled out a little curved needle and threaded some suture through it. It was my first time to learn that skin was tough like hide. Every time Doc pushed the needle through my skin two or three people would go, "Oooh, gol-danged, jew see thet, sure glad it's not me." And overlooking the fact my hand was now painlessly numb, "Thet Tommy's sure enough a game little critter."

After four stitches Doc turned to Homer, "You know he looks a little like heat exhaustion. Take him up to your place, Homer. Give him two or three lemonades and some licks uh salt. Let 'im rest up a bit and cool off. Tom, you come around in ten days, and we'll look to removin' those stitches." Then Doc vaingloriously stuck a new toothpick in his mouth, and a few applauded. Someone shouted, "Make way!" and like celebrities, Homer and I went through the parting Red Sea of a crowd.

"Notice how pale Tommy is?"

"Reckon you'd be pale too."

Doc Chambers had stanched the bleeding, and had sewn me up, regardless of how slovenly he looked. I would have been dumbstruck had someone told me that farther down the road I was to murder Doc in cold blood.

Amzy, the hero of the moment, came along behind us, dragging the big snake. When some saw what Amzy was towing past their ankles, they'd do a quick little two step to move aside. "Gol danged but thet's one big sonuvagun. Why's he a draggin' it aroun'?"

"Why thet's the snake that bit Homer's kid. They say the pool hall kid saved 'im."

When we turned at Homer's Place to climb my thirty-two steps, Amzy called out, "I'll see ya, Tom."

Homer turned and said, "Amzy, I want to thank you. You're a good kid, and I'll remember this."

Amzy turned and walked back down the sidewalk dragging the snake, a jaunty step with an occasional skip to it. His moment had come and gone. He turned up the alley to the backside of the Snooker Parlor, took out his knife, and slowly unzipped the lumpy mystery of the snake's belly. Fur began to appear, the snake had swallowed a small cottontail rabbit whole, had probably killed the rabbit shortly before we had happened on the scene. And like a petulant old dog with a bone, our disturbance had doubly angered it. Amzy skinned the snake and tacked it to the garage door to dry; later on he would present it to me.

Later, when Homer had learned all the details, he called Amzy into his office. "Amzy," he said, "as long as I'm alive you can walk into the Majestic at any time free of charge." Amzy was normally a laid back, cool kid who took everything in his quiet stride, but Homer's gift caught him off guard. No one had ever recognized his good deeds in such a way before. Homer said, "I'm swearing you to secrecy, Amzy, because in all of Winelda only Billy Patton has that special privilege. You're a good man, Gunga Din, and it's my way of thanking you."

The next day Amzy told me what Homer had done, and my admiration for Homer soared. Amzy asked who the hell Gunga Din was and I said, "Hell, I don't know. Maybe we can look it up in the dictionary."

THE BIKE

I don't know if it was because of the warm dry heat so salutary to Homer's physical well being, or because I had made the honor roll five out of six times, or because of my promotion to sophomore, but with gravity suitable for something momentous, Homer called me into his office. Very recently at the Majestic I had done a couple of commendable things on the floor, maybe he was going to speak of those. And he did.

"I liked the way you handled those problems. That's what brings folks back to the Majestic again and again." Homer always said "The Majestic" with special verve as if he were saying The Palace or The

Capitol. Then out of the blue he said, "You still want a bike?" Well, I thought I might faint dead away. He said, "I know where I can get one wholesale."

Like a fool I said, "Is it a red Schwinn with steerhorn handlebars?"

"No," he said, "it's a black and white Nonpareil with chain tread balloon tires." My Schwinn remark visibly irked him and I could have kicked myself. "For your edification," he said, "nonpareil means unparalleled . . . without equal. Of course, if you don't like that . . . ."

"I like it, I like it," I said eagerly.

"Done," he said. "Give me twenty-five bucks and I'll order it."

Now, this surprised me. For some reason I thought a Dad was supposed to buy his kid a bike. This was nothing more than Homer giving me permission to spend my own hard-earned money. I started to broach this but thought better of it. To pop off to Homer was seldom beneficial. So, I savored the moment. It was the very first time Homer had "allowed" a bike and I was determined to have it even if I had to buy it myself.

"I only got twenty in the bank. The rest is in savings bonds."

"Okay, draw out fifteen and give me your promissory note for ten. Pay five dollars a month. I'll give you a break . . . no interest." It was funny how Homer was making me feel "what a great deal!" he was giving me. "But remember," he cautioned. "Come the first of the month, and you fail to make payment, the bike gets impounded in the back of the theater plus a twenty percent penalty."

This was pure Homer, and I was well aware it was the way the Cables did intra-family business—there were few handouts, and no free lunches, and yowling or the slightest hint of insurrection was never permitted.

The following week I had the bike. It added a completely new dimension to my maneuverability. I rode it south to the Cimarron River Bridge, out to Mexican Town and the roundhouse, to the ice plant, and to visit Mert Wright at the light plant. It was as if I had just been checked out in the latest aircraft and had unlimited fuel at my disposal. I even rode the thing the twenty-seven miles to Alva, and then loaded it aboard the Santa Fe to get home in time for dinner. Today I look at kids hanging disconsolately around the malls and I wonder if they're having as much fun, even with the Camaro daddy gave them, as we used to have in Winelda.

Homer—Simply Amazing—Summer 1938

The summer of 1938 launched itself beautifully. I was still euphoric for having made straight A's in English, which had satisfied my pledge to Miss Strickland. People around the Square were remarking that I was growing perceptibly. This made me walk a little taller, and I noticed my voice was beginning to crack. Also, with the simmering summer heat flooding in, Homer was coming into his annual healthy zenith.

One evening, while Homer mashed the potatoes, he surprised me. "You wanted to know how to make money in your spare time?" I never failed to get a kick out of Homer's reference to my "spare" time. "Now that you've invested in the Nonpareil bike, I'm going to tell you how to get a summer job with the Palace Cleaners." I knew Homer could be pretty amazing, but to me it was incredible that what he was about to say had apparently materialized just while he had been mashing those potatoes.

"You go from door to door, see," he continued mashing. "You tell each Winelda housewife about the Palace Cleaners, about their good rates, and their fine workmanship. You pick up their cleaning, and you deliver it to Mr. Stephens. That's called soliciting, and it's as simple as that."

"Did Mr. Stephens say he wanted me?" I asked that because Homer and Mr. Stephens sometimes played afternoon dominoes at the Snooker Parlor.

Homer smiled as he mashed. "Right now, Mr. Stephens hasn't the foggiest idea he has a need for young Thomas Cable. *You* must tell *him* how you will increase *his* business, how *you'll* be an everlasting asset." He slapped the masher against the pot.

I laughed because I thought Homer was putting me on. "Sure, I'm supposed to go right down there and tell Mr. Stephens he needs me and should hire me, and then I'll ask him how much he's gonna pay me."

"Do it like that and he'll turn you down for sure." Homer poured a little milk on the potatoes. "He doesn't need one more employee taking his profit. These days the businesses around the Square can only afford a bare bones overhead. On the contrary, you clearly tell him you *don't want* a salary; you only want to bring in extra business!

Tell him you'll tap the whole town, tap into business currently going to Merle's Cleaners . . . all you want is a mere fifteen percent of what *you* actually bring in. Mr. Stephens has absolutely nothing to lose, has no salary to pay, you bring in nothing, you get nothing. I tell ya, Son, as sure as God made little green apples small, no one can refuse such a proposition. How could they?" I was amazed at how smoothly the plan had flowed out of Homer's mouth. And as Maddy served the pork chops and peas, Homer added some salt and did the last vigorous mashing. He again resolutely cracked the masher on the pot's edge to clean it of potatoes.

What he had said made sense, and he had my full attention. "But what if I knock on doors and they don't want cleaning done?"

"Nothing lost! But immediately let them know how great Mr. Stephens's place is, and that you'll come back another day, and thank the lady for her time and conduct yourself like a responsible person. Maybe the next time she'll spring. Let your thinking be positive. Suppose the lady gives you a suit to be cleaned and pressed. Bingo! When you turn it over to Mr. Stephens, you get fifteen percent of the seventy-five cents which is around eleven cents." Homer immediately equated this into terms he knew I'd readily understand. "In just one call you made a half a box of .22 cartridges, and, I'll bet you money, marbles, or chalk, that's a helluva lot better than slopping hogs at two cents an hour or I pass." Homer's investment in allowing me to take the agriculture course was paying off big time. More and more frequently, he found ways to reference my meager pig profit as an object lesson.

Soon we were sitting down to the table, and as he pulled up his chair, Homer didn't skip a beat. He continued effusively, "But, you gotta be fair with Mr. Stephens. You don't pick and choose around town and only call on the best customers, the very ones he might already have. You start on Cecil and go all the way to the end of the street, door to door, and then work back down the other side, then start another street until you're working every part of Winelda on a scheduled basis."

I said, "Here we are talking about all the money I'm going to make and I don't even have the job."

"Ah ha," said Homer. "That's the first important hurdle, so after dinner let's prepare a sales pitch to convince Mr. Stephens."

Later, as I dried dishes, we worked on my presentation, and

Homer had me practice it several times. I'd enter through the kitchen door as if I was coming into the Palace Cleaners, and I'd walk up to Homer and start my positive spiel.

He raised his hand, "Stop. Stop. It's important to look me right in the eye, no mumbling, and then you start telling me what *you* are going to do for *me* . . . the Palace Cleaners. Lay it on hard, the part about the extra business *you'll* bring in to *me*. *You* are totally insignif-icant . . . *me, me, me*." Homer poked his chest with his finger. "I'm Mr. Stephens; I'm the important one."

After spouting my pitch a dozen times, Homer wished me good luck, and I took off for the Palace Cleaners. It was only a half block beyond the Majestic. Twenty minutes later I ran back to the apartment and took the thirty-two steps two at a time. "Dad, you know the first thing he said? He said, 'We can't afford to take on nobuddy,' and then I gave him the spiel—no salary, I let him know my time was his, absolutely free. I told him why he couldn't possibly refuse my offer. *And he gave me the job!*"

Homer was proud as hell. "There you go! See how easy? And you're just a kid, and this is the Depression. A man gets off his behind he can do anything he wants. You went out there, Tom, and sold your-self. That's a helluva lot smarter than wandering around in the snow in the dark with a big dumb bag of papers, or hauling stinking slop to pigs. Now!" He laughed, and I could see his wheels whirring. He slapped his hands together. "This is doubly terrific. You know why? Think about what you've just done. You're not really an employee. In a genuine sense you've literally become Mr. Stephens's partner! If you work hard at it, you've got fifteen percent of the Palace Cleaners without paying for equipment, or rent, or doing any of the delivery, the cleaning, or pressing. Also, your schedule is yours, not like factory workers. No time clock to punch, no deadline. Your situation is like piecework; you must perform; you must produce. You do something you get paid; you do nothing you get nothing. You have to go out and hit the ball, make things happen, make Stephens glad you had such a great idea." We laughed about it being my idea.

Homer was pretty phenomenal, and his ingenuity was proof posi-tive why no person has to lie down in the arena and wait for the lions to come and gnaw. Like General Patton once said, "I don't care what you do, lieutenant, but for godsakes do something?" or similar words which meant to get off your duff and start functioning.

Then I thought I might probe a tad. "To buy one of those big baskets for the bike is going to cost me about three bucks."

"Not my problem," said Homer turning his back. "Don't suck me into your deal. Buying the basket, a fixed asset, is what's called the cost of doing business."

The Solicitor

The first day out I brought in six suits, a skirt, and four pairs of trousers for a commission of ninety-three cents. That was almost nineteen cokes, or four and a half boxes of .22 shorts in only two hours work. Shortly thereafter, Mrs. Edwin Hill gave me her drapes for cleaning. This was a windfall of a dollar fifty commission in only one call. Mr. Stephens was delighted because she had always been Merle's customer.

And the opportunity to go into almost everyone's home had added a new dimension to my life. I saw how all the other Wineldans lived, and I also discovered most of the ladies liked me. I was building good will. Even if they had no cleaning they usually invited me in for a Kool-Aid, or milk and a cookie. There were also a few rare exceptions when the door was slammed in my face. But most adults liked to hear my pitch, and they'd look around for something, even four neckties—a commission of only nine cents—but it kept the account alive.

At the other end of the spectrum was the nice lady on Church Street who would sometimes remark, "Oh, Tom, you're such a nice looking boy," or some such, and on occasion she'd run her hand—nothing especially intimate—very lightly over my shoulders. She also liked to show me things in her house, how she had done over her kitchen, and her bedroom that smelled of perfume, and before I would leave she always kissed me somewhere on my head or face. It was nothing special, or even deeply personal, just a little brush of a kiss.

I thought she seemed very lonely but I knew her husband. He was a nice guy who worked day shifts at the roundhouse. I'll have to admit that initially I liked her friendly attention, but sometimes her eyes focused on me a little too firmly—like scenes in some movies I'd seen. She always wore a nice smelling perfume, and I must say that her touching and gentle brushes began stirring something mysterious inside me. It eventually dawned on me she was never too interested in cleaning, and that nothing about this was checking out with anything I had learned the past several years in Sunday school. Thereafter, a feeling of genuine guilt crept in every time I turned onto Church Street.

There were a couple of other ladies that always delighted in hugging me and giving me a kiss, inviting me into the kitchen for a cookie, but theirs was different. Nothing more than an Oklahoma momma's greeting—a lot of happy conversation and not remotely as intensive as the pretty lady on Church Street. At least the others sometimes went back to the closet and brought me cleaning, and they never invited me to see their bedroom curtains. I never told Homer or anyone else about the exceptional lady on Church Street, and there was no way I could properly interpret what was happening. So, I finally decided I shouldn't call there. But before I had missed a call, the Santa Fe had already transferred them to Amarillo. The great weight, the responsibility, had been lifted from my sophomoric shoulders.

THE FUNERAL HOME

The job also caused me to call on Floyd's Funeral Home. It was the same huge white Edwardian house on Cecil that Mom and Pop Cable had leased for thirty-one dollars a month when we had first come to live in Winelda. It was the place where Homer had set fire to the back porch roof.

I told Mrs. Floyd I had lived in her house four years earlier. "Over there was my dad's bedroom," I said. "And Mom and Pop Cable were here, and I had that bedroom over there, and this one here was our guest bedroom in case my Uncle Virgil and Aunt Iris came."

"Oh," she said. "That's our guest room as well." Then she smiled and flung the door open. Sitting in there on gurneys were five caskets, their lids yawning open! It chilled me right to the bone. Our guest room was now where families selected a coffin for their deceased member. I thought Mrs. Floyd's reference to dead people as their guests was scary.

I liked the Floyds. They were long time Wineldans who also operated a furniture store on Cecil near City Hall. But despite how nicely they treated me, I felt very uncomfortable in their home. As a funeral home, that fine house would never again be as I remembered it, with Mom in the kitchen preparing sauerkraut and chops, and Pop in the parlor scanning the latest market quotes.

I had inexplicably harbored a fearsome fixation about the business of funerals. Funerals had long given me the creeps, and I avoided them at all costs. Looking in coffins at dead people with waxy hands wasn't my bag. No living person ever had hands like that. And flowers were always stacked everywhere. Over the coffin and along the altar were big sprays that read: "We Love You, Herman." Why did they write words on pretty ribbon? Was that so Herman might peek out of his casket and read those nice words? Or was it really meant to console the living congregation? The flowers most popular at Wineldan funerals were carnations, which was why at that age I referred to carnations as "funeral flowers." Even today, when I smell carnations, I immediately correlate them with coffins and sobs, and black clothes, and dreary hymns, and those unnatural waxy hands.

"Don't Horace look nice?" At funerals people always paid those ultimate compliments, "Just like he's a sleepin' there." I usually averted my eyes, because to me they looked real dead, tremendously different from how I'd last seen them.

And as a kid, I thought it very strange for grownups to put a dead person in a special box that everyone likened to an eternal bed. The thing even came equipped with a fancy pillow and a little frilly coverlet. Yet, instead of following through with the scenario and dressing them for their final bed in red flannel PJs or some such, they always dressed them up in coats and neckties, and with what had been their favorite stickpins and cuff links. One time I even saw the deceased wearing his spectacles! Now, who ever dressed that way for bed? And why did people call it a funeral home, or even a funeral parlor? To me, everything about the funeral ritual suggested fancy and fantasy all sloshed together. I couldn't shake this perspective, and I cannot analyze whatever brought on these thoughts or my bizarre conclusions. Possibly, they had come from a long ago bad movie.

Mrs. Floyd certainly wasn't to blame. She had no way of knowing those few moments by her guest room had caused all my incredible and eerie funeral memories to spew up like lava from a volcano. And what if she gave me a suit of clothes for a next day "special?" I would never know if it were for Mr. Floyd, or for one of their guests. Right there, that very afternoon, I knew Floyd's Funeral Home was one call I would never make again.

Bing—The Black Hearted Critter

Each Saturday morning, right after sweeping the hallway and those thirty-two miserable steps, I knew the Majestic's brass waited for me. I had come to hold this golden metal in the very same low regard as I did those steps.

Every theater had brass cases on its front enclosing pictures of special scenes of the current movie. Those they call stills, and they're put there to pique interest. In addition, an Andy Hardy movie would have a big picture of Mickey Rooney and the names of the cast—the trade identifies them as "one-sheets." A huge highway billboard comprises twenty-four of those one-sheets or a twenty-four sheet billboard. We protected our one-sheet advertisements behind crystal clean glass and shiny brass, and together with the smell of popcorn, their ultimate design was to inflame the people's imaginative interest and suck them inside the Majestic.

In addition to my brass, four large doors opened to the foyer with sizeable copper kickplates. Homer wanted everything to glitter. In his vernacular: "Just like a diamond in a goat's ass." With all this shining, my hands turned black and crinkly, and stunk of my self-made mixture of ammonia and Bon Ami; I later learned this meant "good friend." Ha! I remember that Mom always told me to keep my hands and fingernails looking nice—with Bon Ami it was a challenge.

Every Saturday morning I ordinarily spent two hours shining the cruddy brass and copper until the theater front fairly gleamed. When Homer checked the brass, I would always pray he'd say, "Hey. Now, that's the way it's supposed to look." But that wasn't always the case. There were times when Homer actually hunted me down somewhere around the Square. "No streaks," he'd say as we returned to the crime scene, "no white residue. See those spots of Bon Ami on the sidewalk? Anything worth doing is worth doing correctly." That was Homer's translation of, "Do it again and do it right." And as I shined, I'd see the rest of the lucky guys tooling around the Square on their bikes, and, God, how I came to hate the brass, but there was no ready appellate court for me to address my wrongs. The town's largest majority could hardly empathize because few had ever professionally shined brass. So, for the brass and my regular seven day a week ticket taking, I was paid five dollars. Homer always reminded me that I saw all films for free.

The brass became very personal. Sometimes when people grabbed the side of a brass fixture and leaned forward to scan the pictures, I'd cringe. I thought, *Are they afraid they're going to fall off the Earth? Why was there this nonsensical clutching of brass? Don't they know sweaty hands have acid that causes shiny brass to slowly turn brown?* I was already clearly aware of that phenomenon, and I was just a dumb kid! Thankfully, the copper kickplates were out of the public's normal reach, but not the occasional speckling effect of the Lord's windblown rain.

My real kickplate nemesis was Bing, a sleek, black, terrier-like dog owned by Betty Jean Stephens, the daughter of Mr. and Mrs. Raleigh Stephens of the Palace Cleaners. Betty Jean was my classmate, and because I was now Mr. Stephens's representative, there was no politic way I could protest. That and the fact that kids seldom made protests to Wineldan adults.

So, the silent standoff was strictly between Bing and me. Bing was an alert little devil. He predictably started his mid morning territorial circuit by trotting from the Palace Cleaners toward the Corner Drug. En route were my copper kickplates, and I suppose his pea brain figured the kickplates were part of his territorial property. Bing had corroborated this on occasion by ferociously guarding them from outside dogs. Only he, the great Bing, could pee on my kickplates, which he did resolutely. Any time he passed the Majestic, he dependably raised his shiny black leg, grimaced, and fired a long stream of satisfying pee all over a beautifully shined kickplate. Even if that rascal's bladder was empty, he'd manage a shot from some hidden reserve. And having relieved himself, he'd critically sniff his work then view it as if he were a da Vinci appraising the artfulness of his swish-like strokes.

Bing was obviously unaware he was making a grave error in public relations. While silently doing dumb routine work like shining brass or shelling peas, a lot goes through the torpidness of a person's mind. At such times, Bing's time costly trespass came to occupy progressively more of my idle, sometimes frighteningly psychotic thoughts.

On rare occasions, I'd catch Bing in the act, and I'd wildly thrash my arms and yell. This bizarre behavior never failed to fill Bing with inherent disgust. He'd bristle the hair between his shoulder blades and utter a couple of contemptuous "woof woofs." Unfazed, he'd cockily continue marking his beat as if I mattered little in the scheme of dog things. Apparently no other human around the Square behaved as grossly as I.

Bing marked his territory as automatically as if he were delivering handbills. He'd pee a spurt on this light pole, another spurt for that fire hydrant, a shot for a truck tire, but when it came to my glowing kickplates, there was no such perfunctory treatment. Without exception, he always managed to arrive with an incredibly full bladder. I was convinced it was not personal, that it had nothing to do with my adversarial attitude. I was fully confident it was the warm coppery color that beckoned him to perform his most artful job.

While fingerprints turned brass from golden to brown, Bing's pee changed copper kickplates to a deep imperial green. And Bing always made huge Picasso-like swishes of this green. From Saturday to Saturday there was ample time for Bing to swish and swash all four doors to his satisfaction. But while his casual art took only seconds to produce, to erase it and restore the kickplates to a glowing burnish was tedious work indeed.

So tedious that I even cunningly resorted to inveigling passing kids to stop and shoot some Saturday bull. Not only did it pass the time, but nine times out of ten, the uninitiated would eventually become fascinated with my work. For when I perceived a "live one," I always kept a few extra buffing cloths at hand, just for those strategic moments.

"Hey, Tom," they might say. "Why don'tcha rub it this way?" I would say, "Show me whatcha mean," and very soon I would have Huckleberry Finned the kid into buffing a big section of brass to a high gleam. I'd be quick to admire his work, tell him he had a special knack, and that he could probably shine brass better than anyone in town. Blandishments of this sort had often hooked an unpaid assistant for more than an hour.

Because Amzy Criswell lived nearby, he never failed to visit, but he had long since become savvy to my Saturday morning con job. He would never pitch in unless he needed me to go elsewhere for another project. Because Amzy shined well, I would thirst for those days when he needed me without delay. Amzy had become aware of my enduring tiff with Black Bing. One day, as Amzy stopped by, he said, "Lookit, here comes yer friend now. Step out into the street, I wanta see what you're talkin' about."

Bing was stepping right along, his pink tongue hung out between his flashing white teeth. He was almost in rapture, probably because he was nearing the theater. At the post-office he suddenly veered to the light pole, fired a small volley, and then sniffed to check both accuracy and coverage. Then he would arc his tail jauntily over his back and continue hotfooting it toward my copper. When he reached the theater, he stopped, sniffed a dirty kickplate, rejected it, and went straight to the one I had just been shining.

As he lifted his leg, both Amzy and I rushed mightily onto the sidewalk, yelling and thrashing our arms. This ambush both surprised and scared Bing, and caused him to dribble on his paws. He took immediate evasive action, and dashed to the front of the Rexall. There he took his stand and faced us. Bing lifted his head high and went "Whoooooo, whooo." So infuriated and humiliated because of the dribbled paws, he glared and fluffed out his tail and shoulder hair. Then suddenly, as if we merited no further attention, he checked out with a disgusted "woof" and departed toward the Corner.

"I know Bing," I said to Amzy, "and he knows my schedule. Soon as I'm gone, he'll be back and give my kickplates his best pee of the day."

Amzy said, "You know, I seen somethin' the other day over at the blacksmith. This here rancher south of town was showin' Mr. Lord how he'd rigged up a battry and a Model-T coil so's to keep his cattle outta his wife's flars. Used only one little war to shock 'em. Next Sattiday, I'll pack a battry and a coil over here and we'll teach that black critter a lesson." I had complete faith in Amzy's eminent mechanical skills.

The next Saturday Amzy joined me fairly early. He laid a thin metal sheet on the sidewalk, sheet iron that had once been a Sinclair oil sign with its green dinosaur trademark. He ran a clean copper wire through a nail hole in the old sign, and then made his hookup with the six volt battery, a Model-T coil, and the kickplate. It only needed Bing to complete the circuit. Amzy positioned the metal sheet so Bing would have to stand on it when he addressed the kickplate. By wiping the iron sheet with a damp cloth, Amzy made sure Bing's little pink soled feet would make an even better connection. The trap was set and the suspense was tantalizing.

While I shined brass, Amzy kept a vigil on the Palace Cleaner's front door. Occasionally Amzy would re-dampen the plate, but after waiting half an hour, we began losing some of our edge. Then Amzy said, "Outta here. He jist came out of the cleaners!" Amzy and I retreated to the rear of a parked car.

Bing trotted saucily down the block, his head high, his proud little tail curved over his spine. He diverted to the post-office light pole, sniffed, raised his leg, and fired a token burst. Then he performed a maneuver I had never seen before. After sniffing his work, he began vigorously kicking and scratching his feet on the sidewalk as if he were throwing imaginary leaves and grass into the air. This extraordinary canine action was quite funny, but we maintained a sniper's silence.

Bing approached, but ignored the bright shiny kickplate Amzy had just wired and went directly to a dirty kickplate and peed.

How could he do this?

Again he performed this new tactic, pretending that he was kicking up a cloud of leaves. It was as if Bing were in his very own French Spad, he was making his victory slow roll. While kicking and scratching concrete, he suddenly focused on the shiny kickplate. Such a marvelous opportunity! He went to the sheet iron on the walk, cautiously sniffed this new thing, and examined one of the connector wires. Then as if to weigh himself, he abruptly walked right onto the sheet iron, lifted his leg, set his jaw, and fired.

The surge of current must have jangled every tooth, rib, and dog bone in Bing's body. I'm sure, had it been night, he would've lit up. When Bing's pee arched to the copper plate, it completed the circuit and the strong current flashed through the stream of pee and sizzled right up Bing's little pecker and clanged his *cojones* together like cymbals. Bing catapulted into the air looking as animated as a Halloween cat, everything arched and fluffed. When he returned to Earth, he was howling and peeing uncontrollably, bathing his paws as his blurred legs pumped northward toward Homer's Place.

Old Clarence Morgan, a constant fixture of the Saturday morning square, chugged toward us with his cane in one hand and his antique ear horn in the other. Bing knocked Mr. Morgan's cane skittering to the curb. To no one in particular Morgan said, "What'n tarnation got inta that fool dog!" Amzy and I were all but rolling around on the sidewalk.

There was no doubt that there were Wineldans who would have thought our medieval kid trick wicked and cruel. I for one knew that Homer would have taken great exception. But none of those of that liberal persuasion, including Homer, were polishing copper kickplates for a living.

For two days there was no sign of Bing. We imagined him lying close to home, swelling with pee, but terrified to take another leak for fear he'd blast off again. "Bet his eyeballs are a turnin' yella," chuckled Amzy.

After a few days, Bing recommenced checking his territory. He jauntily trotted to the post-office light pole and made his mark. But when he came by the Majestic his pace slowed, and his tail lost its arc; it drooped hangdog toward the ground. He hung his head just a tad as he peeked peripherally at the glowing copper kickplates, but he gave them wide berth, stepping warily into the gutter. Upon reaching the Rexall, his tail slowly rose and curled over his back, and again he resumed his proud clipped gait. But never again did Bing lift his leg on the Majestic's copper kickplates. There were no two ways about it, innovative Amzy was a prince of a guy.

Tom Cable—Gridiron—Fall 1938

That fall I shelved my dry cleaning business for the football season's duration. Where last year I was thirteen and weighed a hundred and five pounds, I was now fourteen and weighed a robust hundred and twenty-five. I'm sure I was still not the answer to Coach Claunch's dreams, but at least I was ready and almost willing.

All suited up in smelly ancient pads, Coach Claunch jogged us to the vacant lot north of City Hall. It was across the street from where Homer had once collided with the telephone pole. It was the same spot where the city permitted medicine shows and carnivals, and it was the place where I was introduced to scrimmage. "Scrimmage" was a new word for me, perhaps it came from skirmish. In any event, it defined an entirely new encounter. Homer had said it would be fun, but for the better part of that first afternoon, I found myself seeing stars. Like actor Claude Rains in *Casablanca*, I was *shocked!*

I had had absolutely no conception, no inkling whatever that football would be like that. And like a mad man, the coach, who was normally sensible and quiet, kept yelling at us to hit with more vigor. After a jarring encounter, I sometimes experienced the uneasiness of vertigo, and odd singing sounds would occur inside my head. "All right," yelled the coach, "one, two, three, *hike.*" And our two lines would collide with a clattering racket of shoulder pads, grunts, and thudding old leather helmets. A few times someone's cleat would painfully embed itself into my instep. I could not then see the fun in this game!

Unfortunately, from Homer's and pal Aaron Fischer's offices, our scrimmage field was only a short block away. I always knew when Homer was around because I could hear his distinctive cigarette cough. I would stealthily look over on the sidelines, and sure enough, there were Homer and Aaron. And it never went unnoticed when someone knocked me ass over teakettle. Barely able to find the horizon, or to coherently state my name, I'd hear Homer boom, "You sure looked great on that one, Cable."

My frail body had never experienced such wanton violence. And there was no water anywhere; I couldn't swallow or spit because my mouth was like cotton. Had it not been for Homer's presence and my desire for the coveted "W" on my sweater, I'm sure I would've aborted the madness on the very first day. I secretly prayed that the coach would once again give me an official reprieve. "Go grow for another year." But like a mad man, he relentlessly yelled, "*Go Cable, move, move boy, move . . . show me some hate!*" Hate, ppppfffft.

During that very first week of scrimmage, Coach Claunch placed a rare demand on my bony feet. He called it "charging." From continuously charging out of the line, my insteps and arches became so painful they felt fractured. The charging was probably rearranging all the youthful cartilage that connected my many foot bones. After practice, I found walking painful. But like a proud battle scar, I began flaunting this newfound condition. I'd limp around the hallways of WHS, or hobble down the sidewalk to the lobby of the Majestic. I desperately wanted someone to say, "Tom, how come you limping?" Like Billy the beer dregs drinker, no one ever seemed to notice, and I never had the opportunity to announce that I was Cable of the gridiron!

GETTING TO KNOW THE MEXICANS

After school, the Mexicans in our class usually hoofed it north to Mexican Town, giving us little opportunity to mix. Football gave us "of the team" a better chance to know them. During those initial scrimmages, there was fierce blocking and tackling because most everyone fought hard to earn a first string slot. My contribution was solely based on survival. Occasionally a minor scuffle occurred—a heated shoving match by a couple of white kids—and the coach would step in. Despite having heard Mexicans were hot tempered, I don't recall a Mexican having ever been involved. No matter how bruising the contact, the Mexicans were an even tempered, congenial bunch that always smiled a lot.

That first day of football practice was also my very first time to ever shower naked with a large group of guys. We all filed into the smelly locker room and began stripping off our antique equipment—old rib, hip, and dented shoulder pads obviously ripened by Wineldan kids for at least the last ten years. Then all twenty-seven of us piled into one big wall shower area where the great difference between whites and Mexicans became immediately noticeable. Tony, José, and Jesús were brown all over. And José's willie was unusually dark, yet in spite of all the banter nobody ever said, "Hey José, how come you gotta black dick?"

After those initial furtive examinations, I'm sure we'd pretty well concluded without discussion that Mexican dicks were every bit as long or short as white dicks. In the cold showers, none of the shriveled dicks offered much to flaunt or to crow over. All this I learned that first miserable day of football. After four or five of those communal showers, I'm pretty sure we were no longer comparing how our dick stacked up against other dicks. We were all different, but I figured God had constructed us pretty much the same. It wasn't until fall passed to winter that we noticed José, Tony, and Jesús always kept their good looking suntans while we whites looked more and more like plucked steamed chickens.

I attended every scrimmage, knew all the plays as a reserve center, but all that season I had done nothing at game time but warm the bench. It had become my refuge. The battle was out there on the field, but I had become habituated to the civility of the tranquil bench and my fifty yard line view.

I'll never forget the game with Carmen, our last game of the season. Our first string had beaten Carmen so badly the coach was putting in everyone but the cheerleaders. Only ten minutes to go and I was on the bench alongside a huge tackle named Earl Chelf. I unabashedly sought sanctuary. But coach managed to find me. He saw me making myself small and shouted, "Cable for Perry!" I remember I stood rather hesitantly and acted as if I hadn't heard correctly, I pointed at my chest and Coach yelled, "Yes, *you*, Cable!" It was then that I realized how the condemned Thracian gladiators must have felt as they filed into the Coliseum.

On my very first play, Carmen slammed me immediately to the ground with sufficient force to make my brain feel as if it were jostling loose within its skull. And then came the next maniacal play, and surprisingly nothing hurt at all; yet, everything suddenly became like a fuzzy humming dream. I dimly recall my difficulty in determining which goal post was ours. And I wandered around a little until I recognized my teammates and lined up with them. Then, I centered the ball and whammo! Again, I was on my back looking at fluffy cumulus clouds. When the final whistle was blown, I silently thanked God for my salvation. Yet, while riding back in the bus, I realized I was finally a veteran. I knew I was hooked, and that I'd be out again next year. I'd played exactly eight minutes during the entire season which unfortunately was hardly enough for my coveted letter.

WINELDANS NO HABLAN ESPAÑOL

Later in my life, I frequently remonstrated myself for my Wineldan lost language opportunity. WHS offered no foreign language, yet for years we had been surrounded by Mexican kids. But because the Mexicans always used English in school, I acquired virtually no Spanish. Even our progressive school board chairman, Roberta Jackson, viewed foreign language as among Winelda High's least important objectives.

Homer was forever concerned that we should have a first rate education, but the lack of a foreign language seemed oddly to never faze him. Possibly this was because Homer had never been outside America's continental limits. More than a few times, he lamented

WHS's omission of Latin and Ancient History because for him in 1914 these had been *de rigueur*. In his opinion, Latin was the etymological key to so many English words. Yet, he never insisted on making Latin—touted as academia's lost language—an issue.

This was the Depression, and the objective of the board and parents alike was to stress what was essential during those four years in high school. Foreign language was certainly not vital. Where in the world would we ever use it? In the thirties, only the missionaries and the very rich traveled abroad. Who in Winelda would ever visit Spain, France, or Germany? Only aging Wineldan doughboys had been to Europe, none to Asia. Even Mexico was remote. The very fact that the Santa Fe Railroad didn't go to any of those places was proof positive that languages were a total waste of time. Yet, to communicate with good English was paramount, and Wineldan kids, including the Mexicans, learned English, and thanks to Miss Strickland, most of them learned it very well.

We white locals learned smatterings of pidgin, but I can recall no Wineldan, other than the local "Syrians," who facilely rattled off complete Spanish sentences. We had learned, "Adios amigo" which usually came out "Addy-ose a-mee-guh" and "Gracias" became "Grass-ious." We constantly yet unknowingly slaughtered the pronunciation of our Mexican classmates' names. All through grade and high school our star halfback, José Ramírez, and his sister were called Rammer-ezz. José was too polite to say it was really Rah-meer-ez. Even the teachers pronounced it Rammer-ezz, and if a teacher pronounced it Rammer-ezz then, by golly, that made it official. We also managed to butcher the name, Mahn-well. In Winelda, Manuel was called Man-yull as if he were something to read. "Hey, Man-yull, throw the ball over here." And then there was that crazy name, Jesús.

"Dad, why does he call himself Jeezus?"

The whites never felt comfortable in taking the Lord's name in vain, and we allowed that there was only one who was properly named Jesus. We figured the Mexicans had clearly made a mistake in not knowing how to spell their name in English. We figured that perhaps they should really change the J to Q. So instead of saying "Hay-soos" or the anglicized "Jeezus," we Wineldans manufactured something that sounded like "Kuh-soos." Thank God no Julios or Juans were present to endure our incomprehensible logic. And never did a Mexican snort and correct our miserable attempts at Spanish.

We Oklahoma whites slaughtered words of Spanish origin—Vallejo became Valley Joe and the Mojave Desert was the Moe-Jave—to rhyme with gave. In this regard, southern Texas kids handled Spanish quite well compared to their northern, Amarillo counterparts who joined us in massacring the language.

The regrettable upshot: when high school graduation rolled around, the Mexican kids came off decidedly best. They left WHS speaking both Spanish and English fluently while we whites remained in our provincial linguistic capsule. When WWII forced us Wineldans from our cocoon, and beyond American borders, we suddenly became individually aware of our foreign language ineptness. We learned that speaking very loudly to foreigners was no panacea for making them understand. Speaking pidgin was equally ridiculous and demeaning. During Korea, my Greatest Generation invented the disgraceful word Gook. In the Korean language Me-gook meant American, Han-gook meant Koreans. Gook meant country. But this was all so incomprehensible we just called all those people gooks. Not nice. It wasn't initiated as something derogatory, but it became that way. I would imagine that sometime between WWII and Korea it began to register that back in Winelda and other American Podunks, we had blown the perfect opportunity. Spanish had been ours for the asking. Because of those insular times, we had unfortunately ignored it.

WINELDA'S UNWRITTEN LAWS

A myriad of activities divided my attention as I grew up in Winelda, yet not once did I wonder why Manuel, José, Franco, Francisco, or Rosita never hung out on a soda fountain stool. Perhaps at the time I thought Mexicans weren't too keen on ice cream. Perhaps I never really considered. But Mexicans did like ice cream. I was never aware that it was okay for María to fill a prescription at the drugstore, but it was not okay for her to sit at the counter and ask for a coke or a cone. Had she done this, the owner would have politely and quietly said, "María, you're not supposed to sit at the fountain," and María would have quietly disappeared.

But I was oblivious to all this. I was never remotely aware. I had never heard the subject discussed. I never saw a Mexican refused service probably because none ever asked for it. Also, there were no demeaning refusal signs posted around Winelda. Many years later, José told me all about it, and I couldn't believe I had been so blithely unobservant. And the situation was never a topic of discussion.

There was, however, a discrimination that became obvious to me because it was right there at our very own Majestic Theater. We had two seating sections. The large main section was for whites. To the left of the left aisle the irregular left wall created a small nook. This narrow section had a sliver of seats two abreast and eighteen rows from front to rear. We designated those thirty-six seats as Mexican territory, and the aisle separating whites from Mexicans was looked upon as the Rio Grande. No Mexican was expected to cross to the right or white side. Again, there were no arguments and no signs; it was the quiet way Winelda wanted it handled.

Very occasionally I'd put this to Homer, "How come we go to school with the Mexicans, play football, and shower together, but in our Majestic they have to sit in a special section?"

This gnawing and recurring question of mine always annoyed Homer. In retrospect, I believe it annoyed powerhouse Homer because it was something he couldn't correct. "Now pay attention because this is the very last time we're going to beat this dead horse!" He explained that somewhere in the murky depths of Wineldan history, the majority had created the Mexican section. "Some town folks and others out across the river never went to school with Mexicans, and because they have never socialized with them, they have different ideas from yours. When Mom and Pop bought the theater that's the way we found it, and we went along with the wishes of the community. It's a closed subject, okay?" This was Homer's unmistakable signal for "discussion terminated," yet I know he agreed with me.

A few times, with a crowded theater, a white would take a Mexican seat, and Homer would shoot right over there. Homer was fair, and he figured it should work both ways. He'd tell the person that that section was reserved for Mexicans, and he couldn't sit there, and that was Homer's rule.

Homer was no bigot. During the winter, when he occasionally leapt from the wagon, he'd secretly carouse in Mexican Town, chug tequila with Concho and Tony Franco and Ramón. I'd always know when he'd made a Mexican Town foray because he never failed to bring home a Mason jar filled with hot peppers in a spicy brine of vinegar, peppercorns, and bay leaves. Only the Mexicans put them up just that way. Homer loved the peppers, and before supper he'd even sip a teaspoonful of the spicy hot brine. "Great appetizer," he'd say. "Want some?" I later acquired the taste.

Homer kept his gala tequila escapades quiet, and so did his Mexican compadres, and none ever once imposed for a free ticket. And Concho's son never said to me, "Hey, Tom, your father was out at my house drinking tequila last night with my father." Many things in Winelda were never said. But because José was my confidant—he swore me to secrecy—he told me of Homer's carousals at Mexican Town. "We like your dad."

Many of the older Mexicans were Homer's friends. In front of the theater at night, I plainly saw their camaraderie as they bantered with Homer at curbside.

To the best of my knowledge, the subject of discriminatory segregations was never on the agenda at a Wineldan council meeting. Most of Winelda's white folks were good Christians who in their WASP way followed the teachings of the Bible. They felt good about themselves, and probably genuinely believed that virtually no one was persecuting anyone. "So long as those folks live out there in Mexican Town, go to their contrary Cath-lick Church, don't mess with our girls, and sit on their side at the pitcher show, everthing'll work out jist fine." That position seemed very fair to them. Even the ultra-liberal and outspoken Roberta Jackson seemed pleased with the status quo. And not one Mexican free spirit ever stood on a tequila box and ranted, "Down with Wineldan discrimination. Viva Equality! "

Another thing my cronies and I never picked up on was where the Mexican kids had their school day lunch. It never occurred to me that no Mexican kid ever enjoyed a twenty-five cent plate lunch special at Etta's counter. I'm sure Etta was probably faced with the same dilemma as Homer; it was the way some rednecks had wanted it years ago. And come the thirties, there was still no one with the courage to strike a match around all that old gasoline. It had become one of those latently explosive "let-old-dogs-lie" issues.

It was only a few years ago that José told me where the Mexican kids had had their lunch when we were kids. They'd go to Coury's, and to Albert Cohlmia's, the "Syrian" grocers. José supposed it was because the Syrians were a kind of neutral ground because the Syrians themselves were anomalies of a sort. The Syrians weren't really native born, weren't WASPS. They were an ethnic puzzlement, but Wineldans considered them to be white, and fully acceptable. It is not known what rube in town tagged them Syrians, and I never asked. They had all early emigrated from Lebanon, probably from 1905 or 1906 onward.

Because the Syrians were probably Winelda's most tolerant whites, Pacheco and Innocente, shunned by Winelda's eateries, went to the back of Cohlmia's. There they found many other Mexican boys and girls sharing a head of lettuce, bread, cheese, and baloney, and drinking bottled Nehi cream sodas. And the Mexicans never forgot Albert Cohlmia's welcome, and the fact that Albert and his son Sam made an effort to learn and speak Spanish. It was probably why Mexican families bought their groceries almost exclusively from "the Syrians."

Another topic not for public conversation: no one could identify who had previously ordained that Mexicans must live only in Mexican Town, and not in Winelda town. Consequently, up to 1942, not one Mexican lived in town.

The unwritten rule for blacks was infinitely more obscure, yet even more exacting. They were never to be in town after sundown, which is probably why no black family lived within fifty miles of Winelda. Even though there were no posted signs, everyone—even kids—knew Winelda was off limits to blacks.

An old black preacher with a beautiful head of white hair some-times arrived on the morning Santa Fe. He'd stand at the corner of Cecil and Main next to the drawing barrel, and he'd preach the gospel for an hour or more. He'd then walk from store to store to take up a collection. Through the thirties, I must've seen him return to Winelda over a dozen times. A man reportedly of the cloth, both adults and kids always treated him deferentially, but not once did he fail to board the evening train east toward Kansas.

Occasionally a salesman with a black chauffeur would call on Winelda. No kid or redneck ever taunted the chauffeur, or mouthed slurs, but I never once saw a black driver get out and stretch his legs around the Square. They always waited inside their car. I often wondered how they sensed Winelda's unwelcome.

HOMER'S CHRISTMAS SURPRISE

Come Christmas of 1938, Homer did something special. He sent Amzy and me on a great trip—by train to Wichita, then by airplane to Amarillo, and return to Winelda by rail. We spent the night at Wichita's Allis Hotel. At fourteen stories, it was at the time the tallest building in all of Kansas. The next morning we took a taxi to the municipal airport, and upon arrival, I was surprised to hear my name being paged just as they did it in the movies. Homer had taken a letter to the mail car of the Santa Fe train that had left hours after us. He had scribbled on the envelope: "Please broadcast so addressee receives by 9:00 A.M." And what do you know? They announced it throughout the airport's speaker system, and I picked up the message at the TWA counter at 9:10 A.M.

Imagine such magnificent service for three cents! Imagine trying that with today's USPS or today's airlines! It was an earlier, ancient time in an uncrowded nation when special courtesies were not uncommon. Except for the absence of some of today's technology— the dishwasher, the washing machine, the disposal—the old days weren't all that bad.

When I opened Homer's letter, a five dollar bill fell out along with a note from Homer:

> I know you didn't take enuf so herewith is a fiver. Next time you take a trip always add twenty percent, at the very least ten. Sorry for my terrible writing. I cannot use the noisy typewriter, because we have a full house, and I'm writing in a hurry. If this doesn't reach you by 9:30, phone me. We don't want this trip to be a bust. Gives you a chance to get out of Winelda and see what the other world is like. Love, Homer
>
> P.S. I have to run to the train.

The pressure of time obviously rattled Homer because if his letter with five dollars had not reached me by half past nine, how could I possibly have known to call?

Amzy and I boarded the hot new Douglas DC-3 for Amarillo. Even old laid back Amzy was emotionally stirred, especially when the pilot shoved the throttles wide open for takeoff. Once aloft, everything was beautiful, and like country bumpkins, we marveled "gee whiz" when the captain announced we were rocketing at a hundred and fifty-seven miles per hour and were twenty-four hundred feet above the ground! The real thrill came at five minutes to eleven, when we flew over Winelda. We could see our railroad trestle bridge, and off to the right was No-Name Mesa, which we subsequently called Diamondback.

Later on, I was fiddling with our tickets and noticed the airfare was sixteen dollars and ninety-five cents each! I had no idea air travel was so expensive and that Homer had spent so much. When we landed in Amarillo, we took a taxi to the Santa Fe depot, and inside an hour boarded the Scout. We were in Winelda at 6:45 P.M.

Homer met our train, and I sensed an object lesson coming. "Well," he said, "I wanted both of you to get out of the sticks to see how others live. If you two make good grades, probably later on you'll always be staying in fine places like the Allis Hotel and flying TWA." Because we had had dinner in the diner, I went straight to the Majestic to take tickets, and Amzy went above the Snooker Parlor to report to his grandmother.

THE GREAT AND THE TERRIBLE UNCLE ENNY

Through mid February Homer had been doing remarkably well. Oh, there were a few boisterous nights, but nothing riotous. Then one Sunday, Homer's old Kansas University roommate, who I called Uncle Enny—his name was Enfield—drove over from Fairview to visit. I liked effervescent Uncle Enny almost as much as I feared his arrival.

Enny knew all about the Kansas City catastrophe, and he mistakenly thought it good therapy for Homer to commiserate, to occasionally let it all out.

He and Homer would sit at the kitchen table, fill each other's glass, and dredge up that sad event. After a few drinks, Uncle Enny would effusively tell me how much I'd grown or that he'd heard about my grades. He always made me feel like the most important kid for miles around, and then he'd grandly hand over the keys to his new Buick streamliner, "Take 'er for a spin." It was one of the hottest looking heavy cars on the market, and a real kick to drive, and I knew how to drive. Mom had often let me chauffeur her to the grocery, or for a short drive on our deserted highway.

I'd pick up Mean Dean, or Amzy and Jack, and we'd drive Enny's Buick to the Devil's Playground. We'd slowly cruise around the Square, wave at Marshal Patton, and hope a classmate would see us. Enny was big hearted. Still, I secretly wished Enny would stay in Fairview where he sold wholesale groceries for the Polly Parrot Company. He was Homer's best old school friend who never understood Homer's problem as well as he imagined.

I wanted to tell him he caused great harm by encouraging Homer to drink. But at fourteen, I wasn't bold enough to speak in such a way to an adult, especially to an old friend like Enny. Enny would have been offended, and had Homer gotten wind of it, he would have been apoplectic. But long after Enny had returned to wholesaling groceries around Fairview, Homer's pump was still primed, and he'd be chugging his bottle at the kitchen table. Regrettably, Homer never developed or sought a connoisseur's drinking experience, never was he able to quietly sip commendable sour mash, or to whirl it around in his glass so that he could enjoy its special aroma or flavor. Good whiskey was wasted on Homer. He belted the shots back, not for taste, but for a quick solution.

This past winter, Homer had come upon the ultimate quick fix. Lottie was bringing in half pints of grain alcohol. This was ninety-five percent pure alcohol as compared with forty-three percent for ordinary booze! It was the very same torpedo juice used in hospitals. Those little half pints possessed the zing either to numb Kansas City, or to deaden Homer's excruciating sinus pain, or both. At age forty-one, I suppose Homer's body tolerated the powerful stuff up to a point, but then he'd inexorably drift into a comatose condition.

Thank God Mom and Pop were spared learning that Maddy finally had to take Homer to the Alva hospital. They were wintering in Hollywood, Florida, and Maddy opted not to spoil their fun. It was March 1939 when Enny again telephoned. I was looking forward to spring, and the return of sanity to our household. Maddy picked up the phone and immediately started reading Enny the riot act, told him exactly the damage his last therapeutic visit had caused. He drunkenly demanded to speak to Homer. Maddy said, "He can't, Enny. Thanks to your last Kansas City talk, he's strapped to a hospital bed with an IV buried in his arm." Maddy said sterner things, and told him he was no longer welcome. Uncle Enny got the message because I never saw him again.

THE CAR—SPRING 1939

All through sophomore year, I made the honor roll; it was no longer a big deal. Come spring, I would be a fifteen-year-old junior. I had actually won some regional academic contests—mainly in history and science—never in math. And through the winter, I had done well by Mr. Stephens at the cleaners.

As spring brightened to summer, good things began to happen. For example, one day I was shining brass when Amzy happened by with Vern Darbee. Amzy was very upbeat because he had just graduated from high school. Vern was a nice guy Amzy's age, or possibly older, and habitually very reticent. I always thought of Vern as the quiet one. "Hey, Tom," said Amzy. "Vern and I wanta know if you wanta come in with us to buy a used core?"

"A car?" Having just progressed to bicycles, a car was far beyond my comprehension. How could a car possibly be within reach?

"Vern and I are each gonna put in five, and with your five, I believe we kin swing it."

"Fifteen dollars will buy a real car?"

I was quick to sense Amzy's impatience. He wanted me elsewhere to see the car. He didn't want me shining brass, and this always presaged a golden opportunity for me. I lethargically mothered my brass, and continued asking pertinent questions while the two of them impatiently watched.

"What kinda car," I said. "Where is it?"

Amzy, quickly wearied by my questions, grabbed a rag and immediately sprang into action—to hell with this; the three of us feverishly shined the brass. Very soon all the brass and copper had a luster bound to please Homer. The sidewalk was cleaned, and we headed for Hough's Dry Goods to examine the car. While beating it around the Corner Drug, Amzy carefully explained that only one of us should deal with Mr. Hough. And because Vern seldom said anything, I somehow knew Amzy would be our spokesman.

"Yep," said Mr. Hough. "You boys can have her for just twenty dolluhs."

I looked at the big piece of machinery sitting behind the dry goods store—a vintage, stripped down Pontiac from the twenties—no body, no top, no doors, no roof, just a windshield poking up in front of the steering wheel, and the two front seats. It did have wide running boards and a ponderous buckle-down hood over the engine. In the rear, where passenger seats had once been, was a wooden decked flatbed for hauling. It was a real antique with huge wooden spoked wheels, and flaccid tires ready to explode, ancient tires that evidenced considerably more cord than rubber.

Amzy queried, "Will she start, Mr. Hough?"

"'Fraid not, Amzy. Ain't no battry, but then what d'ya expect fer twenty dolluhs?"

"Huh," said Amzy, looking at the heap as if it were something dead in the stockyards. "Core that won't start shouldn't be more than fifteen at most."

Mr. Hough ignored the fifteen remark. He was a wily critter used to deal making, so he just silently gummed an imaginary cud as if he were holding four aces. I was quite proud of Amzy; he came up with some pretty amazing theatrics. He stalked around the heap scowling, lifted each side of the squeaky hood, banged it down, rehooked it, and kicked the tires. Occasionally he'd rap a heavy steel fender with a bare knuckle. Then he said, "Well, Mr. Hough, these days fifteen dollars don't grow on trees. You let us tinker with her a coupla days and we'll let you know if we'll come up with fifteen dollars."

Hough didn't argue. I had the distinct impression that with a tad more of Amzy's histrionics, Mr. Hough might very well have paid us to tow it away. But like good soldiers, quiet Vern and I kept our jaws clamped shut. "Awright," said Mr. Hough. "You boys can tinker, but I don't wantcha removin' no parts, ya hear?" He jabbed his index finger at the sky as if he were making a salient point, "That car's a real piece of Wineldan history."

"Yes sir," said Amzy with another grunt. "It's a piece of some-thin'."

The derelict, in the back lot between the Snooker Parlor and the Majestic, couldn't have been better located. Amzy was just upstairs; I was around the corner; and only Vern lived across town, but that wasn't far. Nothing "across" town was all that far.

I didn't want Vern and Amzy to know I wasn't my own man, that before I could spend my own money, I had to have an okay from Homer. I also didn't want to make Homer appear as an ogre. The fact was that I could spend twenty cents of my savings for a box of rifle ammo anytime I wanted, but for a project of the five dollar magnitude, Homer always wanted to play the entrusted fiduciary role, to advise.

Each of us chipped in a dime and set off to buy a couple of gallons of white gas. Amzy said, "With no battry, we'll have to push her to get her started, then it'll run off'n the generator." To me this was all new information. I knew how to drive, and change a tire, but I knew zip about automotive mechanics. Somehow, I got the distinct impression that my five dollar investment was going to be summer tuition for a seminar on the internal combustion engine, which was okay as I had a hungering interest about cars.

That evening Homer surprised me. He was immediately pleased with the deal because Amzy was the project's prime mover. Homer had always liked my association with Amzy, especially now that Amzy had just graduated from high school, and had never been in any trouble around town. Homer was also pleased because there were no incipient problems—no need for license or insurance. He asked what our plans were for this vehicle.

"We're going into the trash and junk business—cleaning yards, and finding zinc, and brass, and lead, and stuff to sell to the junkman."

Homer smiled and blew a smoke ring. He'd taken to using a cigarette holder with an enclosed disposable filter. When he held it in his mouth at a jaunty angle, I thought my father looked very debonair, and much like our president, Mr. Roosevelt.

"Junk's not particularly good business. You guys are going to discover it's even more unremunerative and backbreaking than farming. If you're smart, you'll forever avoid it as a line of work. But," he said, "at least you should learn what wrenches and screwdrivers are all about." Then we laughed and surprisingly Homer put his arm around my shoulders, hugged me up a little, and said, "Thanks for asking me what I thought."

Homer rarely displayed affection, but when he wanted, he'd do memorable things, like that little hug. I still remember those indelible moments. If at that very instant he had asked me to take a sword and go face a band of wild Indians, I would have charged out the door, saber in hand.

Vern and I got behind the old Pontiac and began pushing it out onto Missouri Street. Amzy, with one hand on the wheel, pushed alongside. When it began rolling at a fair clip, Amzy hurtled over the running board, worked the choke, pumped the foot feed, and then let out the clutch.

Absolutely nothing!

There wasn't a cough, not even a small curl of smoke. The heavy machine came to a clicking halt in the middle of Missouri. After an hour of trying to revive the Pontiac, we were spent and wet with sweat. Thank God when old Mr. Hink rounded the corner in his new pickup, and without a word, nudged up behind the heap and pushed us to the Snooker Parlor's rear.

I asked of Amzy, "Now what?"

"Ain't gittin' no gas, no gas uh tall."

"I don't get it," I said. "We just put gas in there."

Amzy looked at me wearily. "Ain't gittin' pumped up to the carburetor." I marveled at Amzy's automotive knowledge.

Vern and Amzy tinkered and concluded the fuel pump was shot, and with no economical replacement feasible. We spent the next couple of days removing the hood and installing a one gallon gas tank directly over the engine. I must honestly say that I really understood very little of this. But if Amzy told me to remove some screw or bolt, I did it, and then watched to see what followed. It was pretty swell stuff to learn the mysteries beneath a car's hood, and discover words like "slip joint" pliers, and "Phillips" screws, and "hex" nuts, and "ball-peen."

Our small tank worked on the gravity feed principle. But before starting the Pontiac, someone had to open the tank's valve, and be sure to shut it off at day's end. If not, the gas would steadily drip and flood the engine. That was the fundamental set up.

Again we pushed the behemoth out onto Missouri, exactly the same way they do fine racing cars. But ours looked bizarre with the hood removed, and with the little one gallon gas tank poking above the engine. We slowly gathered speed, and then Amzy leaped into the seat and set the gear. The engine coughed, and a substantial cloud of sooty smoke spewed from the tailpipe! Then came a brief uncertain sputtering engine, but it finally caught and roared. Bystanders who had been watching cheered and hooted. Vern and I leaped into the right hand seat, and the three of us zoomed across the Santa Fe tracks, turned right at Lottie's Place, and rocketed up Cedar Street. With no muffler, the Pontiac's growling power sounded truly awesome. It was a charged moment, and at that point, I better understood how Orville Wright must've felt.

Thundering northward, Amzy yelled above the din, "Hey, Vern, you hear thet?" The distinct *knock, knock, knock* was hard to ignore. Vern didn't speak, just nodded his head toward Amzy.

"What's the knock mean?" I asked.

Amzy looked grave, "Most likely a connecting rod's shot. Possible it could fly clean through the block. If it does, then this here core's f'rever dead."

"That knock means more money?" I asked cautiously.

"Yeah," said a quiet but knowing Vern. "Thet and lotsa work."

At that precise moment, Vern's diagnosis meant little to me. The magic carpet thrill mesmerized me as we whizzed out of town scattering idiot chickens. And vital heat began emanating from the engine, and through the floorboard came the good smell of burning oil, and everything sounded very omnipotent. To those of us peering through the windshield, it mattered not a whit whatever work and expense faced us. Like a flying carpet, Mr. Hough's great historic machine had sucked us in!

"Let's go close the deal," said Amzy, and Mr. Hough could scarcely conceal his delight as he pocketed our fifteen bucks.

Over the next ten days, Vern and Amzy feverishly tore into the engine's heart. I handed tools, watched, and asked questions. Amzy played the role of performing an automotive autopsy. He would spew forensic information by me as if I were his recorder. "This here's the ignition harness, that there's the rotor, this's the coil. Tom file thet lead-in's copper tip to a shine . . . ." Eventually we slowly lifted the stubborn head from the engine block.

"Drat," said Amzy. "The gasket's done fell apart. Hafta make a new one." And I felt confident because Amzy was so confident.

And there I was, looking into the shiny innards of a real engine. Next, we dropped the oil pan, its fossilized gasket also destroyed, removed the engine's pistons and connecting rods, and laid them out neatly on an old wooden door.

"Lookit," said Amzy. "These here two valves are burned and here's the bad connecting rod. See?" Amzy stuck the rod under my nose and showed me the missing pieces of Babbitt metal. "That's shot!" he declared with finality. He put it back on the crankshaft and showed me how loosely it fit. "That's why it went *knock, knock, knock.*" Like the master, Amzy exuded triumph while I began to understand the basic fundamentals. Vern seldom spoke but continually worked.

Everyone chipped in a dollar, and at the junkyard Amzy bought two good used valves and a rod. From some gasket material Vern found at Waggoner's "Shivvy" garage, we cut out new gaskets, and two days later reassembled the engine. Amzy had shown me how to clean and gap the sparkplugs, and how to sand the Delco-Remy ignition points. With everything wiped clean, the entire engine and wiring sparkled. Then we canvassed each of Winelda's seven filling stations, rummaged through cast off oil cans, and dripped them dry of their heavy new oil, garnering perhaps a tablespoon from each.

No longer was a car engine a mystery. I knew where all the pieces went and how they worked, and I had become a gasket expert.

"What do we do for a battery?" I asked.

"We ain't," said Amzy. "Battry's too expensive, and used ones ain't worth the trouble. If we kin, we'll always park her on a rise. 'Nuther thing, we're gonna hafta always pack around a coupla gallons uh extra gas 'cause thet liddle tank only holds about fourteen miles worth."

Altogether the car had cost twenty-two dollars and fifty cents and about two hundred man hours of work, but its engine ran like a Rolls Royce.

BLOOD ON THE WINDSHIELD

Born was the CDC—Criswell, Darbee, Cable—Metal and Landscape Company. The remainder of the summer we cleaned yards, and mowed grass, and while doing so made great finds—like the bushel basket of pure zinc Mason jar lids; these brought good money from the junkman. We harvested several pounds of valuable lead connectors from old batteries. Behind a dilapidated garage, we discovered an ancient patinated radiator. This brass treasure brought four dollars. Near the roundhouse, we found almost forty pounds of copper wire with rotted insulation. Amzy built a fire to burn it off. "Don't hurt the metal none," he said. "Copper's still copper." Early on we concluded iron and steel were losers to be avoided—too heavy, too little value, and they agonized the Pontiac.

During all these trips, we had a clean driving record until one day at the intersection of Missouri and Cecil. Luckily, it was a weekday, and there was little traffic. We had just passed Eastman's, and had waved at Cavy, a pioneer cowboy who forever sat in front of Coury's Grocery. Amzy had just begun his right turn onto Missouri toward the Santa Fe Reading Room.

Calamity! The Pontiac didn't turn. It headed straight for the Commercial Hotel!

"Shit far, shit far!" yelled the struggling Amzy. The king pins had failed, and the tie rod had suddenly fallen free. The great machine shot across the intersection and was on a collision course with the fast approaching hotel.

"Whatsa matter, *whatsa matter!*" screamed quiet Vern.

"The brakes, Amzy, the braaakkes!" I yelled.

Amzy pumped furiously. "Gol danged, gol danged!" he said as he tried downshifting. Then we hit the high curb and the Pontiac leaped skyward. "AAAaaaaaay!" we screamed in unison. Amzy was ejected high from his seat, but he maintained his death grip on the steering wheel. His knees were splayed like a bronc rider's in a high buck. We crossed the wide empty sidewalk, glanced off the side of the hotel, and stopped dead, a little cloud of steam spewing from around the radiator cap. We had deeply scarred three of the Commercial's red bricks. In the hotel's lobby, two cheaply framed prints from Kress's crashed to the floor with a tinkling of glass.

Blanche Hawkins, the perfumed owner/madam with rouge and lipstick that flamed, bolted onto the sidewalk with her hands on her hips, her hair piled high atop her head. "Lands sake, what you kids think yer a doin' with ma building? And how come you're drivin' on the sidewalk?"

Amzy, his nose bloodied by the windshield's frame, looked forlorn indeed. "Didn't mean to, Mrs. Hawkins, couldn't steer. She headed straight for yer hotel . . . danged brakes didn't work, nuthin' worked."

Out of nowhere materialized the genie town marshal. About Billy Patton no one could ever say, "When you need him, he ain't never there." Billy had no radio and no patrol car, just a big star and a huge six-gun, but he was everywhere! Ever present, phenomenal Billy was there when needed. This time he was going to be stern to satisfy Blanche and her scarred property. "Uh, huh," said Billy who didn't like arguments or long explanations. "Well, jist back her up boys. Let's get her off the sidewalk. We cain't obstruct the entry to the hotel, now kin we? All rightee, now let's move smartly."

Blanche Hawkins walked over and ran her fingers across the bright red scars on her three bricks. Billy watched her like a hawk. Then she huffed, tossed her great head of red hair, and retreated inside the Commercial. Elna Lou, one of Blanche's girls with no trick at the moment, was standing at the main door with a dustpan full of broken glass. She disappeared with Blanche. Trouble averted, Billy was suddenly relieved. Then he faced us and obviously expected faster action. "Well, well boys, let's start this thing. Let's git it moving, moving, moving."

"It never jist starts, Marshal Patton," said Amzy. "Before any startin' takes place it gets pushed." And Billy, the genuine public servant, and a couple of willing bystanders, pushed and docked the Pontiac alongside the curb. That became our workplace, and by late afternoon, I learned all about the tie rods and kingpins, how the steering mechanism worked, and how our two wheel brakes were adjusted.

By the end of the summer, our earnings had paid for our Pontiac, and its repairs, and fuel three times over. More than a dozen times it had taken us to the sandpit swimming hole west of town. Those six mile trips were always the ultimate adventure. We'd invite Jack Beaman, his brother Milburn, Mean Dean, and Jerry Berryhill—at least eight or nine guys chipping in a dime—but never a girl because no one owned swimming trunks.

As the Pontiac growled along the sandy road straight west of Winelda, it generated its own cloud of white exhaust smoke. Amzy always piloted while wearing an old railroader's cap turned backwards together with an awesome pair of welding goggles fitted with clear glass lenses. He'd hunch over the wheel with a stare as demonic as Baron von Richtofen ready to machine gun the Dawn Patrol. Vern and I, the co-pilots, were squeezed together in the extra front seat. Two guests were on each running board, and the remainder hunkered on the flatbed, where they clung white knuckled to the backs of our front seats. And we all leaned forward as if this would make the Pontiac go faster.

It was yet another scene for Norman Rockwell—the Pontiac's blur of wooden spokes as it flew over those rolling sage covered hills.

Sometimes on down slopes of the sandy road, we'd reach the electrifying speed of forty miles per hour! That's when our flapping fenders would make marvelous clanging and banging sounds, and the phenomenal unmuffled engine would bellow its truly awesome power. Our hair blowing back, shirttails flapping, our jaws rippling from the rush of hot wind, we peered raptly ahead. It was the greatest excitement.

And then, as we reached the banks of the Cimarron, the miraculous geological transition appeared. The rounded sage hills on this side of the river changed to majestic red mesas on the opposite side. Just ahead, near the Santa Fe railroad bridge, lay the ultimate adventure, the sandpit, and already the guys were half shed of their clothes.

HOMER THE RIDICULOUSLY BRAVE

On the third day of July, Perry Phillips needed our service. "If you boys wanta make three bucks, come out to my place early tomorrow morning and haul bales of hay from the barn to the rodeo enclosure. We need 'em for a barrel race, and I'll throw in tickets for the rodeo." We figured that without the tickets, we'd be making about thirty-three cents an hour. As Homer would have fondly said, it sure beat the two cents I'd made slopping hogs.

Every year the rodeo was a major event, and as far as we kids were concerned, the Indians were the best part of it. When they came to town, they'd make camp by the stockyards, put up real teepees for their families and dogs, and at Elm Park they'd sell their jewelry and beadwork.

The rodeo's first event was always Chief Black Bear of the Arapahoes. When he galloped into the arena on his paint pony wearing his beautiful war bonnet, a respectful hush fell over the crowd. "Ladieeees and gentlemen," the loudspeaker boomed. "I give you Chief Black Bear." Thunderous cheers came from the crowd, and then abrupt silence fell because of everyone's great expectation. From a chute at the arena's opposite end, an enraged steer charged toward Black Bear. The cowhands had probably infuriated it by twisting its tail, and for the moment, the chief was the only thing it could see for revenge.

Black Bear calmly reached over his shoulder, pulled an arrow from his quiver, brought it to his bow, and everyone, even wizened old cowboys, was spellbound. Black Bear let the arrow fly, and as always it went straight behind the running steer's right shoulder. In rapid succession, he shot two more arrows and the steer made a pathetic death bawl as it went to its knees. There was much applause as Chief Black Bear's phenomenal accuracy thrilled everyone. Then two yelping braves galloped into the arena, threw their ropes on the dead steer, and dragged it from view. More applause.

Each year the Winelda Saddle Club donated the steer to the Indians, who took it to Elm Park. There they slivered it to dry as pemmican and jerky. When we went to buy Indian belts and other beadwork, we'd see the beef drying under the sun on boards. It was always covered with thousands of black crawly flies. Even today when I eat jerky, I think of the blanket of flies and wonder if the jerky process has ever changed.

After the chief's event, there was calf roping and bulldogging, followed by bronc and steer riding. Over and over we heard the announcements from the judge's tower. "Out of chute number four is Squirrely Jackson on Reno Devil." A sudden crashing of the gate and Squirrely would appear and soon become just an obscure lump inside a cloud of arena dust. "And ladies and gentlemen, one of our greatest Oklahoma cowboys, Dudley Perkins of Nowata, Oklahoma, on Dark Mystery, chute number three." Dudley would explode into the arena flailing his big hat, the bronc snorting and jumping stiff legged. Then there was more yelling, and spurring, and chaps flying balloon-like with each mighty leap. When the whistle blew, a big cheer went up, and Dudley's second would ride out to take him off to the side.

The loudspeakers boomed again: "Now, ladies and gentlemen, this afternoon we have a special Winelda rider, someone we all know well. He'll be ridin' Cimarron Demon. He's not from a ranch. He's a towny, and he ain't wearin' boots, he's wearin' *store bought shoes!*" Laughter and yahoos. "Yessir, he's gonna show these cowpokes a thing or two."

This announcement certainly focused everyone's attention. "Out of chute number one is Homer Cable of the Majestic Theater! Let's everybody give the picture show man a big han'."

I was absolutely mortified!

Homer's drinking always bothered me, but not so much if he were home and out of sight. If he was where my classmates might see him,

I'd want to dig a hole. That's what I wanted to do right then. He had to be bombed to do something this bizarre, even if it was July, and even if it wasn't his time to be bombed. A festive event, I figured Homer was in his cups, had been doing some razzing near the official's box, and had become caught up in a dare he couldn't refuse. I watched intently, and I could hear Homer's horse as it resolutely kicked the hell out of the wooden chute.

"Tom," said Quiet Vern, "it's yer ole man." I was too jolted to respond. So was Amzy, who knew Homer pretty well, and knew how I felt.

There was Homer on the chute's rail dressed in his best double breasted worsted suit, a white handkerchief in his breast pocket, and his new Florsheim wing tips. Thank God it was too hot for spats. But I knew a sober Homer would never have jeopardized his good suit and shoes. There he was, so completely out of sync with all the prevailing Levi's, boots, spurs, and Stetsons. I ducked my face between my knees and hoped for the best. During all the whooping and hollering, Amzy hadn't so much as smiled, and I appreciated that.

Homer's crazy bronc spun out of the chute and all but fell. I was amazed Homer stayed on. But there he sat, like the Rock of Gibraltar. The horse quickly recovered and immediately went into its wild, stiff legged bucking. I'll never forget my dad out there with his right arm way up above his head like a cowhand's, and that silly white handkerchief flapping in his jacket. After two strong twisting bucks, Homer shot high over the horse's neck, his legs and arms all askew, to crash in a swirl of dust while the clown immediately ran out to shoo off the crazy horse.

The tower boomed again, "Ya done right good, Homer! Reckon you boys won't mine if Homer decides to start wearin' boots 'roun the Square. You earned 'em, Homer. Let's have a big han' for Homer Cable."

Everyone could see the fresh steer manure covering Homer's sleeve. When Homer stood up, straightened his tie, and waved, the crowd loved it. I guess it was the straightening of the tie. Homer was in his frivolous stage, it was the Fourth of July, and it was his father's birthday. Later this evening, he'd most likely turn ugly.

Amzy whispered to me, "Surprised me, Tom. Yer ole man done right good. He's got a lotta courage." But having said that, Amzy said no more because he knew Homer, and he could read my feelings.

When the summer was winding down, I knew I'd be starting football, and I wouldn't have much use for the Pontiac, so I asked Vern and Amzy if they wanted my one third share. For ten dollars, they took me out of the trucking consortium. I had learned a lot, even some knowledge that Homer didn't have. I knew how to adjust Delco-Remy points. I knew how a rod was fastened to a crankshaft, how it and the rings and valves functioned, and I knew what kingpins were. That summer with Amzy and Vern had been a great learning experience.

In World War I, Cheek of Winelda had been the town's first killed in action, and when they placed the American Legion building on the south end of town they called it the Cheek Chapter and his name was emblazoned on the building. A few years after the great Pontiac experiences, they changed the sign to the Cheek-Darbee Post. Quiet Vern was Winelda's first to give his life for his country in World War II.

JUNIOR YEAR 1939-1940

My very best Wineldan year was at age fifteen when I became a WHS junior. The courses had become considerably more interesting—chemistry, typing, speech, American History, American Literature, and biology. I also worked on the school newspaper, the *Sagebrush*: "The Sage of WHS." Aaron printed it each week as a scheduled part of the *Winelda Enterprise*.

We started off with class elections, and it humbled me immensely to be elected class president. I could only figure I had strong support from the farm and ranch kids. Homer was impressed and confided he had never been a class officer. This made me ride even higher, because I never thought I could excel Homer at anything. But despite my having conquered the honor roll, I still must not have been a very savvy kid. After the election, I remember meeting Superintendent Pennington in the hallway. He stopped and shook my hand and said, "Congratulations, Prexy!" and I smiled broadly and thanked him and wondered what in hell a "prexy" was.

NO GLORY ON THE GRIDIRON

In the class picture, I finally made it to the row just below the top. I was now five feet ten, and weighed a hundred and thirty-five pounds, and although still not the player of Coach Claunch's dreams, I had become a passable second stringer. Frank Perry, my friend with the pea green kitchen, was the senior class president and first string center. I was Frank's sub.

Looking back, I can candidly say our football was by far more physically demanding than the football played today. We had no offense-defense teams. One team, with only occasional substitutions, played it all. Many first stringers played a full sixty minutes. There were no facemasks, and there were no plastic teeth.

In 1939, the coach used the popular but complicated Notre Dame box. This demanded great skill from me, the center. Probably every team member thought his position was the very best, the toughest, and most demanding. I knew my slot as center was unequivocally the team's most complicated.

It was necessary to contort my body to get my head down to where I could see my four backfielders between my legs. In the meantime, I had no idea where the conniving guard opposite me had shifted. I had to concentrate on centering, and seldom did I center just straight back. There was always a lead angle because my halfback was already running! This was the center's plight. Imagine the pandemonium if I didn't lead him accurately. And upside down, I had to pass accurately on every offensive play. The only time I didn't have to lead was when we punted, and then it was a simple straight back delivery. I see college centers today pass it right over the punter's head.

Compare today's center with the quarterback standing only inches behind. The center literally hands him the ball, which is pretty easy stuff. Before charging, the center today can actually look the opposing guard right in the eye—piece of cake. Not for me, a split second after I centered, I had to charge out blindly, usually to my right or left front, and oftentimes the enemy had shifted, and I'd hit absolutely nothing. There I'd be, stretched out full length on the sod, and I could always hear Homer loudly shouting how great that looked. Or there would be the opposite situation, the instant I centered the ball—*wham*—the unseen guard would knock me ass over teakettle.

It wasn't fair. I would like to have shared a halfback's, or a guard's glory, and at least have been able to see my adversary. But I must say that coach had given me my chance for backfield, but I had failed. My passing was okay, but I lacked the ability to dance and swivel my way through tacklers. So I was relegated to the worst spot on the line, the place where I could never see the man I blocked, and where I spent the game looking upside down through my legs or up at the stars.

Because I was fast enough, I played linebacker on defense, a position very conspicuous to the sidelines. Among the tangled flotsam of the line, no one ever noticed when a guard or tackle miserably failed, but if I failed out there in the open, everyone and his dog could see that fearless Tom had goofed. When some gazelle-like ball carrier managed to avoid all our guards, ends, and tackles, he'd be coming with pointy knees, elbows, and cleats, and at an ever increasing speed. That was Tom-of-the-gridiron's moment to dramatically use his hundred and thirty-five pounds to bring all this inertia to an abrupt halt. When I blammed head on into one of these kinetically wild persons, I oftentimes heard bizarre "tink tink tink" sounds, and I'd miraculously see the infamous thousand points of light dancing around inside my skull. The coach would be yelling "iron head" as the man ran for a touchdown, and the cheerleaders would *never* yell, "Two, four, six, eight, who do we appreciate? Tom, Tom, Tom."

Those discombobulating shocks sometimes caused me to momentarily wander, and all the voices around me sounded like incomprehensible duck talk. But Coach was very perceptive. He was quick to detect when I obviously did not recognize my own teammates. He would promptly send someone to lead me away. I have great respect for a linebacker. It calls for a powerful guy with mass and speed to plug a hole with a devastating, bone crunching tackle. I had speed but very little mass.

There was much punishment in being a center–linebacker and virtually no possibility of a glorious touchdown. But coach, God bless him, regularly pumped me up, told me few could center as accurately as I, and how I had yet to center the ball over the punter's head. Then he'd reward me by letting me play at least a quarter of each game. By Christmas, I was proudly wearing the coveted big white "W" on my black wool sweater. Had it not been so scratchy, I might very well have worn the thing to bed.

José Invites Us for Dinner

After we'd received our football letters, José invited three of us with dates to his home in Mexican Town for a real Mexican dinner. José wore his best suit with a gardenia in the lapel button. Because his father was on shift at the roundhouse, José played head of the house. His mother and sister, Rosita, didn't eat with us because they were too busy cooking the rice, pollo fajitas, frijoles, enchiladas, and tacos.

For the six "native" Americans at the table, it was our first time experiencing Mexican food. Except for my photo atop a sleeping Tijuana burro, none of us had been to Mexico, and Winelda oddly had no Mexican restaurant. José's mom spoke no English, so José translated when she announced the dishes and told us how to eat them and how to use the salsa.

She was obviously proud the Winelda boys had accepted her son, but we'd done that long before the dinner. And there wasn't a kid in WHS who wouldn't have wanted José and his family to sit with us in the middle of the Majestic, but that, unfortunately, was not our decision to make.

I believe everyone in town was aware the Cables never had time for dinner guests, but I thought that perhaps one of the others might have invited José and his folks to a dinner in town—if not José's family, at least José. But no one ever did. We kids had no racial stigma, yet we were equally as thoughtless as we silently shifted the blame onto our folks. Had we been wholly honest, we could have thrown our own dinner at Eastman's or Etta's. Years later, I mentioned this, and José laughed. "They wouldn't have served me at Eastman's or Etta's anyway." Still, we could've had a backyard barbecue or a picnic—funny how thoughtless kids can sometimes be. Only later do we realize our gross oversights, and as adults we still manage to commit them.

Neighborly Winelda

Regardless, Winelda had a special heart. Take this two sentence squib in the *Winelda Enterprise*:

> The Busy Beaver Club met Thursday at the home of
> Mr. and Mrs. Jack McWhorter. The ladies quilted and
> the men sawed wood.

Oklahoma City folks might see this and look upon Winelda as a
real Sticksville, but it spoke of a special level of neighborliness.

McWhorter's friends were Wineldans who cared. They knew his
disfigured arthritic hands were incapable of sawing or chopping
wood. When they met that Thursday, seven Busy Beaver men sawed,
chopped, and stacked enough wood to last over a year. While they
chopped, the Busy Beaver ladies gossiped, cooked, and finished
quilting a Dresden Plate they would sponsor at the church's next quilt
raffle. The community helped a friend, and no one was humbled by
handout welfare.

WICKED WINELDA

The Winelda churches would come down with an iron hand on
anything bringing tarnish on the community's good name. And
while Winelda's city fathers were not always squeaky clean, at least on
Sundays they were paragons of Christendom. They wore their
Sunday best and loved their neighbor and spoke well of the Mexican.
And why not? None of the Mexicans were vagrants, and none ever
attempted to sit in Methodist or Baptist pews. If a little tomfoolery
went on in Winelda, it was okay so long as it didn't burn the ears of
the city mothers. It was only because bootleggers and the ladies of the
night maintained the lowest possible profile that they survived.

Blanche's edict was that her Commercial girls dress and wear
make-up very conservatively. Marvelous Blanche provided the
dichotomy, she with her fulsome paint, powder, and green perfume,
and looking and smelling as whorey as anything out of a Long Branch
Saloon. But if one of her girls occasionally appeared on Winelda's
streets or attended the picture show, Blanche made sure they were like
driven snow, and resembled in no way the bad girl described in my
freshman sex class.

It was several weeks after Amzy and I had crashed the Pontiac
against the Commercial when I learned Blanche ran the best little
whorehouse in Winelda. I learned it from Kylee, the high profile Santa

Fe call-boy. I say high profile because Kylee, twenty-four, drove a Santa Fe Ford dispatched from the superintendent's office, and it was his job to be everywhere. In my eyes, it was a job to envy. Kylee was always scouring the town to tell engineers, firemen, brakemen, and conductors when their train was scheduled to leave the yard.

Kylee was a friend who needed my cooperation because at least once a night he'd rush into the Majestic in search of a railroader. I knew most all the itinerant railroaders by name, and knew where they were seated. This saved Kylee a lot of time, and that is how we became fast friends. Now that I was old and big enough to wear Winelda's "W," he sometimes let me ride with him on Friday nights after I got off work. Even though we'd only go to the Santa Fe Reading Room, or to Etta's, or to Nick's Confectionery, or occasionally deliver an engineer out to the yards, I viewed the whole business as very special. We had an official Santa Fe vehicle, and our missions were of the utmost importance. I particularly liked the excuse to accompany Kylee into Nick's because of the aura of a secret slot machine room in the back. Kylee would say, "Nick, have ya seen Lester March or Orville Broughton . . . they back there?" What Kylee meant was "are they back there playing your outlawed slot machine?"

Nick would thrust out his big hairy hands to support himself against the marble counter. "Orville's down at the hotel, and a half hour ago, I seen Lester havin' a java at Eastman's."

Very little in Winelda escaped Nick Nickerson. We hustled out the door, jumped in the car, and when that powerful V-8 engine burst into action, I felt only one step removed from Elliott Ness. Kylee said he always saved Blanche's hotel for last so's to give a railroader every last minute in the hay. "Down there none of these guys is ever happy to see me."

Most railroaders looked upon the Commercial Hotel as a home away from home, and it certainly had a railroad atmosphere. The hotel's backside was only twenty-five feet from the Santa Fe's main line. Every passing doubleheader set the entire building to rattling and rumbling, and the overhead lights would sway and jiggle. Each room had a bowl and pitcher—no running water—a clean three quarter bed, and a single light with a green shade hanging from the ceiling. The round green shade was exactly like those over the pool tables at the Snooker Parlor. All the rooms opened onto a central hallway with a toilet at each end.

Kylee conferred with Blanche Hawkins at the front desk and all the while she cocked an intimidating eye at me. I was pretty sure she was thinking of our Pontiac, her scarred bricks, and her pictures crashing.

"Yeah, Kylee, Lester's in 204 and Orville's in 209. Poor Lester, he's only been up there ten minutes."

"Cain't be hepped, Blanche. Duty's duty." Kylee and I shot up the stairs two at a time. He told me he figured he'd roared up those stairs more than four thousand times. He also said he'd long since learned never to barge in or to even crack a door. He hammered at Lester's door.

"Yeah, what the hell is it?" said Lester, who had just taken his pants and drawers off and was about to climb into the sack with Sadie Mae, a comely lass newly arrived from Borger, Texas.

"It's Kylee, Lester. You got to be at the yard in forty-five minutes. Number 41 to Wellington."

"Aw, shit, Kylee. Why me dammit! "

"Sorry, Lester. It's your crew. Can I give ya a lift?"

"Naw, I'll catch Norm's taxi." Norm's was a four door Shivvy.

"Don't go to sleep now, ya hear?"

"Kylee, my everlastin' thanks. Now get yerself lost, boy."

Lester said, "Shoot" and stood there indecisively while lightly scratching his belly.

Sadie Mae didn't want Number 41 to chisel her out of her five dollars, and besides, Lester was sure to be a fun frolic. She beckoned with her finger, "Come on, Lester, we got time." She reached and grabbed Lester by his half interested willie and playfully pulled him her way. And there he was, acting the part of a seasoned nineteen year head brakeman, consulting his official Waltham railroad watch while Sadie Mae tugged him toward her perfumed and inviting arms. You might say Sadie Mae had her hand upon the throttle while Lester had his eye upon the rail. And in no time at all, Sadie Mae had his complete interest, and she'd make double sure he didn't miss his train. She didn't want any railroader getting brownies—gigs—because of her. As Blanche always said, "Make 'em happy, Sadie Mae."

Kylee continued on his way . . . Bam, Bam, Bam! "Orville, you in there?"

"Yessss, Kylee, bin here twenty-four hours. Whad'dya want you sucker, as if I didn't know?"

"You gotta nower ta be at the yards, Orv, Number 32 to Canadian. Want I should pack you over there?"

"Okay, Kylee, I'll be at Etta's in forty minutes. Much obliged."

Orville was twenty-six years with the Santa Fe, and one of its senior freight engineers. Orville's responsibility was one of the eight-wheel steel monsters—an enormous 4000 Mikado 2-8-2—that spewed plumes of steam and boiled clouds of smoke. To the kids along the right of way, he was one of the magical men with a red bandanna who looked cockily from his lofty cab window—the captain of the train. Most every kid wanted to emulate the Orvilles of the Santa Fe. And the Orvilles truly cherished their well-paid work. On a big, sweeping curve, they prided themselves by grinning back at their command of a hundred or so freight cars.

In 1939, who could know that times would change so dramatically, that later generations with no dashing Orvilles to idolize, would switch their allegiance to fighter pilots, dotcom entrepreneurs, astronauts, or to swashbuckling Rambo-like characters. Who would have ever envisaged those colorful steam locomotive engineers would become as extinct as dinosaurs?

Elna Lou laid her arm lightly over Orville's chest and brushed her tongue across his ear. "Elna Lou, Honey, I never thought I'd ever say it, but you've plumb near wore old Orville out." Orville stretched. "Yes sir, it's a helluva nice wore out feelin'."

Elna Lou had told Blanche and all her other tricks she was twenty-three, but she was really nineteen. She was three quarters Irish and a quarter Spanish, had dark brown flashing eyes and beautiful long legs. Although a "pro," she was like a vivacious high school girl on her first hayride.

Just looking at her aroused Orville.

But just now, like an old lion on the savanna, he stretched and stared languidly at the yellowed, water stained paper on the ceiling.

"Oh, Orvy," Elna Lou pouted. "You gotta go drive the big choo choo?" Elna Lou was keenly perceptive. She was aware Orville took special pleasure in her tawny legs, so she nestled a soft thigh playfully into Orville's crotch. He touched its chamois-like softness, played his hand lightly across the tiny golden hairs, checked his watch, and figured, "Yes, by golly, I reckon there's time." Orville was always very nice to Elna Lou, and she pleasured him anyway he wanted. If he wasn't exactly certain, she'd manage to come up with something spirited and remarkable. Only at it since eighteen, tossing was a natural sport for Elna Lou. She thoroughly loved turning on good men like Orville. "It sure is a fun business," she'd tell her compatriots, "and they actually pay me!"

It was the irresponsibility of this kind of honest talk that made the other girls think Elna Lou was a lot younger than she let on.

And later, as his big Mikado locomotive pounded up the Curtis grade, Orville would think about Elna Lou's loving, and he'd even feel himself getting aroused. It made him feel good, and he'd lean out, scan the sagebrush, shake his head, and smile broadly. "Gol-danged," he'd say to the prairie, "but that kid's a humdinger!"

Other than the coyotes, if anyone had seen Orville grinning at the prairie, they would've thought Orville was like a kid in love with his locomotive, or that he had taken leave of his senses. But everything was crystal clear, and as he peered beyond one of man's largest machines, and then back at the second locomotive of the double-header and the far-reaching column of freight cars, he thought, *Man! This's as good as it gets. Can't git no better.* Just for the hell of it, Orville reached up and blew the whistle at absolutely nothing but rabbits— "just to blow the damned thing," he yelled. And Orville's fireman glanced at Orville quizzically, but he was sure he knew what was going on in Orville's mind. He wasn't thinking of his wife, which didn't really matter because the fireman knew for a fact that Orville worshipped his Mrs. and their kids.

Blanche Hawkins provided an important Wineldan service. Her Commercial Hotel left most of the railroaders with smiles on their faces. Railroaders spent their entire adult lifetime leaving their families and taking trains somewhere. Had layovers like Winelda been sterile, windblown Podunks, railroading could have been a tedious career of colorless arrivals and departures. Instead, towns like Clovis, and Canadian, and Winelda made them happy, and they felt welcome. Back home when their call-boy told them their train to Winelda had been made up and was ready to leave, their minds were not bogged down with the drudgery of work. Surreptitiously, they'd think of the Commercial and of the likes of Elna Lou, Sadie Mae, or that cutey Bobby Jo. And they'd most likely allow it was a marvelous Depression and "life ain't so bad." Possibly, it's the reason retired railroaders smile a lot and live to be so old.

Nu-Sho—Winter 1939

Good-natured Woods County wasn't always a hundred percent friendly; there was wheeling and dealing. For example, an investment company in Alva, the county seat, owned the defunct theater on the dead side of Winelda's square. The big company had acquired it as collateral in a deal gone sour long ago, and it had become like a festering thorn in the company's backside, an embarrassment that refused to go away.

The investors were hopping mad. "By gol, times are bad enough without carrying unremunerative dead wood that costs us property taxes . . . good money going after bad! Why do you people hang on to the damned thaing?" And slapping the conference table, "We want return for our money, not more debt. Pure and simple, let's have an immediate solution, or we'll start looking for new officers who understand what action means."

In a strategy meeting, Dan Doolittle, the president, was in a blue funk as he chewed his cigar. He knew he had to come up with something evil, else the poorly located old theater in Winelda would never sell. Like a laser beam, the solution came to him, and he said to the other officers, "Try this on for size. Winelda's definitely a one picture show town, right? Now, if we reopen a no frills theater, we know it won't make money, but it'll sure as hell siphon off the Majestic's cream, kill that guy's livelihood . . . what's his name?"

"Name's Homer Cable."

"That's right . . . Homer. Well, Homer don't know it, but he's going to buy us out at our price. If he tries to wait us out, we'll drain that sucker white. We got the resources; he doesn't." Doolittle looked around at the directors who were grinning and grunting approval. "Now then, that should show those hardnosed investors they got innovative management." He struck a match and puffed madly on his dying cigar. "And why in hell didn't we think of this long before?" Everyone around the table smiled, and satisfyingly snapped their suspenders.

It was a downright predatory way of doing business. But business was business, and the Alva company president and directors cared not a *pfffttt* for Winelda, or for Homer and Maddy and me. When you got right down to it, few at the Alva county seat had any special regard for

Winelda. The 1936 dust storms might just as well have blown down-town Winelda clean off the map. Then those in and around Winelda would have had to come to Alva to spend their carefully husbanded dollars.

Homer wouldn't have been the only business affected by Doolittle's decision. The businesses on the hot side—the Rexall, Nick's Confectionery, Miller's Bakery, the Corner, Hutch's, and McBride's Grocery, etc.—all depended on traffic created by the Majestic. A theater on the dead side would siphon off business, start drying them up, tumble their property value, and make them really feel the Depression.

So it was a sad day when reports trickled in that workmen from Alva—they didn't use Wineldans—were over at the long deceased theater with saws, hammers, and paint buckets instituting some bare bones cosmetics. Up went a flimsy plywood marquee with cheap cut out letters that read: "Nu-Sho." It wasn't a bad name because everyone would have referred to it as the "new show" anyway.

The theater's old wooden seats were still okay, but the foyer needed paint, which they were sloshing around. Then they installed thin, unpadded carpeting in the lobby. It didn't feel rich like the Majestic's, but it looked good, and made the lobby smell new. The projectors and sound equipment were operable and had long been on site.

It was a dilemma for Homer because he was in no position to fail. His eighty-five dollars a month rent helped ensure Mom and Pop Cable's retirement. Homer also had Maddy to think of, and on the horizon was my college.

At the moment, Homer was no match for Doolittle et al. At an earlier time, Doolittle would've rued the day he ever attacked Homer. He would've slammed headlong into a brick wall. When Homer was right out of Kansas University, he had been a dynamo in Coffeyville, only to later fizzle because of Kansas City. New Orleans had recap-tured a glimmer of the old Homer, but in the end, even that had begun to sputter. Homer had what it took to joust with Doolittle, but the fire-ball in him was now little more than hardening lava in a dormant volcano.

With the Nu-Sho, Homer faced a monumental test. His family and livelihood were openly threatened. But instead of revving up and roaring out of chute number one, once powerful Homer rolled over pitifully like a bloated sheep. The pressure made him again fall off the wagon, and the crash could be heard all around Winelda. He began slugging down Lottie and Jimmy's hundred and ninety proof grain alcohol, and as he slugged them back and raged, he transcended to an ugly thing neither Maddy nor I recognized. He wouldn't eat. He just drank and occasionally would do his butter thing—eat a full quarter of a pound as ravenously and as disgustingly as a hungry animal. And he'd smoke more Camels, sometimes three packs in a day, and these seemed to trigger his body shaking cough, and rekindle his sinus pain. Everything pained pathetic Homer. It was anything but his finest hour.

As Maddy prepared dinner, Homer sat at the kitchen table clutching his glass on the table as if it would escape. His sticky hair hung down over his glazed eyes, his head weaved from side to side, ashes dribbled on his shirt from the cigarette hanging from his lips, and he ranted.

"*Tom!*"

I was in my room studying and didn't answer. Quite frankly, I was afraid of him.

"*Tom,*" he yelled. "*Dammit,* when I call I wantcha out of your room instantly!"

Having read the same line ten times, I closed the book and walked to the door.

"Ah, there you are." He fixed his bleary eyes on me, and his head bobbed up and down. "Don't give me that insolent look. Stand up. *Stand at attention!* Fasten your eyes on the wall over there." Then he went into another coughing fit with more ashes messing his shirt as well as Maddy's tablecloth. Once the cough was under control, he discursively launched into a series of subjects. This was his tangled, incoherent pattern. Sometimes he'd ramble and slobber for ten to fifteen minutes running.

This time Maddy interrupted. She turned off the gas cook top, took off her apron, hung it on the fridge, put her arm around me, and spoke over Homer's maundering. "Come on, Tom, we're going to the theater." She saw no point, while Homer was in his mood for holding court, to prepare a dinner that we'd never have a chance to eat anyway.

As we prepared to march out of the apartment, Homer said, "You two aren't goin' anywhere," and he rose unsteadily to his feet, stumbled against the kitchen table, and then seized with coughing paroxysms, he sank clumsily to his chair and rested his head on the table. "Ah, who cares where you go? Go on, *ingrates!*" he shouted and violently swept his arm toward the door. His gesture caught his glass and sent it smashing against the kitchen wall, accompanied by a burst of new uncontrolled coughing.

Maddy and I crossed the street to Etta's, sat in a booth, and grabbed a silent bite before going on to the theater.

We knew Homer would eventually drink himself to sleep. After the theater, we'd either find him asleep at the table, or he'd have managed to collapse in bed. Once Maddy had checked after the first show and found Homer sprawled full length on the kitchen floor, where he snored in a deep, stuporous sleep. His nose had bled slightly from falling out of the chair. Between his fingers was charred cigarette paper stuck to a huge watery blister where the cigarette had seared deeply into his flesh. He'd burned his fingers this way several times before. His numbed brain received no signal sufficiently adequate to awaken him.

On a few occasions, he had gone down the stairs, reeled, and stumbled toward the theater. At such times his glazed unfocused eyes recognized no one, and any who saw him pretended as if Homer weren't there. In a town like Winelda—where the word traveled so quickly—it was a painful embarrassment. Yet not one Wineldan ever once made snide remarks to me about "your drunken old man," not one hint from a classmate—even today—and I have always appreciated Winelda for that.

One night I was mortified when Billy, the town marshal, struggled into the theater lobby with Homer. I could tell Mr. Patton was embarrassed for me to see my dad's condition. It didn't occur to him that in the privacy of our three room apartment, I'd often seen Homer in such a way.

"Tom," he said, "your dad was hanging onto the light pole outside. Where can I put him?"

We took Homer into the tiny box-office with Maddy, and he sat slouched in a small chair out of the public's view. Half an hour later, and without warning, odorous urine began seeping through his pants and running down into his shoes. It puddled in his chair and ran off onto the concrete floor in an amber pool. Homer opened his eyes and he became pathetically childlike, "Oh look, Maddy, my God look what

I've done," and he commenced sobbing. There was nothing for Maddy to do but to let him sit there and marinate in his own stinking mess. She called me. I still remember how I felt seeing Homer sitting there weeping like a kid. I threw the *Daily Oklahoman* over the puddle on the floor. Homer slept. Later on, when the box-office closed, Maddy departed for the apartment and brought back dry underwear, socks, and clean trousers. She pulled the box-office curtain, made him presentable, and walked him home.

That night, after the show, Maddy told me to get to bed and not to worry, "Your dad's passed out. Virgil and Esther at the Corner have volunteered to drive Homer and me to the Alva Hospital tomorrow morning. He has to dry out." Maddy didn't cry, but her lip was trembling. She was at the end of her rope. I was secretly relieved that Homer was leaving. He was starving. In the hospital, they would feed him glucose intravenously.

During my high school days, my father had been "dried out" no fewer than seven times. During one very bad bout, when he had delirium tremens, Maddy had sent him to Anthony's Galloway Hospital so that Mom could also keep an eye on him. It broke Mom's heart. She'd see Homer surge against his restraining straps like a mad man and remember how loving and thoughtful he could be when he was Homer. Pop took little part; he hated what alcohol had done to his son. He abhorred the weakness so he refused to visit the hospital.

Through all those episodes that Mom had been made aware of, Mom steadfastly remained the Cable soldier. She never played a wilting passive role. She'd cheer us up; tell us how proud she was that, in spite of Homer, we were operating the theater so well. When Maddy visited the hospital, I'd ask my friend Mean Dean if his older sister Fay would sell tickets for Maddy. I'd manage the floor while Mean Dean ushered. We never once closed the Majestic.

HIGH NOON IN WINELDA

When Homer began coming around from this latest ordeal at the Alva hospital, there was something different from previous bouts. He recalled his hospital nightmare, and almost as if born again, he was both ashamed and angry because of his disgusting behavior. This was certainly a step in the right direction. Most encouraging of all, he came out of the Alva hospital like a driven person. Homer was ready to set the record straight. No longer did he stand in awe of Doolittle's Nu-Sho ploy. Everything had miraculously come into focus, and Homer knew exactly what course of action was necessary. He was mounting up to lead the cavalry. If the Alva moguls wanted to play dirty snooker, then by God, they had met their nemesis. This was the real Homer, and it was going to be *High Noon* in Winelda.

Doolittle and his henchman, Attorney Wilton Schenks, searched for someone to manage the Nu-Sho who was both naïve and easily manipulated. Finding an available theater operator in Northwestern Oklahoma wasn't easy, but they lucked onto Pinky Norcross, a youthful former manager of a small Enid theater. In the Alva company's view, lightweight Norcross was sufficiently capable of holding things together until Homer caved in—six months at the outside.

Doolittle and Schenks didn't want Pinky on contract because they wanted to be able to fire him anytime they were ready. So they tantalized him with a loosely worded lease that gave him cheap rent. As an added inducement, they gave him a "verbal" option to buy the theater at a ridiculously low price, but they never mentioned the price. The option, of course, was malarkey, and the price would certainly be no bargain because they didn't want Pinky to buy it. Pinky had no money. Doolittle and his bandits certainly didn't want to carry Pinky's paper; they wanted to be clear of this property. They wanted to skewer Homer, force him to buy, and make the yapping stockholders happy. After that, they would tie a tin can around Pinky Norcross's tail.

Schenks flicked his cigar ashes and chuckled, "I don't know why we never thought of this before. They'd gotten wind of Homer's delirium tremens from the Alva Hospital and they had celebrated. "The guy's a quick cave-in. By the time we've finished with that poor Wineldan sonuvabitch he'll be crying to buy our building. What the hell's his name again? Homer Cable? Yeah, that's it. Old Homer'll crawl in here, hat in hand, and his cornpone ass will be ours." Dan Doolittle and the board members laughed uproariously.

The Nu-Sho opened, and because it was a novelty in town, it predictably attracted quite a number of Wineldans. In Winelda, when it came to entertainment, or to groceries, or to gas, there was no fast allegiance. Money was hard to come by, and it boiled down to what the public liked, and what it cost. The shows at the Majestic remained high quality, and the air conditioning was far superior, but now that winter was setting in, "air" wasn't important. The Nu-Sho wasn't making expenses, but it was never supposed to. It was doing as planned—draining off enough to make the Majestic a barely break even operation. Something was bound to give.

Homer would give me a dime and send me over to the Nu-Sho to "check their house," and I'd return with a disheartening figure. One that indicated the Nu-Sho was skimming off thirty-five percent of the people who would normally have come to the Majestic. It was the kiss of death, and Homer knew the time had come to launch his own dirty tricks.

One afternoon, Homer intentionally ran into Pinky Norcross at the Snooker Parlor. A few of the regulars noticed and were sure a good fight was about to materialize. So instead of playing, they stood there chalking their sticks and grinning through cigarette-stained teeth. It was a big disappointment when Homer and Pinky sat down to a congenial game of dominoes. "Hell," said one of the bystanders, and they all began shuffling back to their games of eight ball and snooker.

While playing dominoes, Homer discovered Pinky looked upon the Alva company as a solid opportunity to own his own theater. "You can't blame me, Homer. Opportunities are few these days. This thing between you and me is entirely impersonal. Doolittle's attorney laid on a steak dinner, gave me a big soft Cuban cigar, and told me I'd have an option to soon buy the theater at a very attractive price." Pinky smiled, "For me it's a terrific opportunity."

"What price did he name?"

"I never asked. I didn't want to press a gift horse. It was one of those chances of a lifetime."

After dominoes, Homer said, "Pinky, come with me. I want to show you something." Pinky and Homer disappeared down the street to Homer's office at the Majestic. Homer was looking for a deal, and when Homer got on a roll, his salesmanship was powerful and persuasive.

"Pinky, if they were going to give you an ironclad option for peanuts, then how come they gave me this offer?" Homer slid a letter-head paper across the desk. Pinky blanched at the big figure.

"Uh huh," said Homer, "fifty-five hundred dollars. This is outlandish for property on your side of the Square. Can you pay fifty-five hundred, Pinky?"

"Somehow I thought it would be a thousand and that they'd carry me."

"Carry you?"

"Yeah, I don't have a thousand."

"Those people don't want to carry anyone, Pinky. They just want out of that mess. Their stockholders are raising hell. Now, keeping in mind they want fifty-five hundred, let me give you some idea what Winelda property is worth. I bought the prize building on the Square for only thirty-six hundred dollars. My mother bought the Majestic for four thousand, and it was fully equipped and a going concern. Doolittle's demand of fifty-five hundred on the dead side of the Square is pure extortion. It's hardly worth fifteen."

Pinky was quick to see he was just a pawn in Doolittle's fight with Homer. "Hell, everything seemed on the level. I figured they wanted to unload a dog cheaply, and I wanted to start my life." He looked sheepish and gestured with his hands, "Well, you can't fault me. Sometimes good things happen." Pinky lit a cigarette and fiddled with a pencil, "Looks as if I'm just a patsy in this battle."

"Yep," said Homer. "If I paid 'em off today, you'd be out on your ass tomorrow. You did say your lease is null and void when the property's sold?"

Pinky nodded.

Homer went on, "But, even had you got it for fifteen hundred, you and I were still going to be bumping heads in a one theater town. You weren't going to get a life. You and I'd be sucking wind together."

Homer did something very rare. He showed Pinky his books for the past two weeks. Pinky was surprised to see the Majestic had grossed more than twice his take. He was also surprised Homer already knew his house count. Homer had had a checker at the Nu-Sho, sometimes a checker and a double checker, every night since the opening. "You can't make it, Pinky, and it'll be bleak for me. The thirty-five percent you're taking is what we would normally bank; it's what keeps us alive. We'd bleed each other white. The other alternative is that I cave in and come up with fifty-five hundred bucks. I'd be mortgaged to a worthless piece of property, and you'd be history."

The twenty-seven-year-old Pinky could see that the older Homer had five times his experience. Homer had told him of his United Artists position in New Orleans, how he had operated a theater in

Coffeyville, and had helped his parents establish one in Anthony. Homer knew how to exhibit and promote pictures, and he had powerful contacts for buying them.

"Homer, you don't sound as if you're going to buy, and you say we're crashing. What've you got in mind besides handing me my head?"

"Because this Alva outfit's screwing both of us, whad'dya say let's make them sorry they ever tangled with us? Let's you and I get in the driver's seat." Pinky nodded. "Here's what I've got in mind." And for thirty minutes they huddled with Homer's plan.

BREAKING AND ENTERING

Three nights later, when customers came to the Nu-Sho, they found the marquee darkened, and all the doors chained shut. The Alva projectionist, the ticket taker, the box-office cashier, and the usher had been given their final paychecks. Homer subleased the Nu-Sho from Pinky, and took over the obligation to pay Pinky's regular forty dollars per month lease rent to Doolittle. Homer was also responsible for paying Alva ten percent of gross, which was an additional percentage rent. But because Homer shut the Nu-Sho down, there would be no gross, and there would be no percentage to pay.

Homer wanted Pinky far from Doolittle. To seal the deal with Pinky, the two of them flew out of Oklahoma City on a Lockheed Electra for a week of celebration in New Orleans. But before leaving town, Homer and Pinky told the right people around the Square the true facts. This assured the story would spread out across the Cimarron like a prairie fire.

The Alva company had no legal right to reopen the theater because it was Homer's. Schenks had never considered a no sublease clause in Pinky's brief lease, nor had he contemplated the contingency that if the theater were closed there would be no percentage rent. Doolittle and Attorney Schenks were furious.

Most crippling to Doolittle and company was that they had contractually rented—cash in advance—the first three months of films—a sizeable amount of money. This had been a part of their deal with Pinky because he had no money. They'd rent the film, and in return would get ten percent of the take plus Pinky's forty dollars per month lease money. It was virtually a break even deal for the Alva Company, which was now stuck with three months of films and no theater to show them in. It was a situation bound to exacerbate the displeasure of stockholders.

"Now goddamit to hell," seethed Attorney Schenks. "Sub-leasing and closing the theater was never the intent of our lease! We paid through the nose for all that film, and now Homer's not even going to show it. It's not sposed to work that way."

"Homer's a dirty sonuvabitch," said Doolittle. "Unethical as hell. We'll sue that Norcross so fast it'll make his head swim."

"Sue him for what?" said Schenks. "He isn't defaulting the lease; goddam Homer's paying it. Unfortunately, the film rentals cost us five times as much, and we're getting nothing in return. Not only that, we're also on hook for Norcross's advertising."

"Advertising?" wailed Doolittle.

"Yeah, we did it because we weren't sure Pinky would do a good promotional job. Remember, we wanted the Nu-Sho to be a killer? So we prepaid three months advertising in the Alva, Winelda, and Wood'ard papers."

Doolittle, thinking of the stockholders and the darkened Nu-Sho, poured himself some stiff shots of Old Quaker.

When Homer and Pinky returned from New Orleans, they drove down to Seiling where Homer knew that, due to a death, a theater was up for grabs. Homer liked Pinky and had faith in him. On a handshake, he staked Pinky to a thousand dollars—a considerable amount of money at the time. After six months, Pinky was to begin making restitution to Homer of at least seventy-five dollars a month. Homer asked his Oklahoma City United Artists friends to support Pinky's Seiling debut. Within a year, Pinky had repaid all the money with interest, and Homer had a lasting friend in the newly successful Pinky Norcross.

Meanwhile, the Nu-Sho's darkened marquee and its chained doors became a leg slapping story that spread its way throughout Forrest County and across the river into Major County. Quite a few folks in the area suddenly recalled stories of how this same hard-hearted company had either threatened or foreclosed on their friends—and the stories multiplied.

"Ya know, this here Homer over in Wy-neldee, he subleased the Nu-Sho, chained the doors shut, and then took Doolittle's manager clean outta town. Heh, heh, right smart the way Homer handled them slick Alva fellers."

Wineldans, and curious out of towners, drove around the Square just to see the dead Nu-Sho and its array of chains and locks hanging from the doors. Among the curious were a few of the irate investors in the Alva Redlands Investment Company. They were losing a bundle, and Doolittle et al. were back on the griddle. Duped by Homer of Winelda, they were desperate to turn this embarrassing defeat around. But, until the six months lease expired, Schenks knew Doolittle and his banditry were legally dead in the water.

So Schenks planned a fast one.

They located a new manager in Wood'ard and wanted to show him the Nu-Sho set-up so he'd be ready to roll the day Homer was out of there. Schenks would handle this new man differently. There would be no lease. They'd promise the Wood'ard man a substantial salary and nothing else. If he was incompetent, they could give him the boot any time they wished, but there'd "sure as hell be no sub-leasable lease for Homer to manipulate."

Schenks and the Wood'ard man were spotted entering town one noon from the south in the backseat of a big dusty green Buick. The driver was a beefy guy with a black felt hat and cauliflower ears. The man to his right was a good sized workman in bib overalls, a hacksaw at his side. They drove around to the quiet side of the Square and parked in front of the Nu-Sho. The man with the hacksaw hopped out and immediately went to work on one of the chains. Because the loose chain was difficult to hold and saw at the same time, it created a clanging racket. This caught Cavy's attention, the Winelda pioneer who often sat and sunned himself in front of Coury's Grocery. He alerted retired cronies in front of the Commercial Bank, and because everyone was aware of the gritty details, they ambled over to see the action. It was an event that would surely spice up their otherwise vacant day.

"Hey there, fella! You tole Homer you was a bustin' into *his* place?"

The hacksaw man kept working, but the beefy driver got out of the car and approached the oldsters with no smile. "Ain't his place," he said. "B'longs to our company. Now move on."

"Oh, is thet so? Then howcum you ain't got no key?" and everyone began scraping their feet and guffawing. The big driver backed off.

The Alva worker didn't want trouble and stopped sawing. He looked over at Schenks sitting in the car. After all, when it came right down to it, he was the only one breaking and entering. Schenks shouted, "Ignore them, Roscoe! I told you it's our propity. We got every right."

One of the hecklers, a man who Homer had given the privilege of charging tickets at the Majestic, immediately hustled around the block to Homer's office.

Homer's sublease from Pinky still had over four months to run, and he had carefully paid Doolittle's investment company its lease checks by certified receipt—return mail. Homer had turned this expense into promotion. He figured since so many people had their eye on the Nu-Sho, he'd plaster the Majestic's coming attractions on the Nu-Sho's front.

Homer found Billy Patton watering at the Rexall, showed him his notarized sublease, showed him that if the rent were paid the lessee would get quiet enjoyment, and pointed out there was no provision for the owner to come onto the leased property for inspection.

Billy Patton took off his spectacles, "Yes, sir, Homer. It all looks legal and proper, sure 'nuf does. Yes, siree bob."

"Well, Billy," said Homer. "Orly here says they're breaking and entering my leased property, taking a hacksaw to my locks. Isn't busting in still a jail offense?"

Billy looked at Orly, who corroborated Homer's story by nodding.

"Well, it's a jail offense so long as a judge sends 'em to jail. I can only hold cantankerous people in jail a short time while they're being charged, or until Ken Greer comes down and gits 'em." Billy wasn't going to become a bull in a China closet until he was sure of his ground.

"Well then," said Homer, "if they're trespassing, let's go arrest these cantankerous people, throw them in jail, and let Greer come down and pick 'em up."

Billy was now confident, and he suddenly had duty, honor, and country written all over his Stetson. "Alrightee, let's go!" Four eavesdroppers under the Majestic's marquee joined Orly and Homer in the vigilante-like march. As they marched, Billy periodically patted and adjusted his six-shooter to make certain it was still hanging from its belt. As they rounded the Corner Drug, four more joined the group—

"What's happenin'? Where're yuh goin'?" Another three joined at the Snooker Parlor.

When Billy sternly arrived at the scene, thirteen onlookers were at his side plus Cavy's original contingent of six seniors who had stayed at the Nu-Sho. It looked like a horseless posse. The big driver assumed a low profile by sitting glumly behind the Buick's wheel. Billy could see the chain had been sawed through, and he could see the workman was just then unthreading it from the handles of the big doors. It was the kind of red handed situation Billy loved. He knew his boots were planted on solid terra firma, and his big gleaming star seemed ever larger.

"Well, Sir," said Billy to Roscoe, the hacksaw man. "I am the law here, and it 'pears you are breakin' and enterin', and I'm placin' *you* under arrest."

The agitated workman was quick to back paddle, "Whoa, Marshal. I only done what he paid me to do, and he pointed to Schenks in the back of the car.

"Makes no difference, mister. What wouldja say if he paid you to shoot somebuddy?" Billy whirled to face Schenks, "And you, Sir, I would say you're aidin' and abettin'. Yes, siree. Yer jist as guilty." To the driver, "And you driver, as wheel man, you're an accomplice." Billy had swiftly and authoritatively covered all the bases.

Schenks, unperturbed, immediately put all his oily legal eagling to the fore, "Marshal, now for heaven's sake, let's be sensible." Schenks sat up tall to intimidate Billy and handed over his calling card—no one in Winelda used such cards. "I am Wilton Schenks, attorney for the owners in Alva. This is our propity, and we are only trying to gain our rightful access so that I may show it to this potential lessee. This is Mr. Ramsey Bartlett of Wood'ard."

"Uh, huh," said Billy who was peeved because Schenks had told him to be sensible. "I've heard of the owners, and you got no rightful access. This here's Mr. Cable's notarized lease, and it proves it's his place, and his rent payments are certified and not in arrears. You cain't come on to his premises breakin' his locks unless you're the law with a warrant, and you ain't the law. *I'm* the law in this here town! Yer breakin' and enterin', pure and simple, and as a lawyer you oughta know better." Schenks started to protest, but Billy, knowing distasteful lawyer ways, cut him off at the pass. "You'd best get sensible, lawyer-man. Start arguin' with me and you'll also be disturbin' the peace and resistin' arrest." Billy virtually stuck his head inside the car window. "Am I makin' mahself perfectly clear?"

Wilton Schenks was no fool. In his lifetime, he had had more than his share of experiences with small town marshals. Yet he registered his displeasure by snapping, "Alright, Marshal, we shall leave."

"Nah sir. Not 'til I say ya will, ya won't. If I decide to charge ya, you won't go anywhere but the Winelda jail . . . to be held there till such time as you can be turned over to Sheriff Greer. Now if that's clear, you've got some clearing up to do." Billy had become as obstinate as a goat. "*First*, I believe you should pay Mr. Cable here ten dollars for replacement of this here lock and chain and the marring of the door. Wouldn't you figger ten dollars was about right, Homer?" Homer nodded. Billy turned back to Schenks, "Yes, ten dollars. As a lawyer man I'm sure you're well aware that I got no authority to force you to pay Mr. Cable ten dollars. However, if you refuse, I'm puttin' y'all in jail to wait for Ken Greer to take y'all up to county where a judge will have you pay punitive extras."

Wilton Schenks quickly opened his wallet and took out two five dollar bills, which he handed to Billy Patton. "Oh, not for me, Mr. Lawyer," said Billy raising his hands. "Pay it to Homer Cable; it was his property you destroyed." It killed Schenks to hand money to Homer, who smirked faintly. "Now, that done, I want y'all to git straight outta mah town, and don'tcha ever come back 'lessn you behave yerselves." Billy eyed Schenks carefully, "We understandin' one another?" Billy could be terrific!

RAMSEY BARTLETT

Four months later, Ramsey Bartlett came to town and legally reopened the Nu-Sho. Ramsey was a boozer, and a disingenuous person not remotely approximating Pinky Norcross's capabilities. With a hollow guy like Ramsey, money talked, and it could temporarily buy his ill defined loyalty. Homer decided to buy a piece of Ramsey's tarnished allegiance and chalk it up to the cost of doing business.

Two weeks later the new chains were back on the Nu-Sho's door and the marquee darkened. Homer had Ramsey in an L14 Super Lockheed Electra en route for a week of festivities in Miami. The classy air travel had intrigued Ramsey as well as the thought of the wicked women that Homer said they'd surely find. Unlike Norcross, Ramsey was on no legal hook with Doolittle and Schenks. He was merely an uncontracted employee who had walked away from his salary.

Doolittle and company went absolutely ballistic. This time there was no lease for Homer to take over, but finding yet another theater operator was no easy matter. To lay on a replacement plus the projectionist, ushers, et cetera would take the Alva company at least another expensive month. And like a faucet that wouldn't turn off, expensive films arrived every second or third day, never to be shown.

Word was getting around that the Alva company was having its problems screwing with Homer and Winelda's marshal. Also, because the word was getting around, no projectionist or responsible manager wanted to work at the Nu-Sho. And the Alva company was again caught with a new three month contract for film rentals as well as stale advertising, all of which would cost another bundle. Apoplectic stockholders, who couldn't believe the company had again been skewered, besieged Schenks and Doolittle.

The whittling boys in front of the post-office were saying, "Them fokes up in Alva don't know if they're the screwer or the screwee. Har, har, de har."

Surprisingly, the trip with Ramsey wasn't as onerous as Homer had supposed. Dishonorable Ramsey was personable, had an interesting line of gab, and Homer didn't have to trust him. Ramsey appreciated the trip to Miami Beach, something that was far far from his reach. And the woman Homer had found through an enterprising Shelburne Hotel bellman had captivated Ramsey.

Ramsey was so thoroughly enthralled by this Florida siren that he disappeared from the beach for three continuous days while euphoric Homer teetotalled and sunned himself, dried out his sinuses in the Gulf Stream, and commendably improved his health. When pallid Ramsey eventually dropped in on Homer to have breakfast, he had a happy smile and looked blissfully depleted. "I've had a great time down here with you, Homer." He rolled his eyes like a high school kid, "I mean that Patsy is some woman." Homer smiled, sipped his coffee, and handed Ramsey a bus ticket to Key West together with an envelope containing thirty ten dollar bills. Ramsey grinned at the stack of green money. It represented almost two month's pay. Within the continental USA limits, Key West was as far as Homer could geographically remove Ramsey from Winelda.

"You're pale, Ramsey. Go down there and have some fun and sun. They say it's some of the world's best fishing, and they also run a coupla good games. I've got to get back to Winelda. If you return to Oklahoma, drop in to see me. It's been a pleasure vacationing with you." Neither Homer, nor Doolittle, nor Northwestern Oklahoma ever saw Ramsey again.

I BEGAN TO WONDER ABOUT MADDY

W hen a suntanned Homer returned to Winelda on the last day of April, he was laden with gifts—a large bottle of Chanel No. 5 and two pair of I. Miller high heels for Maddy, and a brand new pair of Wilson football shoes for me. Homer had come in late on the Mistletoe Express bus. By the time he had told us of Ramsey and the trip, and had shown us the gifts, it was midnight. He looked wonderful. He was Homer!

Homer yawned and Maddy said, "Homer, we have a surprise for you. Come with Tom and me." Maddy went to the hallway, looked back, and motioned to Homer, who was still sitting at the table.

He said, "It's after midnight for God's sake. Where are we going?"

"Just down to the corner. Come on. You surprised us, now let us pleasure you."

At the bottom of the thirty-two steps, Maddy turned left. Except for Etta's, everything in Winelda was sound asleep. The three of us walked past the darkened Snooker Parlor to the corner of the Commercial Bank at Cecil and Missouri. Maddy stopped and turned. "Here's your surprise!"

Homer's jaw dropped. Across the street was the blackened ruins of the Nu-Sho. Entirely gutted by fire, there was no front, no rear, and no roof. Only parts of the left and right walls remained standing. It had pretty well scorched Karl Hemple's Barbershop next door. "Jumpin' Jehoshaphat," said Homer. "When did this happen?"

"Night before last. Some immediately speculated you did it but you were far far from Winelda. Some wondered if possibly an irritated Main Street merchant, Nick or Hutch, with something to lose got tired of the seesaw. Some even wondered if the befuddled boys in

Alva decided to collect insurance, and there were some who even suggested I did it." Maddy laughed, "Which as you know is ridiculous. I wouldn't even know how. So, it's a big big mystery." Then she added sweetly with a sensuous smile, "Now, isn't this the greatest kind of surprise?"

Homer grabbed her up in his arms. "Couldn't have happened to a better building," he said and kissed her. "You sure you didn't do it?" said Homer still holding her.

Smiling mischievously, Maddy said, "I'd never tell."

I was just standing there taking in all this hugging and speculation, but then even I began to wonder about Maddy. I followed them as they walked arm in arm back to our apartment. There were only three cars on the entire street. One was Kylee's official Santa Fe car parked in front of Etta's, where the jukebox was forever blaring its current favorite: "Ma, She's Makin' Eyes at Me." A huge tumbleweed completed its roll down Main and lodged itself in the darkened entry of Hank's Place. South on Main, the Rexall Drug Store sign squeaked and squawked in the relentless wind. Each night, after we darkened the Majestic's marquee, the Square was pretty much this way.

DATING AND MARL THE GREAT TALKER

Because of our Cable lifestyle of going to the Majestic every night, I rarely dated. There were very few parties, and absolutely no jukebox joint allowed dancing. Other than the Majestic, and Etta's, and Eastman's, nothing much happened in Winelda at night. I never knew if this was because of the Depression or religion. Consequently, having to work at the Majestic never made me feel as if I were missing out on big social events.

The spring of 1940 in mid April I turned sixteen, and more than ever, girls began wandering into my thoughts. During recesses, I'd talk to one girl or another. They smelled good, and I sensed mysterious and ill defined delightful things waiting to happen. Girls could do a lot with their eyes. At the desk to my left, I began noticing Betty Jean's legs, which only recently had become beautifully shaped. The skin was clear and soft and not marred with mosquito, or chigger bites, nor were the knees doctored with mercurochrome and adhesive tape. I also noticed how her dress would sometimes inadvertently creep eight or nine inches above her knees. I'd pretend to be absorbed in history while with a racing heart I'd shade my eyes and peek down at those long, beautifully tanned legs. I wanted to reach out and lightly touch them, see if they really felt like chammy—chamois. I found these new discoveries, these stolen moments, considerably more electrifying than the droning of our history teacher, Mr. Elvyn Page. Girls were certainly different from the year before.

Some kids used their family car or pickup for dating, and they'd drive aimlessly around Winelda Square. Sometimes they'd park on Main and watch the pedestrians walk by, or go for a soda in the back booth of the Rexall or the Corner. Afterwards, they might take in a show at the Majestic. Other than the Majestic, there was little else. Even if I had a date, and a family pickup, and a rare night off, I certainly wouldn't want to spend it at the Majestic. Which made me wonder: how did two people on a date spend those night hours? Conversation certainly couldn't last forever. I wondered if a girl expected a guy to do stuff. I wanted to know. But there was no one, not a single guy, capable of a forthright answer. In any event, I was never too keen on revealing how naïve, how utterly ignorant, I was.

And despite the erotic attraction of sensual girls, subliminal fear constantly lurked inside me. I still remembered the scary freshman year sex talk. I still remembered Jack's story about girls sometime locking on to boys and the horrible loss of the all important willie. No one had yet dispelled or disproved that theory, and where there was smoke there was certainly fire. The path to girls was fraught with obstacles. There were those who said that some girls supposedly got pregnant at the drop of a handkerchief. I figured how shameful it would be to have to move in with a girl's folks, how it would permanently terminate life as I'd come to know it.

Regardless of how powerfully I was being drawn to girls, I figured they were currently a dead issue—perhaps at college. Right now, I had neither car nor pickup and no prospects. Just what was I to do? Was I to pedal up on my Nonpareil and go sit around on Betty Ruth's porch swing, her folks hovering and peeking through the curtains, the people across the street getting an eye full?

One afternoon I came upon a farm girl riding her horse on the edge of town. I knew her well and she invited me to climb up behind her. Once up she said, "Tommy, you gotta put yer arms around my waist or yer gonna fall off. Haven't you ever done this before?" I hadn't; it was her idea, and I discovered it was a very special experience. As we galloped, I could feel her warm lissome body move beneath my fingers, and I could smell her mix of sweat and cologne. She'd encourage me with, "Hang on." It was my unvarnished invitation to touch! Her midriff was slim and firm. All kinds of erotic sensations rushed through me. How could they not? But nothing ever came of it. Let's face it; my timetable left me few opportunities to fraternize with the girls of Winelda. Homer said my time would come, but any "now" solution was slim indeed.

I'd heard Marlin Shotwell, one of my blasé football teammates, talk about his nocturnal exploits as impassively as if he were describing how to dribble a basketball. Marl was a couple of years older than I, and a big man on the WHS campus. I envied his offhand "cool Luke" way of talking to girls. It was as if he were Rick in *Casablanca*, with his occasional sigh as if he were bored, his utter nonchalance. I couldn't talk to girls that way; I was always trying my damnedest to think of those remarkably clever things in the movie scripts. I thought Marl doesn't have a family car either, so how does he do all the things he says he does? I knew if I asked his advice, he'd curl his lip and give me his condescending "Gosh, you-don't-know-anything" smirk. A year later, I discovered Marl had never gotten to first base with any girl. He'd been all talk and no conquests.

I asked myself why I was fretting over this. Why couldn't I just continue my happy, uncomplicated life of taking tickets and tooling around on my bike? Why this sudden overwhelming concern about social things? Finally, I went to Amzy who was nineteen and asked him if he'd had any meaningful dates. He hadn't—neither had Mean Dean or Jack. Nothing other than the eighth grade graduation banquet—that kind of chaperoned thing. I was feeling more and more like Lt. Zebulon Pike, wandering around the Great Plains without a compass and conquering neither canyon nor peak.

While Marl was a great talker, there were at least three seniors who demonstrated their prowess. They could always be seen disgustingly mooning around WHS's hallways, sauntering hand in hand with their one and only. They'd look at each other soulfully as if they were coming down with the flu. It was disgusting. One couple actually married before graduation. This was indeed scary! I figured how fortunate I was to have been saved by the Majestic from such a final purgatory.

My Bonehead Decision

When spring graduation came, it was traditional for the president of the junior class and his girl friend to lead the procession of gowned seniors with mortarboards down the main aisle of the school auditorium. When we reached the proscenium, my date and I were to turn around and face the single file of seniors as they took seats. This was a very high profile event. I hadn't given much thought to it but what girl wouldn't want to be a part of it? To be the one to wear a bright taffeta evening gown, and to literally be in the spotlight before an auditorium packed to overflowing with schoolmates, parents, teachers, and the graduating class? I dragged my feet asking a girl to share the occasion.

I remember that I received three secret notes, "Tom, have you given any thought to . . . ." What an ego trip! Girls were actually writing me for a date. I foolishly focused on one of those three note writers, a popular girl who had her eye solely on "the event," and didn't really give a fig for me because she was steadily dating a senior. I was just a vehicle but like a colossal dope I chose her. It was my single most misguided social move in all my sixteen years. I had ignored those of the home-ec class—Albertine, who had baked cherry tarts for me, and Deva, who was positively beautiful. And I had ignored those who had always been happy to gab with me in the hallways. I also thought of the girl with the phenomenally long sensuous legs. And for that big "event," my truly solid friends had been too proud and ladylike to ask.

Even Homer got involved. "Why on earth" he said, "would you ask her?" and he mentioned Deva. "Now she's a looker," he said, "and as sweet as a sandhill plum. How about the girl who's always slipping you stuff from the home-ec class? What the hell's the matter with you, Son?" I could've killed myself! Homer was so right. Unfortunately, there was no retreat. I had impulsively taken the plunge and there was no honorable remedy to extricate myself. I deserved to be excommunicated from WHS.

Homer was determined his air-headed kid wouldn't further screw up the year's grand event. He would personally see to it that I was at least turned out properly. He suggested I wear a white double breasted suit, white buck shoes, and a sky blue tie and handkerchief.

To me it sounded like Gatsby rags, far too radical for me, or for Winelda. Not a soul in Winelda owned a white suit except Reverend Treat of the Congregational Church. He owned a crinkly Palm Beach that looked slept in. Obviously, he had never sent it to either Stephens's or to Merle's for pressing. Regardless, when it came to tailors, I always passed to Homer. He had flair and impeccable style. He said, "Trust me, son. The white will be terrific."

He marched me down to Mr. Stephens, who flicked out his tape and swatches. He immediately selected a white closely woven gabardine because it would hold a razor press. Mr. Stephens gave me a special price of twenty-seven dollars, and Homer, true to form, smiled and said, "He'll write you a check, Raleigh." Homer made a present of the tie, shoes, and handkerchief.

HOMER COMMENDS COACH FOR COURAGE

Toward the very end of the year, we had an experiment in chemistry that I wanted to show Homer. From the school lab I brought home a large glass bell jar. In its top was a rubber stopper with a piece of glass tubing running through it. I bought a couple of ounces of fuming sulfuric acid from Mr. Lloyd Curtis at the Rexall. Homer, seated quietly on the edge of my bed, watched as I poured the syrupy acid over several zinc pieces cut from a Mason jar lid. The mix immediately bubbled and smoked and fizzed, and when a white cloud materialized in the jar, I plugged the stopper in tightly.

Quite importantly, I told Homer that this was hydrogen gas, and if pure, it would burn. But I cautioned importantly, if not pure, and mixed with air, it would become as explosive as the Hindenburg. "That's the point of this experiment," I said almost loftily. "An explosive mixture of air and hydrogen is coming out of the tube now, once all the air has been expelled, and we have only pure hydrogen, I can light it, and it will burn like a candle." And because Homer was there, I waited much longer than we had in the school lab to make triple certain only pure hydrogen remained. Then I struck a match and brought it toward the escape tube.

BAM!

I shall never forget the ear ringing force of that explosion, how the concussion blew all my bedroom windows out onto Cecil Street; some of the glass tinkled almost as far as Etta's Café. Also, the frosted glass of the sealed door in my room blew all over the dentist's hallway floor. People across the street, arms akimbo, were looking up at where the windows had been.

To gauge the damage, Homer stuck his head out the window, and someone across the street yelled, "You shoot someone, Homer?"

"No, LeRoy, just a little skeet practice," and Homer came over to me.

"You okay?" he said looking me over. "Must've still been explosive. You hadn't removed all the air, huh? And now, the acid's making your sweatshirt holier by the minute. Better get in the kitchen and wash your face and hands with laundry soap. Then go find someone to put new glass in these three windows." And he walked out. My hands were beginning to burn, so I quickly washed my hands and face with soap, and then added a tad of ammonium hydroxide to neutralize the acid. As I did this, I couldn't figure the explosion. Why had it happened? How come that huge thick jar disintegrated into hundreds of tiny pieces of flying glass? Maybe my zinc wasn't pure zinc. How come neither Homer nor I suffered a single cut? It was enough to make an atheist believe.

The experiment made the front page of the *Winelda Enterprise*: "Explosion in downtown Winelda." Homer presented me with the eighteen dollar glazier's bill. I had clearly caused the accident, and there was no point in whining about it. I wrote the check.

A week later, I won the Bausch and Lomb Science Award, which they presented annually to the school's top science student—biology and chemistry. I was quite frankly surprised. I secretly thought I had won it, but I was sure my well publicized home experiment had literally blown whatever chances I had for this junior Nobel sans gold.

Homer thought the award was wonderful, and he did something decidedly unusual for the Cable family. He and Maddy invited my science teacher, who happened to be Coach Claunch, and Mrs. Claunch to Eastman's Restaurant for an early T-bone steak dinner. Having dinner with a teacher was embarrassing. I told Homer this might be bad form, people would think we were apple polishing. He said, "What's the difference? You don't have any classes under him next year. Besides," he smiled, "I want to commend him for his courage in having had you in his chemistry laboratory."

The dinner wasn't ordinary. Homer reserved Eastman's very best table, and paid for a special centerpiece of flowers. When Coach introduced Mrs. Claunch, Homer pinned a little corsage on her suit, which obviously pleased her. Homer had the panache to do grand things—like the dinner. In my eight year memory of Winelda, it was the only time the Cables had ever formally invited anyone to dinner.

SENIOR YEAR 1940-1941

Winelda buzzed right on through the Depression without soup lines or vagrants sleeping in doorways of closed shops. Even when the terrible dusters tried the patience of everyone's Job, most Wineldans wasted little time making trifling complaints about hard times, or the hated blister beetles, or the hordes of marauding rabbits and grasshoppers. Everyone went about his business. Years later I concluded that Wineldans suffered no glaring poverty because of their inherent work ethic. There was truly a Spirit of Winelda!

"Hell, we didn't know we wuz bad off till the guvmint tole us."

There were no fancy clothes or furs in Winelda, which was probably why I was always in awe of the fantasy world portrayed in the movies. Fred Astaire, Adolph Menjou, Warner Baxter, and George Raft seldom appeared without their tuxedos. I sometimes wondered how Winelda would've reacted had I debonairly strolled into Etta's Café with top hat, cane, and tuxedo. I doubt if there was a tux within a hundred miles of Winelda. The first one I ever saw was during WWII at a formal ball at Washington, DC's Statler Hotel.

The Depression was still with us, but no one sold apples at Main and Cecil. There were times when we had slumgullions for three or four consecutive days. After a couple of days, Homer would add a load of potatoes, onions, chuck meat, peas, and more pinto beans. He always made a point of cheerily saying, "This stuff gets better every day, doesn't it?" And I was always quick to say it certainly did.

Homer and Maddy worked hard to gross—before expenses—twenty-five to thirty-five dollars a night; sometimes up to a hundred and forty dollars on Saturdays. During the Depression, Maddy and Homer had lived frugally, yet they bought two of the best located buildings in town, and Maddy continued to tuck money away. She kept a goodly amount in the safe because Homer didn't want local bank employees to know what the Majestic was actually grossing. "Their tongues wag," said Homer, "and the town is small." The Nu-

Sho experience had made him especially wary of competition.

Mom had predicted my pathetic academic syndrome would eventually correct itself, but Homer wasn't convinced until I made that very first honor roll. That's when he began salting away my college money. Pop had given Homer his chance in life, and he in turn felt responsible for mine.

HOMER'S HIGHS AND LOWS

By my senior year, everything was going academically and fiscally as Homer had wished, and he had a jewel in Maddy who, in spite of his frailties, loved him very much. Yet for reasons locked up in Homer's misty psyche, he continued to live his erratic lifestyle.

At the Menninger Clinic in 1928, they diagnosed him as a double or triple person—manic at one time, and depressive at another with normality in between, but not a schizoid. Unlike a schizophrenic, his keen intellect never deteriorated. It was indeed unfortunate Winelda had no specialist to comprehend Homer's complex problem, to prescribe some miracle drug. Did they even have lithium? However, I seriously doubt Homer would ever have wanted a shrink probing his mind. He wanted privacy. He knew the Kansas City curse arrived and fled with the seasons. He realized there were often blank spots when the curse made its visitation. However, I'm convinced Homer was never aware he could become as horrible as Mr. Hyde. Had we tried to tell him what Hyde had done, he would've summarily cut us off at the pass. But I'm sure Homer lamented that he wasn't always in full control of his mysterious side. It was indeed a vexing curse. It must have often torn at Homer.

When Homer was "manic," it was the hundred and eighty degree opposite of Homer the "depressive." The manic Homer possessed the exuberance and confidence to handle any situation. He'd awaken with infinite joy and with the expectation of a wonderful day. His boundless enthusiasm was so contagious that it uplifted all those around him. Manic Homer was kindly, and considerate, and with his assertive way and his facility with words, he could cause Maddy and me to virtually worship him. We loved him because all his cards were faced up. There was nothing phony or mean about manic Homer.

His leadership was natural and he made Wineldans—who sensed

he was different—feel unthreatened and happy. They took pleasure in hearing Homer's views. And despite the fact he sometimes wore spats, Homer wasn't a fop. One day Winelda would see him painting the theater front, a bandana tied over his hair, paint spattered on his face and hands. The next day he'd come down Main wearing the spats and flourishing a cigarette holder. He was the only man in town who wore spats; on Homer they looked as proper as boots on a cowboy. For a small western town, he indeed had remarkable flair.

Not only was manic Homer softhearted toward little animals, he was thoughtful toward people. If condolences were in order, if some old lady he knew was in poor health, he'd quietly send a bouquet of flowers.

During grade school, I know I was a big disappointment to Homer. Sometimes I wasn't completely certain he wanted me around. However, this was my own misconception. Later on, I knew I was important to Homer, and that I hadn't disappointed him.

But with very little warning, the depressive Homer could suddenly appear, and we'd become strangers. Early on, I had become fully aware of the correlation between the onslaught of bitter winter and Homer's slumps. The depressions would manifest themselves very gradually—sometimes the transition lasted three to four days—but by day four the ugly Mr. Hyde would be in full charge, and everything became hell at Homer's Place. He'd complain of great discomfort in his sinuses, which in turn made all his teeth excruciatingly sensitive, and his chronic cigarette cough predictably increased until he was seized with body shaking coughing fits. Then would come the bottle, and the gradual indifference to food, followed by lack of hygiene—no bathing or shaving. If his drained bottles weren't quickly replaced, it was hell for Maddy. Jimmy would hippity hoppity to the apartment to deliver a bottle, see Homer's condition, and say, "It's the last one Homer; no more." But Homer would explode, and Jimmy would relent. Jimmy knew he'd return, as did we.

Homer would reign in the kitchen, his elbows on the table, and his painful head clasped between his hands. Sometimes—with me standing at attention—he'd look through his disheveled hair like an old English sheep dog, a little drool appearing at the corner of his mouth.

Did I hate him for this? Certainly. He often rocked back on his chair to rail. I'd imagine kicking the chair suddenly out from under him and valiantly announcing, "I've had enough of this shit." During the winter's gloom period, I daydreamed this a number of times. But once on the street, where was a sixteen-year-old kid to go during the Depression? What if I ran off to Flagstaff? How would I get in school? Where would I live and eat? Who would want me? Besides, this was my last year at WHS. I wanted to graduate. I didn't want to become a dropout with no future.

How about duking it out with two hundred pound Homer? Ha! That would be the day, unless I played the coward and got him while he was falling down drunk. I could never bring myself to strike Homer. And while thinking of this, I'd remember what Maddy said, that this wasn't the real Homer. And then, all the fine memories of how great Homer could be would flood over me.

If Maddy and I thought he had verbally abused us, the hospital staff sighed whenever they saw Homer Cable being wheeled into their establishment. "Oh my God, here he comes again!" His aggressiveness was well known, and even though he was usually comatose, they were quick to strap him down. And as he came around, he would rage and surge against the straps, and he'd cry and shake. For days later, he would upbraid the doctors and nurses. Recovering six to ten days later, he would charm the nurses, send them flowers, and compliment the attending physician. Everyone would be happy because they had restored this marvelous man to the productive world. Such was Homer's remarkable power when he climbed out of depression to hover in his limbo world somewhere between normal and manic.

KITCHEN SCRIMMAGE

One evening in October of 1940, after the football game with Fairview—I was sixteen and first string center/linebacker—the three of us were in our apartment kitchen. At the game Homer had nipped a little hundred ninety proof alcohol, and now he sat at the kitchen table becoming progressively unfunny with his sarcastic remarks. Maddy and I knew that this was the harbinger, the initial swirling of a threatening depressive storm, clearly another downward glide.

Homer began criticizing my game, that I had missed a couple of important blocks. This in itself was unusual because no matter how poorly I played, Homer usually acted as if I were a burgeoning All-American. We both knew this was our in-house joke. Unfortunately, Homer was on a roll and wouldn't let it go, kept nagging about the missed blocks. I attempted to explain that as the center looking at my backfield upside down, it was impossible to see the man I was supposed to block.

"Excuses, excuses," bellowed Homer. "What you did wrong, Cable, was you didn't charge hard enough. Come over here, I'll show you." I rose from the table thinking how I disliked Homer when he was such a stranger. "All right," he said. "I'm going to say 'one, two, three, hike,' and you charge out. See if you can block me off to the left."

"That's not the point. Sure I can block because I can see."

"That's *my* point, Cable," he slurred sarcastically. "I don't think you can block with your eyes right on me."

When he was going downhill, Homer's judgment was never too sharp. I told him blocking in the kitchen was silly and he immediately recoiled.

"Damn you, Tom," he said slamming the tabletop viciously with his hand. "Don't *ever* speak to me that way!" And regardless of my being a senior and now six feet tall, he grabbed my shoulders and shook me hard. I saw Maddy gasp and raise her hand to her mouth. She was sure Homer was going to strike me. "Now, dammit, get into position and I'll count." There was nothing friendly in Homer's instruction. Maddy gave me the high sign to humor Homer, but this was one of those times where I would have liked to march right out of the apartment and never seen Winelda or Homer again.

"Okay now," he said, "and one, two, three, *hike!*" I moved out half heartedly and collided very lightly with Homer, but he had charged drunkenly, and had put his bony knee solidly into my shoulder.

"Well, whoop de doo. Just like a little girl at a maypole dance. No wonder you looked so sorry this afternoon."

I resented this sarcasm, this innuendo in front of Maddy.

"Now, dammit," he growled. "Get back down there. When I give the word, don't look like a goddam tap dancer; *charge* like a football player! "

I got down into the standard three point position. I was tired from the day's game, and angry as Homer again commenced his count, "And one, two, three, *hike!*" I wore tennis shoes with good traction, and I charged out low and up with the same drive I would have used at scrimmage. I slammed the two hundred pound Homer up against the kitchen door.

The frosted glass in the door broke and clattered to the hallway outside. "Oh God!" said Homer with a look of surprise. As if shot, he slowly began slipping to the floor. "Oh God," he grimaced, "Tom, my leg's broken. Maddy. Oh, Jesus!" I helped him slump to the floor. With the broken leg it was a painful descent.

Doc Chambers

The stilt-like Doc Chambers soon arrived with his satchel, the usual toothpick in his mouth, and his aroma of old beef and onions. He checked Homer quickly, "Yeah, Homer, your lag's broken. Now how'n hell did you manage that?" Homer looked so pathetic on the floor propped up against the G.E. refrigerator, unable to move. I felt terrible. I had known better. I should have refused and run from the apartment. This should've never happened.

"Homer," said Doc Chambers, "I'm givin' you a little shot to make you feel better." He mouthed the toothpick, "Fussin' with yer lag is gonna hurt some." Very shortly the morphine was a blessing to Homer's pain. Then Doc said, "Now we have to slide off yer pants or we kin cut 'em off, what'll it be?"

"Perfectly good worsted trousers, Doc. Maddy, go get a towel to slip under me and the two of you slip my pants off."

Homer held his body up with his arms and we slipped off his trousers, all the time I couldn't believe what I'd done in anger.

"Well, Homer," said Doc, "don't you go away. I'll run to my office and get a splinting gadget, and some plaster and gauze."

"You being funny, Doc?" joked Homer. "I'll be right here." Maddy and I both noticed that the shock of the break had sobered Homer, and had brought him back to complete normalcy. It was a helluva shock therapy.

As Chambers went out the door, he said, "Homer, ya broke it just below the knee. How in the world did you do that up here?" Without waiting for an answer, Doc scurried down the stairs.

I said to Homer, "Dad, I feel awful."

"Tom, the asininity is wholly mine. I asked for it." He winced at a twinge of involuntary pain. "I had it coming. And Homer," he said to no one in particular, "don't take on yer linebackin' son; yer too old." Then he looked at the odd twist in his leg and sighed. He looked so pitiful propped up against the fridge, and I never felt so low.

Maddy said, "Tom, you go on over to Etta's and order a couple of hamburgers and a glass of milk then go open the show. You work the box-office and have Mean Dean take tickets until I get there." She gave me fifteen cents and kissed me on the cheek.

As I was leaving, Doc Chambers returned. "Maddy, git me a big bowl or a bucket to mix up this here plaster?"

At the moment, but only for that moment, Doc Chambers was a savior. For the long run, however, he would become an ogre. The shot of morphine he administered that night would be the first of very, very many; so many that every time Doc gave Homer a shot either Maddy or I would write the date on the bedroom wall next to the swamp cooler. Later on, I remembered counting fifty-three different dates. Homer had often demonstrated that his self-discipline threshold left a lot to be desired, and he grew to like the effect of morphine.

Early on, this became a major point of contention between me and Doc. One day on the street, I asked Doc about all the shots, and he surprised me by becoming testy. I had regrettably crossed the kid-adult threshold, and was unwittingly questioning his competence. "Does Homer know you're talkin' to me? You know yer fixin' to git in over yer head?" he scolded. "You leave the doctorin' to me. Homer'll come around." And he abruptly left me standing on the sidewalk wanting to ask more.

In my view, when Doc faced Homer, he should be a take charge doctor. He should start weaning Homer of this new habit. Chambers was like putty in Homer's hands. He'd come to the apartment and Homer would ask for a shot, and Doc would say in a whiny voice, "Homer you hadn't oughta . . . ." Nonetheless, he'd go right ahead and give Homer another hypo.

This went on for several weeks, and I knew it was wrong. In between shots, Homer would be okay for a day or sometimes even two then he'd get a morphine monkey on his back, and in a few hours the thing would be the size of a gorilla. He'd be yelling for Maddy or me to get Doc. "Where in hell is he? What have you done to contact him?"

"He had to make a call out in the country," I reported.

"Goddamit, Tom! You get him up here as soon as he returns." And then to ease whatever pain—by this time it should only have been imaginary—Homer resorted to alcohol. This wasn't his depression thing; this was different. He'd become hooked on Doc's morphine, and Maddy and I both knew it. I'm sure Homer knew he was hooked, but like other things, he wouldn't face up to it. He liked it. He didn't want to discuss it with Doc. He didn't want to risk a discontinuation of his shots of morphine, his fix.

The real problem was Doc, who was professionally remiss. This was a grave charge in such a small community where doctors, preachers, and teachers were held in such high regard. Neither Maddy nor I knew what course to take. Wasn't there some state regulatory agency? I was patently sure of one thing: Homer would have been furious had he known what Maddy and I had churning around in our minds.

Consequently, Doc continued arriving, sucking the toothpick, always sucking his toothpick. I began to loathe the sight of Doc Chambers, and I'm sure he sensed my vibrations. He shut me off completely by never looking in my direction, never acknowledging my presence. Sometimes, as Homer railed, I'd see Doc's disdainful smile as he shuffled around in his black satchel. Possibly I imagined this but ever after, when I'd visualize Doc, I'd see his evil little smile. And he didn't mask his sneer at me, it was like a dare. "Go ahead, Tom, say something now while Homer's yelling his fool head off, go ahead and pop off."

Homer was strong willed, and could argue very convincingly, "Damn it, Doc, the leg hurts. Maybe you didn't set it right."

"Now, Homer," he said soothingly. "We went up to Alva, had it X-rayed, and the danged thing's set absolutely perfect. Nuthin' wrong with your lag 'cept you let your imagination run away with you."

"I'll be *damned* if that's so," and Chambers would recoil and never stand up to Homer's fury. "Don't give me your crap, Doc. You're talking to Homer Cable. Don't *you* talk to *me* about imagination as if I were some goddam imbecile! *I resent that!* The pain's real, and I don't intend to suffer when you can relieve it. Now give me the goddam shot! "

And Chambers would shrug and say, "You're the doctor, Homer. It's your money."

Doc was a coward. Doc was unethical. He should've pulled up

Homer sharply. In my view, he had no business practicing serious medicine.

"Goddam right it's my money." And then Doc would fill the syringe and plunge it into Homer's arm, and Homer would soon relax, and peace would incrementally return.

One day I followed Doc down the stairs to his office and asked him straight out if he should be doing this. After Homer's ass chewing, he clearly resented accusations from a kid, and not surprisingly, he flared up. "Oh," he said sarcastically, as he threw stuff into his satchel, "so you're a doctor now, eh Tom? You're talking about something you don't know a damned thing about. Now let me tell you something, kid. You keep your goddamned nose out of my business, or I'll tell Homer you're pesterin'." He snapped his satchel shut, "You understand me?"

It was my first time to have a Wineldan adult cuss me, and he was on record that he'd tell Homer. If Homer discovered I had talked to Doc in such a way, I knew I'd pay. Doc finished off my presence with, "Now get the hell outta my office." I was afraid of what he was doing to Homer, but I was also afraid of Doc's threat, and he obviously detected it. One thing for sure, despite all those Methodist Church teachings, I had begun to hate Doc. I had never before felt this way toward another human being.

I figured if Doc couldn't face down Homer, why couldn't he cleverly give Homer shots containing less and less morphine. Wean him, so to speak, and still charge his fee. A harsher way would've been for Chambers to have kept himself unavoidably detained. But he did none of those things. I knew Homer—the last of my biological parents—wasn't faring well.

Aaron Fischer and the *Winelda Enterprise*

During Homer's lengthy bone mending, he'd have good days when he would put on his camelhair overcoat and walk to the theater on his crutches. Homer struck quite a regal picture as he made his way toward the Majestic, the cigarette holder poking jauntily from his mouth. The good leg had a nice shoe covered with a silver gray spat; the other was a huge cast with autographs from all around the Square. Only Chambers, Maddy, and I knew that he had become a bona fide dope addict. Homer at only forty-three, was also becoming paunchy, his face flaccid as if he were Ray Milland on a continuous *Lost Weekend*.

"Hey, Homer," yelled *Winelda Enterprise* Fischer from across the street, "with that cigarette holder you look like FDR. How's the leg? Come on over. I want to show you a copy of tomorrow's *Enterprise*." Aaron Fischer and Homer had a special rapport, and Aaron sometimes liked to bounce an article off Homer.

It was Wednesday, February 12, 1941, and Aaron's news item seemed to prophesy new Wineldan progress. Actually, it spelled doom, but neither Aaron nor Homer saw it coming. Unflagging Winelda, that had survived the Depression in its spirited way, was about to be wrestled to the ground and stomped. All its gutsy, bubbling verve of the thirties was destined to fade and disappear.

Aaron was running a superlative caption under a picture of a huge four unit diesel locomotive:

> The Santa Fe's new Diesel locomotive, the first of its kind in the world, was in Winelda Thursday. It's America's largest locomotive.

Aaron and Homer analyzed this event as remarkable progress. In the late thirties, the huge 4000-series Mikado locomotives had come and they'd certainly improved things with their phenomenal steam power and speed. When supplanted by the even larger 5000-series, it was yet another progressive step. What had been good for the Santa Fe had always been good for Winelda. Now the new 5400-horsepower diesel, America's largest, forecast an even greater onward and upward thrust for Winelda.

In retrospect, it is easy to see why Aaron and Homer's enthusiasm had not clouded. It seemed as if nothing short of civil war could ever depreciate the mighty Santa Fe's tremendous investment in Winelda's roundhouse, the ice plant, its huge marshaling yards. Winelda was railroad oriented, had been since what seemed to have been forever. Wouldn't it always be that way?

Neither Aaron nor Homer noticed the correlation with the night flying Douglas DC-2 airplane that suddenly appeared in the thirties and eclipsed the venerable Ford Tri-Motor. The Douglas was able to fly right over Winelda, and overnight Winelda's airline industry became history. They dismantled the huge hangar, reportedly the nation's third largest, and erected it anew in Little Rock, Arkansas. Wineldan pride momentarily wilted, but it was just a fleeting blip. Few local jobs were lost, and without hesitation, they put the airdrome to the plow and planted wheat. Wineldans soon forgot the easy-come, easy-go aviation episode. The philosophers in front of the post office seldom mentioned it.

Aaron had just ridden a special press train to Amarillo, Texas, where they had permitted him to ride in the cab. He wrote in the *Enterprise*:

> The engineer didn't wear overalls or a Casey Jones cap,
> the gentleman wore a white shirt with a white collar,
> and he sat in a nice soft seat with upholstered arms.
> There was little noise in the cab, and no dirt or soot.
> All the engineer needed to add to his comfort was a
> radio and a window box full of flowers.

Homer laughed.

"You like that line, Homer?" Homer grinned approval. "You know, Homer, the only thing that disturbed me was perhaps the lost nostalgia. When we came to crossings there was no mighty whistle. There were no plumes of white steam like the big 5000s. The obscene blaring of the diesel's bus-like horn seemed to fizzle the romance of steam and rails. Do you think I can get away with saying 'romance' or am I being too maudlin for Winelda?"

"Romance is just the right word," and Homer clapped Aaron on the shoulder because Aaron's enthusiasm was always a pleasure to Homer. When Homer was down on Winelda because of its occasional provincialism, he would seek out Aaron and go away feeling uplifted. And when Homer was manic and the two of them were together, there was little in Poland or Czechoslovakia that they couldn't solve.

THE HEADLOCK

Homer had some bad days. Even after the cast came off he'd mix hundred and ninety proof alcohol with the morphine shots. His weight climbed to two hundred and ten pounds, and his face looked puffier. Always so trim, his waistline now at age forty-three appeared full. When en route to the theater, Homer had begun stopping at McBride's to buy small bags of sugared orange slice candy. He'd eat the slices throughout the day. Later on he switched to the larger bags. From week to week, I could see his physique degenerate. I couldn't discuss it with him. Homer didn't like negativity, and Maddy wanted peace at Homer's Place.

What the hell was wrong with Doc Chambers? Couldn't he see Homer's condition? Once again I approached Doc, and he snapped, "I'm not telling you anymore, Tom." He shook his finger at me. "One more nosy word from you, and I'm telling Homer. Now be on your way, boy. It's not your place! "

It was my place! Homer was my dad. I knew nothing about medicine, but now my distrust for Chambers was total. I began looking at Doc differently. Each time I saw him around the Square, he looked as sly as a fox and twice as smelly. Doc surely knew how I felt; it was sticking out all over me. My feeling toward this adult was like heresy in Winelda, but to others I never criticized Doc. In a town like Winelda, I was savvy enough to know that any derogatory remarks I might make about Doc would soon land smack in Homer's lap. It would not have pleased him.

There were many good days. Tuesday, the fourth of March was one of them. It wouldn't be long until spring, I would turn seventeen in April, and in May the great WHS graduation would become fact. Late that afternoon, Homer and Maddy and I talked about college. I had resolved to study petroleum engineering at Oklahoma University, but Homer put his foot down gently.

"It's a good field, but I think you're awfully young for OU. Don't forget, some boys in your class are nineteen going on twenty. I'm not so sure that I want you girling around down at Norman. Take it from a pro, I went to KU too early and spun my wheels. I think I want you to go to junior college at the Oklahoma Military Academy. There's less horsing around there. You take your basic pre-engineering subjects, and when you're a junior you can go on down to Norman for your serious work. It would help us out, Tom, because the academy is only nine hundred dollars a year for your room, board, uniforms, and books. OU's pretty spiffy; you have to have clothes. It'll probably cost us twice as much.

"In the meantime, I'll get together with Aaron, and we'll work on your appointment to West Point. Now *that*, my boy, would really be prestigious." Ever since freshman year, when I had started making the honor roll, Homer spoke more and more of West Point. The military certainly appealed to me, even though I had absolutely no concept of what Army life entailed. "But," Homer cautioned, "I don't want you building any air castles about West Point. The chances of you getting in there from out here in the sticks are next to impossible. I've mentioned it to Aaron, and we'll give it our best shot. Wouldn't that make Mom and Pop proud?" I began to feel that West Point was a possibility.

That evening, after the first show, Homer, with a cane, came into the lobby at 9:45. "Well, Hot Shot," he said, "time for you to wrap it up and hit the hay."

Just then a Main Street cat with a bobtail—everyone called him Bob—brushed into the lobby. I petted old Bob, and to get a rise out of Homer, I pretended that I was going to lift Bob by his stubby tail. "Hey, hey," said Homer, who loved all little animals, and he snapped a headlock on me until my ears rang.

"Okay, okay," I yelled, "calf rope, *calf rope!* Joke, joke, I wasn't really going to pick him up."

Homer laughed, "Let that be a lesson to you. You don't like the headlock and old Bob doesn't want you foolin' with what's left of his tail." He looked at his watch, "Okay, John Leeper"—I never knew who John Leeper was among Homer's Ellinwood lore—"take off for home, see you in the morning, and you kill 'em at school tomorrow." This was Homer at his best.

THAT GRAY MORNING

The next morning I got up and quietly went through Homer and Maddy's bedroom to use the bathroom. At that hour they were always sound asleep. As I turned into the bathroom I looked down at Homer. He didn't look right, and a piece of orange slice candy was hanging halfway out of his mouth. I didn't want to awaken him, so I momentarily continued, but then I stopped and went back to the bed.

I watched. *Homer wasn't breathing!*

It was then that I noticed his eyes were not completely closed as they should've been.

"Maddy, Maddy." I said in a hushed tone, still not wanting to awaken Homer. She sat up with a start, her eyes wide yet sleepy. Her hand clutched the sheet against her naked bosom.

"What is it, Tom?" she was wide eyed and startled.

"It's Dad; look at him. He doesn't look right, and I don't think he's breathing."

Maddy turned to Homer, noticed his odd pallor, and shook him. She shook him harder, but Homer didn't stir. She quickly placed her hand over Homer's heart and said, "Oh, Tom, *quick*, run to Doctor LaFon's! *Run!*" Dr. LaFon was a new young doctor in town who lived only two and half blocks up Cecil at the Campbell Apartments.

I shot down the stairs, sprinted the two blocks, banged on the doctor's screen door, and yelled, "Doctor, doctor!"

"What is it, Tom?" Dr. LaFon already knew me because he'd come to every change of picture.

"It's my dad, Doctor LaFon. He's not breathing."

LaFon drew a pair of trousers up over his pajama bottoms, "Here, let's jump in the V-8." It started promptly, and we were back down at the Square within a few tire burning seconds. Together we bounded up the thirty-two steps of Homer's Place.

Maddy was dressed and looked shocked, "Oh Doctor I think it's something terrible."

Dr. LaFon immediately began pushing on Homer's chest with the heel of his hand. He quickly placed his stethoscope over the heart and again pummeled his chest. Maddy and I stood over by the air cooler and helplessly watched this action. Then the doctor speedily rattled in his satchel and pulled out the longest hypodermic needle I'd ever seen in my life. He filled the syringe with a liquid from a small rubber capped bottle. I couldn't believe it when the doctor jammed this long needle straight down into the part of Homer's chest where the heart is located. "This should kick it over," said LaFon, and with both hands he again began pumping away on Homer's heart. But after four or five minutes of this frantic effort, and another examination with the stethoscope, Doctor LaFon turned to Maddy and me and said, "I'm afraid Homer is gone. There's absolutely no sign of life."

On March 5, 1941, Homer Cable at age forty-three was pronounced dead of cardiac arrest. There would be no autopsy. Autopsies in Winelda were unheard of. No one would ever investigate why there were fifty-three lines of dates next to the air cooler. It was simply a tragic case of what was believed to have been a heart attack, but provoked by what?

"Maddy," said Dr. LaFon softly, "with your permission I will call Russell Floyd to come and take Homer to the funeral home."

God! There certainly was no reprieve from that!

I remember how terribly final it had sounded. He hadn't said, "I'll drop by this evening and see how Homer's doing." LaFon drew the sheet up over Homer's face as if he weren't there. Homer was gone. So final. Homer wasn't there anymore.

Maddy nodded her head to Dr. LaFon, sat down next to her dressing table, and very soon her body shook with sobs. Dr. LaFon left. I put my arm around Maddy's shoulders and kissed her on her cheek. She moved her head back and forth as if what had just happened was too momentous to possibly comprehend. As Maddy sobbed, my own tears welled up. I knew I wasn't doing Maddy any good, so I left her in the bedroom with Homer.

That was Tuesday. I didn't know what to do. I knew I didn't want to be there. I went off to school as I had always done. I had never missed a day. I thought the classroom work might take away the awful reality, but it didn't work. I sat in my first class numb with shock, and I told no one what had happened. I heard none of the teacher's words. I could only think of this morning's terrible blow. In my head I kept replaying the events after I'd passed Homer's bed. Then suddenly it dawned on me that Homer wouldn't be in the office when school was out. He'd never be there again. I barely heard the drone of the teacher's voice, and my eyes began to swim. I knew class was not where I should be. As the teacher lectured, I rose from my desk, walked down the aisle, and went out the door.

"Well," said the teacher to the class, "what a peculiar thing for Tom to do."

"Looked like he was about to cry," volunteered one of the girls, and the members of the class looked at each other—"How strange!"— and the class continued.

I went over to Elm Park and sat on the same merry-go-round where three years before Homer had taken his uninspired stab at telling me all about sex. I thought about all the good times we'd had and some of the bad times. But whatever kind they were, I knew there would never be any more Homer times, and this line of thinking made things well up inside me. I saw a couple walking my way so I got out of there. What would the guys say if they heard I was bawling like a kid? I was sixteen about to be seventeen, a WHS senior, a letterman.

I walked through the brush along Dog Creek and my self-discipline fizzled. Try as I may, I couldn't stave off the tears. I sat at the base of a big remote elm in an area where people seldom walked. I sat there all day and let it all out. Around five o'clock, I was certain I had myself under control. I crossed Dog Creek and walked back to the Square, hoping everything was really a bad dream but knowing it was for real. I even looked through Homer's office window. It was dark in there where there should have been light. There was his chair, his typewriter.

Just as I was going up to the apartment I ran into Aaron Fischer who had heard from Doctor LaFon. The news had spread around the Square like sheet lightning races across a hot summer's night sky. Aaron was obviously distraught. Just the look on his face was more than I could handle, and the lump in my throat grew to a knot. He put his arm around my shoulders, "Tom, I'm so very sorry. I feel like I lost a brother." Aaron's voice broke and that did it. Without speaking I tore away and ran up the stairs. I'm sure Aaron understood.

That night Maddy made soup and laid out some cold cuts for sandwiches. We sat in our chairs around the kitchen table, and Maddy said, "Homer would have wanted us to open the show; we've got to do that. He always said, 'no matter what happens, the show must go on,' so we have to be down there tonight, and the night after that, and the one after that." And then we ate without much to say, and I realized Maddy was doing the same as I; we were staring at Homer's empty chair. When Homer had been on a trip or in the hospital, I never noticed that chair, but now I did. It was so quietly empty. It nearly yelled out for attention. It was almost as if Homer were over by the fridge watching us, taking us in, and quoting something cogent from Omar Khayyam: "Ah take the cash and let the credit go, nor heed the rumbling of the distant drum"—that kind of thing.

Then Maddy asked me for a judgment and years later I would wish I had never made such a self-centered, unthinking decision. Maddy suddenly asked, "Where do you want your dad buried?"

More logically, I could've said, "Probably up in Ellinwood next to Uncle Virgil." But without thinking, I said, "Couldn't we bury him over at Coffeyville next to my mother?" What I said was almost cruel, but at the time, it seemed right to have both my biological parents in the same place. I didn't think. I wish she had never asked me. I would've done whatever she had thought best. It has plagued my thoughts for these many years.

Maddy said she would look into it and see if there was room. She would call Mrs. Ross, my maternal grandmother, and see if it was all right. She knew of the past Ross conflict. But in all this, Maddy was totally selfless. She loved Homer Cable, and he was now a memory. If she sent his body off to Coffeyville, she was giving up any solace that an occasional visit to the Winelda Cemetery might yield. Now she was giving him up to the ghost of the first wife, whose memory had so many times come darkly between her and Homer. She would be truly alone, and would become in reality only a transitory part of Homer's life. Then again, considering Maddy's youth, possibly it was for the best. But how would I as a sixteen-year-old know how best to handle this situation?

She might have said to me, "Well, Tom, how do you think that makes me feel?" Later in my adult life, I thought of that so many, many times, and how selfless Maddy had been. It would have made not a whit of difference to Homer if we had placed him in the Winelda Cemetery. I sincerely doubt that Homer knows he's resting next to my mother. I doubt if my mother knows Homer is buried only inches from her. In crisis times like that we do a lot of very final inexplicable things—things never discussed beforehand.

Thank God Mom and Pop were in Anthony and not in California or Florida. I hated calling them, telling them their last son was dead, but it was an obligation, and there were no alternatives. Those are everyone's miserable moments. I also called Aunt Lillian, who was still in San Diego and not yet remarried. Over the years, Homer had battled with his older sister. Each of them was strong willed and held strong convictions, but deep in her heart she loved her brother very much. She would be present for the funeral. That was what was left of the Cable family who had helped pioneer Ellinwood, Kansas: Aunt Lillian who was forty-eight; Pop who was eighty; and Mom now at sixty-seven. They were the last of the progenitors who had started what might have become a big family of Cables, and now I was the last to carry on the Cable name.

GOING TO SEE HOMER

A couple of days later, Mr. Floyd, the mortician, called. "Tom," he said, "if you'll come up to our parlor on Cecil, I want you to see your father." I didn't particularly want to do that. I wanted to remember him the way he was that last night when I had played with Bob, the Main Street cat, how he had used the headlock to roughhouse with me. If Mr. Floyd only knew how much I detested the death rituals and the whole morbid atmosphere. Why on earth should I want to see Homer dead? To me there was absolutely nothing beautiful about death; it was so remote from life.

But I also wanted to do whatever was expected of me, what was right. Maybe it was written somewhere that the son was supposed to go view the body. Why hadn't Mr. Floyd asked Maddy? Perhaps he had. I wanted no indication of disrespect, anything that might reflect on Homer. So I walked up Cecil past the Campbell Hotel to the Floyd Funeral Parlor across from the Congregational Church. It was the same house where Homer, Mom, Pop, and I had all lived together eight years before. God how I hated that two block walk.

It was my second time to visit the old place after we had left it. The first was when I was soliciting dry cleaning and Mrs. Floyd had invited me in to look around. That was when Mrs. Floyd had innocently joked about Mom's guestroom as also being their "guestroom." It was dark humor because the guestroom had become the Floyds's room for casket display. Spooked, I had since avoided coming anywhere near the Floyds's place.

But here I was, on my way to see Homer.

I wondered if they'd have him up in the guestroom. For some reason this sent a chill down my back. Mrs. Floyd answered my knock, "Oh, Tom, come in. I'll call Russell. Won't you wait here just a moment?" I stood by the door in what had been our living room and what was now the Floyd's living room as well.

From out of the room that had been Mom's knitting and Pop's reading room came Russell Floyd. "Hello, Tom," he said with a reverential smile, "come back to the parlor. I have Homer there." I at least preferred this way of talking better than formal funeral language where they sometimes said, "your father's body" or possibly even used the word "it."

Unfortunately, I was not prepared for what followed.

Mrs. Floyd was in the parlor crocheting at a table. Over in the corner of the parlor was a foldup type Army cot with a large white blanket draped over its canvas top. On top of the blanket was Homer, wrapped tightly, almost bound in clean sheets up to his armpits. His naked shoulders, arms, neck, and head were in clear view. It was as if he were in a hospital room instead of our old parlor. Mrs. Floyd continued to rock back and forth as she crocheted. Russell Floyd smiled, "Tom, you notice that Homer has just a hint of the smile he always wore?" All I noticed were his ashen shoulders, how deadly white my father's fingers were, how their nicotine stains contrasted sharply against the white waxiness of his blood drained hands. Was it necessary they look so marble white?

Mr. Floyd must have noticed that I was uncomfortable, and he said, "Would you like a coke or somethin', Tom?" I could tell Mr. Floyd wanted so much for me to see what a nice job he'd done on Homer. It must have been a surprise to him when I turned on my heel and rushed out the front door and bolted down the steps. I ran across the street and through the Congregational Church property, across Broadway and out into a field where I continued running until I reached the willows bordering Puppy Creek. It was a quiet place where we kids used to catch tadpoles. When I ran, I hadn't thought of this place. All I wanted to do was get the hell away from the funeral home.

Later on, one of the funeral home's helpers came to see Maddy. He needed to pick up the clothes Mr. Floyd would use to dress Homer. Maddy carefully selected a beautiful dark brown worsted, his rodeo suit, and then she took down some shoes. "Ah, that's okay, Mrs. Cable, we don't have no use for the shoes. Nobody can see down there, so it don't make no difference." These were just facts but nothing I wanted any part of.

THE *ENTERPRISE* AND SNAKES AND MEAN DEAN

I graduated from WHS two months after Homer's funeral. I had just turned seventeen. I still remember that April birthday. Esther and Virgil Clemans of the Corner Drug gave me a lifetime Schaeffer fountain pen along with a card that read: "Today. You are a Man!"

I suppose I should have been on top of the world. But, just beneath my usual teen-age countenance, I was saturated with uncertainty and turmoil. I hoped no one would perceive this. I wanted to appear to be in charge of myself. It was particularly good for me that that summer was jam packed with action. Aaron asked me to be circulation manager for the *Winelda Enterprise*. He gave me the keys to his V-8 and told me to cover the countryside. Within a fifteen mile radius of Winelda, I went around every square mile. I knew almost everyone, and because they all welcomed me, I soon learned never to carry a lunch. It was harvest time and each place had extra hands, and I was invited to an unending spread of fried chicken and dumplings, gravy, string beans in bacon fat, potatoes, and loaves of homemade bread. Those mammoth lunches were invariably served outside on a large plank table under a spreading elm. Sometimes Mean Dean accompanied me to share the camaraderie of the road. His company always swept Doc Chambers and Homer's death far from my consciousness.

One afternoon we had picked up a few worn out tires for the nation's rubber drive. Aaron encouraged this small act of patriotism. Evidently, one of the tires had been home to a five foot king snake. While tooling up the hill from the Cimarron River bridge, I looked in the rearview mirror to see the king snake flicking its tongue and cautiously beginning to move along the top of Mean Dean's seat— very close to his neck. Dean was rattling on about baseball and his pseudo-deity Mel Ott. I immediately let off the foot feed, brought the car to a crawling ten miles per hour, and then casually told Dean, "Don't look now but . . . ."

The reaction was as instant and as explosive as lighting hydrogen gas.

Dean flung the door open, dived and rolled from the shoulder down the embankment of the ditch. I slammed on the brakes, and shooed the snake out. The snake was anxious to leave, but headed straight for the recovering Mean Dean. Dean gave the snake a wide berth. He was shaking just as he had after his wild stallion ride at Hammerhead's ranch. We climbed back in the V-8 but for the last three miles to town, Mean Dean divided his furtive view between the windshield and the pile of tires on the back seat.

That early summer in 1941 Mean Dean and I had many good laughs, and I sold a lot of subscriptions for the *Enterprise*. Upon returning to Winelda each evening, I'd do my normal work with Mean Dean at the Majestic.

Later in the summer, Virgil Clemans, at the Corner Drug, asked me to plow his hundred and sixty acre wheatfield with his John Deere "Johnny Pop" tractor. I knew nothing about plowing or tractors, so Virgil stuck with me most of the morning. It was generally around and around the field, nothing an aeronautical engineer couldn't handle. Occasionally the three bottom moldboard would cause a minor delay when entangled with weeds. Virgil showed me how to handle that. As the sun came up, my biggest challenge was starting the Johnny Pop. I had to rock the big flywheel back and forth and before I ran out of muscle. I yearned for it to go pop, pop, pop, pop. Virgil paid me four dollars a day—great money—would pick me up around sundown, and take me to Eastman's, and treat me to a sixteen ounce T-bone. It was another of the summer's great new experiences. It almost seemed as if Aaron and Virgil and a couple of others were surreptitiously doing their level best to play a part of Homer's role until I got off to college. None of them ever spoke of this, but I knew, and I appreciated what they were doing. It was unparalleled Wineldan friendship.

While plowing and chugging around and around Virgil's quarter section, my mind often turned to Doc Chambers. I tried to look at it with honest objectivity and weigh the fact that when depressed or in pain, Homer could be very difficult. Regardless, Homer had deserved much better. He didn't deserve an untimely death. He deserved a doctor's sworn professionalism. By not preventing Homer's addiction to morphine, Doc hadn't been professional. Even so, I gradually came to the conclusion that although Doc was an irresponsible bastard, killing was perhaps too drastic. Having arrived at this conclusion, I felt relieved. I felt absolved of some day having to assassinate Doc Chambers for Homer.

JUNIOR COLLEGE AND REFORM SCHOOL

When Esther and Maddy drove me across Northern Oklahoma to study at Claremore's Oklahoma Military Academy, I harbored irrepressible inner turmoil. I was also in a mild state of disquiet. I was leaving home for the first time, and with Homer no longer around, I was beginning to feel like a castaway of sorts. I knew absolutely no one at OMA. That enrollment day everyone else seemed to have a father. True, I had Maddy and Esther, but neither was a blood relative. There was still Mom and Pop, the remains of my revered family, but now they seemed old and tired and were of a much different time. Had Homer still been standing in the wings, had I been able to write to him in the event something unusual came up, I would have felt better. That first night in the barracks as Cadet Detar played taps, I looked at the ceiling and figured I'd better damned well start swimming hard because no one was standing around with a pole to fish me out.

I was convinced the Oklahoma Military Academy would be a collection of Little Lord Fauntleroys. To the contrary, many seemed to have been exiled to OMA to avoid reform school. In any event, we were all in the ROTC horse cavalry program. We wore boots and spurs. Goaded by gnarly cavalry sergeants of the Regular Army, we rode horses hell for leather in wild cross-country Russian rides— down steep slides, over log jumps and across streams. After the first year, and after the experience of four or five runaways, I felt that I'd finally become a fairly passable horseman. This military training suddenly seemed even more important when, during a Sunday parade in December of 1941, the president of the academy announced that the Japanese had just bombed Pearl Harbor. I immediately signed up for what the Army called the Enlisted Reserve Corps.

MADDY AND DOC

It was about this time Esther wrote that Maddy was rapidly sliding downhill. Surprise of surprises, she had taken up with Doc Chambers! Maddy was young and beautiful, and I thought, "Anybody but him!" According to Esther, the Doc was doing Maddy no favors. Esther wrote that Maddy seemed to be on some kind of drug and had taken to hard liquor. With Homer, her worst vice had been to occasionally smoke a cigarette. No wonder my letters to Maddy had gone unanswered. She hadn't written since my first month at the academy. Worst news of all, Doc had moved in with Maddy! And there was absolutely no reason to doubt Esther, who was both Maddy's and my old and loyal friend.

Evidently Doc had been seen on a number of occasions coming down the stairs of Homer's Place around seven in the morning and then across the street to Etta's for breakfast. Evidently, Doc had taken over Homer's Place and was sleeping in the same bed Homer had died in. Anyway, that was the news that spread like galloping horses around Winelda's square. To make matters even worse, Esther wrote that it appeared Doc had begun managing most of Maddy's business. He collected the rents.

In corroboration, Mom Cable's letter had a postscript that Maddy had ceased paying the Majestic's rent. Mom had called Maddy to ask if there was some problem, and found her quite hostile. There were bad words, and Maddy had snarled that if push came to shove, she'd see Mom in court! That was clearly not Maddy. Maddy had always loved Mom.

Mom spoke to her attorney, Marvin Halbower, who in turn hired a Wichita investigator to check Maddy's situation. He discovered Doc had Maddy's unlimited power of attorney, all legal and proper. Maddy had even deeded over the piece of Homer's property known as Hank's Place to Doc for the payment of one dollar! The investigator also reported that it was common knowledge around town that Doc was cohabitating with Maddy, that Maddy's health had deteriorated dramatically, and she was on drugs and drinking heavily. Doc had recently moved her out of Homer's Place to a very small cottage he owned on South Missouri Street. Doc had supposedly given a long time lessee of the cottage, an old widow, notice to quit the premises. For years she had been paying Doc ten dollars a month, which lends some indication as to what kind of a property this combination cottage and outhouse was. Doc sometimes stayed upstairs at Homer's Place or at his own house. Observers had seen his car occasionally parked overnight at Maddy's tiny cottage.

A couple of weeks later, Esther wrote that when Doc had refused to renew Virgil and Esther's lease for the Corner Drug, they had made an attempt to contact Maddy at her cottage. At ten in the morning, Maddy had come to the door with glazed eyes and was virtually incoherent.

Mind you, when this information filtered through, I was only seventeen. It was even more disconcerting than when Doc had ordered me not to butt into his business while he was negligently killing Homer. Quite naturally, my old hate for Doc rekindled. I was very disappointed with both Maddy and Chambers. Something was very wrong, and I knew I should be doing something, but I wasn't worldly enough to know what it was that I should do. In my naïve way, I thought the marshal and the townspeople of Winelda would right the situation. I'd always depended on Winelda. But, in retrospect, just what was Winelda to do? What were Virgil and Esther or Aaron Fischer to do? In the eyes of the law and the community, Maddy was a consenting adult. I felt remarkably helpless. I was in the northeastern part of the state; the problem was in the northwestern part. For want of anything noble or constructive to accomplish, I played ostrich and turned to my studies.

Come summer vacation of 1942, there was obviously no room for me at Homer's Place, so I stayed in Anthony with Mom and Pop. One day I drove Mom's Plymouth down to Winelda and stayed with Esther and Virgil, and visited with the Fischers at the *Winelda Enterprise*. The following morning, Esther and I sat in her kitchen, and she spoke of Doc. She was understandably exasperated with Doc and very sorry for Maddy's deterioration. Still, she remained the calm, pragmatic, and dependable Esther I had come to know.

Quite unexpectedly, she asked me if I knew the combination to the Majestic's safe. I pulled out my wallet and showed her that I had always carried it there in a code. She said she was concerned for my future. She said, "Do you realize that you can be left with absolutely nothing at a moment's notice." She said that the success of the Majestic had been partly due to me; that for years I'd spent many hours there. Then in a hushed tone she clutched at my shirtsleeve, and as if there were people in the living room, she whispered, "You better get down to the Majestic, open the safe, and take some money for your future."

"But that's stealing," I said. "What if I get caught?"

"You might say it's stealing," she said. "Right now there's a question of who's stealing from whom. If you don't look out for yourself right now, you'll hand over all that Homer worked for to Doc. Now, get down there and play it smart, look around, and get to the safe."

I went to the Square with considerable trepidation. I certainly didn't want Doc to catch me with my hand in the till. I had seen Doc at Etta's, only a half block away, so I sauntered around Thorne's Hardware. Eventually he came out of Etta's, got into his car, and motored south, possibly he was going out into the country. I slipped into the Majestic's lobby and listened for someone's sounds, but the theater was deadly quiet. I hustled into the Majestic's office and popped the safe open on the first try. I was amazed to find stacks of twenty dollar bills. I took what seemed quite a lot, but I left considerably more. I slammed the door shut, twirled the knob, and went directly to the Plymouth. Had any one seen me on the sidewalk, I would've looked guilty enough to indict.

At Esther's house I counted it out. I had taken thirty-five hundred dollars! When you consider my junior college with books, food, and uniforms were nine hundred dollars per year, it will reflect the buying power of thirty-five hundred dollars at that time. It was more money than I had ever seen at any one time. Esther smiled, "Don't give it a thought. It's truly yours. Now go straight back to Anthony and put it in a savings account." I thanked her, she kissed me, and I left.

GREETINGS FROM UNCLE SAM

Come November of 1942 the Army called up the enlisted reserve corps. I was eighteen and Uncle Sam pointed his finger and said "I want you to report to the horse cavalry at Camp Maxie, Paris, Texas." I was definitely leaving Winelda and going to work for the federal government. This was the grand cutting of my Wineldan umbilical cord. I left Claremore for Anthony, Kansas, and because I looked upon Winelda as my home, I went there briefly to say my goodbyes.

When I boarded the Mistletoe Express to start my trip to Texas, I knew I was out in the world and on my own—no Mom, no Pop, no Esther, no Virgil, and no brothers. No one out there knew that I was Homer's son. No one had ever heard of Homer or the Majestic. No one knew that I had been on the football team, had made the honor roll, had been president of my class, and had been gainfully employed since the sixth grade. I was suddenly a nobody without portfolio, and it was lonely out there. I was nonplussed to discover that a hundred miles down the road, no one had even heard of Winelda! I couldn't believe it. I had always considered Winelda to be the center of the universe! For whatever it was worth, my little slate was absolutely clean; there were no truly outstanding achievements yet there was also nothing bad. I was literally at square one in my life. I was an unknown quantity to all others and I had to prove myself all over again.

The Army folks gave me quite a number of immunization shots and my very own serial number: 18023448. Already I had rank and position: Private, U.S. Horse Cavalry. The supply sergeant handed me a set of dog tags with a chain to wear around my neck. The war was just getting started in North Africa and I had yet to hear about these tags. I asked, "Why two?" He said in case I was killed one tag stayed on my body and they'd send the other back to the unit. For an eigh-teen-year-old that was pretty sobering stuff to discover. Regardless, I was at last becoming somebody in this new world; my name was stamped in steel; I had a number no one else in America had. I was in the real Army with the august title of Private, United States Army; my blood type was B; and I was again drawing pay.

When I reported to the first sergeant, he asked where I was from. I said, "Oklahoma." He asked if I could ride. I volunteered yes, and without hesitation, he said, "You'll do." Someone had told me to never volunteer. I suddenly realized I had just committed that grave sin. In no time at all I was en route to the stables with a profane staff sergeant and two other bewildered buck privates. I began to correlate the sergeant to the black goat at the stockyards. It's the goat that leads dumb cattle up the chute and into the boxcars for eventual slaughter in Kansas City. I learned that Camp Maxie just received a new delivery of horses from Oklahoma's El Reno Remount Station. The sergeant simply said, "some are skittish, and need attending to." What he really meant was that we'd be breaking horses. I rode quite well, but I'd never broken obstreperous animals. Early on at OMA, I learned that even broken horses can take the uninitiated on a wild ride.

The sergeant took me to a gelding named Reno Pride, and as I saddled that four legged psychotic, he kept switching my face with his tail while clicking his big yellow teeth at my left elbow. Horses can be mean critters, and they're wily and cunning. As I put on Reno Pride's blanket, he delighted in bumping and pressing me against the stall wall. When I tightened the cinch, Reno Pride inhaled mightily, this to cleverly insure that as I mounted, the McClellan saddle would fall off as soon as Reno exhaled. Reno Pride was a devilish critter with a bagful of nasty tricks. I knew about the inhaling technique so I stuck my knee in Reno's side and tightened the cinch with all my strength.

Because they issued me a bridle with a simple snaffle instead of a curb bit, I figured I was in for big trouble. I got the distinct impression that this obnoxious animal couldn't wait for me to mount up. The other guys were nervously saddling, and every now and then from an adjacent stall I'd hear, "Whoa, whoa, now, be nice."

To shorten a long story, we three guys spent our first hour divided equally between the saddle and sprawled on the equitation circle's poop impregnated ground. The designing horses were having one helluva good time.

The sergeant, a piece of straw in his mouth, just hunkered on the fence and spit tobacco. Periodically he'd yell leadership things like, "Come on men, don't be afraid! Ride with yer knees . . . assert yerselves! Show 'im who'n hell's boss. Holy Mackerel McDermott! You hit right hard, Son. Don't worry none, just dust off and try her again." And at eighteen, when we believed we could do virtually anything, we'd get back in the saddle. By noon, I was actually trotting Reno Pride around the perimeter and doing circles left and right.

After lunch, they gave me Star of Reno, and within an hour, I was working yet another, a feisty mare called Western Pearl. Pearl was a real piece of work. If I put my hand back of the saddle's cantle on her rump, she'd go absolutely berserk and do her little resentful bucks all around the fence. That night I slept like a bruised rock. I went to bed before taps, and tossed around for a time in search of a good resting position. I closed my eyes and concluded that for the first day, I had already learned much. Never, never volunteer. I drifted off quickly and never heard the scratchy recording of taps. The next night I heard it, but it wasn't nearly as sweet as Cadet John Detar's rendition at OMA.

BAD NEWS AND GREAT NEWS

Near the end of the first month at Maxie, Esther wrote that Maddy had died in her sleep. She was almost twenty-eight when they buried her. Doc had swindled her of everything, including her life. She died intestate and penniless. Mom's attorney closed the Majestic and put it up for sale. I can thank Esther for her keen understanding and decisiveness. Because of her I was not flat broke. I would never have to hit up Mom or Pop for a fifty. I had thirty-five hundred dollars in an Anthony bank drawing interest. It was all I had, but it was nice to know it was there. By now I had convinced myself this was my rightful legacy from Homer and Maddy, and the thirty-five hundred dollars would never line Doc's pockets.

In my view, Doc was definitely a sonuvabitch that deserved the worst. Because of the Maddy episode, I had become determined that I couldn't let it pass, that I'd surely have to set the record straight. No court of law could do the situation justice. I decided I'd wait. There was plenty of time to do it right. I'd do it when things were settled, and I better understood life and the lay of the land. I realized that what I had in mind was vengefulness, serious business not condoned by the Methodist Church. I made a pact with myself to eventually get Doc, but right now I was too busy with sergeants.

On 19 May 1943, the first sergeant told me to report to the regimental sergeant major. I had orders from Headquarters Eighth Service Command in Dallas, to report to West Point as of 3 July 1943. What a grand surprise on the day before Pop's birthday! Aaron Fischer of the *Winelda Enterprise* had fueled it; he had made Homer's dream come true. With the stroke of someone's pen, the Regular Army suddenly became my permanent home and career. I was no longer adrift, and Mom and Pop were very proud.

I never saw it, but perhaps something of my short Camp Maxie record followed me because the entire time I was at the United States Military Academy, they forever exempted me from horsemanship training. This was just as well because about the time of my arrival, the Army decided to abolish the romantic old horse cavalry. It seems a group of officers headed by a general named Adna Chaffee had pragmatically concluded that a cavalry charge against German Tiger tanks would never be a sound match. Yet, tradition continued. Years later, when I reported for duty in Japan, senior U.S. Cavalry officers with no horses, but still wearing gleaming Dehner boots, nub spurs, and carrying riding crops, gripped hands and dined together at the Meiji Club, a cavalrymen's club festooned with colorful yet historical guidons of famous horse units. Ah, tradition! It brings a tear at the sound of tattoo.

Because of West Point's fierce regimentation, coupled with a schedule set to a rigorous timetable, there was precious little time to kindle any additional hate for Doc Chambers. West Point was its own nightmare, a treadmill of activity that would be difficult for a civilian to imagine. I quickly discovered my peers were all quite smart and competitive. Completing dog eat dog West Point would become a true survival of the fittest. One of Homer's favorite homilies constantly echoed in my head: "No rest for the wicked."

Each morning at reveille, the Hell Cats, a fife and drum band located in the dark just outside our windows, literally shot us out of our warm beds. Their thundering martial music rattled the windows. Ratty-tat-tat drums, piercing fifes, and blaring bugles issued forth in fast tempo. They achieved far, far more action and decibels than Tchaikovsky's 1812 "Overture" ever duplicated. The last note of their bugles demanded we be in formation. Winter reveille was even worse as we stood in the darkness like frozen sheep while senior people took roll. Yard long icicles hung from the area clock, and a frigid wind whined down the ice clogged Hudson River, and snapped and popped a flag we couldn't see. I was sure this very same, high pitched, fife racket energized General Washington to get the hell across the Delaware. We loved the Hell Cats; we hated the Hell Cats.

After reveille, we returned to our respective rooms, abluted, shaved, made our bed, and again assembled in the area outside to be reported present or absent—they were always counting us—before marching off to the cavernous mess hall. All twenty-one hundred of us sat down upon command: *"Taaaake Seeeats!"* After breakfast, they actually permitted us to return unattended to our rooms. We did not stroll; upperclassmen were watching. We walked briskly, and in a military fashion because only a few minutes remained to prepare our three man room for inspection. Time, time, time—a never-ending contest.

Rooms prepared, we again assembled in Central Area, this time for academics, and we marched off to German, calculus, or thermody-namics. Each formation provided yet another opportunity for some passing officer to report the blemish on our uniform, or that we hopped into formation three seconds late. We arrived at class, saluted the instructor—a uniformed officer—and took seats. They scrupu-lously tested us each and every day.

We reassembled for lunch and still again for afternoon classes, followed by the athletics formation, followed by marching off to dinner, and finally we had somewhat tranquil study time until taps. Even bed provided no sanctuary. In my permanent file exists an infraction written by some eager tactical officer: failed to sleep in pajamas. Among my most unreasonable gigs: soiled laundry in laundry bag, wastepaper in wastepaper basket. At first, these infractions were mind boggling, but after a time we became inured to life's unfairness. Let's just say that no ROTC cadet at Berkeley or elsewhere has the slightest conception of how tightly engineered the regimentation on the Hudson can be.

After the Saturday inspection and parade, it was little wonder that many cadets fell into the sack as if drugged. Only as an infant had I ever slept in the daytime. I always thought Winelda was jam packed with action, but in my lifetime, I've yet to find anything that matched West Point's beehive of activity. Only at West Point have they discovered perpetual motion and its perfection to the nth degree.

What was the single most important lesson I learned while there? Unquestionably, it was the code of honor. It was far more important than calculus, or spherical trig, or even tactics. It was so important, they emblazoned it on our class rings, on our diplomas, and forever in our hearts. We new cadets hadn't been at West Point a week before an upperclassman gave us our first "honor" lecture: "What West Point expects of a truthful and honorable person." In quick succession, there were many subsequent lectures until it dawned on us that this was no ho-hum passing exercise. This was the incontrovertible way of life at West Point. The cadet must always strictly adhere to the well defined Honor Code. He does not lie, cheat, or steal. Quibbling with words, parsing to twist truth and mislead is a breach of honor. It earns a one-way ticket to the South Gate within a week's time.

At WHS, the Golden Rule had been our all important guideline, but not honor per se. At my Claremore junior college—where there was rampant cheating on quizzes—cadets proudly proclaimed that the school had the honor while the cadets had the system. At West Point, honor was paramount; in short, it became our way of life. Its most beautiful dividend: No one at West Point ever asked, "Is that the truth?" Everyone knew that if you said it, then it must be the truth. That was probably the greatest dividend the honor system paid. We all lived from the same ethical rulebook. The families of some new cadets had always lived these rules and had passed them on to their progeny. Some had not, but the new cadets learned and lived West Point's ethics without delay. If a cadet violated the code, the Academy officials didn't initiate the dismissal action. The cadets themselves took the action because it is "their" honor code. Well before a dozen sunsets, the silenced former cadet is out the South Gate, and on his way to where ethics aren't paramount.

It is difficult to quickly explain the code to those who haven't lived its non-negotiable ethics. Every ten years or so, some committee from Congress decides it has to look into the Academy's honor system, a system that has been working beautifully since almost 1802 without a lesson in ethics from pork barrel politicians.

The West Point academic grind was a bestial hell for strugglers in mathematics. In light of that, my greatest day at West Point was graduation day. I must say that I am proud to have come from the banks of the Hudson. However, I'd quickly volunteer to take the rigorous six week parachute course four dozen times rather than march up to West Point again. They've since reduced the dominant focus of mathematics at West Point and have provided courses more applicable to a well rounded education.

In light of the foregoing, it should be easy to understand that during those busy years I had little time to think of Doc Chambers. Sometimes just after taps, when my mind might drift off to Winelda, and to Homer and Maddy, I'd think of Doc and his toothpick, and I'd grind my teeth while searching for solutions. I thought of the monomaniacal Captain Ahab who had his own pathological obsession of the white whale. I wasn't sure if mine constituted a pathology, but I sensed my thoughts were not altogether healthy.

NELLIE WAY AND FORT BENNING

After our West Point graduation in 1946, I was a salaried second lieutenant—a hundred and fifty dollars per month—en route to the excitement of Fort Benning on a Harley-Davidson motorcycle. That full year at Benning was particularly enlightening, and I greatly admired our dynamic instructors. All were WWII veterans with DSCs, Medals of Honor and Silver Stars, and each had a wealth of information to impart to us. At Benning, my classmates fired for record every kind of weapon in an infantry battalion. By default we knew our weapons backwards and forwards. When not on the range, we were forever attacking some hill somewhere on the reservation. Live ammunition whistled around us, the smell of cordite was heavy on the morning air, and we hoped we were all watching out for each other. Overhead artillery support and flamethrowers accented our dependability on each other. We also stomped and stumbled around the reservation on night problems.

To attack a make-believe enemy across the Chattahoochee River, we rode in antique gliders loaded with weapons and jeeps. I was game for everything except the gliders. We'd load a jeep inside, tie it down, and once aloft, I vividly remember hitting air bumps and watching the wooden bottom of that glider actually bend. In my opinion, the Galileo-like gliders were inventions that had to go. I felt safer parachuting at night from nine hundred feet than I did watching the floor of my glider bend. I sometimes fantasized the entire glider floor popping loose and all of us plunging bizarrely in a jeep strapped onto our very own plywood flying carpet. Later in the year, the Mayor of Columbus, Georgia, and other civilian dignitaries were killed when given a VIP ride in one of our gliders—the wings had fallen off, which I imagine was as bad an experience as having the bottom fall out.

One evening at the Benning Officer's Club, I met Miss Nellie Way, the honey blonde daughter of M. Sgt. Way. She became my first true love. Sweet Nellie Way. She affected me in such a way I could hardly wait for the 4:30 trucks to deliver us from Kelly Hill's pungent smell of cordite and phosphorous back to barracks. There I'd peel off sweaty field clothing, shower, splash on Old Spice, put on sharply creased khakis, and jump on my Harley-Davidson. I couldn't wait for the damned sun to set—the precursor for seeing Nellie. We were perfect for each other, and in secluded leafy spots around the Benning reservation, we made wild passionate love. Had they not assigned me immediately to Korea, I most surely would have asked Nellie Way to marry me.

OFF TO THE FAR EAST

For a twenty-three-year-old Oklahoman far from Winelda, it was an unforgettable experience to fly out of Fairfield-Suisun Airbase in California. There were no seats, and the crew chief distributed blankets to each of us eighteen second lieutenants. "When we take off," he said, "stick your middle finger through those round tie downs and hold on." We came into Honolulu's Hickam on three engines. The flight sergeant said, "This captain always loses an engine coming into Hawaii." Lt. Dick Kinney and I looked at each other skeptically. "We'll lay over a couple of days." We flew on to Johnston Island, and as we came over Sand Island, I was sure the pilot was going to land in the water. When the brakes squealed to a halt, there were waves crashing to our front. After refueling, we took off for a midnight stop at Guam, a Quonset hut surrounded by palms. There was no food or drink on our plane. At Guam they served us baloney sandwiches and buns liberally covered with rancid butter. Then we headed for Kwajalein where we discovered shellfire had clipped off every palm tree on the island. The sergeant told us Kwaj's dogs were half nuts looking for a proper place to pee. We flew all night to make a dawn landing at Tokyo's Haneda. A bus took us to our Yuraku Hotel where we showered and waited a couple of days for onward orders. We strolled along the bomb pocked Ginza Avenue in occupied Tokyo. Only an occasional U.S. Army jeep or truck were there dodging the Ginza's bomb craters. Japan was the first distant foreign land for me to see. It was overwhelming with its rickshaws, the flood of unusual Oriental faces, different dress, the pervasive smell of men's pomade hairdressing, a thousand merchant stalls lining the Ginza's curb. Everything was very foreign, even the men's belts, which they wrapped almost twice around their waists. It was even stylish for men, who could come by them, to wear two or three wristwatches on the same wrist. Nothing in Tokyo reminded me of the Winelda Square.

My stay in Japan was short. In an old C-54 [DC-4], they whisked us from Tachikawa to the very end of the supply line, a country everyone called Frozen Chosen, or Korea. The redolence of night soil was pervasive. It was indeed ancient, and pleasantly quiet, and decades behind the times. Euphemistically they called it the Land of the Morning Calm, but in 1947 it was anything but calm. There were riots and bloodshed, and there was an ever bubbling, seething volatility. The Koreans were at last free of the Japanese and they were eager to elect their first president, but there was a lot of dangerous jockeying for position.

I found myself on a train bound for Pusan at the southern tip of Korea. I met our Sixth Division commanding general, Maj. General "Pinky" Ward who acquitted himself bravely at the Kasserine Pass. He said welcome and sent me back north to Taegu to meet the First

Infantry Regiment's commander, Col. "Command Post" Evers. Once again I found myself on a train, bound this time for Pohang-Dong. A jeep from First Battalion picked me up and took me to report to the battalion commander atop a windswept hill. The battalion commander was drunk. I was immediately assigned as first platoon leader of A Company of the First Battalion of the First Infantry Regiment. In my convoluted way, I figured that my rifle platoon must've been the very first platoon in the United States Army.

I remember well that first reveille in the dark. Old First Sergeant Jetta was drunk; to formation he carried a five gallon can filled with saké. The company stumbled out of the barracks, stretching, yawning, and cursing. That's when an extremely powerful looking first sergeant stepped out of the shadows and blew a rather strident whistle. "Good morning, gentlemen, I am your new first sergeant. My name is Bull Claytor. Now when I blow this whistle, I want you all to double time back into the barracks." I could see round shouldered soldiers straightening up. "When I blow the whistle again, I want you to pile out here double time and fall into attention, and if you're not standing at attention in twenty seconds, it's going to take a wrecking crew to get my foot out of your ass." This was more like it. Perhaps the Army hadn't gone to hell.

But, with WWII just finished—the war to end all wars—who would have thought I'd be right on deck for the Korean War? Homer would have described it as, "A grand awakening!" It would commence with a poorly trained occupation Army that had no training ammunition. An Army at barely fifty percent strength, and with worn out WWII equipment. Some soldiers went into summer battle wearing tennis shoes because combat boots weren't available. Washington hadn't funded us, but Washington had been quick to lead with our chins. Even so, patriotic folk would shout and mindlessly chant, "We'll whip their asses." We were unprepared for what would happen. Yet, they always say, "This will never happen again."

Part Four

Welcome Home Soldier

Four years later, April 1951, I had just turned twenty-seven, had fought a war in Korea and was returning to the States aboard the USNS *General Aultman*. Looking out on the waves, my thoughts turned momentarily to Nellie Way. They were happy, wonderful memories and she had always been in my thoughts. A year after my departure, she had married an Atlanta doctor and was already the mother of two children. I shook my head; much had happened since leaving Winelda. I suppose some would say I was more serious, less outgoing, not quite the same effusive kid who had taken tickets at the Majestic, and who had remembered everyone's name within a fifteen mile radius of Winelda.

For all of us aboard that old ship, the return to the States was a tremendous event. We considered ourselves our nation's gladiators returning from the battlefield. I believe everyone aboard naïvely assumed that the entire nation must have been aware we were docking that morning. When the president had ordered us to fight a so called police action in a place few could find on the map, he had said our resolve was of great consequence to him personally and to our nation. He had said it almost like a father, and it had stuck in my head. And because it had obviously been a considerable moment to the nation's president, and to this shipload of men who had risked so much, I was convinced he would personally be on hand to greet us at the pier.

However, when we docked at Port Angeles in Seattle, I could hardly believe how routine it was. Not only had the president not come, but also nothing festive was happening. Down on the pier there were just a few squawking sea gulls and some disinterested civilian stevedores operating forklifts. There were no flags, no bunting, and no band. Hell, no one was down there—no general, no governor, not even the Mayor of Puyallup! Just a sergeant barking over a megaphone as he lined up buses. That was it!

Korea had all been deceptive, political bullshit, including the appellation: "Police Action"—a less than candid political equivocation. We had obviously never been of any personal consequence to the president; we were only tools for a Capitol Hill ploy that miserably failed. The day the Chinese called the president's vacillating hand and surprised us, suddenly our gutsy, scrappy president was no longer flamboyantly brave. My newly discovered cynicism had made it easier for me to shrug off the miserable way we were winding up what had initially been the great Korean crusade. While aboard ship, I also learned the president had just fired Douglas MacArthur. MacArthur had been an exceptional general for thirty-three years— one of America's greatest generals in history.

Consequently, it was the height of naïveté for me to have imagined the president or his representative would really greet our shipload of men. I suddenly felt foolish. It should have been obvious he didn't care. Which was probably just as well; we were in no mood for some windy political palaver. After all, down there on the dock was America, and it was safe, and it smelled a helluva lot better than antiquated Korea. As I stood at the ship's rail, I silently thanked God Korea was behind me and that I had passed that momentous test of battle. I looked forward to the gangplank, to plant my feet on real American soil. I may be faulted for my first objective, but I wanted to go to a bar and see this new thing they called television.

At twenty-seven, I had begun to recognize that life was clearly to be one monumental test after the other. My first time to make the Winelda honor roll had been a nerve wracking test. Going out for football had been an enormous physical test, and one of will. Going into the Army had been a trial because no one initially cared much about me per se, or how many of life's tests I'd already passed. To

Army sergeants and West Point upperclassmen, I was an untested item—just a warm body with a serial number and dog tags around my neck. It seemed they were always testing me, trying to get inside my head to flip switches.

I remember before Korea—at West Point and Fort Benning, Georgia—the thought of fear rattling me in combat had disquieted me. Combat was going to be the mother of all tests, because this one would involve death! I was young and gung-ho, but God how I feared and hated death—such a final thing. Even today, when I hear a man brag, "Why, I have absolutely no fear of death," I feel he's either uncommonly lucky or a damned liar. I'd often wondered that if face to face with death, how would I handle myself while leading my men? Would I be paralyzed with fear? A troop leader can't afford temporary paralysis. Combat is no longer a Benning training exercise; it's the real thing. All those Koreans and Chinese out there actually wanted to kill us. Consequently, I knew my men would be looking to me to make all the right calls.

But the commanding officer is just a flesh and blood guy. What happens if imminent death scares the hell out of him? Will he lead or just fold up? I wondered about those situations countless times. Would I meet that great test, or would I be scared out of my wits? I prayed I'd measure up, and I fully expected some kind of positive heavenly response, yet no clear encouraging answer ever came from out there. Consequently, my praying gradually disappeared.

Then one day, I was suddenly in combat with my company of two hundred men, and all my chips were in the pot. I remember the radio was on the fritz, I couldn't contact battalion or anyone else, and there were screams, and ricochets, and mortars exploding. The air was a smother of pungent white phosphorous, cordite, and the fecundity of freshly exposed earth. I had been scared absolutely numb, yet I had done just fine.

For seven full years before the Korean action, I had been subjected to countless sandbox problems together with actual company sized field exercises with live ammunition. Virtually by rote I knew the principles and the logical responses to virtually every conceivable combat contingency. In Korea, I was amazed at what the Army's often maligned training system had done for me. In each special battle situation, my reaction was swift, and the correct responses proactively spewed from me, almost as if I were bionic. In Korea, they had said,

"Captain, you looked as cool as steel under fire," but no one really knew my inner turmoil, and I never told them otherwise.

Except for the Congressional Medal of Honor, I was awarded every combat medal there was to have: the Distinguished Service Cross, a Silver Star, three Bronze Stars with V for valor, a soldier's medal and two Purple Hearts. Not many of my rank—even those of old military families—could claim that. They'd given me a battlefield promotion to captain, and although wounded and scarred, I still had good sense and all my systems were go. Inwardly, I was very proud for having made it through another of life's tests.

So as I looked over the railing at the Seattle pier, I was pretty much at peace with myself, and abundantly confident. Other than to see an actual TV, my most important thoughts were to visit what was left of the family. Mom had died in 1946, the year I'd graduated from West Point. She had been seventy-two and much too young to die. Her mind had remained very sharp, but there's no doubt that losing Virgil and then Homer had hastened her along. In 1946 Pop had been eighty-five, and with Mom gone, Aunt Lily had dependably returned to Anthony to watch over him.

When World War II started, Lily had found an excellent government position in Washington, D.C. She had loved Washington, its museums, and countless cultural opportunities. As a Life Master, she competed in frequent duplicate bridge tournaments. She had always abhorred small towns, but when Mom died—out of loyalty to Pop—Lily sacrificed her beloved Washington. She packed her things, and at age fifty-three and in the prime of her life, martyred herself to insure Pop was properly cared for. She exiled herself to provincial Anthony where Pop became her single interest. Aunt Lily had started life fitfully, but she had become a great lady! I looked forward to seeing both her and Pop.

Virgil's widow, my Aunt Iris, occasionally wrote to me after Virgil's tragic death. When World War II came, she immediately volunteered for the Women's Army Corps. She was in the initial test platoon of WACS at Des Moines, and during the war years, she rose to the rank of major. I always admired her *joie de vivre* and her patriotism, and she had been very taken by my appointment to West Point. I think she knew I was proud to have her as my aunt, which was probably why she took the time while I was a cadet to occasionally write to me. Shortly after the war, she inexplicably suffered a massive heart attack and was dead at age forty-seven. She and Virgil left no children.

Ever since I had known Pop, he would complain of dizzy spells and loss of memory. "Oh, this senility is terrible," he'd say. But then he'd shoot out the front door and go play a morning of horseshoes. As far as I know, Pop was never confined to a rocking chair or bed for even one day of his life. Now he was ninety and still pitching horseshoes and visiting his downtown club of senior men. Mentally alert, he knew the names and numbers of all the U.S. infantry divisions deployed in Korea, and Lily said he kept abreast of the grain and cattle markets as well. His chief complaint was that he missed Mom and wanted to be with her.

I've already recounted Maddy's slide at the hands of Doc Chambers and her early demise. Lily had come down from Anthony in 1944 and had sold the Majestic. I thought perhaps all this death portended exceptionally bad luck for the few remaining Cables, but then I'd think of Pop's longevity, his good health, and at ninety, he seemed indestructible.

WINELDA: MY HOMETOWN

I really had nothing in Winelda. There were no cousins or uncles, no dwelling with my old room, no revered letter jacket hanging in some closet, none of my books. Winelda held nothing for me except old friends and the fact it was the only hometown I had ever known. During WWII, over half my WHS classmates had moved elsewhere. Jack Beaman was a lithographer, married and lived in Topeka. Amzy had bought the farm in a burning tank near Bastogne. Still, before reporting to the 82nd Airborne at Fort Bragg, North Carolina, I had to revisit Winelda for a very special reason.

First I'd go to the *Winelda Enterprise*. I knew I'd find Aaron and Louise Fischer there. That would be the next best thing to Homer and Maddy, and then I'd go down to the Corner Drug and visit Esther and Virgil Clemans. Virgil had a great dog he called Hector; maybe Virgil would invite me for a quail hunt. And there were several other Wineldans I wanted to see again.

For the trip around the Square, I'd wear a razor sharp uniform and show off my ribbons. I'd let folks see how I'd fared since leaving

Winelda High. Strutting a smidgen is criticized but it's okay. I figure that if we all leveled with ourselves then we'd have to admit there's a little, of the show-off in each of us. It's the reason a soldier proudly displays bright "accomplishment" ribbons on his chest. It's why we send invitations to our graduations and weddings; it's why we display our plaques and trophies; and why Ph.D.s always put Ph.D. on their calling cards and call themselves doctor. It's why we bore people with our wallet pictures; everyone in Korea showed off his wallet pictures. They were actually saying, "This is what I've accomplished. See this one? That's my son, this is my hot sports car, and this is my wife." And even if she were plain, we'd always say, "Ah, yer really lucky, Henry. She's very pretty."

It would have been wonderful to return to Winelda to hug my real mom, or Maddy, and to show off a little for Homer. Being an only kid had never bothered me. There had always been people—old friends or relatives—around me, but now I missed not having anyone. I was fully independent and that was fine, yet right now I could've used a little Cable praise. I considered it a perfectly normal reaction.

I often remembered my West Point graduation. All the sisters, parents, and classmates around me were reveling, kissing, patting each other's backs, and congratulating. I should have come off the parade ground in my dress uniform and have said, "Well, Dad, I made it. Thanks for all you've done." That would've been a terrific experience, but Homer was dead when he should've been forty-eight and standing there. No Cable had come to that important graduation. Mom was dying, and Pop and Lily were at her side. Pop sent congratulations and added, "Too old, can't travel."

The return to Winelda from Korea should have been my moment of infinite glory had not Doc Chambers haunted my thoughts. If not for him, these family disappointments would probably never have happened. For countless months, Doc had burned indelibly into my mind. I remembered clearly how Doc had told me to keep my nose out of his business, had scoffed at my pleas, had run me out of his office, and had gone right ahead with his destruction of Homer that ultimately sent me off to a wrenching funeral.

I had later been willing to absolve Doc of Homer's death only because Homer had so willingly allowed himself to become addicted to morphine. Then came Doc's sordid and unpardonable involvement with Maddy, almost as if he were being doubly spiteful to Homer's memory. Chambers had wantonly and irresponsibly killed Maddy and had indirectly hastened Mom's death. He did this as surely as if he'd plunged an ice pick into their chests. My self-conceived charges against Doc were damning. Countless times I had analyzed those charges for equitableness, and each time the verdict for Doc was always the same: Guilty!

I hate to reveal how many times I sat in a Korean bunker and thought of facing Doc Chambers in a great shootout at the OK Corral. In my reveries, I must have blown that sucker away fifty or sixty times—a tad differently each time. Sometimes I wondered if my fixation was because of the carnage that I had witnessed around Taejon and again when the Chinese poured across the Yalu. I wondered if these events fueled my macabre obsession. It wasn't until I started carefully calculating precisely how I would kill Chambers that I realized my thoughts had turned to an inordinate and perhaps unhealthy zeal. Now here I was on Doc's turf and facing yet another of life's major tests.

When I actually began this planning, I implemented the same professional killing skills that I had learned at Benning's Infantry School. I followed the logical sequential steps of the Army's time-honored "Estimate-of-the-Situation." We always used that systematized estimate in analyzing the feasibility of eliminating or seizing an objective. At the Infantry School, the objective was normally an enemy troop unit, or possibly the critical terrain the enemy occupied. In this instance, the objective was Doc Chambers. I sometimes wondered what Colonels Linnell and Meyer, my mentors at the Infantry School, would have thought had they known that I was using their plan-to-kill techniques in such a personal and bizarre way? They had honed me into a professional killer, so why not apply those same skills to exterminate Doc Chambers.

I actually enjoyed my cunning cerebrations because, during those moments, they had blanked out Korea. I didn't really give a damn that my thoughts had become a little cock-eyed. I wanted Chambers dead! I had remarkable self-discipline. I knew I had the power to stop the ghastly thoughts anytime I wished. They were thoughts that I knew were not complimentary to me as an officer, as a human being, but I must admit I relished them, and I permitted them to run rampantly wild. My associates never knew what was in my head, and I offered revelations to no one. Anyone aware of the weird machinations taking place inside my skull might well have had me packed off to the shrinks.

If this sounds quirky, just let me say it wasn't something that occupied all my time. While in Frozen Chosen, I had little spare time to sit and dwell on Doc Chambers. He probably didn't cross my mind more than once every other week. But when I conceptualized, it usually commenced with Doc saying, "Now get the hell outta my office!"— that to a sixteen-year-old kid worried about his dad. From there I'd fantasize my first meeting with Doc. It was never a chance meeting, but rather a very well planned encounter. I'd always remind Doc how he hadn't given me the time of day, how it had cost Homer his life, and that was exactly why I was blowing him away. I tried to imagine his expression; I always savored that part. Then I'd coldly blow the sonuvabitch away.

No matter how potentially tense our combat situation, my fantasy seemed so very real—as if it had actually taken place—and it actually made me feel good, extraordinarily good. Afterwards, I could turn over and fall sound asleep until another Chinese incoming awakened me. This bizarre insanity might very well have been what kept me sane during our hectic, sometimes muddy, sometimes frozen, marches up and down that crazy Korean peninsula.

This nagging urge to even the score for Homer, to meet that ultimate test, never lessened. It grew exponentially. I figured Chambers had killed both Homer and Maddy as surely as if he had been slowly poisoning them with arsenic. In Homer's case, he had used morphine. Homer had become ever bloated, ever dependent upon Doc's unrestricted drugs. Even when I had urged him to stop, Chambers had made no move to curtail the morphine. He killed my father when I was sixteen. I believe the day Chambers heard Homer had been carried down those thirty-two steps—his last trip—Doc must have been incredibly relieved. No longer would he have to deal with either Homer or me.

Why? Because I remember at that miserable funeral, the only face I searched for in the congregation was Doc Chambers's, but he wasn't there! Wouldn't you say that was odd? After Homer's death, Maddy and I received a huge stack of condolatory notes from my classmates and other Wineldans, but Chambers, who had been up to Homer's Place more than any other outsider, never spoke to me or to Maddy— never sent a note. He just sent a bill for his last call. At the time, I thought his behavior strangely insensitive.

A week or so after the funeral, Maddy told me that, on Homer's last night at the theater office, Chambers had given Homer a shot not more than an hour after I pretended to pull the cat's tail. That shot was never recorded on the wall, and learning about it made me wonder how many other shots possibly had not been recorded. By that time Homer had probably built up quite a tolerance to morphine, and Chambers must have been giving him ever larger doses so that Homer could experience the effect he craved. All the while, Homer's body was crying out for a decent doctor's expert professionalism, but he wasn't getting it.

Months afterward, when I began focusing on this, I wished Doctor LaFon had demanded an autopsy. Neither Maddy nor I knew how a person went about asking for medical investigations, and Marshal Patton wouldn't have known. By the time this had grown heavy on our minds, Homer was already in the ground in another state. Then, after Homer no longer posed a threat, after a few months had passed, Doc made his shameless move on Maddy.

GETTING DOC

As soon as I could finish processing at Fort Lawton and spring free, I went to Seattle's nearby McChord Field and hitched a ride on a sparkling B-25 "Billy Mitchell" bomber to Vance Air Force Base at Enid, Oklahoma. I rented a car and made some key purchases—purchases I had planned for many months. Soon I was on my way to Winelda, a distance of only seventy-four miles.

My old friend, Mean Dean, had the perfect welcome home. We double dated, took our girls out to the Devil's Playground, lay on blankets under the spring moon, had a few drinks of coke spiked with Southern Comfort, and listened to the radio's "Saturday Night Hit Parade."

I hadn't seen Wanda since going to the Army over seven years ago. From a freckle faced gangly kid she'd certainly developed into a truly fascinating beauty, and there was instant electricity between us. But sometime during the evening, when we were quietly talking about the old high school days, out of the blue she mentioned how sorry she'd been when Homer had died so unexpectedly. "I just couldn't believe it," she said. "He was so young. I'll never forget how I felt."

With this, my full attention immediately swung from Wanda and uncontrollably locked onto Doc Chambers. For the remainder of the evening, I was preoccupied, and paid scant attention to Wanda. She was so pretty and our interaction so perfect. I've since wondered what she must have thought of my abrupt change. For the perfect murder, I wasn't playing my role well.

It had been my original intention to hang around Winelda for at least a week in order to reassess the lay of the land before making my move. But Wanda's remark, kindled with a little Southern Comfort, made me think, *What the hell, my plan's perfect. Why not get the show on the road!*

After we took the girls home, and Mean Dean and I had told old stories for thirty or forty minutes, we promised to see each other the next day. I said goodnight, and then to purposely kill time, I drove aimlessly around Winelda. Because the great moment was near at hand, I kept getting more and more agitated about Doc Chambers. For me this was an uncommon nervous reaction, and I was disgusted with myself. Damn! I didn't want agitation; I wanted equanimity. I even considered aborting, for a better calmer day.

I wasn't a boozer, but I had a pint of Southern Comfort under the seat, and I recall I began nipping on that bottle like a lush in a B movie—not big swigs, just little frequent nips. I drove up and down Cecil and Santa Fe Streets, down Main, and back to Cecil. Always back to Cecil, because that's where Doc lived. All the while I'd nip a little of the Southern Comfort. Why I let myself get sloshed, I'll never know because it wasn't something I needed for courage.

I parked in front of Doc's house. I could see an inside light. It was the same house where he'd lived his bachelor existence for as long as I could remember. I often wondered why he never married. I figured it was pretty obvious that no woman wanted him as he was, and Doc certainly wasn't about to change his ways. He was one of those slovenly guys who always had the hip pockets of his shiny pants hanging close to the back of his knees. Doc had plenty of money, but he was far from a haberdasher's dream. Then there was the toothpick that hung constantly from his mouth, and his chronic onion breath. No doubt about it, he'd be a bachelor till the day he died, and tonight was his night.

All the while I drove, I called on myself to get off the dime. I'd manicured my logical plan for months. There was no question whether it would succeed; so, after a few more swigs, and the fourth stop in front of Doc's, I got out of my car. I'd like to make it clear that I was not drunk; I had a high tolerance for alcohol.

Unfortunately, just as I stepped toward the curb, the heel of my shoe caught in my cuff. My head came down hard against the concrete curb. I remember the explosion of little lights inside my skull, and I lay in the gutter for what seemed to have been a few seconds—it was probably more like several minutes—and then I got to my feet. My forehead was bleeding. Back in the car, I checked the mirror and collected myself. I had a nasty cut. It's a wonder I hadn't broken my fool neck. I licked my handkerchief and wiped at the wound, and then I figured, what the hell. It will fit perfectly with my story. I let some of the blood ooze down over my eye and went toward Doc's place.

When he snapped on the porch light and opened his door, it was as if I were meeting the devil, and as if he were seeing a ghost. Doc was still skinny; his face sagged a little because he must have been around fifty-five. I did not remember him having so many curly nose hairs or the frizzy tufts growing atop his ears, but there indeed was the toothpick, and the obvious need for a haircut and wash.

"Well I'll be darned," he blinked, "if it isn't Tom Cable. What a nice surprise," he said with a phony yet somewhat cautious ring. He was obviously ill at ease. "But what's this?" he said. "You've got a nasty cut on your forehead."

That's when I told him there had been a bad accident south of town at Bouse Junction and he was needed there immediately. This was more than plausible because people had been killing themselves at that junction for years. Since the invention of the automobile, Bouse Junction had had one unbelievable wreck after the other. It was a lonely four way stop intersection where the Fairview to Wood'ard highway crossed the one from Winelda to Seiling.

Doc didn't invite me in. He darted back inside, grabbed his satchel, and returned to the porch, stuffing his nightshirt inside his trousers. Assisted by the porch light, he dug into his bag, wetted a square of cotton gauze with peroxide, and wiped it across my forehead.

"There," he said, "that'll do till we get some time," and then we went on to my car.

I could tell Doc was pretending that he was glad to see me. I could sense the fear beginning to emanate from him. Only he would know why and how he had finagled his way into Homer's bed. He initially made small talk: "My how you growed. When did you get back to town?" Then, as the road wound southward through the sagebrush covered hills, the two of us just peered through the windshield without having much to say. By the time we had gone the four and a half miles to the Cimarron River Bridge, I could smell Doc's acrid nervous sweat, and I smiled. Everyone wore the same special scent on a lively bugle blowing night on the front slope of a Korean hill. I wanted Doc to sweat.

As a kid, I had posed virtually no threat to Doc. Even so, I always imagined he must have been relieved that day in late 1942 when I briefly visited Winelda en route to Camp Maxie in Paris, Texas. Doc never said goodbye as so many had done. I had seen him near the Corner Drug when I was in front of Etta's Café, and I know he saw me, but he never made a move to wave or yell. Doc certainly knew me well enough; he had sewn up my hand the day Amzy slashed my artery. Doc's behavior hadn't really been strange when considered in light of his scheme for Maddy, her bed, and her assets. Doubtlessly, he hated the sight of me, probably figured the sizeable dint in the safe's contents was because of me. He probably could not wait until I was long gone from Oklahoma. What with the war, and because I no longer had blood family in Winelda, I probably would never return. Good riddance and goodbye! To him I was history, and he had pointedly ignored me.

But here I was, back in Winelda!

I'd popped up again, and I was no longer a lanky kid. I was a hundred and seventy-five pounds, almost six one, and lean, and I had just spent the past fourteen months exterminating humans. The silence in the car grew ominously. My only misgiving was that Doc must have been twice my age, but I really didn't care if he was old.

As we traveled the thirteen miles south to the junction, I wished for extrasensory perception. I was confident Doc was dredging his memory's rusty depths. I wanted to listen, and I actually believed I was reading his brain waves. He was reviewing the many times he had been to Homer's Place, how on the night of Homer's death he had gone to the Majestic Theater office and had once again negligently used his death needle. Had he used too much morphine that night?

Doc was probably thinking about that awful March dawn when Homer had died, and about me sprinting to the nearby Campbell Apartments to bring Doc LaFon. I'll bet he had had mixed feelings about LaFon.

On the one hand, he was probably grateful he had been spared Homer's last act. On the other hand, he may have been very uneasy at the thought of Winelda's eager new doctor examining the dead Homer. I would bet Chambers had constantly been on pins and needles as he waited for some sign from LaFon, the man who was to sign Homer's death certificate. Every time he saw LaFon approaching, he probably feared he'd say, "Oh, Al, I want to ask you a few things about Homer Cable." I would say Doc probably didn't rest well the whole time Homer was at Russell Floyd's mortuary.

For the new doctor to call for an autopsy would have been relatively simple, but old Chambers was probably confident there would be none. In Oklahoma's early forties, autopsies were for the movies. Yet, anything was possible. But when Doc learned Homer was safely under six feet of earth in Coffeyville, Kansas, he probably locked his doors, ran off to Okie City, and tied one on.

After all these years, I figured Chambers had never quite wiped Homer entirely from his mind, but who was to know? Possibly, in Doc's despicable irresponsible way, it had been an easy chapter to forget. But just as I was probing the air for his thoughts, Doc said, "Tom, I've always felt bad about your dad and I want you to know his dying was no fault of mine."

Now isn't it funny Doc would say that and ignore Maddy's early death completely? I let just enough silence intervene to put him on edge and then said, "Nobody ever said it was your fault, Doc. How come you to say that?"

"Well, I remember each time I gave him a morphine shot, Homer used to have you write the date on your apartment wall. I remember you once mentioned that you thought mebbe it was too much morphine." Doc clearly remembered that, but he made very light of our four brittle confrontations.

I said, "Well, Doc, after all, what would I know? I was only sixteen. Quite frankly, I never dwelled on it. I figured my dad was always in good hands with you, and you'd know whether fifty-four or fifty-five shots were too many."

"Oh, 'twasn't that many."

"Oh, yes it was, Doc. Remember? I'm the one who wrote each one down. It was a long, long string of dates that didn't even include the one you gave him the night he died. Remember the one in the Majestic's office?"

"But, but, but" he said quickly, "I told Homer he shouldn't have so many. You know how willful Homer could be. Tom, this is Bouse Junction, how come you turnin' right? Where's the wreck?"

"Accident wasn't right at the junction, Doc. It's west about two miles on this Wood'ard road."

Since picking up Doc, I had been running on automatic pilot just as I had often done in Korea. Ever since the river bridge the adrenaline had commenced surging through my veins. The moment of retribution was at hand, and I was on the edge of exhilaration. From the Pusan Perimeter to the Yalu, all of this had been planned very carefully.

Was I overlooking anything?

I certainly didn't want to be discovered. If I were, then Doc's ghost could revel for having taken down both Homer and me. No, this was good; everything was good.

I glanced at Doc and although it was cool at 3:00 A.M., I could see perspiration bathing his face and I liked it.

Here was the spot! Here was that ultimate test.

Homer and Mom and Maddy were going to get some belated justice.

I pulled onto the left shoulder of the road and stopped. Doc said, "This is where the bat cave is at. Where in hell's the accident?"

"Get out, Doc. I didn't know you knew about the cave, but it's exactly where we're headed." That was when Doc saw my .38 Smith and Wesson, and his worst fears suddenly materialized. He didn't try to get cute; he obeyed instantly. In bright moonlight, we walked down the craggy gypsum and limestone gulch to the mouth of the cave, which was hidden from the roadway.

"Well, now what?" he said as he turned in front of the cave.

I said, "Doc, as a kid I begged you to take care of my dad. You told me to keep my goddam nose out of your business. Remember? Four times you used that language, and then you finally killed him. Next you went after Maddy. You couldn't wait to jump into Homer's bed. You took advantage of her vulnerableness, fed her drugs, swindled her out of her and my possessions, and put her in an early grave.

You're a real dandy, Doc, and tonight I'm settling the score."

I got the look I wanted. For an instant, he opened his mouth as if to speak then changed his mind. I was surprised how effortless it was. I fired. He never cried out. As he was going down, I squeezed the trigger again. That round must've been a little off center because it spun Doc around so that he fell face down. Shooting Old Onion Breath had been as easy as any garlicky North Korean. Very easy. Easy as it had been for Doc to shove that last deadly hypo into Homer, and to later make his plans for Maddy.

I knew weapons well but was surprised on that still night at the tremendous noise the .38 had made. I wasn't prepared for all the echoes, and hoped that if the folks up by Bouse Junction had heard it, they would take it for a hunter. In any event, I didn't think they would get up at 3:00 A.M. to investigate.

I knelt and felt Doc's carotid. The sonuvabitch was as dead as road kill.

IT WAS PERFECT FOR DOC

I returned to the car and brought back the Coleman lantern, and the entrenching tool I had purchased at the Enid Army-Navy store. I went inside the cave and lifted my lantern to light the cavern's fifteen foot high gypsum walls. Nothing had changed since Mean Dean and I had so often explored it. Because of the lantern, a few bats clinging to the walls began squeaking and making small jerky movements. The thousands upon thousands of bats that had left at sundown for their nightly mosquito kill wouldn't return until dawn. When they did, they would thunder back into the cave in a black squeaking tornadic cloud.

And the smell! God! I hadn't been in that cave for ten years, but with thousands of bats eating and defecating tons of digested mosquitoes, and moths, and other arthropods, there must have been truckloads of the smelly stuff. That matchless odor! It was not as repulsive as a pigpen's, nor as stinking as a cattle enclosure's, but it was pungent. The thick spongy carpet of dung was not clingy nor did it collapse with each footstep. It was like walking on an endless mattress, except that each foot imprint would well up with annoyed insects.

I took the lantern to the far left corner of the initial cavern and set it there. That was where I'd planned to plant Doc. I returned and grabbed his wrists and dragged him toward the lantern. I hadn't looked forward to this personal part. Having been in there so many times with Mean Dean, it wasn't so much the bat guano's odor, it was the fact it was alive with beetles, roaches, and waves of other crawly insects, many of which looked so protohistoric, I doubt if they had all been entomologically cataloged. Farther back in the cave were cleaner rooms with no bats, the dank places where Mean Dean and I used to search for albino salamanders.

Digging in the guano was as easy as digging in moist sand. After awhile I forgot the stench, and the bugs, and got into the rhythm of rapidly throwing bat guano over my shoulder. I moved a load of it, and when I was down about four and a half feet, I hit rock. I laid down the shovel, cleared Doc's pockets of identification, relieved him of a fifty dollar bill, and rolled him into the hole. He landed on his back. I lifted the lantern. His open accusing eyes riveted squarely on mine. It was as if Doc were going to speak. I stared for a time, and then I shrugged it off.

I made several trips to the mouth of the cavern to collect flat pieces of gyp rock to cover the body. I must have carried enough rock to have filled a steamer trunk. I don't know why I went to all that trouble. Doc wasn't going anywhere, and I doubted if a coyote would ever pick up Doc's scent through all that bat dung. Still, a coyote is a resourceful critter, and I didn't want a famished one screwing up my perfect plan. It got personal again when I threw on the first rock. It landed on Doc's stomach and bounced slightly. No sound, Doc just stared back at me. The eyes, the expression, they remained the same. Uncomfortable, I quickly began throwing in rocks without looking where they landed, and then I filled the hole with guano.

When I'd finished, I was very aware that I had just completed a grisly chore, but in my heart, I knew it was one that had been long overdue. I couldn't think of a more ignominious place for Doc's final resting spot. To me the sonuvabitch was a real devil, and as a final touch, I should've thought to cram his mouth full of toothpicks. The bastard deserved a cave slithering with salamanders, and bugs, and bats—bat shit up his nose and in his ears and mouth, and he'd ferment in that mess for eternity. It was perfect for Doc! I caught myself gritting my teeth.

After smoothing, there was no sign of a grave, just footprints that I leveled as I backed out. When a few thousand bats returned near dawn, they'd spring a flurry of new stuff so that the cave floor would appear as never having been disturbed.

I went back to the car, wetted a cloth with Southern Comfort, and wiped anything and everything that Doc might have touched. I checked Doc's floor mat for evidentiary trash. There was Doc's satchel. I opened it. It contained his stethoscope, bandages, tongue depressors, a syringe, syrettes of morphine sulfate—Doc's favorite remedy—naloxone and atropine, and various bottles of pills. I threw in Doc's wallet and scooped in three large handfuls of road gravel. On the way back to Winelda, I'd throw it all in the Cimarron River. Nothing else in the car would ever indicate Doc had been there.

The natural thing would have been to turn around in the middle of that gravel road, but I didn't want to leave a suspicious track. According to plan, I drove ahead a mile, then I made my u-turn. It was half past four in the morning when I tossed Doc's satchel and wallet, and my fine Smith and Wesson, in the swollen Cimarron—no *corpus delicti*, no identification, no murder weapon. I met no car during the sixteen mile drive back to town.

I don't know why I did such a foolish thing but I drove back to Doc's house on Cecil and sat there in the dark for a time. I felt as if a great burden had been lifted from my shoulders. I smiled . . . Doc was finito. I actually fell asleep parked by the curb, enjoyed dreaming the entire gory sequence, and didn't awaken till dawn. I looked in the rearview mirror and my face was a mess. There was dried blood down to my cheekbone. I quickly cleaned it up, and via the football field, I drove twenty-six miles to my Ranger Motel in Alva.

I had slept but a few hours when someone banged incessantly on my motel door. I carefully peeked through the drawn shades. Three policemen!

For godsakes! The Law! How was it possible?

At that moment my blood pressure would have destroyed a sphygmomanometer.

My perfect plan? How could a solution have come so swiftly? When I opened the door my heart was pounding out of its cage. The sergeant—he held his cap in his hand—quickly reported that three Alva kids had stolen my rental Ford. They were returning it undamaged, and apologized for Alva's tawdry welcome. I think they were all pleased when I pressed no charges. I shaved and got in the car. By reflex I felt under the seat for my pistol, but it was gone. Then I suddenly remembered having thrown it in the Cimarron and smiled. By noon I was back in Winelda.

I thought I was as cool as ice, but Mean Dean sent me into shock when he said, "I'm sorry you're leaving so soon, Tom. I'd planned a picnic lunch, some cold beer, and I thought we'd drive out and re-explore our favorite cave. Haven't been there since your junior year." It reverberated in my head: Our favorite cave! Our favorite cave! Haven't been there! Haven't been there!

There was one of those scrimmage hums in my ears, and Mean Dean was grinning broadly, and staring knowingly into my face. His jaws were working, but I heard nothing. In my limbo world, I was transfixed. Mean Dean's friendly face had suddenly metamorphosed into some hideous thing from a Frankenstein movie. Then, just as quickly, the galloping of my heart in my ears, and the hum in my head, stopped. I heard Mean Dean say, "What's the matter, you okay?" I looked at him carefully for subterfuge, but there was nothing guileful. *Damn!* It was another of those screaming coincidences, pure happenstance on Mean Dean's part. First the Alva police and now this. I thought, *My God, am I losing it? Has my Korean composure fizzled? Where's old Cool Luke?* I quickly recovered, patted Mean Dean on the back, asked for a raincheck, said I had too many good-byes to make, and I got in my car. It was the only time in my memory that I was ever glad to take leave of Mean Dean.

I drove by Doc's office and noticed some fretting rancher, both his hands up to the glass shading his eyes as he peered through Doc's locked door. No doubt he was wondering, "Where'n hell is Doc?"

Doc wasn't there.

Doc was over in Major County under a load of gyp rock and crap, his heart ripped apart by lead, his mouth, nose, and ears crammed with bat shit.

WINELDAN MYSTERIES

Two weeks later, I reported to my new unit, the 82nd Airborne Division's 505th Parachute Regiment at Fort Bragg. Col. Trapnell, famous for Bataan, was my commanding officer. I immediately picked up the mail they held for me. Once in my Spartan quarters, I searched out the copies of the weekly *Winelda Enterprise*, the paper Aaron had been sending me without charge ever since I entered the Army. I literally ripped through those *Enterprise* pages, but there was nothing, absolutely nothing about Doc. I had been confident Doc's disappearance would be major, major—worthy of a bannered headline.

As the days passed and subsequent *Enterprise* editions had nothing; my curiosity intensified. Then, two weeks later, the *Winelda Enterprise* carried a story almost as large as the results of the weekly city council meeting. There it was virtually yelling from the page:

Doc Chambers Mysteriously Disappears.

I devoured every word. I felt so guilty the hair stood up on my arms.

Since the bat cave, I had re-examined every detail. I figured the only thing that could tie me in with Doc's disappearance was the fact that I had been in Winelda the night he had disappeared, but then so had two thousand other Wineldans. Had anyone seen my black rental Ford V-8 parked in front of Doc's house? Could they connect me with it? Every other car in Winelda was a black or gray Ford or Chevrolet.

As to motive, Doc was indubitably not my favorite character, and because of that I never once discussed him with others. Consequently, no one was ever aware of the hard thoughts that seethed in me for Doc. Only Maddy was witness to hearing me castigate Chambers, and she was no longer alive. Not once since that 1941 morning when Homer died had Maddy and I ever mentioned malpractice. In the forties, the word "malpractice" was a rarity. And if there were a few curious Wineldans probing—and there were always a few—they were already aware that Doc LaFon attended Homer the morning of his death, not Doc Chambers. So no shadow, no correlation, no motive was ever cast on Chambers for Homer's death; no gossip that I had ever been told or heard of.

No one was aware that Doc had slowly but surely killed Homer. Had there been dirt like that in Winelda, it would've spread like a prairie fire. Even I hadn't realized Homer was being pharmacologically murdered until it had happened. Besides, that was March of 1941, and this was May 1951. It was so long ago, and there was no

reason to link me with anything. Homer was said to have unfortunately died in his sleep due to cardiac arrest. It sounded okay if you
overlooked his young age—forty-three—and the fact he had had no
previous cardiological disorders. Consequently, Homer's odd passing
went without forensic laboratory analysis.

According to the *Enterprise* article, the housekeeper had found
much of Doc's clothing missing, there was no luggage in his closets,
and his four-year-old Buick was not in its garage. There were burglar,
kidnap, and robber theories. Then, Court Washburn, the local banker,
volunteered to the County Sheriff that Doc had withdrawn more than
twelve thousand dollars in cash three days before he was last seen.
The *Enterprise* intimated it looked very much like Doc had flown the
coop. But this explanation made little sense to most people around the
Square. Doc had property. He had the house on Cecil and another
rental property, and he also owned the office property and equipment
on the Square. Altogether, his real possessions were estimated at
roughly sixteen thousand dollars. A man just didn't walk away from
that kind of money! I wondered if someone were pulling off a scam.
The bank clerk perhaps? I knew damn well that Doc hadn't run off
with any money. The twelve thousand must be around somewhere, or
someone had made off with it. In mysteries, the butler always takes
the fall. Why not the cleaning lady? Who had the money? Like Rhett
in *Gone With the Wind*, I frankly didn't give a damn.

Following editions revealed nothing except for three or four letters
to the editor scolding Doc for leaving his long term patients in the
lurch. Of course, there must have been a good number who were
happier than hell. If Doc never returned, their past due bills were
forever closed.

As time passed, something deleterious to my psyche occurred: I
began awakening in the middle of the night thinking of what I'd done
and the true ramifications of "cold blood!" I'd lay there and fret: *So
what, Tom? In Korea, killing was your middle name. Yeah, but those in
Korea had been required, legal killings while this one wasn't.* In those
thoughts, I equivocated with myself that I wasn't totally at fault. I had
become obsessed with a long-standing family situation. Eventually
this weak self-flagellation irritated me, because I had resolutely killed
Chambers with a measure of honor, and with my eyes wide open.
Then my thoughts would drift to Homer and Maddy, and like a
morning fog, the remorse would suddenly burn off—my conscience

would be miraculously salved. I'd indeed done the correct thing. This worked until the next time my thoughts decided to wander. Also, after battling these brain wave episodes, I might toss and turn for an hour or two before falling asleep, and this annoyance began happening ever more frequently.

PIPER BELLE

The following spring, 1952, while I was busy parachuting from C-119s and C-46s at Fort Bragg, a new Chambers story appeared in the *Enterprise*. At the Alva Courthouse an attorney disclosed that he had been sworn to secrecy for a period of one year, a restriction that no longer applied. He announced that if Piper Belle Zollinger could prove she had had a child during the month of September 1951, Doc's houses and his office property were now—after taxes—her legal property. But what was this Piper Belle Zollinger's nexus, and who the hell was she?

Quoting other sources, the paper explained that Piper Belle had been Doc Chambers's patient from December 1950 to January 1951. She had made several visits to Doc's office. The article stopped short of full implication, but it must have elicited many "Ah hahs" from in and around Winelda and the Winelda trade territory. For a community like Winelda, buzzing spice of this genre over the party lines and around the Square made life worthwhile.

I wrote Mean Dean, brought him up to date on the Army, and casually asked about the Piper Belle article. He was delighted to fill me in, and added many asides that the *Enterprise* would never dare print.

He wrote that I had never known Piper, that she was the winsome, blue-eyed daughter of Emil Zollinger. He further explained that Emil had cattle southeast of Winelda near Twenty-One Crossing on the Cimarron, and that Zollinger was a hard worker and a God fearing man who could quickly forget his allegiance to the Bible if defamatory meddlers trespassed on his privacy.

Once, back in the thirties, on the busy Winelda Square, a man revealed some questionable dirt about Zollinger; he had in fact referred to Zollinger as a no count sonuvabitch. Women within earshot gasped. It had been a charged moment because in Winelda the use of such abusive language was tantamount to demanding a duel.

Word of the incident traveled quickly, and it wasn't long before Zollinger showed up in town with his .44, spotted the rumormonger emerging from City Hall, pulled out his piece, and winged him from across Cecil Street. Zollinger reportedly ambled over, kicked his prone prey hard in the ribs, and said, "Now you best fergit thet you ever lernt thet awful SOB word." Nobody in Winelda ever again dared call Zollinger a sonuvabitch, not even in a whisper. Tombstone justice like this squelched the ultra liberal application of the First Amendment in Winelda. There was a limit to public accusations or acerbic remarks.

Winelda's best sleuths began working overtime on the Piper Belle jigsaw. After all, this was a town where everyone knew everyone's name, including their kid's and dog's, the make of their car and its license number. Bits and pieces began leaking around town. Were they from Doc's imperfect lawyer? Probably not. From Piper Belle to an untrustworthy confidante? No one knew. However, the fact that Piper Belle had had a minor bladder infection soon became common knowledge. Chambers had attended to her regularly in his office. Yes, Piper's visitations had begun in December 1950.

One day Piper Belle was on Doc's examination table (no doctor in town had a nurse) and Doc's practiced anatomical eye quickly noticed the perfection draped under Piper Belle's loose cotton housedress. He must have been titillated when he discovered how his slightest private touch could send this lovely specimen into tantalizing gasps and squirms. Such provocation was much more than most unprincipled men could endure, especially someone as flawed as Doc; it was no surprise for Old Devil Sex to take over.

Doc had supposedly said, "Just a moment Piper Belle, Honey," and he locked the office front door, turned the sign to "Out to Lunch," and pulled the shades. When he lifted Piper Belle off his examination table and gently placed her on his leather chaise longue, she was already in a state almost as uncontrolled as Doc's, and Doc began fumbling so feverishly he was popping his fly buttons all over the linoleum floor. And that was how it had happened.

Evidently, from a later examination, Doc learned the awful truth; his child was growing inside this delectable waif. He knew it was only a matter of time before the tornadic story and subsequent fury would break. Knowing Emil Zollinger's eye for an eye reputation,

Doc started packing his bags and drawing out his money. Doc's debouchment measures had taken place in April of 1951, just as I was returning from Korea.

I sat in my bachelor officers' quarters at Bragg and re-read Mean Dean's letter, and the watered down versions from the *Enterprise*. Reading between the lines of the flurry of angry and often speculative letters to the editor as well as the court report, I began to think that only in Winelda could something like this have happened. All this humming gossip about Doc's flying the coop. Most thought he was probably fat-catting it in Florida or Southern California, but there I was in the driver's seat. I knew exactly where old Doc was. He had been about to fly all right, but I had interrupted it. But whatever became of all that money? I eagerly awaited the next week's *Enterprise*.

BUGS AND DREAMS

I also had become concerned with discovery at the cave. What if some jerk decided to go in there and start bagging guano? I had often wondered why an entrepreneurial Wineldan hadn't started a fertilizer company years earlier. Bagged steer manure had certainly made it big with corporate offices in Tulsa and Wichita. Why not designer bat guano—richer, finer, and filled with natural chemicals to induce plant growth?

I figured that with just a little more time, it wouldn't really matter if someone eventually decided to mine the nitrogen and phosphate rich guano. The cave's awesome collection of carnivorous bugs would soon make it virtually impossible to identify Doc Chambers's mess in the cave. Also, bear in mind that none of the speculative rumors suggested Doc was dead. Everyone had concluded he'd fled to Florida to avoid Zollinger.

Wouldn't that be a bizarre twist?

Take the worst case scenario: A body is discovered by chance in the cave and identified as Doc's? Not to worry. Every sign would superficially point straight to old eye-for-an-eye Zollinger. Couldn't be more perfect. Moreover, there would be no real harm done to Zollinger other than a little inconvenience. The district attorney would investigate exhaustively, but would never be able to prove conclusively that Zollinger was the perpetrator. Zollinger would have an ironclad alibi because he had never been near the scene. Yet, everyone in two counties would babble that old foxy Zollinger was most likely guilty.

It was this useless cogitation that had allowed Doc to devil my sleep since my arrival at Bragg. Regardless, I was doing an outstanding job at Bragg as commander of a parachute infantry company. Despite my gnawing anxiety, I had not taken to booze or anything stronger than perhaps a couple of milligrams of an innocent tranquilizer known as milltown.

Yet, when I turned in, I'd know in ten or fifteen minutes if another parade of kaleidoscopic scenes would commence marching through my brain. There was always a recital of that trip with Doc to the cave, the discharge of my Smith and Wesson, dragging the body into the cave, and burying it. The Doc of my dreams would groan every time I threw on a shovel of guano. That's when I'd come out of any half-sleep and stare at the ceiling. Groans? Could there have been groans? Certainly not! I was positive there had been no groans. When I buried Doc, he had been quite dead. And there had been no resurrection, no Nicodemus had come and spirited him away, and although guano wasn't all that heavy, there was no possibility of Doc having crawled through all those rocks. Besides, I'd hit him square in the middle of his chest—twice; his heart no longer functioned.

My chaotic half sleeps often veered in other absurd directions. For example, I'd be a fly on the wall observing the spirited boardroom of Winelda's new fertilizer tycoon. In my recurring dream, this was always Mean Dean, with eyes as creepy bright as foxfire. He'd become the corporate president of a sleek multi-state manure consortium, and as a Northwestern State graduate geologist, he was well aware that underground streams, sinkholes, caves, concomitant bats, and slithery things characterized a true karstic region. Consequently, Mean Dean and his staff had scoured real estate across the Cimarron, studied the area's geomorphology, located quite a number of caves, and quickly controlled them through cheap leases and easements.

This Mean Dean of my dreams was always standing at the end of an enormous mahogany conference table, his reflection mirrored in its burnished surface, as he discussed cave number thirteen with his board members. Of course, cave thirteen would unfortunately have to be Doc's cave. He would say, "Gentlemen, we're lucky to have glommed onto that cave. I explored it as a kid with my friend Tom. I know first hand there's tons of guano. It's a gold mine in there!" Then I'd hear Doc's hollow spectral voice, "Now they'll surely f-i-n-d m-e."

This eerie dream was so bizarre yet realistic, and so patently absurd, it insulted my intelligence. I began to wonder if I were losing it. Doc was as dead as a doornail, and those bugs out there were feasting like they had never feasted before. Ghosts and voodoo are for a strange religious sect in Haiti—certainly not for me! Go to sleep.

SOMETHING UNEXPECTED

I suffered on. I had a tour in the Pentagon with Army Intelligence and a somewhat perilous Bangkok assignation. I married Julie in 1959, a full eight years after I had nailed Doc, and we were stationed at the Presidio of Monterey in California. One evening I picked up the *Winelda Enterprise* and was thunderstruck!

> Doctor Aloysius Chambers, 66, Formerly of Winelda, was killed in a freak car accident in Lone Pine, California, at the corner of Main and Cerro Gordo.

Impossible! I was absolutely dumbfounded! How could that possibly be?

Lone Pine is a remote little desert town east of the Sierras blessed with beautiful geology. It is the magic location where they had filmed *Gunga Din*, and *A Bad Day at Black Rock,* and at least forty other films. Still, how could this possibly be? I read on. This Doc had evidently retained an attorney from Bishop, California. Immediately after Doc's death, part of the attorney's obligation had been to send a letter to the *Winelda Enterprise* containing his obituary from the local *Inyo Gazette*. When Doc died, he wanted Winelda to know where he had been all these years, and what he had accomplished as head of a remote California county clinic. It was nothing less than a posthumous ego trip for Doc.

This Lone Pine Doc was still a bachelor, but he had left a will. He had made it crystal clear that he wanted ten percent of his estate to be spent in bettering the Inyo County Clinic, and ninety percent to go to a Miss Charlsey Belle Zollinger, a minor, of Fairview, Oklahoma. Doc had kept track of Piper Belle. He'd known she had given birth to

Charlsey Belle at the Fairview Hospital and had later married. Charlsey Belle, Doc's daughter, was eight years old, and would inherit a hundred and twenty-five thousand dollar trust account. Possibly along with Doc's ego trip, he must have felt some gnawing responsibility for his love child. This was certainly not true to form for a scalawag, but stranger things have happened. The *Winelda Enterprise* editor added her own note, stating she had often wondered why the Inyo County Clinic, in a remote part of Eastern California, had for years subscribed to the *Enterprise*.

I was nonplused—absolutely flabbergasted.

I immediately secured a three day pass to drive from Monterey out across the High Sierras via Tioga Pass to Lone Pine. At Lone Pine's local paper, *The Advocate*, I asked if they had a photo of Doc Chambers. Sure enough, it was Doc who was looking back at me. If it wasn't Doc, it was a helluva clone! However, he looked more cosmopolitan; gone were the tufts over his ears and the proliferation of curly nose hairs. I then went to the Inyo County Clinic and was shown Doc's office. I looked at his desk, his chair, and his fountain pen desk set. His presence seemed everywhere. His portrait hung in the hallway with some black ribbon tacked to its frame. There was no doubt about it; it was Doc. Then I went out to the cemetery, and there was a fresh mound, some flowers as dead as the grave, and a modest headstone. Carved into the granite was "Denzel Aloysius Chambers." I had never known his name was Denzel. Also on the stone was a caduceus and the simple dates "1894-1959."

In Korea, I had proven to myself and many others that the pressure of the worst kind of combat had not affected my ability to command. I had always felt I was in total control, but not at this particular moment! If Doc Chambers had indeed begun to molder away in Inyo County's dirt—from the photos it certainly appeared to be Doc—then who in hell was in the bat cave? This was a jarring, inexplicable, new turn of events.

In just three weeks, the Winelda High School Alumni was holding a reunion. It was the perfect excuse for me to take four days leave and do some on site checking. After all, I was practically a lieutenant colonel; I'd have no problem swinging four days from Gen. Carl F. Fritzsche. I flew to Oklahoma City and secured a rental to drive the hundred and thirty-five miles to Winelda.

Seeing my classmates for our eighteenth reunion was revelatory.

We were all thirty-five to thirty-eight; I noticed that some had begun to bald and fill out. There were a few I couldn't recognize, and that was really bad. The embarrassing failure to recognize is the prime reason I'd probably never become a reunion aficionado.

That Mean Dean didn't attend was a big disappointment. Instead of digging guano in cave thirteen, he was running for state senate in his chosen state of Georgia. He had lived in Macon for the past six years. Because of his witty personality, and his innate intelligence, I was quite sure Mean Dean would win. Mean Dean could do anything. He could ride wild stallions; he could sell overcoats in Tahiti. If he failed as a Georgia Cracker, there was always cave thirteen. I missed seeing him, but right at the moment, he was far from my central purpose for being in Winelda.

After the banquet, I attended what they called a mixer, a time for impuissant punch and the renewal of old acquaintances. I hung around until eighty percent of the attendees had cut out, then I sauntered toward the men's room, casually looked around the hallway, and then drifted toward the parking lot.

One thing I had already decided: I was not going to be outfoxed. I would be exceptionally aware of anything and everything around me. We have all read of the perfect crime, and of the hapless perpetrator who returned to the scene where the law waited. Just one wrong move and out of the woodwork would pop a ton of FBI and State Police! I got behind the wheel and surreptitiously checked everything in view. While I casually engaged my seat belt, I checked the rearview mirror before slowly gliding out of the parking area. Two miles out of town, a place everyone locally referred to as "the end of the pavement," I cleverly spun the car around the shoulder in a cloud of dust and headed back toward Winelda. This I did to craftily foil any sleuths possibly following me. But there was no one. Fully satisfied, I made another u-turn and headed for the cave.

The mystery was killing me as I drove toward Bouse Junction because I *knew* the events like my service record. I had taken him from his own home in the middle of the night. It had unquestionably been smelly Doc Chambers—no chance of an interloper. As I drove I reminded myself that just *eight* years before I had taken this very same route.

In spite of all the pictures and the tombstone in Inyo County, I might only *assume* Chambers lay buried in California. It was indeed a clever ruse, but without exhumation, I would never know for sure. After all, I hadn't seen him in his casket; I hadn't seen him shoveled under the California desert dirt. On the other hand, I *knew* I'd put Chambers in his bat cave grave. I personally dragged him there, piled twelve inches of flat rocks on top of his body to ward off coyotes, and buried him under three feet of bat guano. I didn't really know why I was even going to the abominable cave. It was a disgraceful exercise; I was insulting myself. Regardless, in the face of the conflicting information, I had to check.

Once again, as I slowed to a stop on the shoulder, I scrutinized my surroundings. I went to the trunk and pulled out the lantern and the shovel I had bought in Oklahoma City, and within five minutes I was digging. I'd forgotten the odor, such a fetid Stygian smell, but the moment I stepped near the cavern opening, I was quickly reminded.

I dug down three feet where I should have touched the mantle of rock that I had laid over Doc, but there was only more of the bat stuff as well as the angered army of horrific beetles et al. I figured that after eight years, the extra accumulation of guano was entirely logical.

Finally, I struck a rock, I dug around it but it was large, much larger than a bushel basket. I certainly had not carried that in there. I dug on the opposite end of what I remembered to be the grave. Estimating the location wasn't difficult because I'd dug it in the far left hand corner. I looked around. That's precisely where I was now. However, on the opposite end I hit an even larger rock. Where were the thirty or so flat rocks I'd piled on top of Doc? I stopped for a moment to consider. Where in hell was Doc? I chuckled at the thought. It was as bizarre as Edgar Allen Poe's *The Cask of Amontillado*.

Finally, I looked into the yawning hole and wiped the sweat from my forehead. Jesus! I'd come all the way from California; consequently, I wanted to be absolutely positive. I didn't want to return to the Coast and then start wondering if I'd dug in the wrong spot. I carefully oriented myself. No, *this* was indubitably *the right spot!*

I had thought this evening would be gory, and I hadn't really wanted to thrust my shovel into Doc's bones and maw. I didn't really want to see his putrid crawly remains, but this turn of events was mind boggling. As I climbed out of the gulch to the roadside, I felt as if Doc's ghost were playing games with me. Had I lost my sanity? I was mystified.

THE MISERABLE PUZZLE

The next day in my DC-7C airliner, my eyes were transfixed on the Arizona desert slowly unfolding fourteen thousand feet below. Just as my baffled mind tried to make sense of the dead thing that had been plaguing me these past eight years, the captain announced we were flying over the Canyon of the Dead. This was why my eyes weren't really seeing the desert's gorgeous coral outcrops of Coconino sandstone or the Cañon del Muerto.

The answer to my miserable puzzle was hopelessly gridlocked.

When we were over Lake Mead with Las Vegas to the right, I spotted the High Sierras in the lightly hazed distance, and I could identify Mount Whitney. As we drew nearer, I could see the salty crust of Owens Lake at its base. I knew at the northern extremity of the lake was the barely discernible town of Lone Pine. Doc was incontrovertibly buried down there because he sure as hell was not in the bat cave. And if he wasn't in the bat cave, then by God *I hadn't been there!* And if I hadn't been there, I hadn't killed Doc.

But I knew I had!

The many contradictions made my temples throb. I asked the stewardess if she would bring me three aspirin. I didn't know if I was suffering from the glare of the snow on the High Sierras, or the tangle of what was congealing in my mind.

As soon as we passed the crest of the Sierras, we began letting down over Yosemite for the approach to San Francisco. Once in the terminal, I had precious little time to hustle to my Convair twin engine connector flight that would whisk me down to the Monterey Peninsula Airport.

When the pilot started going out to sea, I knew that dense fog blanketed Monterey. In such instances the pilot flew seaward in order to lock onto checkpoint Munso before making his ninety-eight degree ILS—instrument landing system—approach to runway 10R. While the pilot was carefully readying to make his localizer intercept, I relaxed by turning back to the nagging Doc Chambers.

That night I had definitely been outside Doc's house. I had knocked on his door, and he had gotten into the car.

Or had he?

I remembered tripping and smashing my head on the curb, and I also remembered awakening in my rental car at dawn, still in front of Doc's house. Blood had dried on my shirt, and blood had caked from my forehead to my jawbone.

My God! Is that it? After cracking my head, did I pass out in the car? While passed out did I hallucinate the crystal clear concatenation of events, events rehearsed so many times in Korea: shooting Doc, dragging his body, digging the hole, covering him with rocks? One major flaw: I had definitely come to Winelda with a Smith and Wesson and, after the killing, I had thrown it into the river! If, in fact, I had had a hallucinatory dream, why on the following day wouldn't my pistol still have been in the car? I distinctly remembered feeling for the pistol at the motel and it was gone. Had the pistol been there the next morning, it may have tipped me off I had dreamed all those details.

So, how about that pistol?

The three kids! The ones who had stolen my rental car in Alva. *Voilà!* They had ripped it off. Damn! That certainly made sense; I had never disposed of the pistol.

I absentmindedly pinched my lower lip with my thumb and fore-finger and stared at the airplane's bulkhead. I was in a deep, deep introspection. I concluded: *The murder and burial had been so incredibly clear. Moreover, for eight miserable years I've been agonizing. I've been letting that flat-assed sonuvabitch haunt me all this time.* And instead of me vindicating Homer and Maddy, it had been some weirdo from the Land of Fruits and Nuts who had lost control of his car at twenty-five miles per hour in the little town of Lone Pine. Some jerk in Lone Pine had handed Doc his just reward and *not me!* SSShhhii! I wondered if that miserable Doc had had a toothpick stuck in his mouth when the collision occurred.

Then I sensed the Convair turning to lock on for its final approach toward the runway; it was steadily descending through the solid fog guided by an invisible localizer. Landing in the dense fog at Monterey always made me pucker and white knuckle my arm rest as I thought of the exceptionally deep and cold ocean beneath me and the shrouded coastal mountains just ahead. At three hundred feet above ground, we broke through the fog; tall Monterey pines were jutting up on either side. Almost immediately the tires screeched on runway 10R and I exhaled a long sigh, not from the superb landing, but because *now I knew.* I knew about Doc! It had been just like Sinatra's last four words of the famous ballad, *Laura*. At last, his ghost was forever off my back.

A Promise to Homer

Two months later I was in our car driving across country for my new assignment at The Command and General Staff College at Fort Leavenworth, Kansas. For a couple of weeks my wife, Julie, was visiting her folks on Long Island. I decided to sidetrack a bit, go through Coffeyville, and briefly visit with Homer. When I traveled up busy 8th Street, I stopped briefly at a package store near the Carnegie Library. From there I skirted around the south border of the old Sherwin-Williams zinc smelter. Its formerly boiling smokestack had once symbolized progress in Coffeyville, but if the wind had been wrong, it could make that entire West Side of town stink to high heaven. Now, smoke no longer came from the huge stack, and the air was as sweet as spring flowers.

I drove on to Fairlawn Cemetery and was surprised at how well I remembered the little graveled lane that led to my mother's and Homer's graves. I stepped out of the car with the memory of Homer's gloomy graveside services—the black umbrellas, the long black dresses and black shoes, the veiled faces. While recalling this, I wondered why humans forever make such a fetish of death. We make a roaring production to further shatter ourselves when the circumstance calls for every conceivable lift and comfort we can find.

Looking down upon Homer's mound of grass covered earth was more moving than I had expected. There he lay, well before his time, resting beside my twenty-eight-year-old mother. He had constantly blamed himself for her death that drizzly Kansas City night. Now that I had absurdly hounded myself for eight years by carrying around the murder of Doc Chambers, I better understood Homer's own nagging inner turbulence, the burden that had so discombobulated him. Now I understood what the mind could do. I was well aware that Homer's anguish must have been twenty times worse than anything I had ever experienced.

And I spoke softly, "Too bad, Homer, our life together was so plagued by Kansas City. I wonder if you ever comprehended how much that single drizzly night would eventually affect Maddy and me? When you were troubled, you could be among the very worst.

But I also remember so many days when you proved to be the best damned Dad in Winelda. Had not that dark cloud constantly moved in and out, it could have been so different between us. Worst of all, we had precious little time to enjoy each other's adult company. There was virtually none . . . you missed a lot; we both missed a lot." Then I briefly told Homer how I had mistakenly thought I had avenged him with Doc Chambers. "I know you're having a roaring good laugh from that one."

Suddenly, I halted my reverie with Homer. I realized I had been addressing him for several minutes as naturally as if we were standing there together. Beneath my eyebrows, I did a furtive Jack Nicholson scan to determine if anyone were watching, to see if anyone with a net and a white uniform were advancing stealthily toward me from tombstone to tombstone. But there was no one lurking. It was just Homer and me.

I shook my head and smiled at my exchange with Homer. Quite frankly, I very seriously doubted we were communicating; I doubted Homer was even aware I was there. While in Korea, I had come to doubt a lot about the Lord and my religion. Religious cogitations often produced a somewhat romantic story, but I didn't really believe Homer or my mother knew they were lying side by side. Yet, we had spent an entire day transporting Homer's remains so that he could be here. We try to cover all the proper bases, sometimes at great expense, and months afterward, we privately wonder: "Was all that really necessary?"

All of which reminded me of my Chinese friend in Chieng Mai, a Harvard graduate and a Catholic. In the northeast corner of his Northern Thailand backyard, he had shown me his gold leafed teak Buddha, his image of the Virgin Mary, and finally the quasi-animistic spirit house cluttered with fresh offerings of rice, tangerines, and smoking joss sticks—this to make lurking spirits happy—all were in close proximity to each other. Here was an exceptionally intelligent man surrounded by religious objects of different beliefs.

He told me he was a devout Catholic yet he paid equal respect to each of these icons. He had laughed sheepishly as he proclaimed he couldn't ignore the distinct possibility of some other god's viability. He wanted to be sure not to slight any of them; therefore, he covered all the bases. These were his passports to multiple allegiances. Doubtlessly, a parallel syndrome had drawn me to commune at

Homer's graveside. I didn't really believe, yet I had traveled miles to come here and stand beside a mound of grass.

And having briefly reflected on these contradictions, I went ahead and complicated it by doing something Homer had asked of me long ago. I returned to the car, reached into the glove compartment, and surreptitiously pulled out a little brown paper bag. I popped the seal and poured the half pint of alcohol over the head of the grave. I said, "There you go, Homer; enjoy." And I felt good, but I also felt like a damned fool.

EPILOGUE

NO MONUMENTS

In 1985, when I was sixty-one, I wanted to see Winelda again. Over the years, my wife Julie had heard the Wineldan lore so often she had become curious to see the actual places, and Winelda's special people. I wanted to show her Homer's Place, and take her to old WHS with its main hallway lined with pictures of every class since the school's inception. I wanted to look into my homeroom where Ila Strickland had gently nudged me to honor roll status. I wanted Julie to see Lottie's Place, and where the secret liquor stash had been stored. I wanted her to see where we'd kept our snake collection, and the site of Amzy's monumental bag swing. She had to see those beautiful red mesas across the Cimarron, Diamondback Mesa, where a rattlesnake had snagged me, and of course, I wanted her to visit the infamous bat cave. I also wanted to visit the Majestic, and have a coke at the Rexall. That would just about wrap up Winelda.

Next spring we were to visit Principia College, her school at historic Elsah, Illinois. I too had heard her many stories, and they had kindled my imagination. I wanted to see those great old buildings she had so often described on the bluffs overlooking the mighty Mississippi.

As Julie and I drove nearer to Winelda, I could hardly curb my mounting inner excitement. I realized I was running off at the mouth about inconsequential things. I'd point to a farmhouse and tell her who had lived there. I decided to check myself, and not become a raging bore. After all, those names meant nothing whatever to Julie.

My first shocker was the sign on the northern entry: "Entering Winelda—Pop. 895." Through all the dust storm years, the population had always been around two thousand! I knew that the loss of the railway center had been devastating, but now that the nation's economy was booming, why would fifty-five percent of the town be wiped out? Despite this initial disappointment, I knew that all Winelda's bones—its key places—would still be intact. We would lunch at Eastman's and have one of their famous T-bones.

My first disappointment was Mexican Town.

There was no sign of it. It had been completely wiped off the earth!

Not a trace, not a foundation, not even a derelict shed remained to give evidence of a once viable community of three hundred—no Catholic Church, no little houses scattered beneath the cottonwoods, no little Mexican children cavorting through the brush. There was nothing but weeds, trees, clumps of sage, and sandy soil. It was like an unmarked grave. "Is this the place?" I mumbled to no one. Yes, it was certainly the place.

Back through the huge cottonwoods, I could see a vast weedy area where the brick roundhouse had once been. Not a solitary brick remained. A stern sign announced "No Trespassing. This is Santa Fe Property." The roundhouse, the heart of the yards, had long been such a vibrant focal point. Four or five locomotives had always been there with maintenance workmen crawling over them. There had always been the clanging and banging of wrenches and hammers, and the all pervasive smell of steam. Now, except for a male quail somewhere in the weeds calling to its mate, and the soporific droning of a bee, it was deadly still, everything as silent as the moon. There was no José Ramírez, no Concho Concepción, no Manuel, no Tony Franco, no church, and no kids.

I looked just beyond. The ice plant had disappeared. It had been the largest ice plant west of Chicago, a place that had once vibrated with the shouts of teams of men dumping huge blocks of ice onto clanking conveyer belts to cool eighty or ninety waiting vegetable cars. Now the site was a tangle of dense underbrush with the wind sighing funereally through the tall cottonwoods. A bereft hound's mournful howl would have completed the description.

"Come on, Tom," Julie said, "look at the bright side. Now that man's been erased and everything's returned to the wild, the Sierra Club environmentalists, and that quail, must be ecstatic."

"I can't believe it," I said. "We've seen a jillion historical signs on this trip. Most of them were inconsequential. You'd think a spot like this, where so many people once lived, where for years people were born and some had died, would at least rate a dumb little sign . . . some vestige of what had helped Winelda be great."

"What do you want?" she teased. "A bronze statue of a Mexican railroader? This cottonwood grove is monument enough; it's beautiful."

"Just goes to show," I said as we got into the car, "how fleeting our mark on earth is."

Here I was returning with my San Francisco wife to show her effervescent Winelda. I had imagined a triumphal entry with everything humming as I had long remembered. But when we turned the corner onto Cecil, the town was absolutely stark dead! There were only three or four parked cars, and the sidewalks were virtually empty. The Campbell Hotel no longer looked prosperous. They'd closed George Barnett's Eason filling station; its main glass window was broken, and its faded sign hung askew.

Pop's horseshoe grounds—the arena of hard fought games—was as quiet as a cemetery. What the hell! Didn't today's Wineldans play horseshoes? The old Wagner Motor Company's Chevrolet showroom was empty. Its windows were grimy, and tumbleweeds and shifting sand covered its once busy concrete apron. This formerly bustling intersection reminded me of *Grapes of Wrath* architectural relics, of Arizona's decadent Route 66, where around Seligman, we'd seen ancient boarded up motor courts and derelict service stations. Like tired monuments sprinkled along what had once been the renowned highway of the thirties—the Great Okie Highway across the Mojave—all its action had now moved over to a much newer I-40.

As we drove toward the Square, Thorne's Hardware, Winelda's largest store, had sheets of plywood nailed over its huge plate glass windows—windows that had once displayed fancy saddles, and decorated harnesses, and Remington rifles. As if the plywood were not sufficiently tawdry, some progressive ding-a-ling had covered it with graffiti, one misspelled message on top another.

Homer's Place actually took the wind out of me. Its plate glass windows had been sealed with concrete blocks. Jutting like warts through its windowless skin were dripping air conditioners, ugly and sterile. Wineldans had effectively killed the business district. They'd even replaced the original ornamented streetlights with new skinny poles strung together by unsightly wire; previously the wires had been underground.

Homer's Place, the town's hottest commercial corner, had atrophied to dreary, unimaginative apartments. This corner had been the epicenter, with the drawing barrel chained to the central light pole, and the Corner Drug humming with customers and whining Hamilton Beach malt machines. Mean Dean had scooped chocolate ice cream here, and had made the place come alive with his colorful remarks; the very same Mean Dean who had mistaken finger cots for condoms, and who was now a senator in Georgia. What a miserable transmogrification of Homer's Place! On the top floor, I had grown up to the accompaniment of the non-stop jukebox at Etta's Café. Up there is where Homer had lived his last. Now, just like old cemetery flowers, it had wilted and was strangely quiet.

There was also no Seaman's Barber, no McBride's Grocery, no Nick's Confectionery, no hardware, no Stiller—the official Santa Fe watch repairman—no Doc Wright's Drugs, and no Etta's Café. For so many years, Etta's had been the town's pacemaker. It had been the twenty-four hour sanctuary for Wineldans escaping blazing summer heat, or the winter's sleet and swirling tumbleweeds. Now, the Square was as dead as the hackneyed doornail—not a pedestrian in sight; I was stunned. It was like *High Noon* revisited; I fully expected to look up and see Gary Cooper stalking stiffly down the middle of deserted Main Street.

Hank's Place had become a vacant lot. Eastman's Restaurant, Winelda's finest—where Irish Lily had flattened Blacky Bronson with a heavy water pitcher, where Homer had feted my chemistry teacher—had become a sleazy tabernacle with a flickering neon sign proclaiming the "Word of Life Center" and "Jesus Saves." No longer was the great Eastman's the purveyor of succulent seventy-five cent, sixteen ounce T-bones. Its tables with starched linens had made room for a tawdry Mecca for impassioned reborns, a dissolute place where they could spin their nondenominational prayer wheels.

I looked down Main and then down Cecil. There was not a single drug store, not a solitary restaurant in view. They had closed the

Snooker Parlor; its windows were opaque with dust, as were those at old Mr. Hough's Dry Goods store.

I felt my wife's arm coming around my shoulder. "Don't be down, Tom. Just think of Times Square; it too fell on hard times."

We walked toward the Majestic. The Rexall Drug, which had once been alive with its whirring Hamilton Beach malted milk machines and the scent of nutmeg, was now a weedy vacant lot strewn with tin cans and yellowed *Daily Oklahoman* pages. No longer did its busy ceiling fans rhythmically whap-whap the air. Where the doorway had once been, there remained, like a tombstone, the white tiled entryway with blue letters that spelled "Rexall." It was the place where "Doc" Lloyd Curtis revived Boyd McGurn's wife after winning the hundred dollar drawing. Whatever had happened to Lloyd, who during the war could always find an extra pack of Dentyne chewing gum? Some said he had retired in Texas.

And then there was the Majestic, Winelda's last real "picture show." I wanted to show Julie the box-office, the lobby, and the office where Homer had once created show bills to deliver from door to door. But Homer's monuments were as unrecognizable as Mexican Town. Someone had removed Homer's great one hundred bulb marquée; the Majestic looked naked. Locked tightly was the place where all of Winelda had once come to be entertained and comforted by ice cooled air. Now there was a simple doorway with a sign that read: "Antiques Bought and Sold. Your Junk is Our Treasure." I speculated how Homer might have reacted had he been with us. Filmy, fly-specked windows had replaced my glistening brass. I shaded my eyes and peered through the inner darkness at the jumble of dusty junk. The junkman was obviously buying nothing, and Main Street apparently had little treasure left to sell. I looked in the direction of the dry cleaners and for some reason thought of Bing, the abominably proud dog who had once ruled this sector.

How come this degeneration: windows covered with graffiti, the burned out lots littered with tin cans? Even the western look of the handful of men around the Square had changed. Where were the macho Perry Phillipses, or the Ten Gallons, or the Hods with their Justins, and Stetsons, and Bull Durham tags dangling from their shirt pockets? Now, creeping along the sidewalk in Wal-Mart walking shoes, were softer looking dudes wearing Howdy Doody feed company caps. No longer was there a Cherokee Strip aura around

Winelda's square.

The Main Street post-office had always been an important meeting place, a part of the glue that had made Winelda a viable town. It was no longer there. Strange that while the shadowy bugler was readying himself to blow taps over this dying town, the federal government had diddled away "pork" money on a new post office. Strange because the new post-office was twice the size of the old one, yet with only half as many people to serve. Think about it; instead of placing it centrally, they built it off to the dead side of the Square where the new crop of ancient whittlers refused to congregate.

With no Santa Fe crews, the Commercial Hotel had boarded its doors. I wondered whatever became of Blanche and her ladies. The world's most resilient profession had abandoned Winelda and had scattered to survive in livelier places. I'm sure the resourceful girls—probably all grandmothers by now—had survived. Huzzah for Billie Joe and Elna Lou.

Once bustling Coury's Grocery had faded. So had mortal Cavy, the old pioneer who had perennially sunned in front of the store while watching a more vibrant Winelda pass in review. What would Cavy have thought of today's Winelda? I suddenly wondered if any research scholar had ever sat with him and methodically extracted the exciting history filed inside his head. He had known Winelda from the days of Indian Territory, and boardwalks, and horses, and no paving around the Square.

I drove across the tracks to Lottie's Place—the place where Sheriff Ken Greer had made his raid, and where our school principal sometimes made his shadowy appearances, his snap-brim pulled almost to his nose.

Lottie's Place was gone!

All that remained of her building was a charred foundation and part of one wall. I remembered how this place had sometimes been my sanctuary when Homer was in his other world. According to a passerby, Lottie's had fallen into disrepair, and only two months before, had mysteriously burned. Still intact was the back wall; Lottie's kitchen screen door was hanging on one hinge. It was the same door Hod Phillips and so many others had often passed through to enjoy Lottie's sour mash sippers. I wondered if Hod's brightly suspendered ghost watched over the place. Then I conjectured whatever became of Lottie and Jimmy, two fine people who had raised and loved other people's children as if they were their very own. I had personally been sadly remiss. Unfortunately, young people start their lives and rudely forget those who helped them make their start.

I parked near the slab of concrete that had been Jimmy's garage floor. Weeds, now burnt and twisted, had grown up through its cracks. My Winelda extravaganza was flopping badly; I had to produce something for my wife, at least show her where Jimmy had kept the stash of liquor. And there it was in the concrete slab: the bootlegger's secret, the cache area. The concrete cover, no longer there, had allowed the hole to fill with shifting sand. I actually heard myself droning, "Jack said the runner from Arkansas would come in the garage late at night and unload." Imagine; I was reduced to showing Julie what had been a hole and was now filled with sand. It was my very best effort to substantiate at least one of my stories. And Julie tried her level best to be interested in this ridiculous sand filled hole, and I loved her for it.

Just then, its horn blowing, a four unit diesel with eighty boxcars sped northward. It swirled dust across the Broadway crossing and clattered on. What a contrast to the majestic arrival of those stately old 4000-series locomotives! With their strident whistle at the crossing, their cylinders spewing geysers of steam, they would proudly puff and clank through town like mighty Caesars returning from war. Then they would switch to the marshalling yards and be swarmed over and pampered by a platoon of slave-like maintenance people who oiled and wiped them, manicured their every part. And new, refreshed crews with bright red bandannas would board and continue driving the valuable cargo on toward Chicago. The arrival of a 4000 double-header had always been an event! But this speeding diesel driven freight irreverently thumbed its nose at Winelda, as if Winelda were just another insignificant part of the prairie. It clattered northward.

Court Washburn's bank on Missouri Street, the dead side of the Square, had been managed well and had survived despite Winelda's glaring demise. Across from it was the burned out Nu-Sho, the site of Homer and Maddy's dramatic victory, the only burned out lot that looked good to me. It was a hollow monument to the Alva bastards who tried to hogtie Homer. Winelda had briefly been a two theater town, but now there was none.

Old Ben Taul's overstuffed chair was no longer in front of his unpainted wooden store where for eons his family—a distant Taul had been Winelda's first mayor—had sold pain killing liniments, Day's

Work Chewing Tobacco, Golden Grain roll-yer-owns, canned sardines, coal oil lamps, nails, and Wings factory made cigarettes. His wooden, unpainted store, one of Winelda's original pioneer buildings from the days of the Wild West, had been obliterated.

And bulldozed *not* to make way for progress! It had become just another unsightly vacant lot filled with weeds and cans. It would have been better to imaginatively effect some cosmetic surgery on Ben's Place. Better to have placed a historical sign reading: "Original Wineldan Store: Prop. Ben Taul, ca. 1889"

I wondered how small western towns could ever make their historical mark if nothing was ever preserved? Certainly there are very few modern people who would ever wish to live in Paul Revere's cramped, creaky house in Boston, but at least Bostonians hadn't bulldozed it. They maintained that part of America's history, and now thousands of Americans visit it every year. Even at tiny Langtry, Texas—far smaller than Winelda—the leaders had preserved Judge Roy Bean's simple frame bar and courtroom. It's become a national showplace, and it's no larger, and constructed not one whit better than had been Ben Taul's quintessential general store. How come there had been no palpable civic interest in Winelda, no solution other than the bulldozer?

Julie finally said, "Restoring the old general store would have been an improvement over this weedy lot. Now they've got nothing."

Austin Cue's filling station had closed, as had the dusty Ford agency. Amazing! Now that unprecedented prosperity had arrived in America, the Shivvies and V-8s, which during the Great Depression had sold well in Winelda, were no longer locally available.

I was ready to leave the dismal square. Having saved the best for last, I swung east toward Winelda High School. I told Julie, "Now for the *pièce de résistance*, my high school. I remember in our science room, Mr. Claunch, our chemistry teacher, removed a windowpane and covered it with wax. With a stylus each class member signed his name. Claunch then etched our signatures into the glass with hydrofluoric acid. With luck, that pane will still be intact." But when I turned the corner, old WHS was gone; it had become a vacant windswept lot! For a time, I peered speechlessly through the windshield.

We finally found the new school with its truly forgettable architecture located far from the city's center. Old WHS had been two short blocks from downtown; this one was out among the wheat fields. It seemed to be beyond Winelda's city boundaries. It was as if Wineldans had wanted it as distant from their homes as possible; it was as if they had forgotten how on twenty degree mornings, those whipping Oklahoma winds could make walking to school a bitter experience.

I wondered why there hadn't been a revolution when Wineldans heard of the plan to tear down WHS. Since 1928, it had long been the focal point for recitals, school plays, basketball tournaments, lectures, and graduations—even Homer's funeral. It had lent purpose to Winelda's Square because kids and teachers spent their noon hour lunching "downtown." I'm sure the school's relocation hastened the disintegration of downtown Winelda. It had been an urban explosion outward as opposed to a concentrated implosion.

The Square had always *been* Winelda. Never before had anything been established along the highway. Now, it was as if an immense meteor had splashed the town and had left a huge hole where the Square had been. Downtown was a shambles with no restaurants, no drugstores, few stores, and fewer local services. The newer city fathers had performed outlandish urban surgery. They had cut open Winelda's chest, pulled out her heart and other vitals, and distributed them far from the corpse—cored the apple; gutted it. Gertrude Stein might now say of Winelda, "There's no longer any there there."

We walked into the *Winelda Enterprise* for a short visit. It had vacated its original site on the east side of the street and had moved across the street into what had once been Miller's fantastically aromatic bakery. But I must say hurrah for the *Enterprise*. It had not shut down; it had not fled to some metal pre-fabricated building out on the highway. Even though transposed from one side of the street to the other, it was still the very same. It still smelled of good printer's ink. Its ancient press and Linotype continued its familiar clink-clanking as it ran off "Farm and Farm Equipment Liquidation" notices.

The new editor, Raymond, said most of the western part of town—across the tracks by Lottie's—was generally abandoned. Its street maintenance had become an ever larger drain on the city's coffer. The town council was considering bulldozing it and returning it to natural sagebrush.

Raymond told me passenger trains were history; the once active depot was shut tight. No longer was it possible for Wineldans to watch the Scout passengers do their evening promenade on the platform. There was no Scout. Today there are no buses, planes, or trains. A person who travels to Amarillo, or to Wichita, must drive, which is okay if you're not too young, or too old.

Old Nelson Otterbein, once a Santa Fe brakeman, dropped in while we were at the *Enterprise*. Nelson was the earth's salt, a representative of Winelda's very best asset; its down to earth people.

"Well, I declare, sure I remember you and yer dad, Homer. Well, well, if it ain't Tommy Cable. I'm seventy-nine now, Tommy, wouldja bleeve it?" And then, "Yep, I heard you askin' about the railroad. Remember when you fokes were here, how the railroad was Winelda's heartbeat? Lookit today, the Santa Fe gave up on Winelda, and now we've given up on it. Mexicans all left because there are no jobs. Remember those locomotive whistles? I never thought I'd miss 'em, but they sure was like music."

I asked Nelson, "What's the town's biggest industry now?"

"Well, sir," Nelson scratched his head, "I reckon there's two major industries. I would say the demolition business is pretty important as fokes steadily bulldoze the town. Not being funny, but I supposed the undertakers is the most solid business. Heh heh, now isn't that some-thin'? Yessir, we're mostly old here so it figures the undertaker thrives. So, there you go. We have the fokes that bulldozes the town and then the undertaker that buries old Wineldans who had once built the town. Now ain't thet a pretty turnaround?" Raymond, the editor, smiled and shook his head in agreement.

"Well," said Raymond, "every Easter the funeral home runs a big ad that lists the names and date of interment of every Wineldan buried over the years. It's almost an anniversary thing, and I think it's a right fine memorial tribute . . . don't you, Tom?" I quickly nodded.

Nelson chimed in, "Yeah, and it heps. Sometimes fokes up in years fergit where a friend is, and then they read that Easter paper and they say, 'Oh, I plum fergot Leon died in 1967. I wunnered why I didn't see 'im no more.'"

"Another sign of Winelda's modern times," said Nelson. "What if I was to tell ya that with half as many people we got *four* uniformed poe-licemen, and a five thousand dollar drug sniffin' dog . . . would you believe it? And they got three or four patrol cars, fancy Motorola radios, and seven hundred dollar pagers. Remember how Billy Patton was always on foot, had no office, yet seemed always to be every-where? Our poe-lice today costs a real heap but there's sure 'nuf a need for the law, cause fokes just aren't the same any more."

I asked where in town we could lunch. Nelson said, "No more

Etta's or Eastman's. Nowadays you have to motor south outta town; you'll see it out there on the edge of the highway—Miller's Café. Once you get there, the food's right good. Nothing much left here in town for strollers, which is why you don't see many strollers. By moving everything out, you'd think we were worried about some atomic bomb. Gol danged wonder the guvmint didn't build the new post-office out on the highway. Maybe you heard we moved the school to hell and gone. And speaking of the school, I heard it rumored the other day that they're talking about bussing all the kids to Alva . . . close down Winelda's school altogether." Nelson winked, "Winelda don't have enough kids, and as you know, old folks don't have kids."

I smiled and looked at my watch. Julie and I had to get on toward Taos, so we said our farewells. We silently drove south out of town until finally I said, "You know, Julie, that old aphorism is right. Unless you have relatives or graves, you shouldn't go back. Winelda was one helluva memory, and I shouldn't have disturbed it. Everything has changed, even those mesas over there. They don't seem to be as high or as far as when Amzy and I climbed them. Just ahead is the Cimarron River . . . even it doesn't appear to be as wide as it was."

As we crossed the bridge she said, "Nothing's wrong with you, Tom. You're just disappointed with Homer's Place, and the Majestic, and the fact they tore down the Rexall, and your school. You're right. We shouldn't have come back; we shouldn't have fooled around with great memories. And just to convince you that you haven't gone bananas, I'll be the first to admit that Winelda didn't look at all like the place you've been describing these many years. Except for the people; those we met were very nice."

After we crossed the Cimarron River Bridge I said, "You know it just occurred to me that its entirely possible—probably not in our life-time mind you—but, like Mexican Town, many little towns will just pppfffft disappear . . . wiped clean, not a trace left of them." Julie laughed.

"Oh, you laugh. I'll bet the Enids will steadily absorb the Hopetons, and Carmens, and the Avards. People already run to Enid to buy a screwdriver, nails, or to see a show, or have dinner. Winelda's population is dominantly senior and dwindling; there are few children . . . eventually no school, no people. I'll bet today that only a small percentage of the kids who go off to college ever return to Winelda." Julie enjoyed viewing Eagle Chief Creek and the red mesas while I droned on.

"You want to hear my fixed opinion? Winelda's going to go full cycle. Ultimately they'll plow it under, eradicate it just like Mexican town—return it to quail, Herefords, and sagebrush. Won't that make the environmentalists ecstatic?" Julie just grinned as I gathered steam.

"It's not all that difficult to imagine the corner of Main and Cecil just as it was in 1860 when the Indians went there to hunt buffalo. Why not? In 1932, who would have ever thought the once bustling airport with its huge hangar would have ever reverted to a wheat field? Who would have thought that the virtually timeless roundhouse would have ever been dismantled?

"Can you imagine that future picture. Not a single brick or concrete block. Just sagebrush, and if lucky, a solitary historical sign proclaiming: "This was the site of Winelda, Oklahoma: A pioneer ranching and farming community, once the home of the railroaders football team."

Julie laughed again, "Oh my God, Tom, you just killed Winelda."

"Yeah, it'll become as dead and unnecessary as the Phoenician's Baalbek, or the Khmer's Angkor Wat. Except those places have truly interesting ruins to draw tourists from thousands of miles. I don't really believe there'll be a Wineldan ruins—no ghost town. Winelda will be more like Carthage, or Mexican Town—absolutely *nothing!* Whatever survives will either be carted off to Enid, or plowed under. It's the wave of the future for small, unnecessary Western towns that have outlived their original purpose."

I looked at Julie. I could tell she was grinning as she listened and noncommittally viewed the beautiful gyp hills as they drew nearer. "So, what's the smirk for? I suppose you think my rocket's gone out of control?"

"Yes, you fool," she laughed. "Your guidance system is all screwed up, and I'm about to hit your self-destruct button. Now," she said with a smile, "take my advice, Boy, and delete today! Erase all today's data . . . all of it. Leave everything in your head just as it was yesterday. Now come on, get this thing going, let's go West."

At Bouse Junction I turned west and gave it the gas. About the time we passed Doc's cave I said, "How about it, are we going to Principia next spring? Are we going to visit your old school in Elsah, Illinois?"

Julie laughed, "After today, I'm not so sure. Probably not."

ABOUT THE AUTHOR

Harlan G. Koch was born in Anthony, Kansas and raised in Oklahoma's Cimarron Country. He received an Associates degree from the Oklahoma Military Academy Junior College, a Bachelor of Science from West Point, Masters in Science from University of Illinois (Southeast Asian specialization), and a Masters in Arts from University of California, Berkeley (Northeast Asian specialization). He served as a regular U.S. Army officer in general staff, and in infantry, armored, and airborne divisions His overseas duty included Korea, Japan, Taiwan, Iraq, and all of Mainland Southeast Asia. He graduated from Leavenworth's venerable Command and General Staff College. He resigned from the service and became chairman of the board of the Thai-American Steel Corporation, Bangkok. He and his wife, Judy (a Principia graduate and a former Pan American Stewardess), then opened their own corporations in Hawaii and California. They retired from business in 1994 in San Francisco. Koch is currently wrapping up a novel about the lethal intrigue and infighting among diplomats in our American Embassy in Bangkok, and among foreign agents in the jungles of Southeast Asia. Entitled *Deception,* and soon to be completed, the protagonist is the same Tom Cable that appears in *Homer's Place.* Formerly an avid marathoner and 10K competition runner, Koch has tapered to writing, pushing a little iron, and riding his Harley.